The Mapmaker

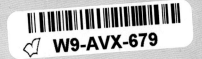

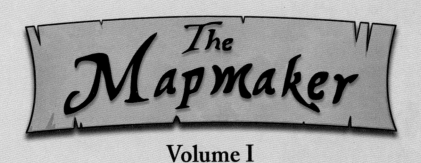

Volume I

The Mapmaker

Writer
BEN SLABAK

Artist
FRANCESCA CARITÀ

Letterer
HdE

Scout Editor
WAYNE HALL

Scout Production
RICHARD RIVERA

Brendan Deneen, *CEO*
James Pruett, *CCO*
Tennessee Edwards, *CSO*
James Haick III, *President*
Joel Rodriguez, *Head Of Design*

Don Handfield, *CMO*
David Byrne, *Co-Publisher*
Charlie Stickney, *Co-Publisher*
Richard Rivera, *Associate Publisher*

 FB/TW/IG:
@Scoutcomics

LEARN MORE AT:
www.scoutcomics.com

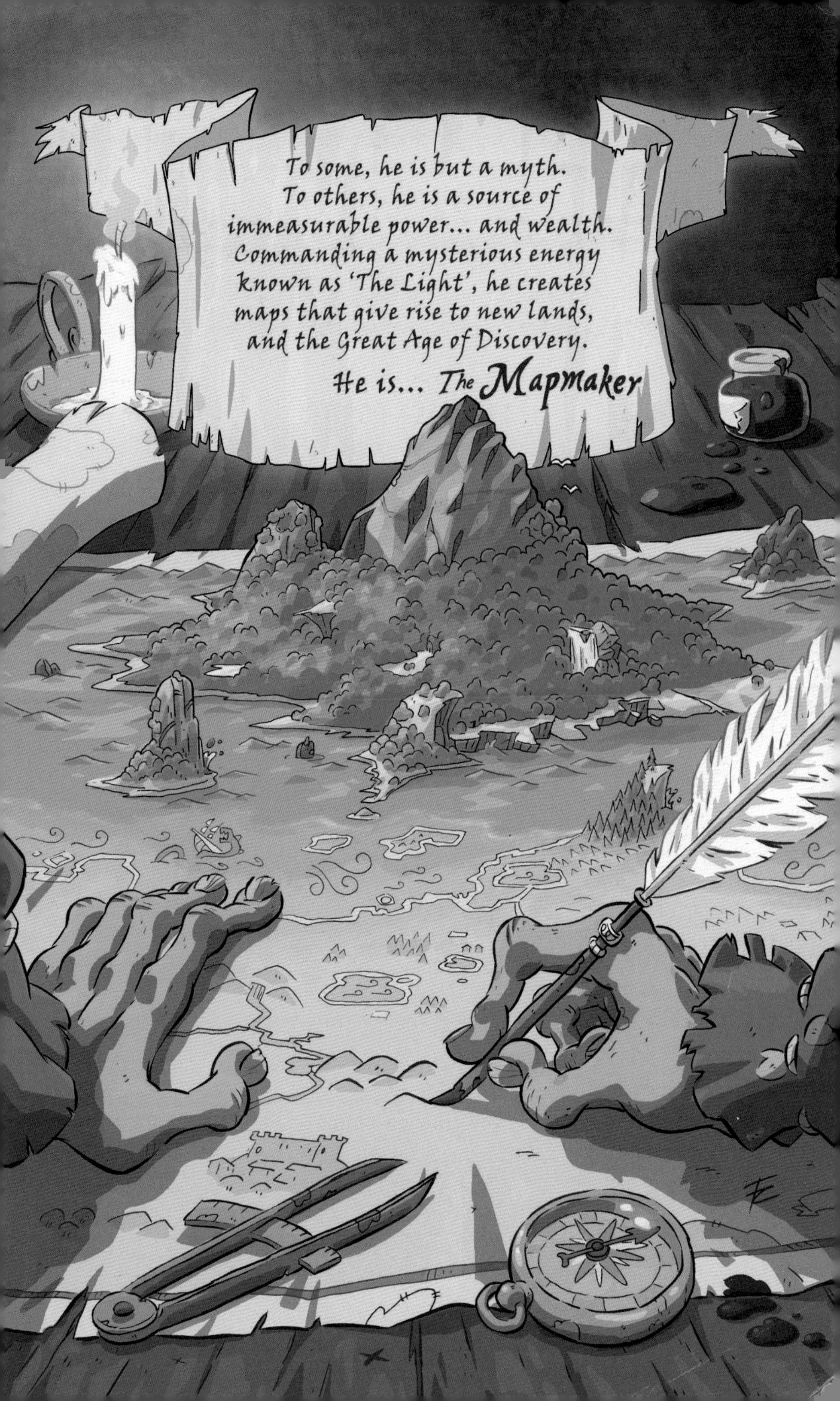
To some, he is but a myth.
To others, he is a source of
immeasurable power... and wealth.
Commanding a mysterious energy
known as 'The Light', he creates
maps that give rise to new lands,
and the Great Age of Discovery.
He is... The Mapmaker

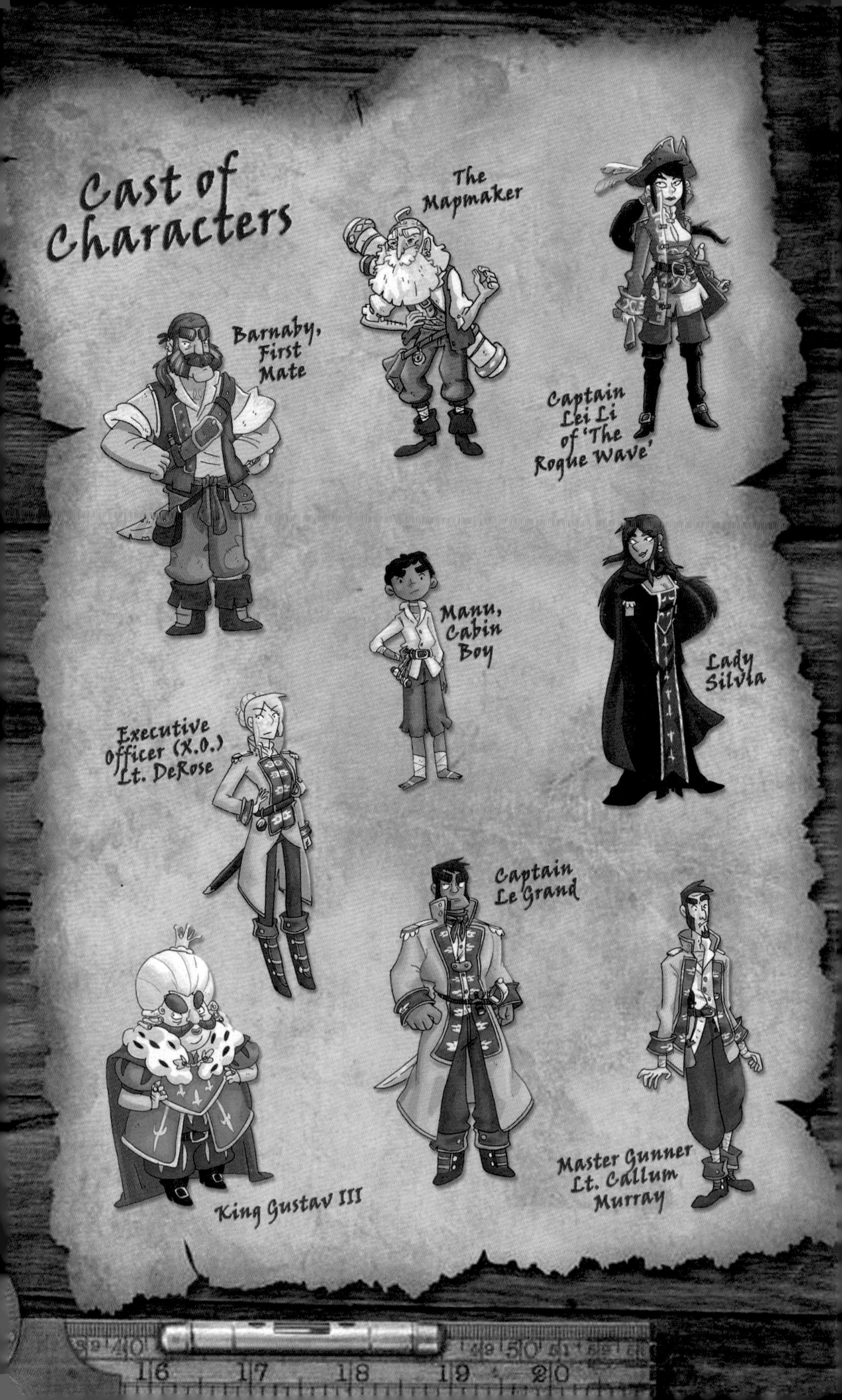
Cast of Characters
The Mapmaker
Barnaby, First Mate
Captain Lei Li of 'The Rogue Wave'
Manu, Cabin Boy
Lady Silvia
Executive Officer (X.O.) Lt. DeRose
Captain Le Grand
King Gustav III
Master Gunner Lt. Callum Murray

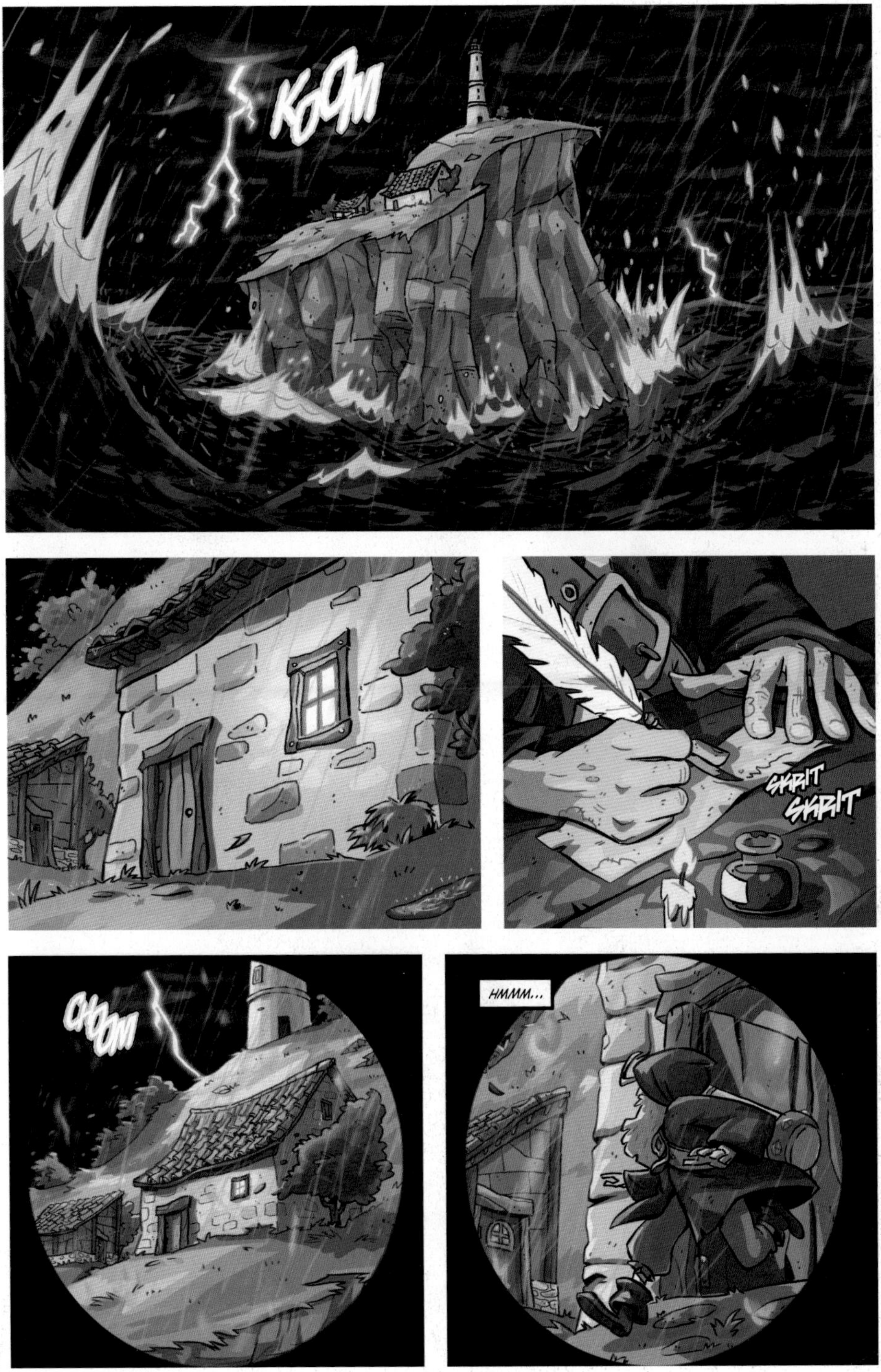
KOOM
SKRIT
SKRIT
CHOOM
HMMM...

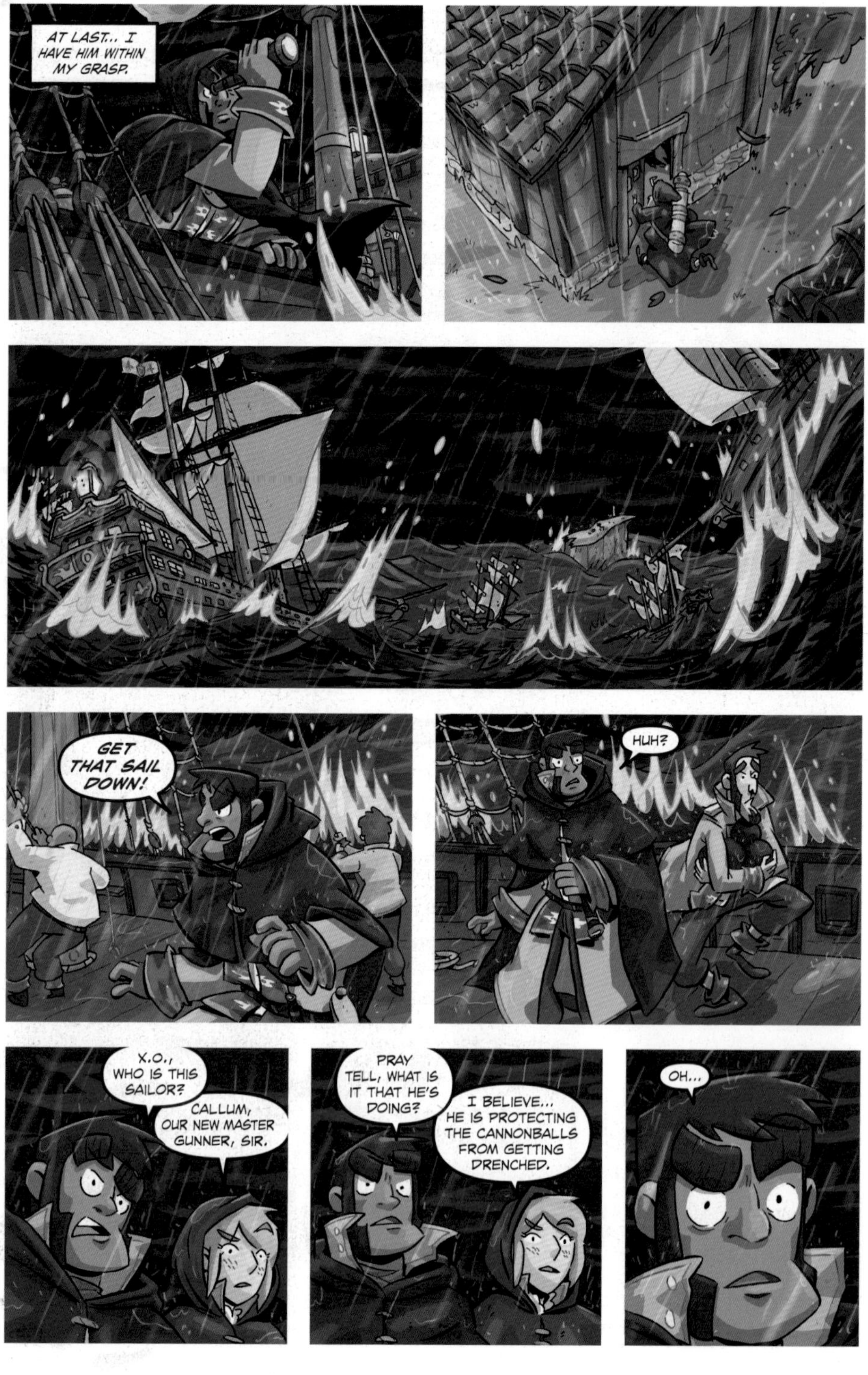
AT LAST... I HAVE HIM WITHIN MY GRASP.
GET THAT SAIL DOWN!
HUH?
X.O., WHO IS THIS SAILOR?
CALLUM, OUR NEW MASTER GUNNER, SIR.
PRAY TELL, WHAT IS IT THAT HE'S DOING?
I BELIEVE... HE IS PROTECTING THE CANNONBALLS FROM GETTING DRENCHED.
OH...

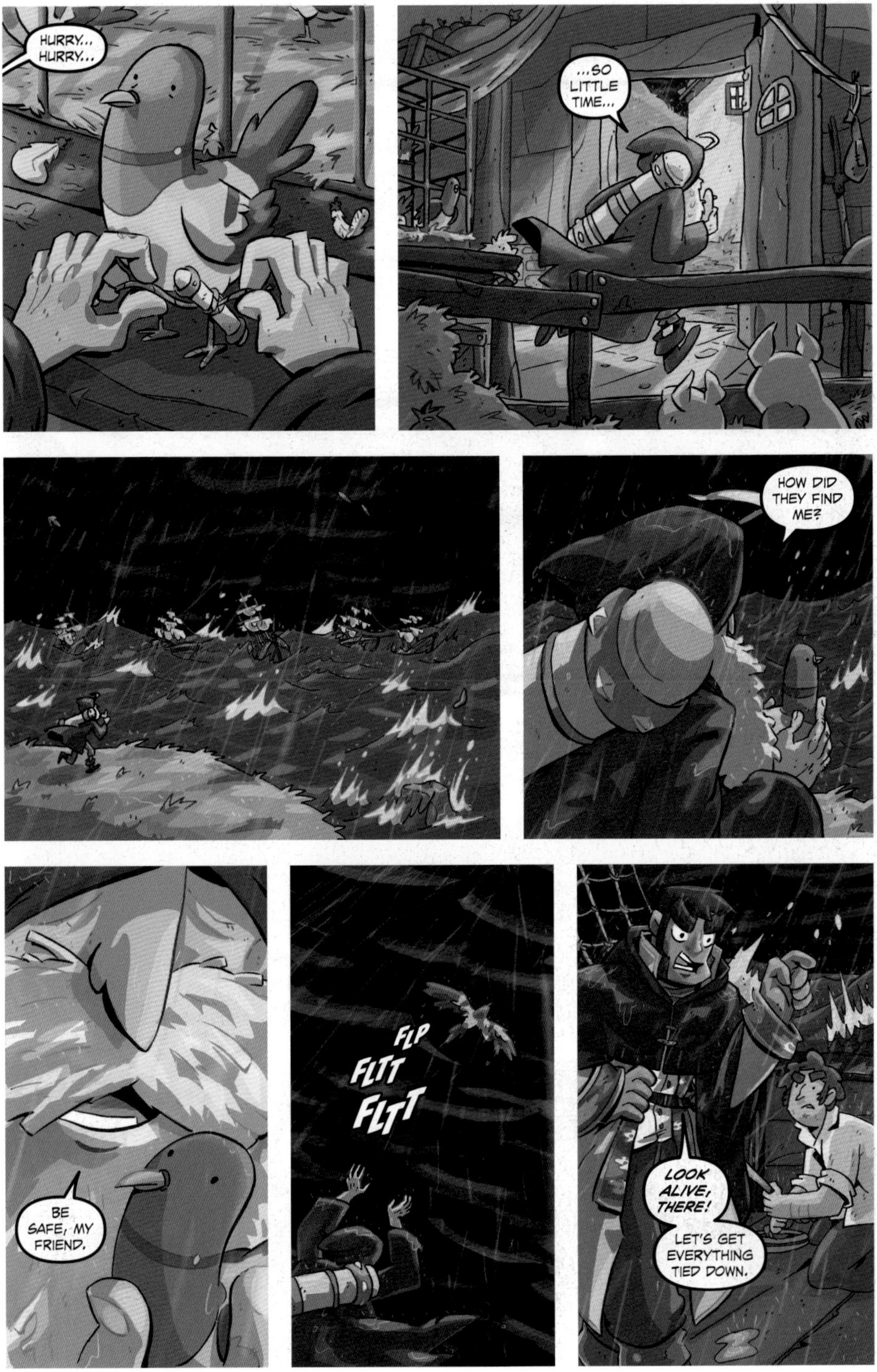
HURRY... HURRY...
...SO LITTLE TIME...
HOW DID THEY FIND ME?
BE SAFE, MY FRIEND.
FLP
FLTT
FLTT
LOOK ALIVE, THERE!
LET'S GET EVERYTHING TIED DOWN.

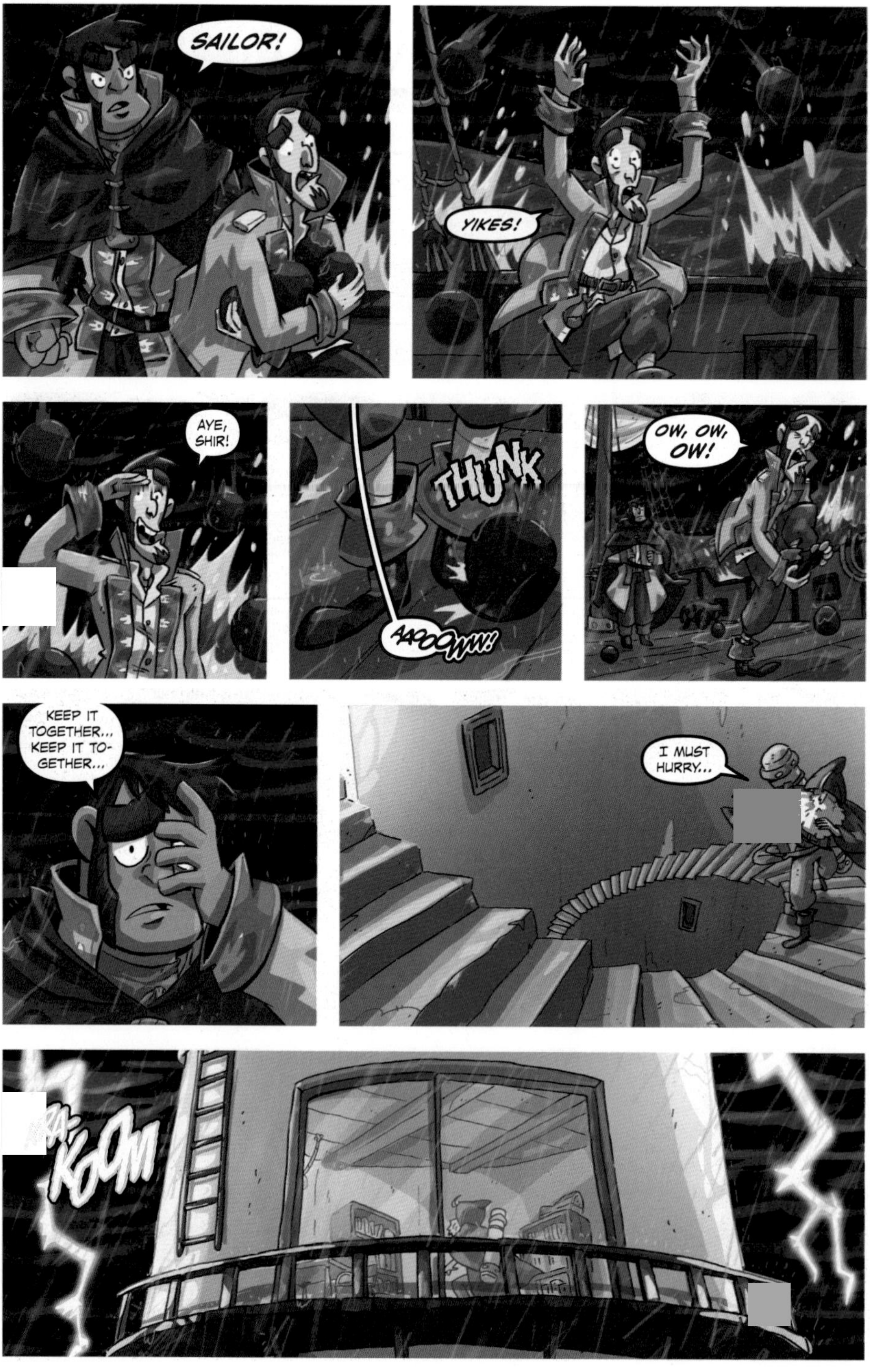
SAILOR!
YIKES!
AYE, SHIR!
THUNK
AAAOOWWW!
OW, OW, OW!
KEEP IT TOGETHER... KEEP IT TO-GETHER...
I MUST HURRY...
KOOM

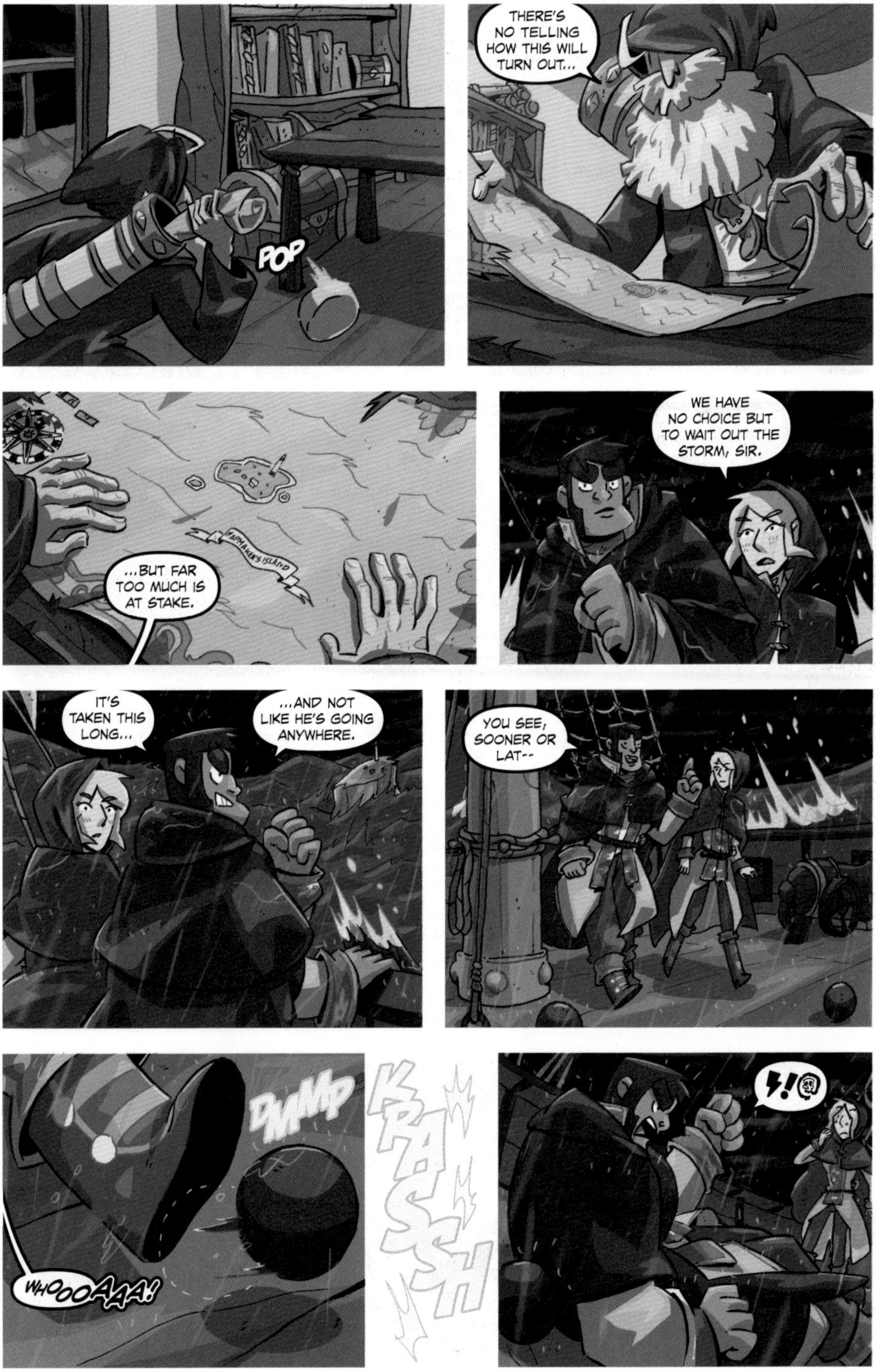
POP
THERE'S NO TELLING HOW THIS WILL TURN OUT...
MAPMAKER'S ISLAND
...BUT FAR TOO MUCH IS AT STAKE.
WE HAVE NO CHOICE BUT TO WAIT OUT THE STORM, SIR.
IT'S TAKEN THIS LONG...
...AND NOT LIKE HE'S GOING ANYWHERE.
YOU SEE, SOONER OR LAT--
DMMP
WHOOOAAA!
KRASSH

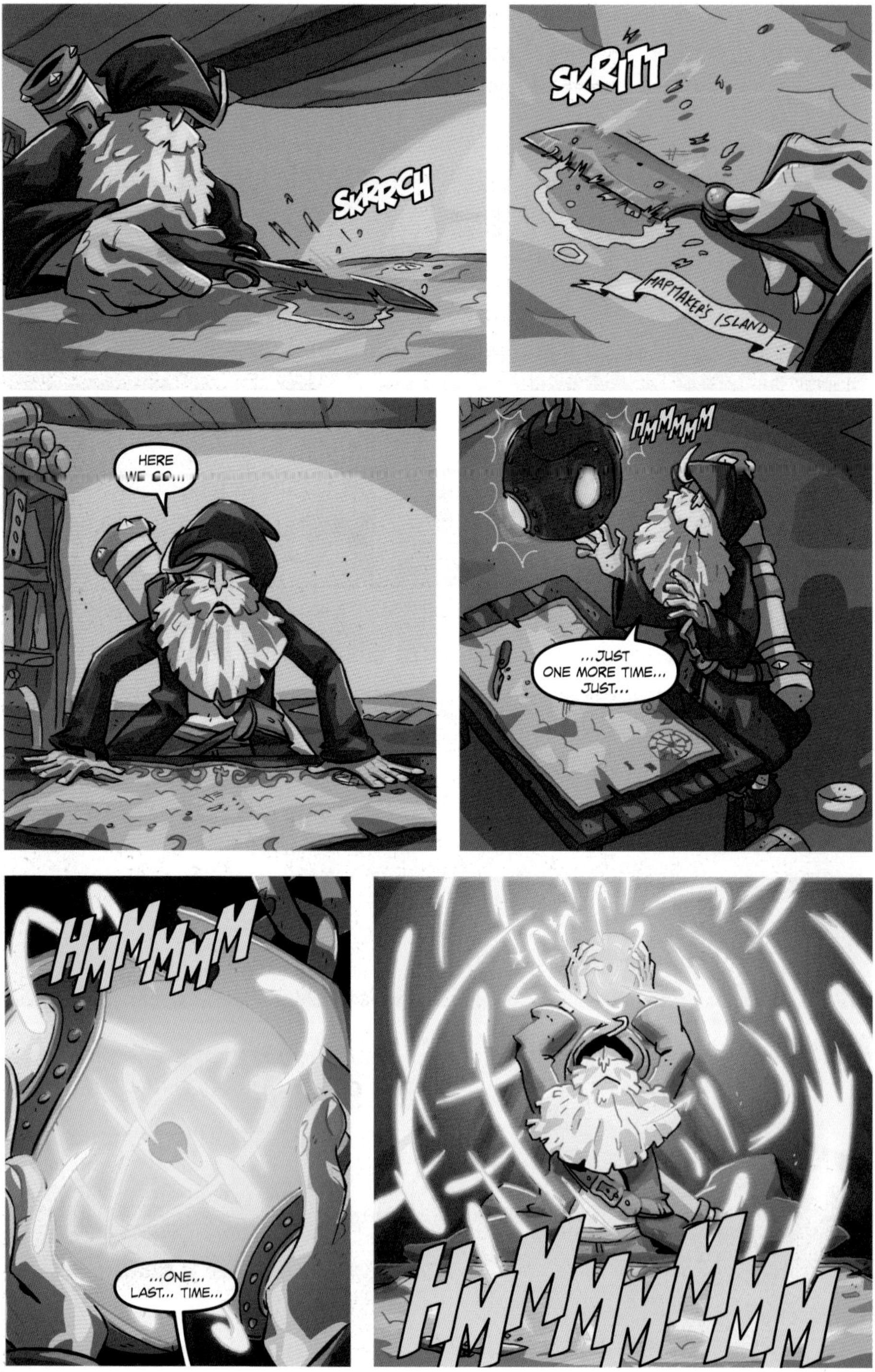
SKRRCH
SKRITT
MAPMAKER'S ISLAND
HERE WE GO...
HMMMMM
...JUST ONE MORE TIME... JUST...
HMMMMM
...ONE... LAST... TIME...
HMMMMMMMMMM

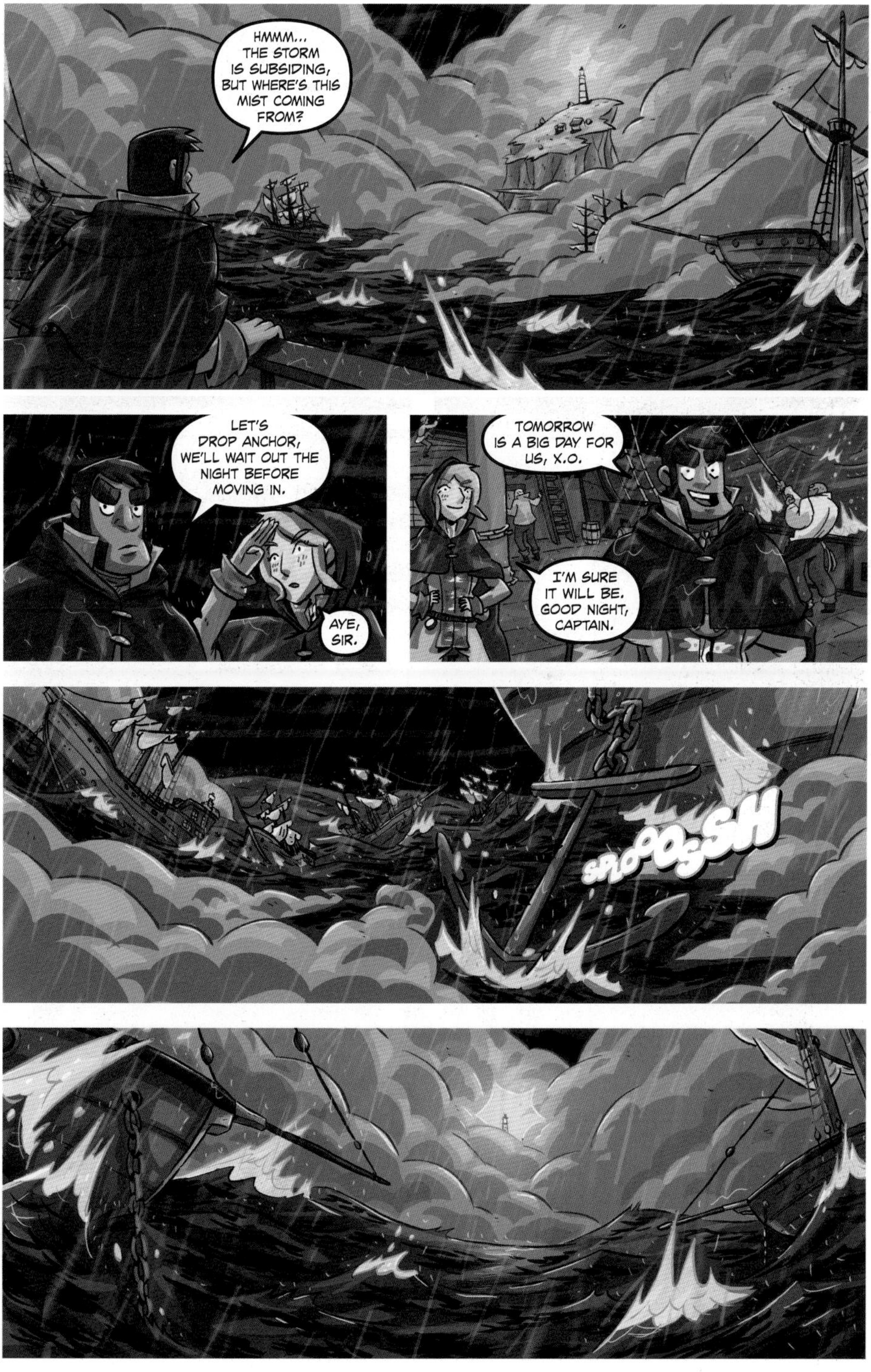
HMMM... THE STORM IS SUBSIDING, BUT WHERE'S THIS MIST COMING FROM?
LET'S DROP ANCHOR, WE'LL WAIT OUT THE NIGHT BEFORE MOVING IN.
AYE, SIR.
TOMORROW IS A BIG DAY FOR US, X.O.
I'M SURE IT WILL BE. GOOD NIGHT, CAPTAIN.
SPLOOOSSH

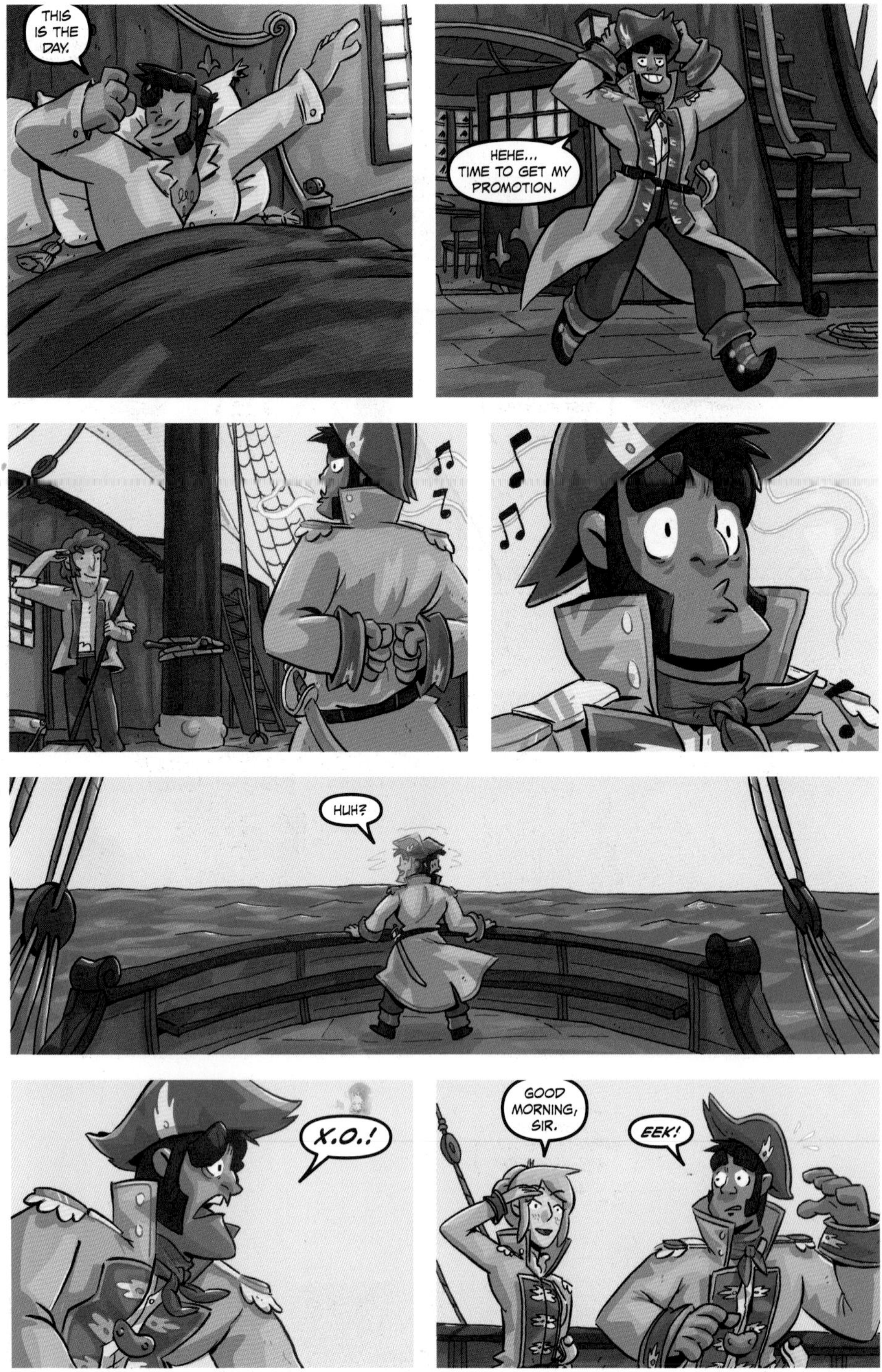
THIS IS THE DAY.
HEHE... TIME TO GET MY PROMOTION.
HUH?
X.O.!
GOOD MORNING, SIR.
EEK!

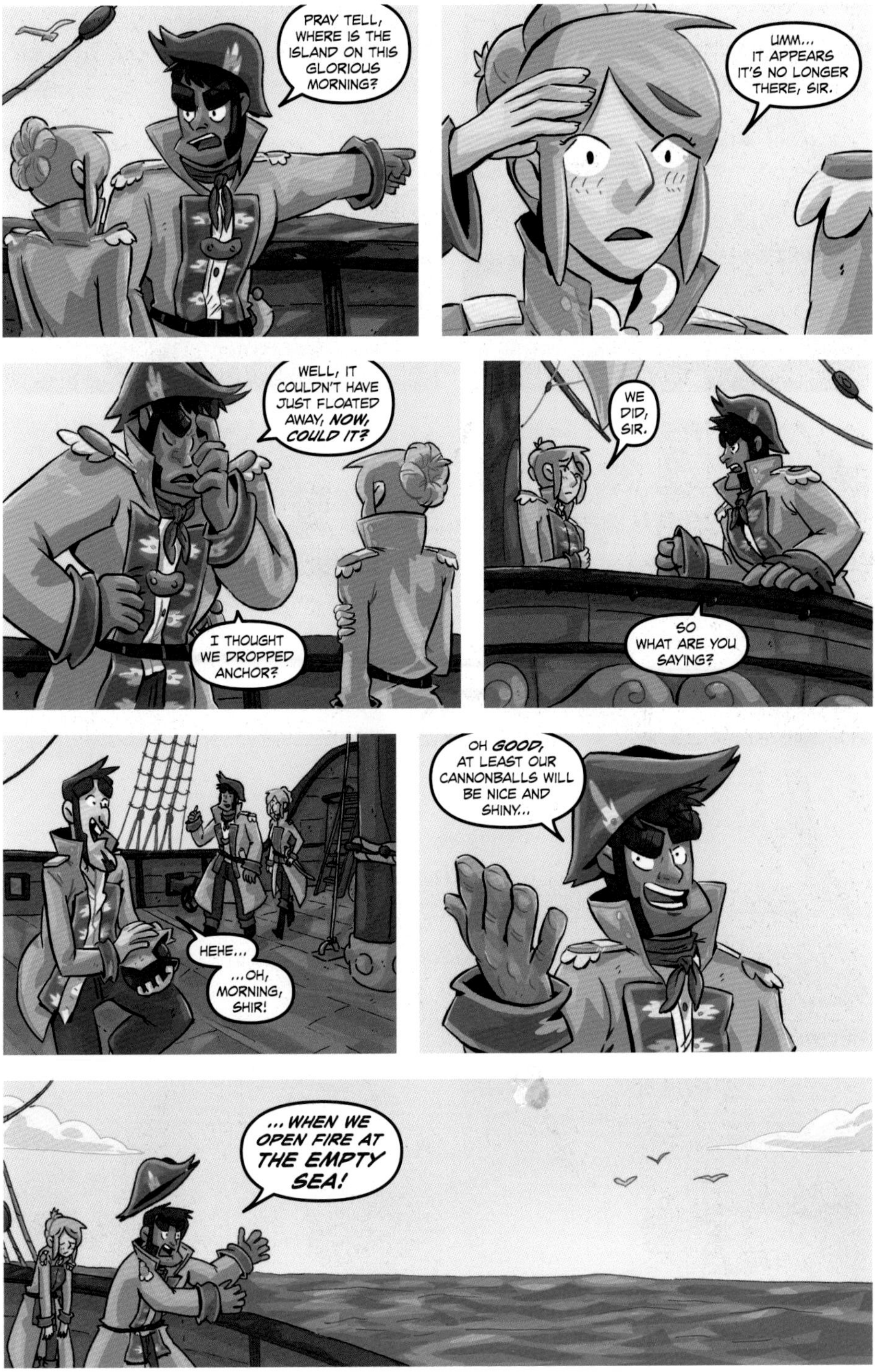
PRAY TELL, WHERE IS THE ISLAND ON THIS GLORIOUS MORNING?
UMM... IT APPEARS IT'S NO LONGER THERE, SIR.
WELL, IT COULDN'T HAVE JUST FLOATED AWAY, NOW, COULD IT?
I THOUGHT WE DROPPED ANCHOR?
WE DID, SIR.
SO WHAT ARE YOU SAYING?
HEHE...
...OH, MORNING, SHIR!
OH GOOD, AT LEAST OUR CANNONBALLS WILL BE NICE AND SHINY...
...WHEN WE OPEN FIRE AT THE EMPTY SEA!

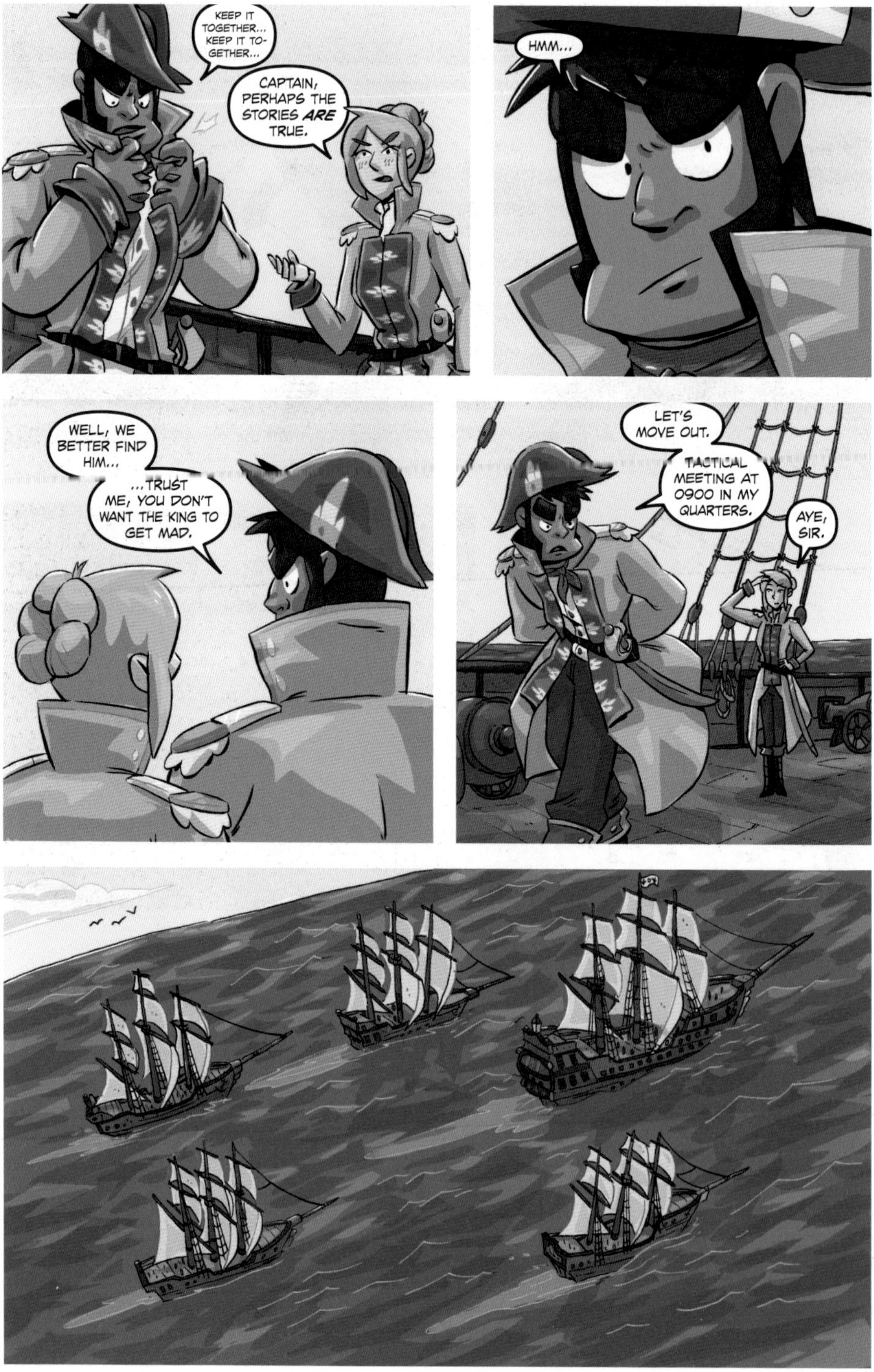
KEEP IT TOGETHER... KEEP IT TO-GETHER...
CAPTAIN, PERHAPS THE STORIES *ARE* TRUE.
HMM...
WELL, WE BETTER FIND HIM...
...TRUST ME, YOU DON'T WANT THE KING TO GET MAD.
LET'S MOVE OUT.
TACTICAL MEETING AT 0900 IN MY QUARTERS.
AYE, SIR.

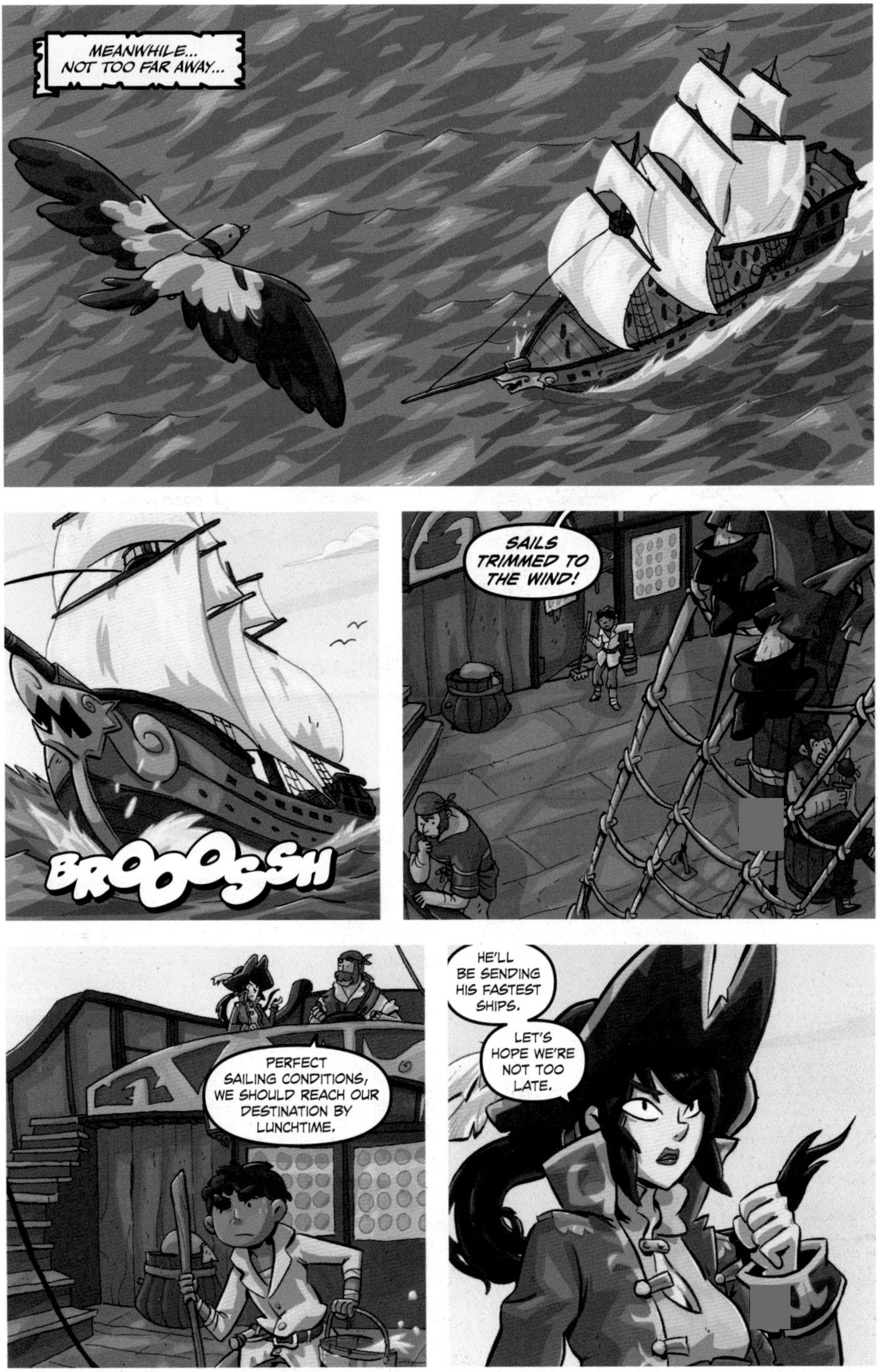

MEANWHILE... NOT TOO FAR AWAY...
BROOOOSSH
SAILS TRIMMED TO THE WIND!
PERFECT SAILING CONDITIONS, WE SHOULD REACH OUR DESTINATION BY LUNCHTIME.
HE'LL BE SENDING HIS FASTEST SHIPS.
LET'S HOPE WE'RE NOT TOO LATE.

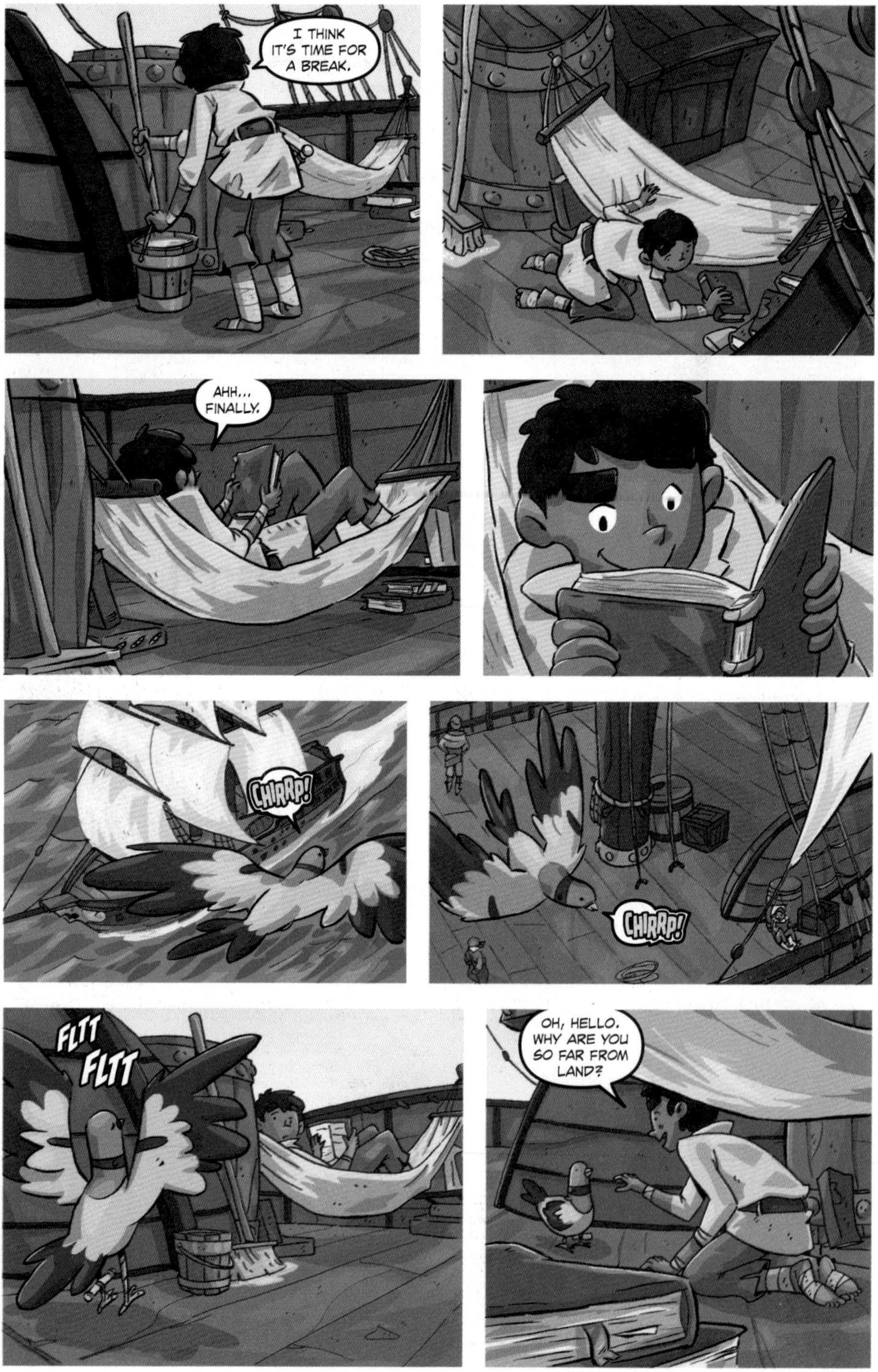
I THINK IT'S TIME FOR A BREAK.
AHH... FINALLY.
CHIRRP!
CHIRRP!
FLTT
FLTT
OH, HELLO. WHY ARE YOU SO FAR FROM LAND?

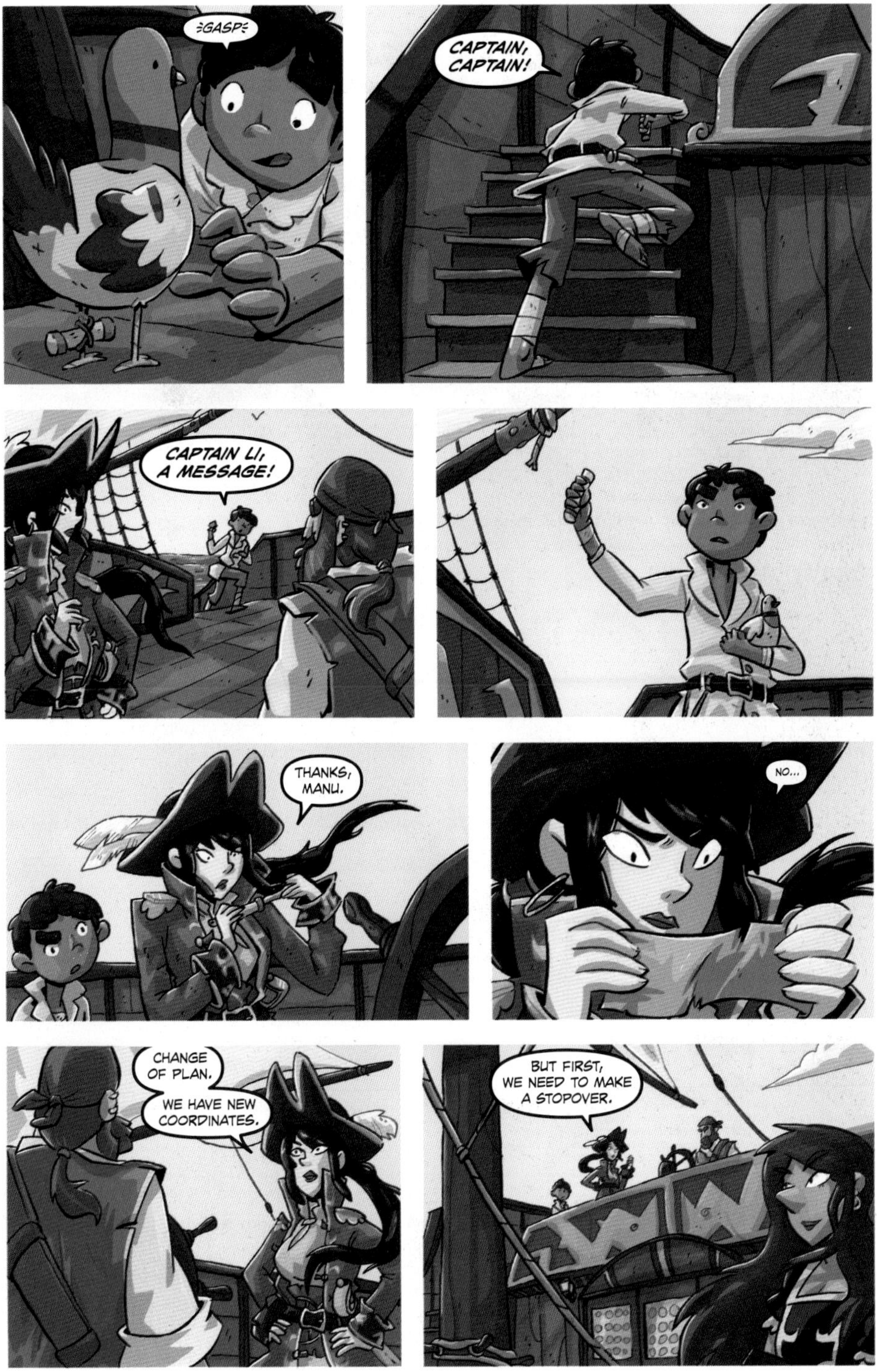
GASP
CAPTAIN, CAPTAIN!
CAPTAIN LI, A MESSAGE!
THANKS, MANU.
NO...
CHANGE OF PLAN.
WE HAVE NEW COORDINATES.
BUT FIRST, WE NEED TO MAKE A STOPOVER.

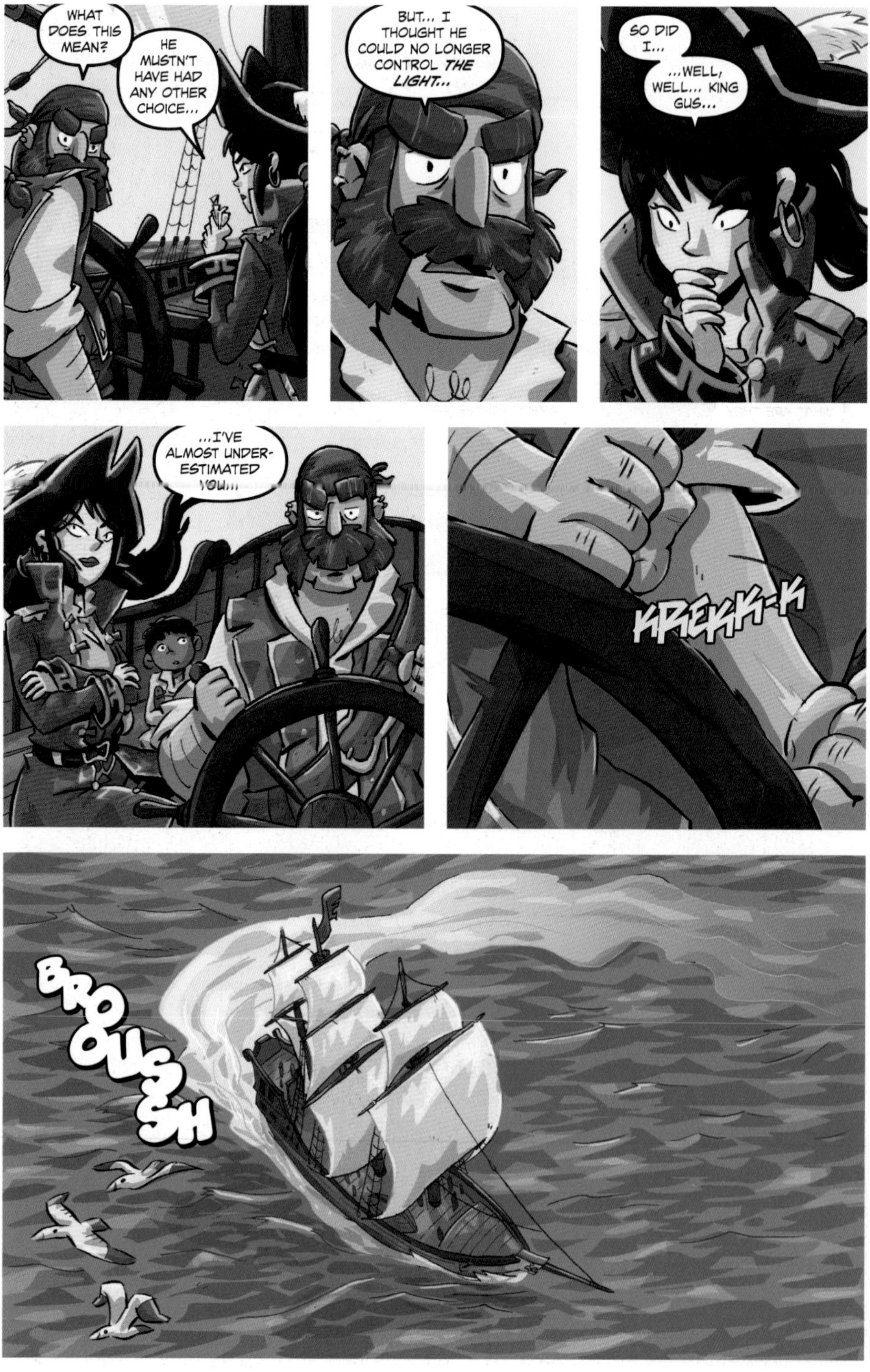
WHAT DOES THIS MEAN?
HE MUSTN'T HAVE HAD ANY OTHER CHOICE...
BUT... I THOUGHT HE COULD NO LONGER CONTROL *THE LIGHT...*
SO DID I...
...WELL, WELL... KING GUS...
...I'VE ALMOST UNDER-ESTIMATED YOU...
KREKK-K
BROUSSH

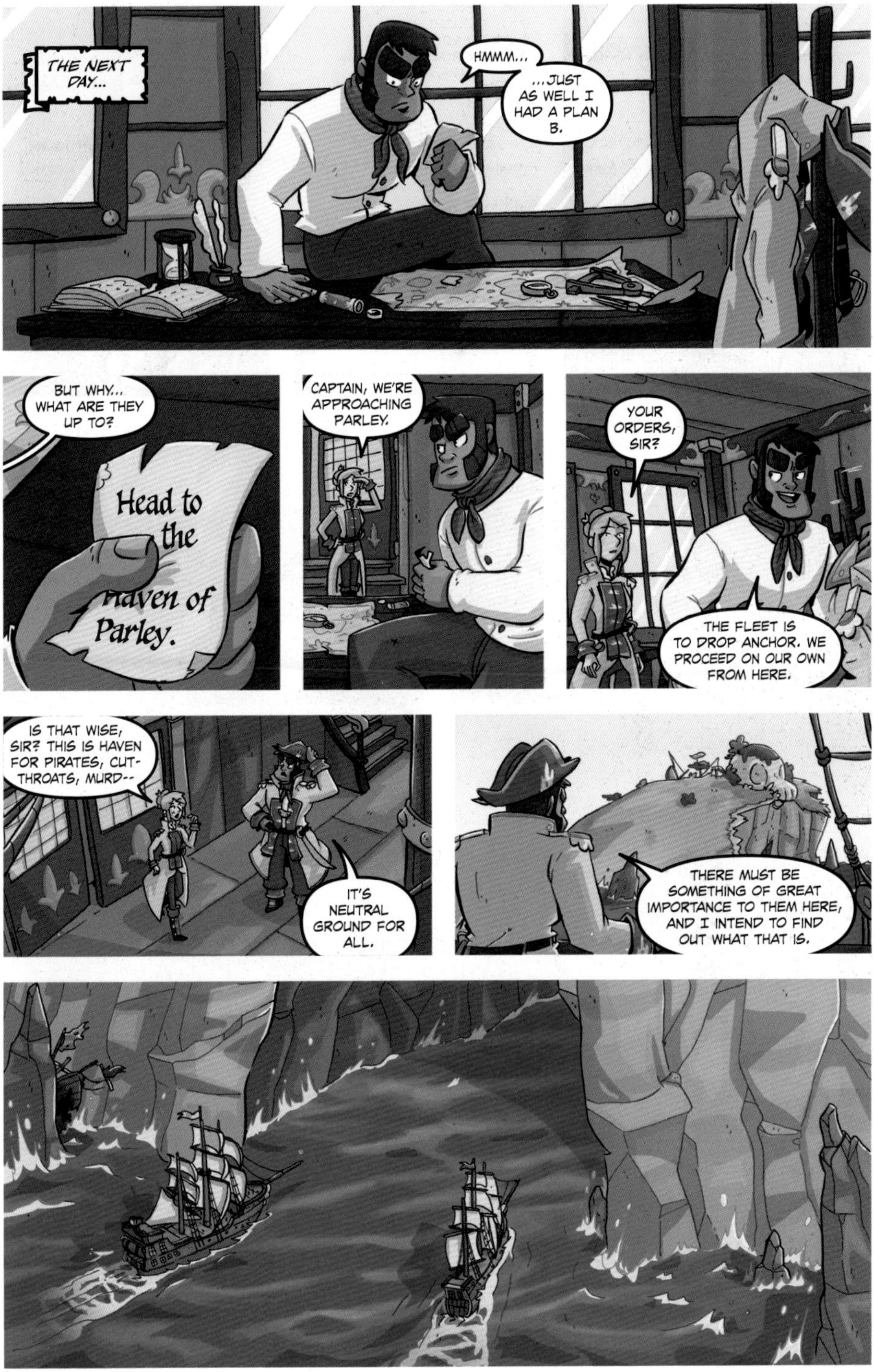
THE NEXT DAY...
HMMM...
...JUST AS WELL I HAD A PLAN B.
BUT WHY... WHAT ARE THEY UP TO?
Head to the Haven of Parley.
CAPTAIN, WE'RE APPROACHING PARLEY.
YOUR ORDERS, SIR?
THE FLEET IS TO DROP ANCHOR. WE PROCEED ON OUR OWN FROM HERE.
IS THAT WISE, SIR? THIS IS HAVEN FOR PIRATES, CUT-THROATS, MURD--
IT'S NEUTRAL GROUND FOR ALL.
THERE MUST BE SOMETHING OF GREAT IMPORTANCE TO THEM HERE, AND I INTEND TO FIND OUT WHAT THAT IS.

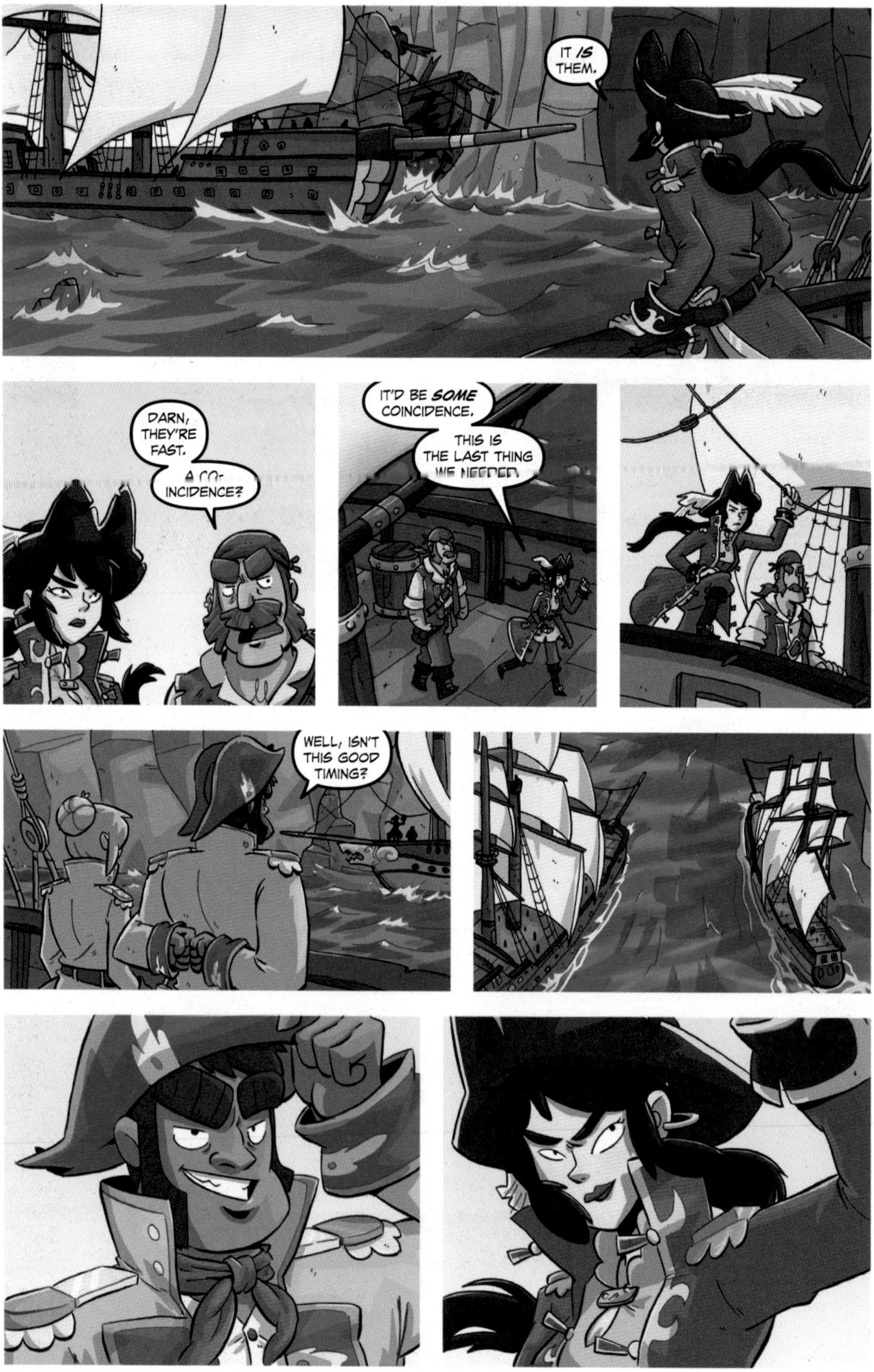

IT *IS* THEM.
DARN, THEY'RE FAST.
A CO-INCIDENCE?
IT'D BE *SOME* COINCIDENCE.
THIS IS THE LAST THING WE NEEDED.
WELL, ISN'T THIS GOOD TIMING?

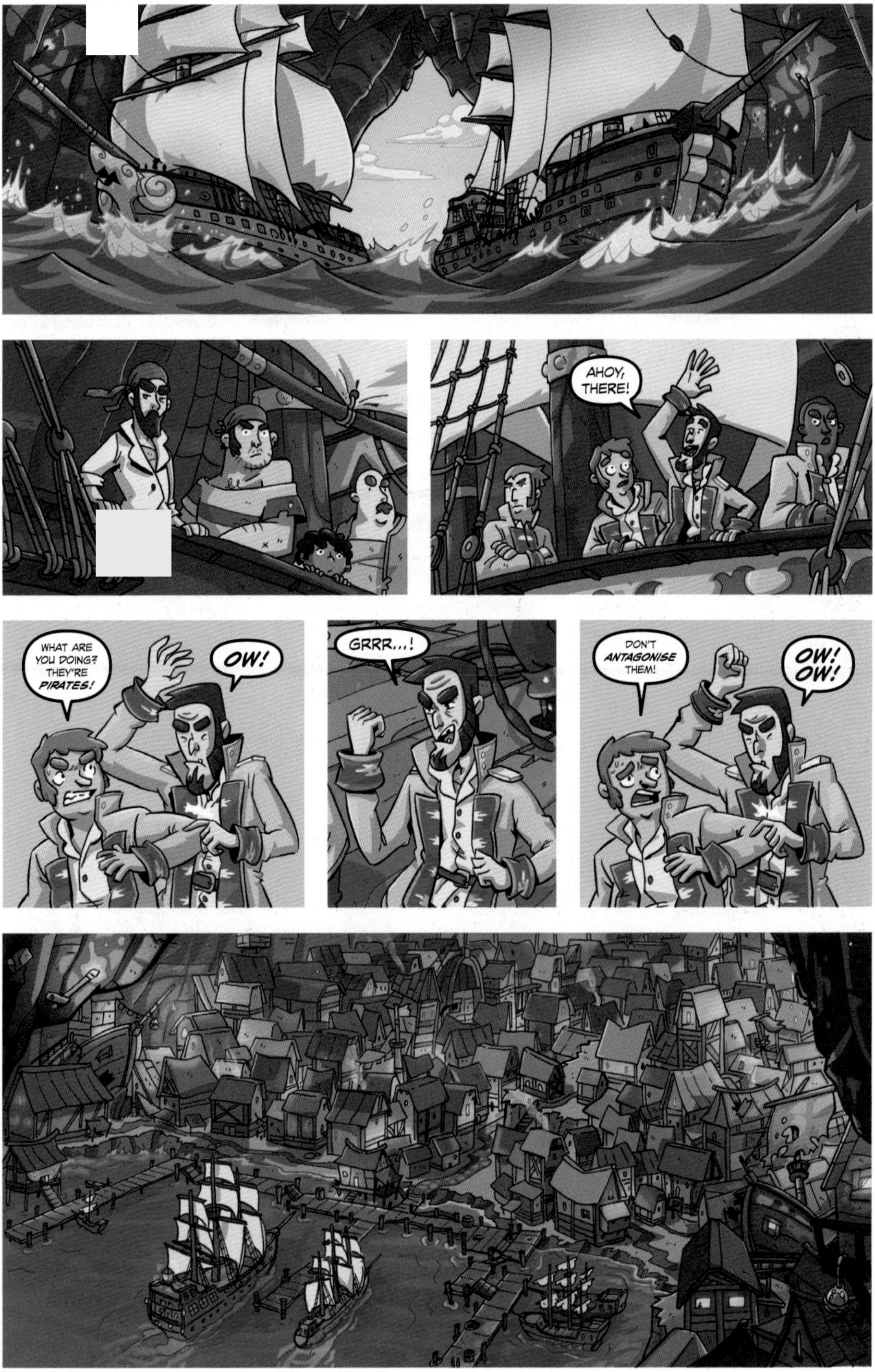
AHOY, THERE!
WHAT ARE YOU DOING? THEY'RE *PIRATES!*
OW!
GRRR...!
DON'T *ANTAGONISE* THEM!
OW! OW!

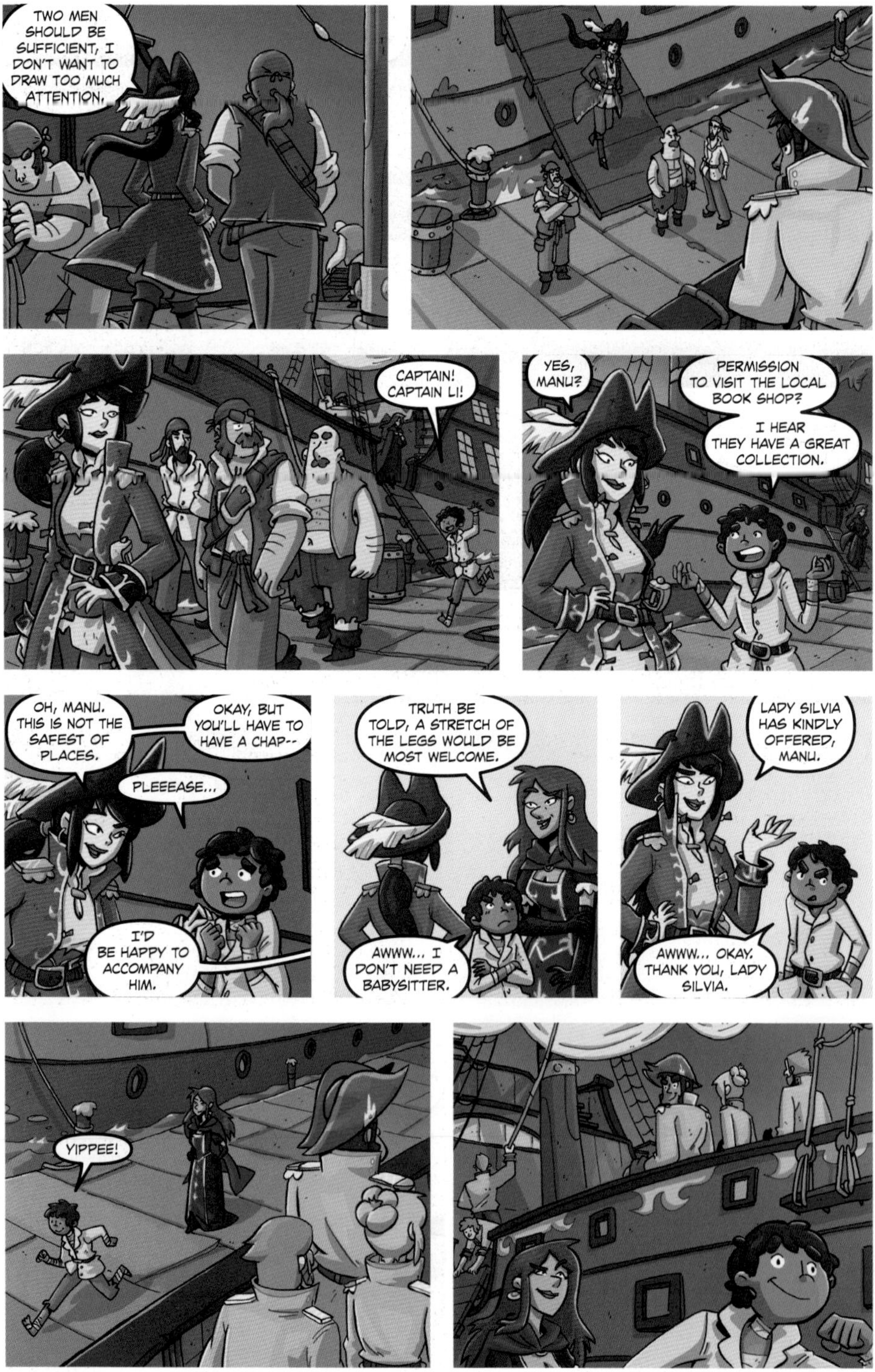
TWO MEN SHOULD BE SUFFICIENT, I DON'T WANT TO DRAW TOO MUCH ATTENTION.
CAPTAIN! CAPTAIN LI!
YES, MANU?
PERMISSION TO VISIT THE LOCAL BOOK SHOP?
I HEAR THEY HAVE A GREAT COLLECTION.
OH, MANU. THIS IS NOT THE SAFEST OF PLACES.
OKAY, BUT YOU'LL HAVE TO HAVE A CHAP--
PLEEEASE...
I'D BE HAPPY TO ACCOMPANY HIM.
TRUTH BE TOLD, A STRETCH OF THE LEGS WOULD BE MOST WELCOME.
AWWW... I DON'T NEED A BABYSITTER.
LADY SILVIA HAS KINDLY OFFERED, MANU.
AWWW... OKAY. THANK YOU, LADY SILVIA.
YIPPEE!

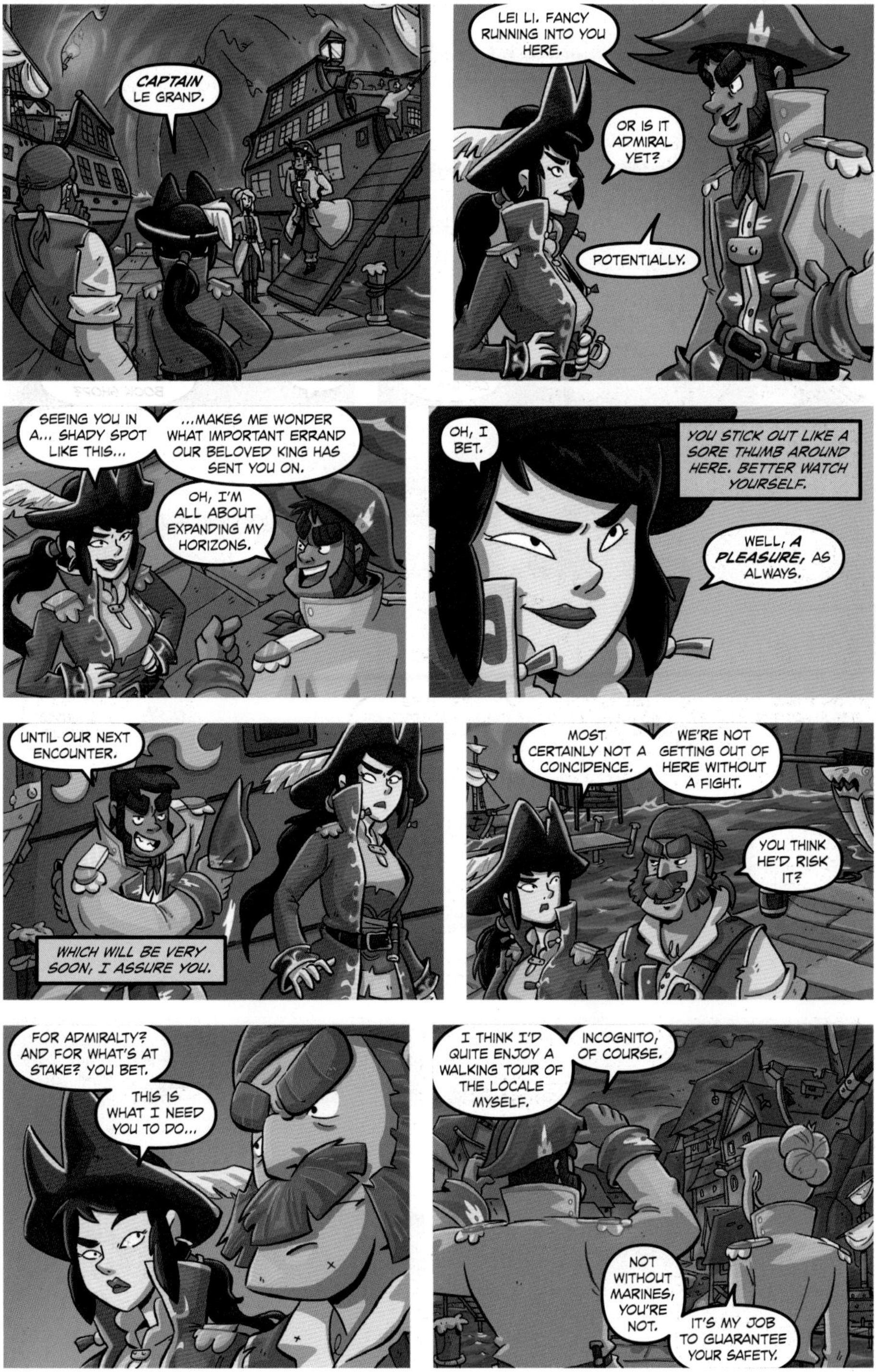
CAPTAIN LE GRAND.
LEI LI. FANCY RUNNING INTO YOU HERE.
OR IS IT ADMIRAL YET?
POTENTIALLY.
SEEING YOU IN A... SHADY SPOT LIKE THIS...
...MAKES ME WONDER WHAT IMPORTANT ERRAND OUR BELOVED KING HAS SENT YOU ON.
OH, I'M ALL ABOUT EXPANDING MY HORIZONS.
OH, I BET.
YOU STICK OUT LIKE A SORE THUMB AROUND HERE. BETTER WATCH YOURSELF.
WELL, A PLEASURE, AS ALWAYS.
UNTIL OUR NEXT ENCOUNTER.
WHICH WILL BE VERY SOON, I ASSURE YOU.
MOST CERTAINLY NOT A COINCIDENCE.
WE'RE NOT GETTING OUT OF HERE WITHOUT A FIGHT.
YOU THINK HE'D RISK IT?
FOR ADMIRALTY? AND FOR WHAT'S AT STAKE? YOU BET.
THIS IS WHAT I NEED YOU TO DO...
I THINK I'D QUITE ENJOY A WALKING TOUR OF THE LOCALE MYSELF.
INCOGNITO, OF COURSE.
NOT WITHOUT MARINES, YOU'RE NOT.
IT'S MY JOB TO GUARANTEE YOUR SAFETY.

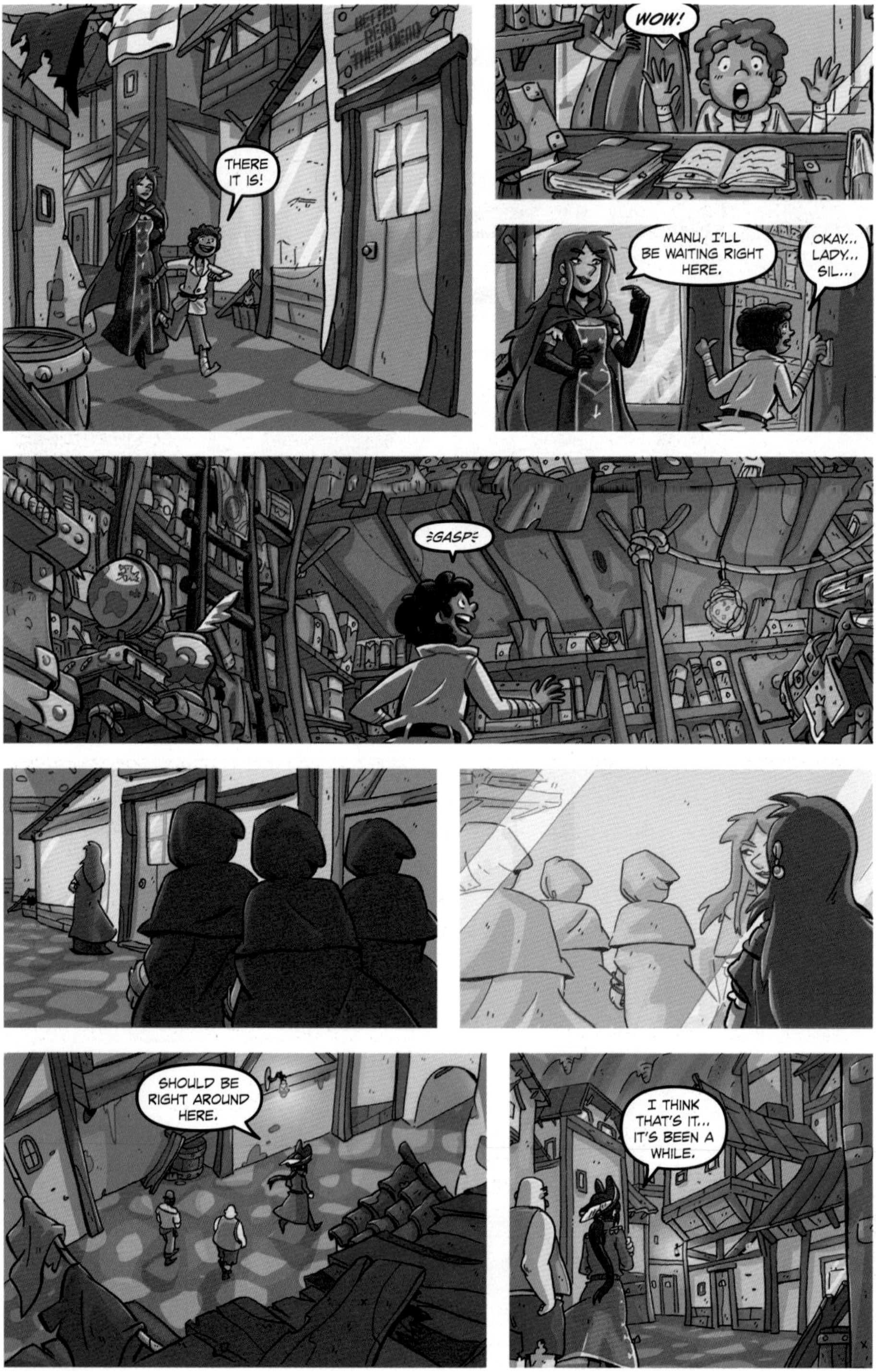
BETTER READ THAN DEAD
THERE IT IS!
WOW!
MANU, I'LL BE WAITING RIGHT HERE.
OKAY... LADY... SIL...
GASP
SHOULD BE RIGHT AROUND HERE.
I THINK THAT'S IT... IT'S BEEN A WHILE.

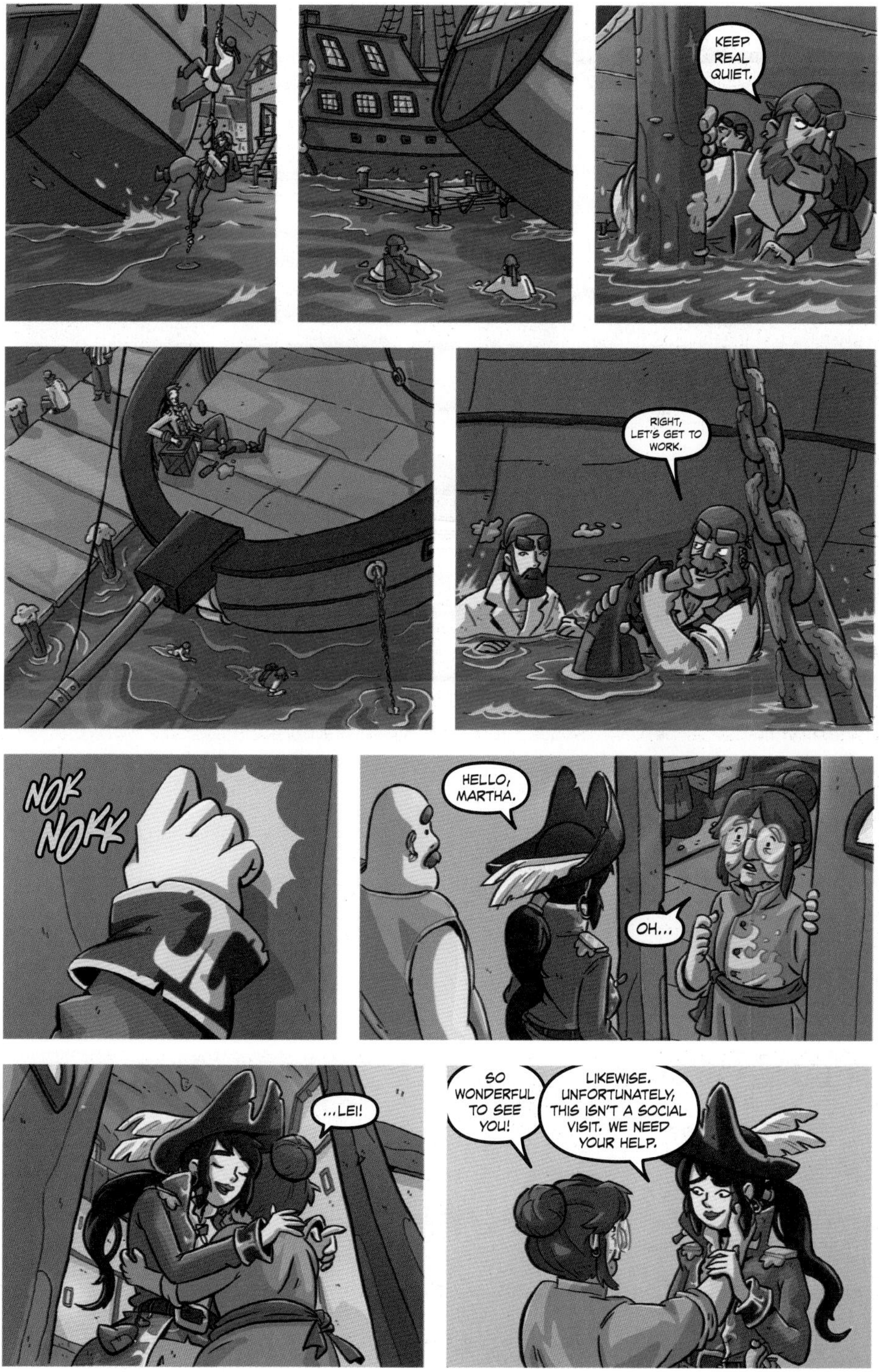
KEEP REAL QUIET.
RIGHT, LET'S GET TO WORK.
NOK NOKK
HELLO, MARTHA.
OH...
...LEI!
SO WONDERFUL TO SEE YOU!
LIKEWISE. UNFORTUNATELY, THIS ISN'T A SOCIAL VISIT. WE NEED YOUR HELP.

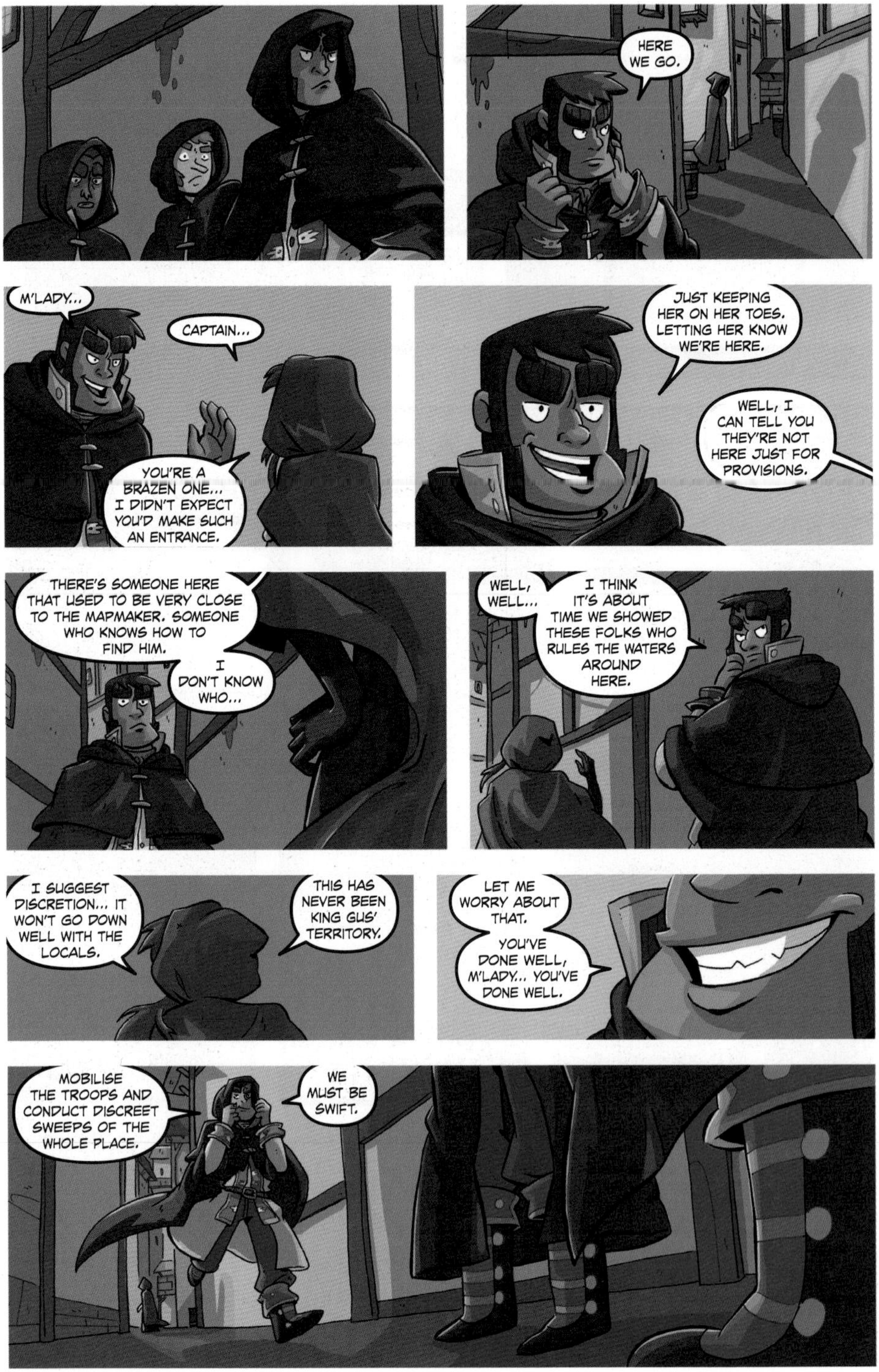
HERE WE GO.
M'LADY...
CAPTAIN...
YOU'RE A BRAZEN ONE... I DIDN'T EXPECT YOU'D MAKE SUCH AN ENTRANCE.
JUST KEEPING HER ON HER TOES. LETTING HER KNOW WE'RE HERE.
WELL, I CAN TELL YOU THEY'RE NOT HERE JUST FOR PROVISIONS.
THERE'S SOMEONE HERE THAT USED TO BE VERY CLOSE TO THE MAPMAKER. SOMEONE WHO KNOWS HOW TO FIND HIM.
I DON'T KNOW WHO...
WELL, WELL...
I THINK IT'S ABOUT TIME WE SHOWED THESE FOLKS WHO RULES THE WATERS AROUND HERE.
I SUGGEST DISCRETION... IT WON'T GO DOWN WELL WITH THE LOCALS.
THIS HAS NEVER BEEN KING GUS' TERRITORY.
LET ME WORRY ABOUT THAT.
YOU'VE DONE WELL, M'LADY... YOU'VE DONE WELL.
MOBILISE THE TROOPS AND CONDUCT DISCREET SWEEPS OF THE WHOLE PLACE.
WE MUST BE SWIFT.

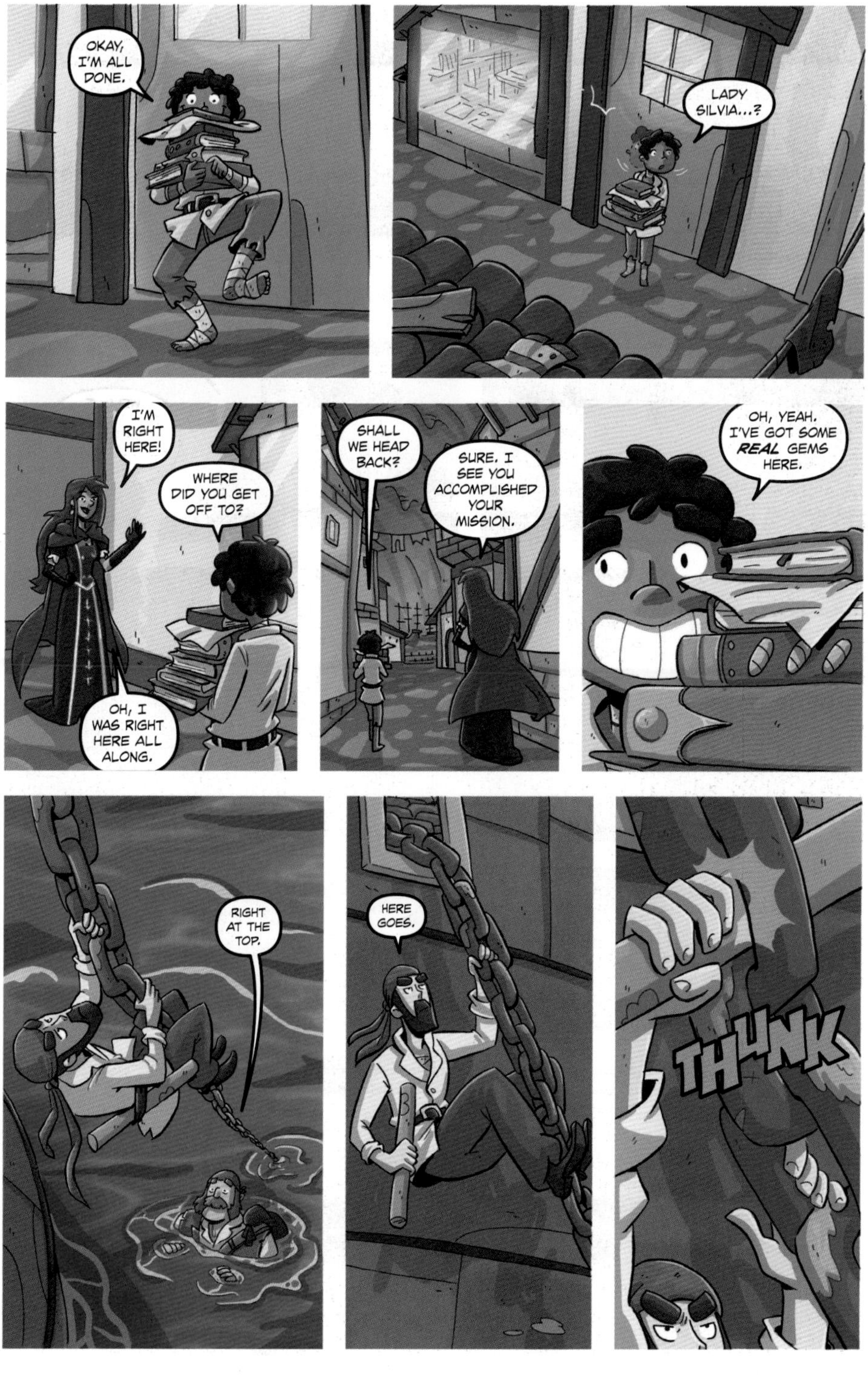
OKAY, I'M ALL DONE.
LADY SILVIA...?
I'M RIGHT HERE!
WHERE DID YOU GET OFF TO?
OH, I WAS RIGHT HERE ALL ALONG.
SHALL WE HEAD BACK?
SURE. I SEE YOU ACCOMPLISHED YOUR MISSION.
OH, YEAH. I'VE GOT SOME REAL GEMS HERE.
RIGHT AT THE TOP.
HERE GOES.
THUNK

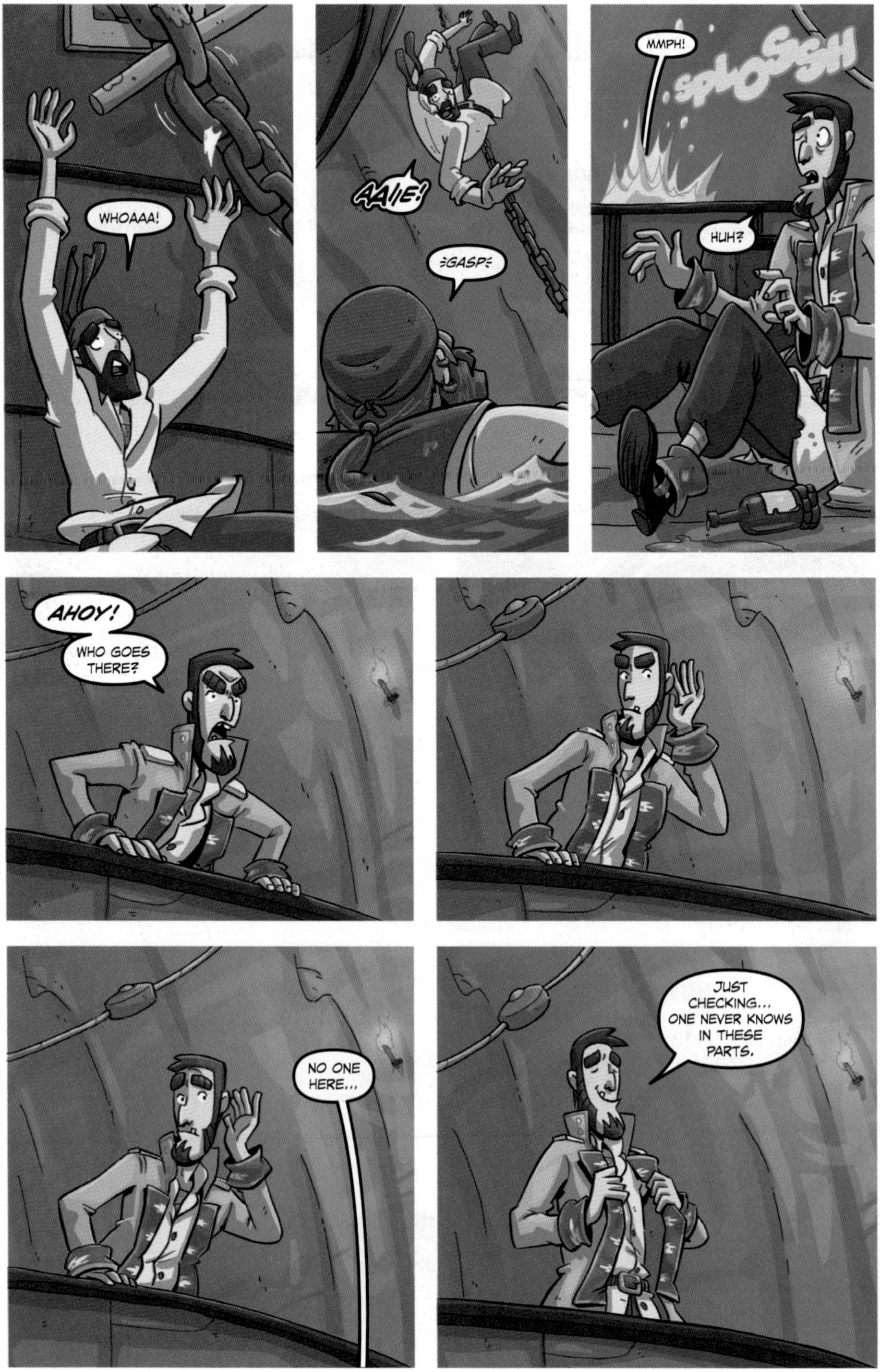
WHOAAA!
AAIIE!
GASP
SPLOOSH
MMPH!
HUH?
AHOY!
WHO GOES THERE?
NO ONE HERE...
JUST CHECKING... ONE NEVER KNOWS IN THESE PARTS.

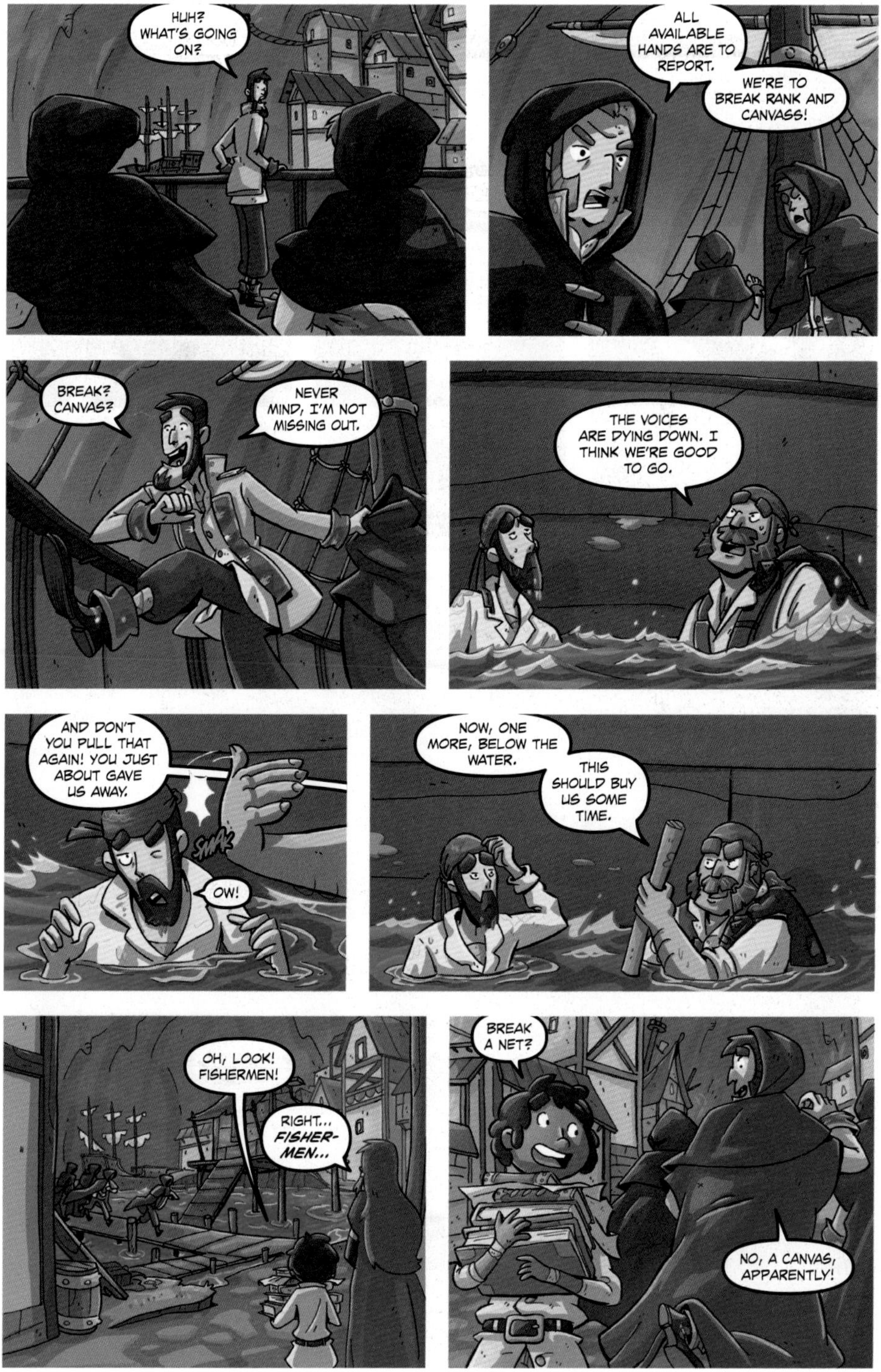

HUH? WHAT'S GOING ON?
ALL AVAILABLE HANDS ARE TO REPORT.
WE'RE TO BREAK RANK AND CANVASS!
BREAK? CANVAS?
NEVER MIND, I'M NOT MISSING OUT.
THE VOICES ARE DYING DOWN. I THINK WE'RE GOOD TO GO.
AND DON'T YOU PULL THAT AGAIN! YOU JUST ABOUT GAVE US AWAY.
SMAK
OW!
NOW, ONE MORE, BELOW THE WATER.
THIS SHOULD BUY US SOME TIME.
OH, LOOK! FISHERMEN!
RIGHT... FISHERMEN...
BREAK A NET?
NO, A CANVAS, APPARENTLY!

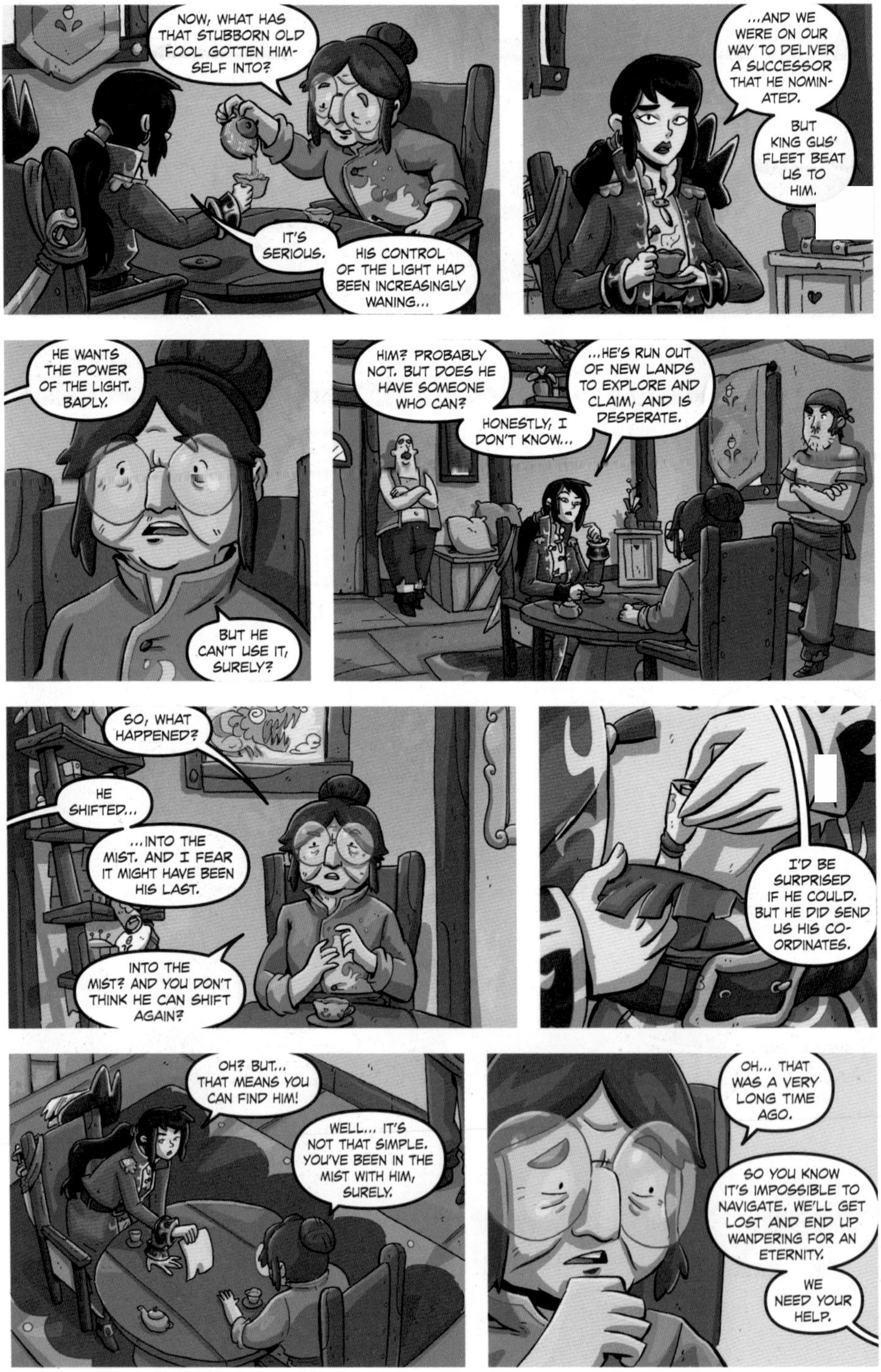
NOW, WHAT HAS THAT STUBBORN OLD FOOL GOTTEN HIM-SELF INTO?
IT'S SERIOUS.
HIS CONTROL OF THE LIGHT HAD BEEN INCREASINGLY WANING...
...AND WE WERE ON OUR WAY TO DELIVER A SUCCESSOR THAT HE NOMIN-ATED.
BUT KING GUS' FLEET BEAT US TO HIM.
HE WANTS THE POWER OF THE LIGHT. BADLY.
BUT HE CAN'T USE IT, SURELY?
HIM? PROBABLY NOT. BUT DOES HE HAVE SOMEONE WHO CAN?
HONESTLY, I DON'T KNOW...
...HE'S RUN OUT OF NEW LANDS TO EXPLORE AND CLAIM, AND IS DESPERATE.
SO, WHAT HAPPENED?
HE SHIFTED...
...INTO THE MIST. AND I FEAR IT MIGHT HAVE BEEN HIS LAST.
INTO THE MIST? AND YOU DON'T THINK HE CAN SHIFT AGAIN?
I'D BE SURPRISED IF HE COULD. BUT HE DID SEND US HIS CO-ORDINATES.
OH? BUT... THAT MEANS YOU CAN FIND HIM!
WELL... IT'S NOT THAT SIMPLE. YOU'VE BEEN IN THE MIST WITH HIM, SURELY.
OH... THAT WAS A VERY LONG TIME AGO.
SO YOU KNOW IT'S IMPOSSIBLE TO NAVIGATE. WE'LL GET LOST AND END UP WANDERING FOR AN ETERNITY.
WE NEED YOUR HELP.

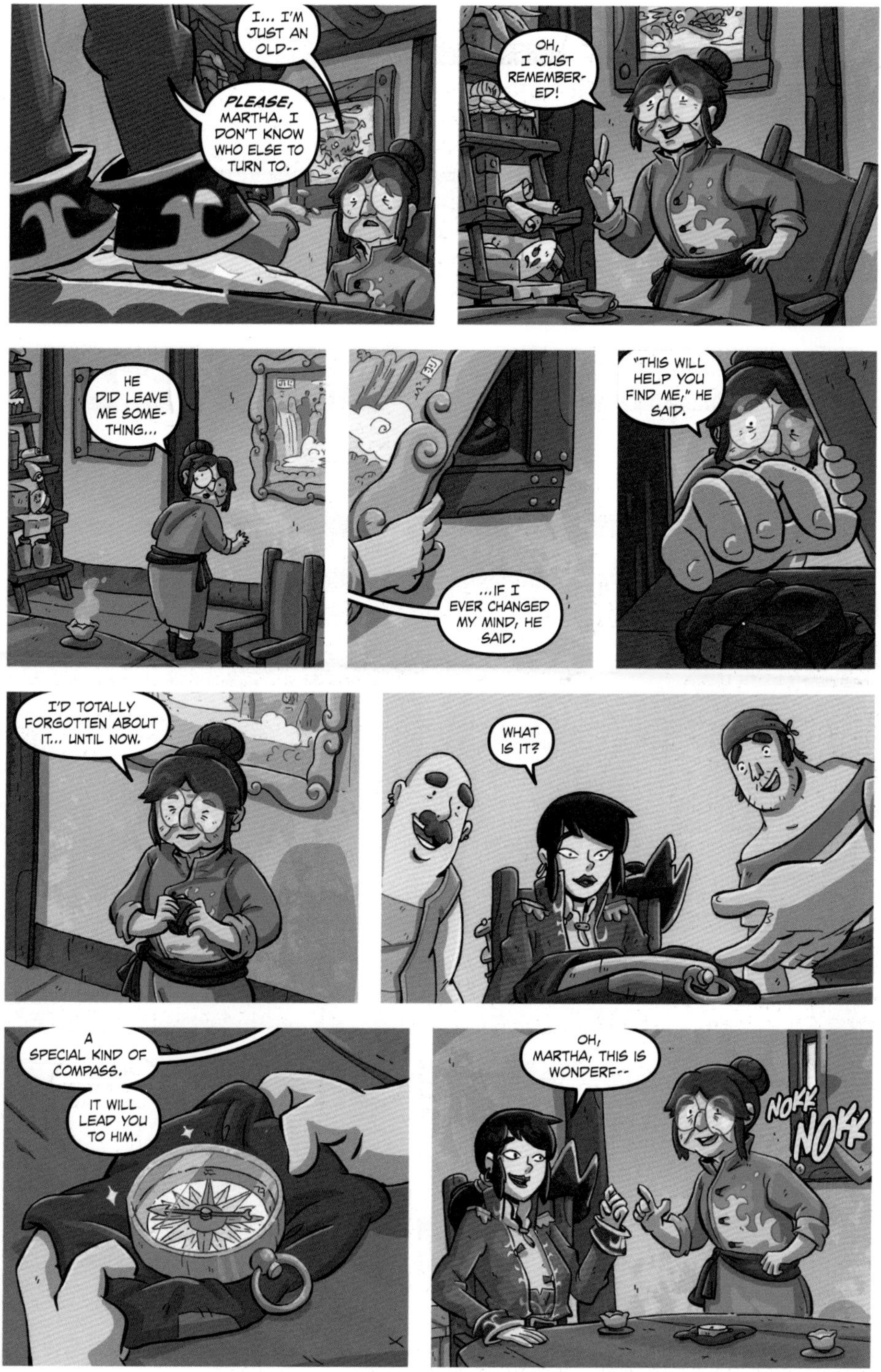
I... I'M JUST AN OLD--
PLEASE, MARTHA. I DON'T KNOW WHO ELSE TO TURN TO.
OH, I JUST REMEMBER-ED!
HE DID LEAVE ME SOME-THING...
...IF I EVER CHANGED MY MIND, HE SAID.
"THIS WILL HELP YOU FIND ME," HE SAID.
I'D TOTALLY FORGOTTEN ABOUT IT... UNTIL NOW.
WHAT IS IT?
A SPECIAL KIND OF COMPASS.
IT WILL LEAD YOU TO HIM.
OH, MARTHA, THIS IS WONDERF--
NOKK NOKK

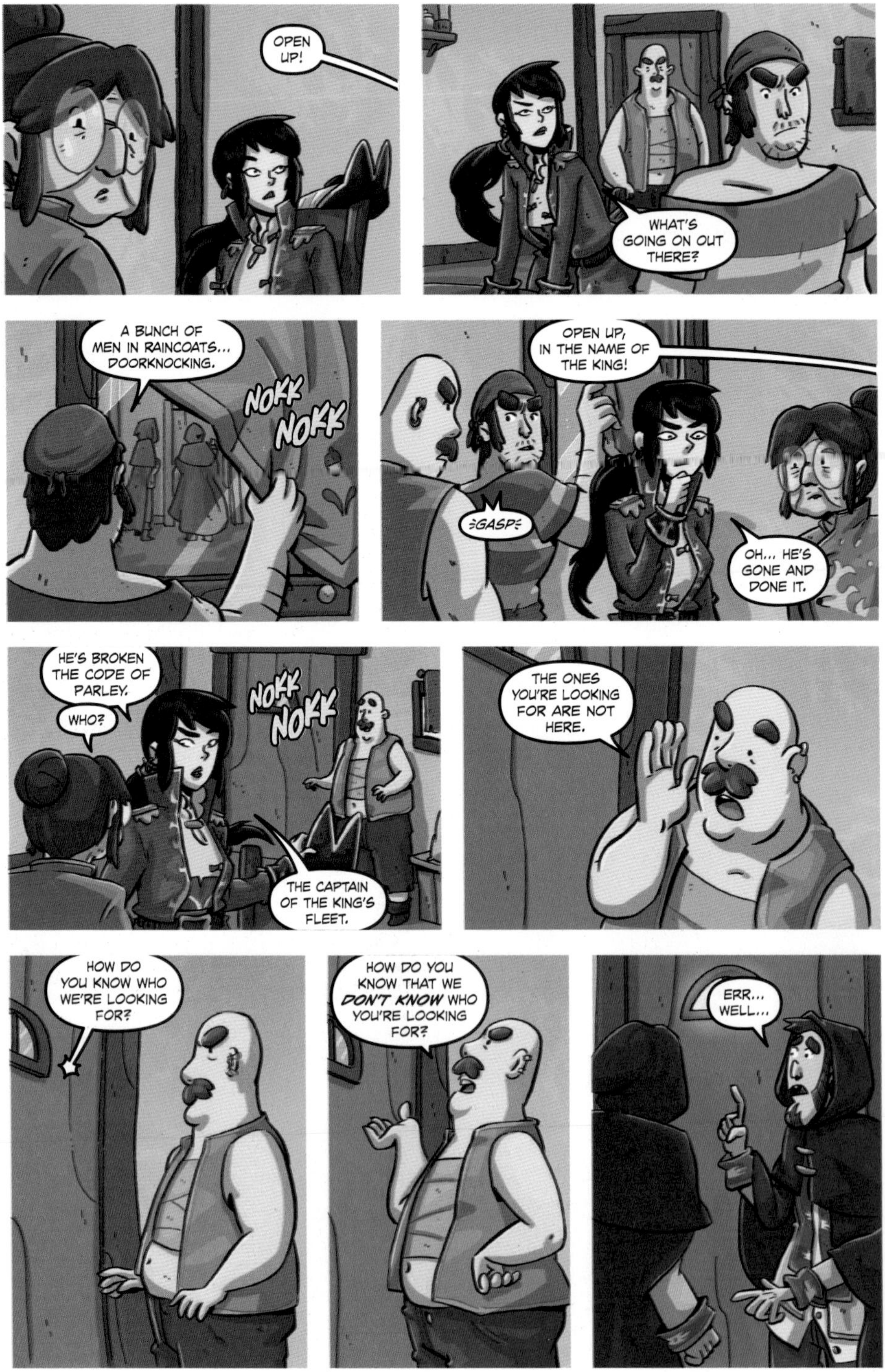
OPEN UP!
WHAT'S GOING ON OUT THERE?
A BUNCH OF MEN IN RAINCOATS... DOORKNOCKING.
NOKK NOKK
OPEN UP, IN THE NAME OF THE KING!
GASP
OH... HE'S GONE AND DONE IT.
HE'S BROKEN THE CODE OF PARLEY.
WHO?
NOKK NOKK
THE CAPTAIN OF THE KING'S FLEET.
THE ONES YOU'RE LOOKING FOR ARE NOT HERE.
HOW DO YOU KNOW WHO WE'RE LOOKING FOR?
HOW DO YOU KNOW THAT WE *DON'T KNOW* WHO YOU'RE LOOKING FOR?
ERR... WELL...

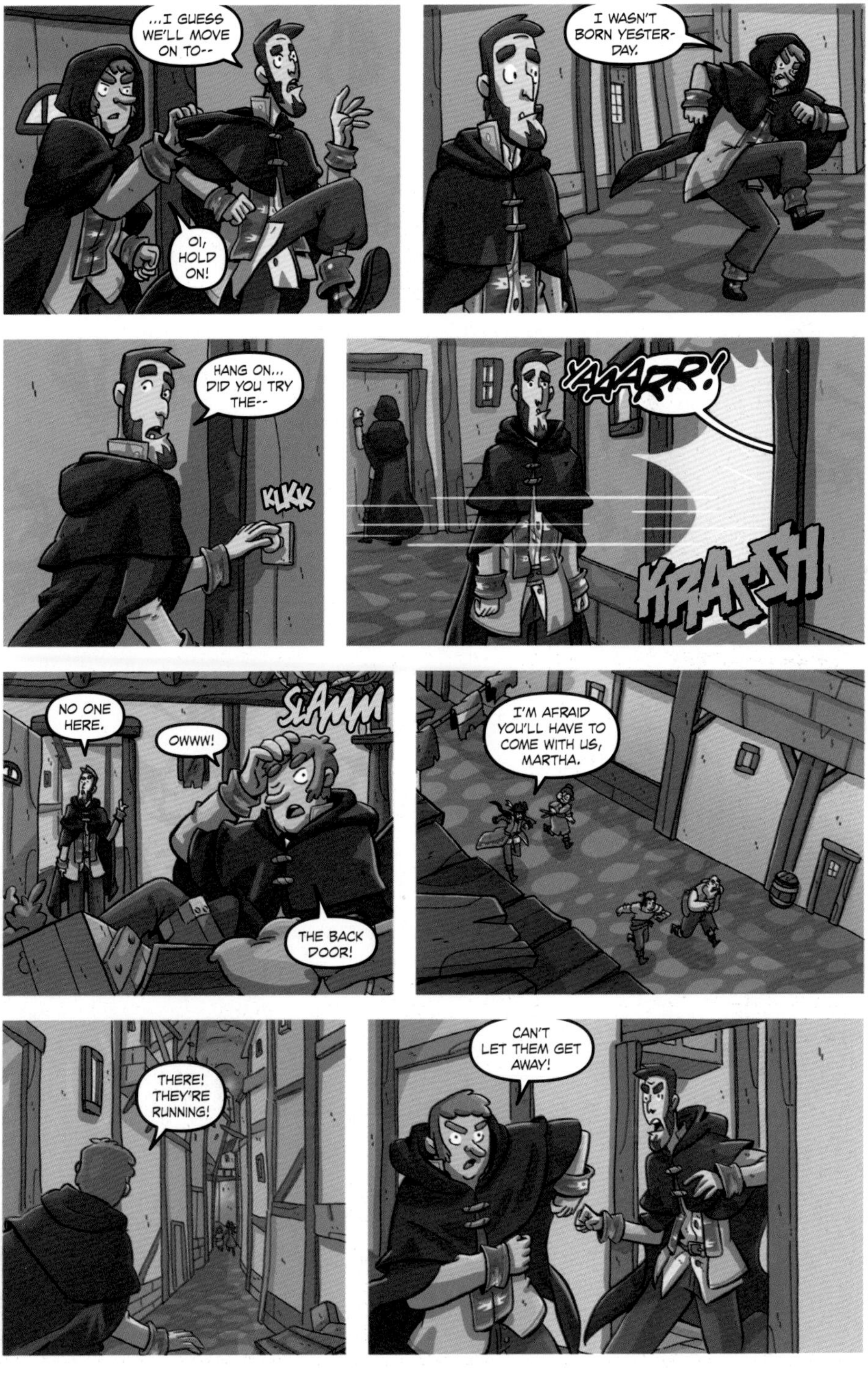
...I GUESS WE'LL MOVE ON TO--
OI, HOLD ON!
I WASN'T BORN YESTER-DAY.
HANG ON... DID YOU TRY THE--
KLKK
YAAARR!
KRASSH
NO ONE HERE.
OWWW!
SLAMM
THE BACK DOOR!
I'M AFRAID YOU'LL HAVE TO COME WITH US, MARTHA.
THERE! THEY'RE RUNNING!
CAN'T LET THEM GET AWAY!

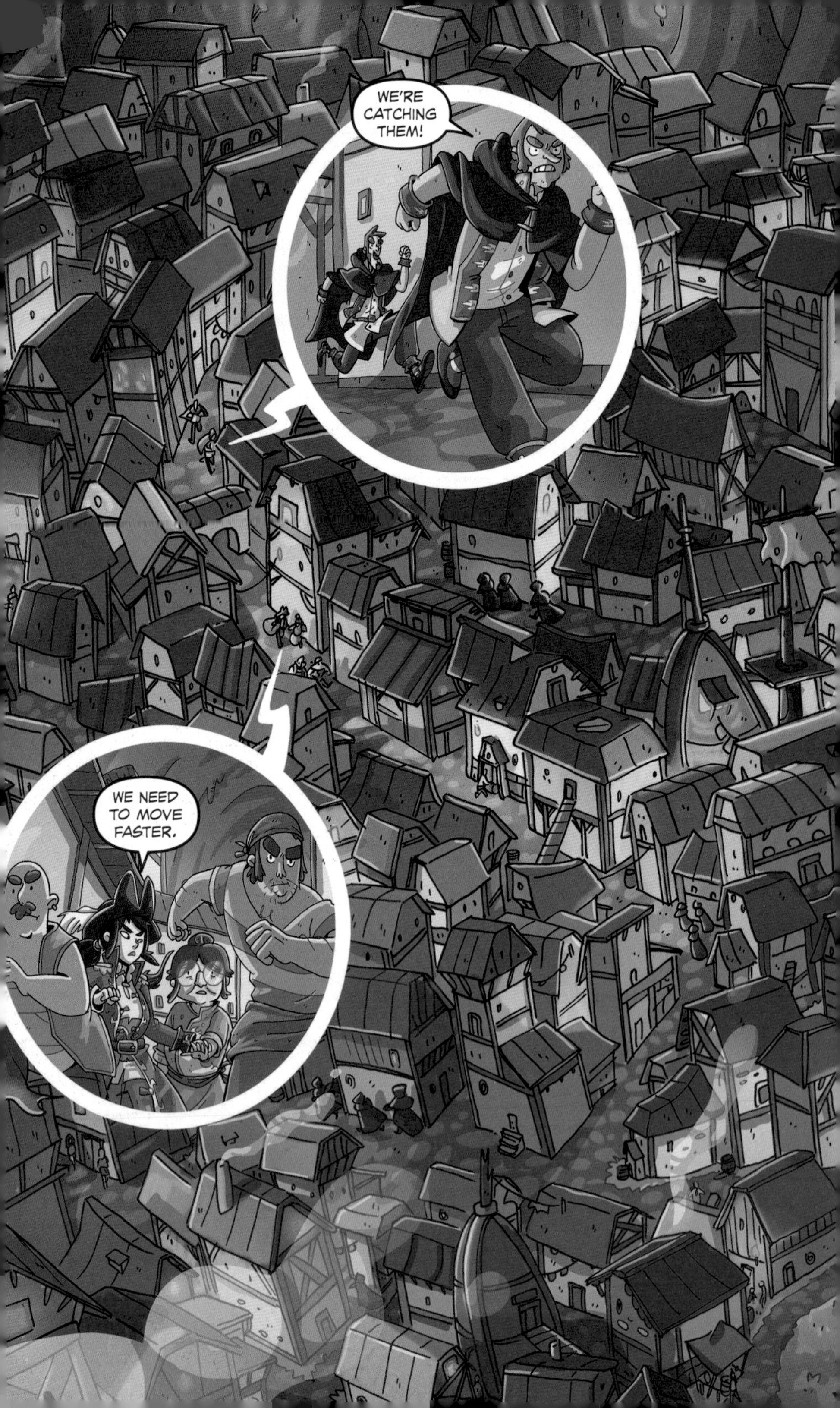
WE'RE CATCHING THEM!
WE NEED TO MOVE FASTER.

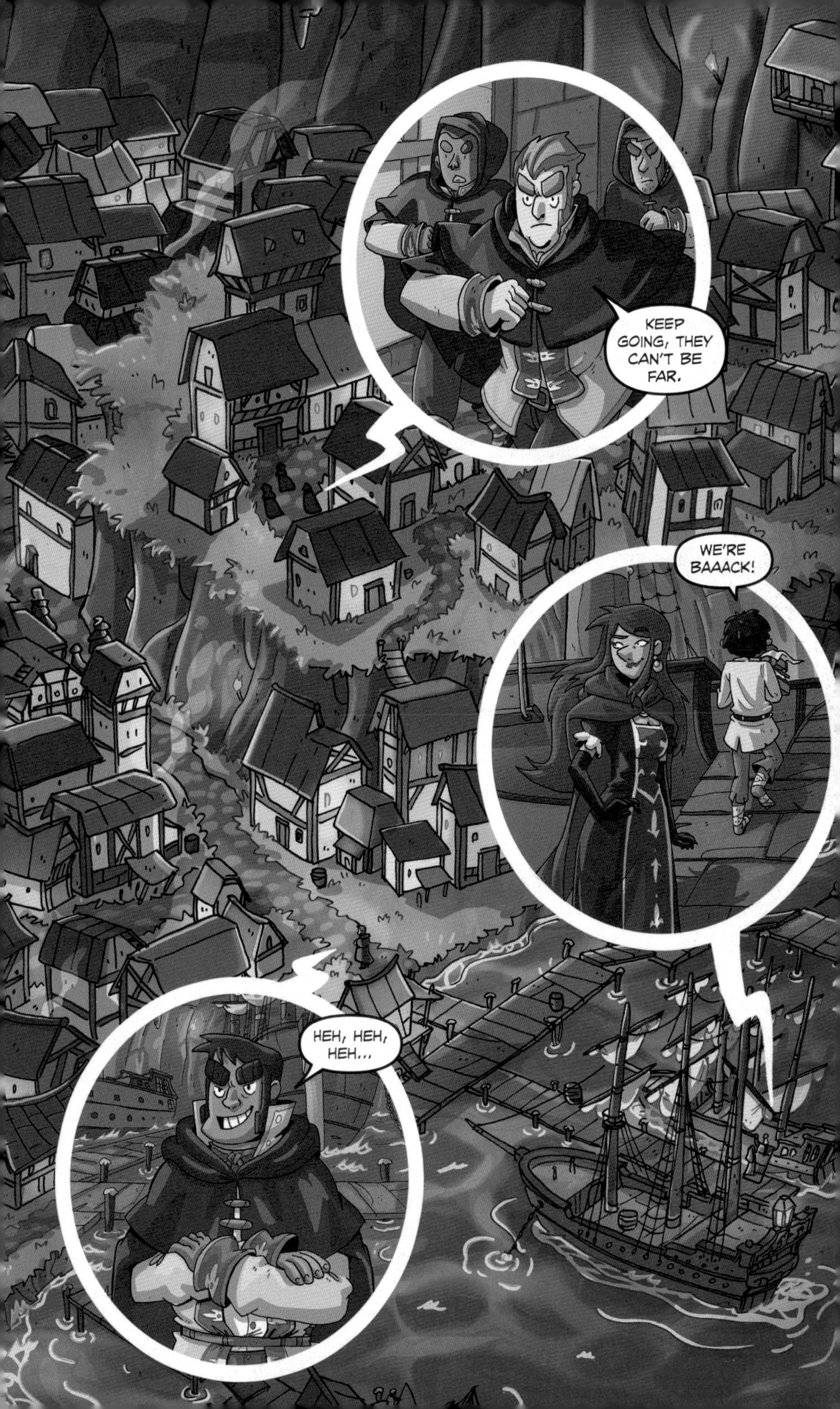

KEEP GOING, THEY CAN'T BE FAR.
WE'RE BAAACK!
HEH, HEH, HEH...

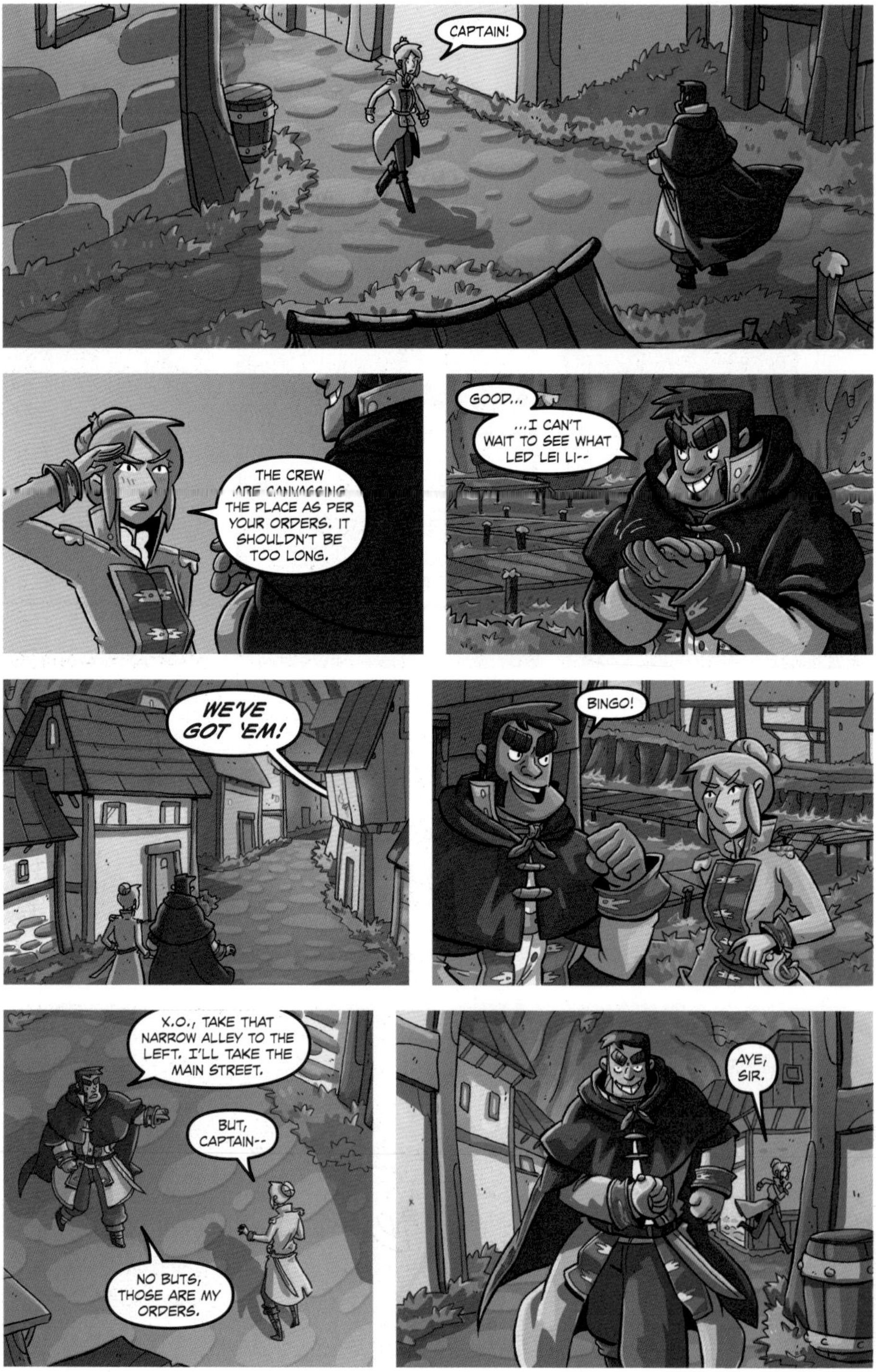
CAPTAIN!
THE CREW ARE CANVASSING THE PLACE AS PER YOUR ORDERS. IT SHOULDN'T BE TOO LONG.
GOOD...
...I CAN'T WAIT TO SEE WHAT LED LEI LI--
WE'VE GOT 'EM!
BINGO!
X.O., TAKE THAT NARROW ALLEY TO THE LEFT. I'LL TAKE THE MAIN STREET.
BUT, CAPTAIN--
NO BUTS, THOSE ARE MY ORDERS.
AYE, SIR.

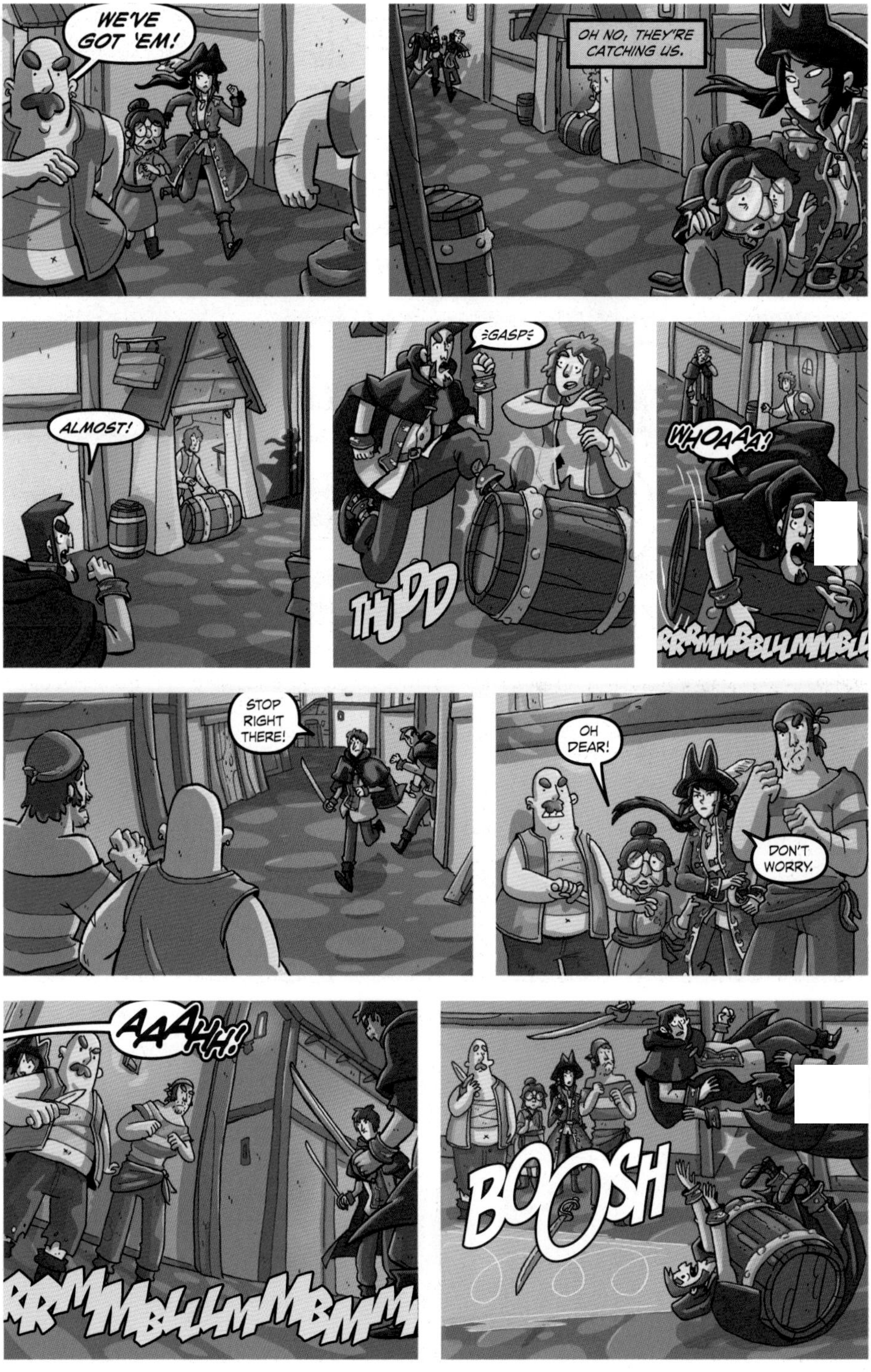
WE'VE GOT 'EM!
OH NO, THEY'RE CATCHING US.
ALMOST!
GASP
THUDD
WHOAAAA!
RRRMMBBLLLMMBLL
STOP RIGHT THERE!
OH DEAR!
DON'T WORRY.
AAAHH!
RRMMBLLLMMBMMM
BOOSH

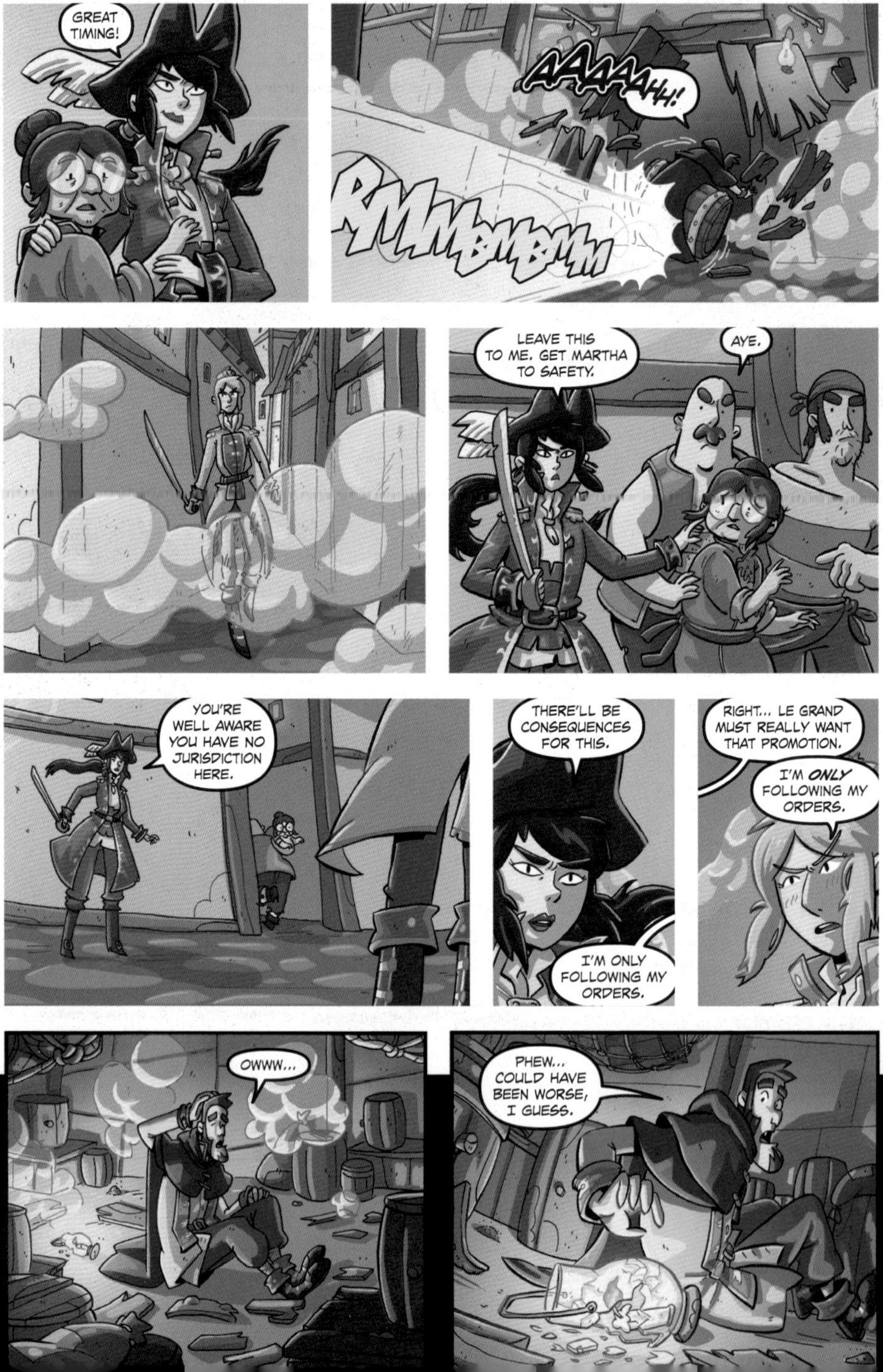
GREAT TIMING!
AAAAAHH!
RMMBMBMMM
LEAVE THIS TO ME. GET MARTHA TO SAFETY.
AYE.
YOU'RE WELL AWARE YOU HAVE NO JURISDICTION HERE.
THERE'LL BE CONSEQUENCES FOR THIS.
I'M ONLY FOLLOWING MY ORDERS.
RIGHT... LE GRAND MUST REALLY WANT THAT PROMOTION.
I'M *ONLY* FOLLOWING MY ORDERS.
OWWW...
PHEW... COULD HAVE BEEN WORSE, I GUESS.

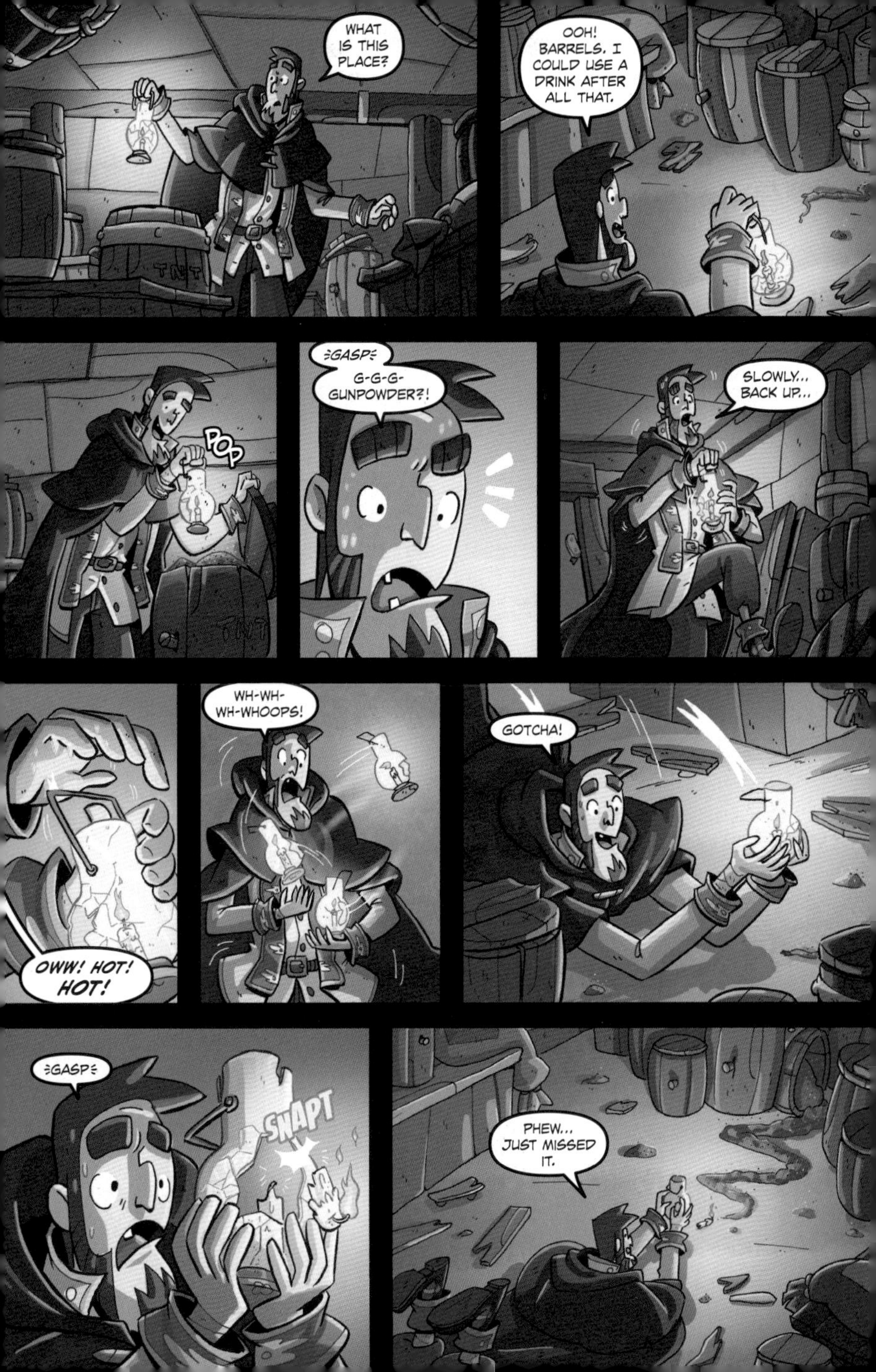

WHAT IS THIS PLACE?
OOH! BARRELS. I COULD USE A DRINK AFTER ALL THAT.
TNT
POP
GASP
G-G-G-GUNPOWDER?!
TNT
SLOWLY... BACK UP...
OWW! HOT! HOT!
WH-WH-WH-WHOOPS!
GOTCHA!
GASP
SNAPT
PHEW... JUST MISSED IT.

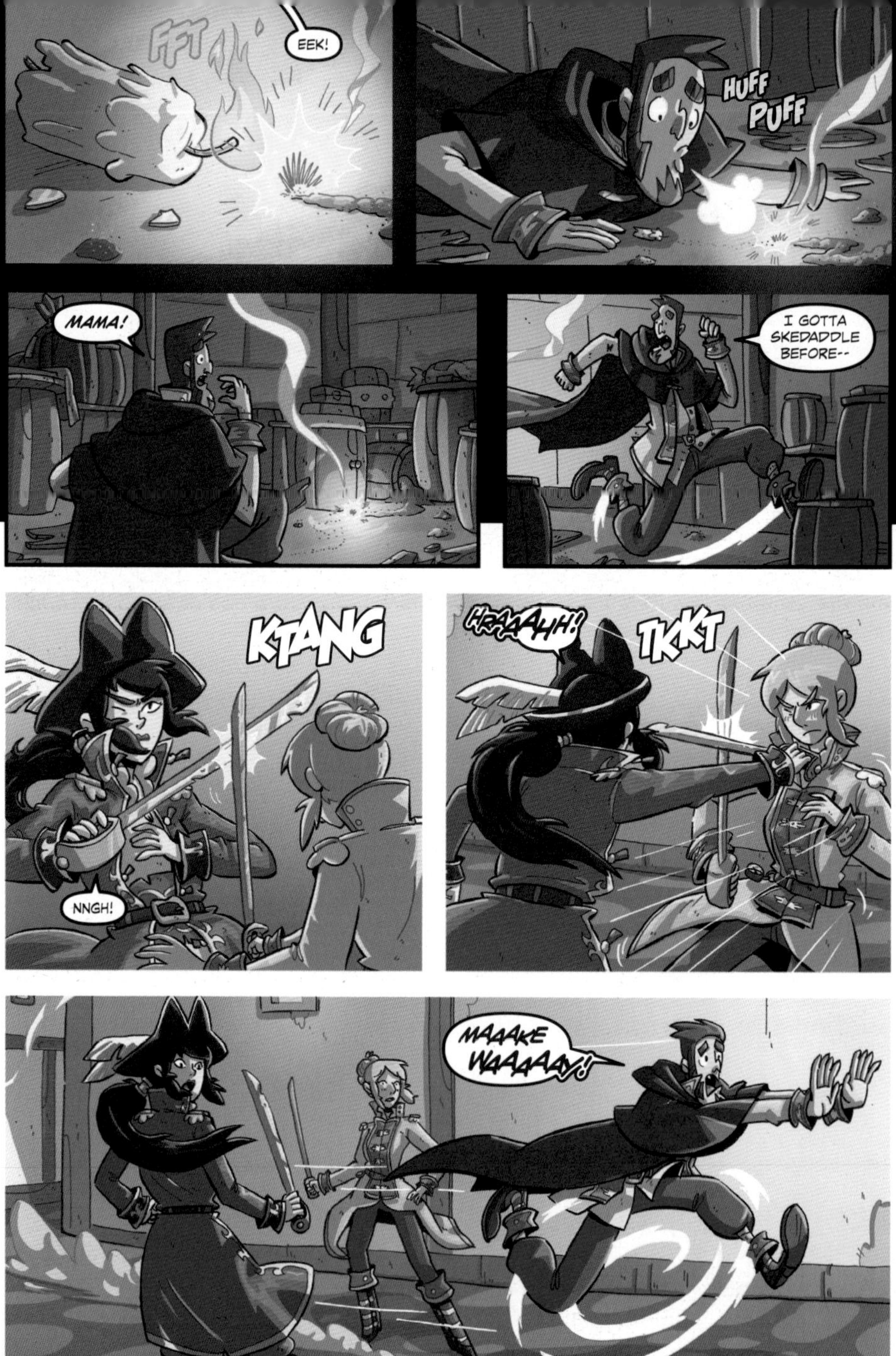

FFT
EEK!
HUFF
PUFF
MAMA!
I GOTTA SKEDADDLE BEFORE--
KTANG
NNGH!
HRAAAHH!
TKKT
MAAAKE WAAAAAY!

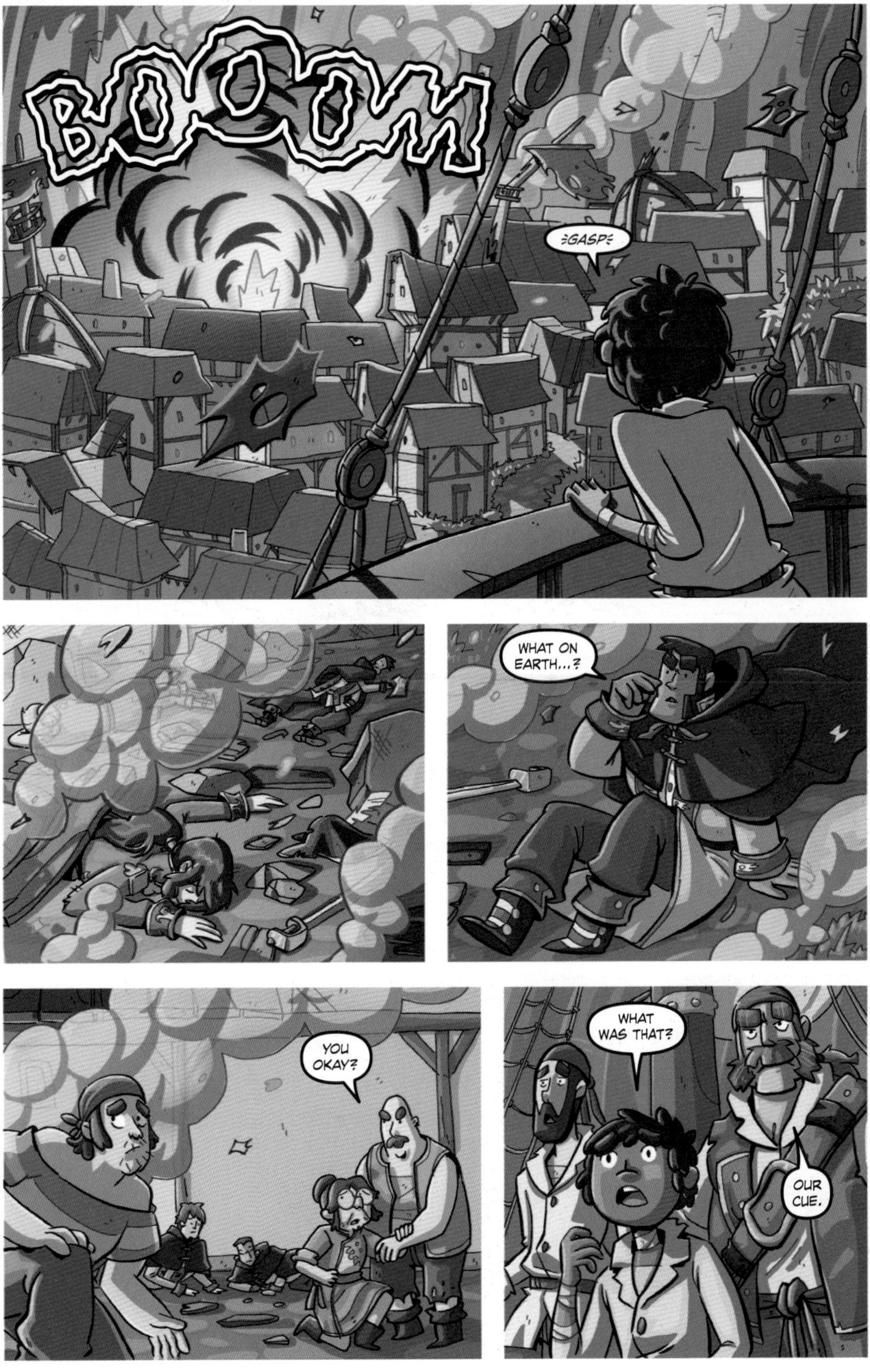
BOOOOM
GASP
WHAT ON EARTH...?
YOU OKAY?
WHAT WAS THAT?
OUR CUE.

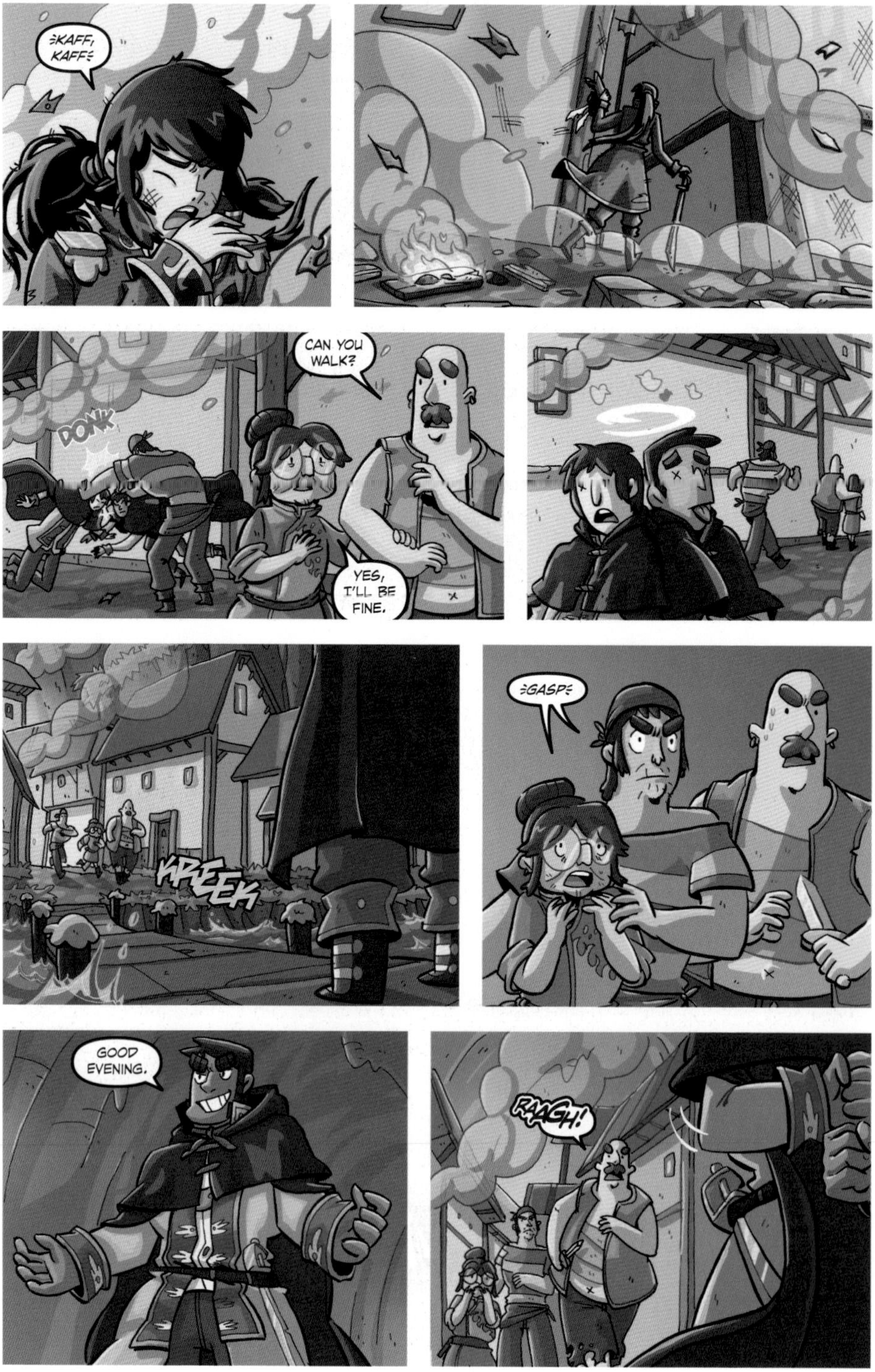

KAFF, KAFF
CAN YOU WALK?
DONK
YES, I'LL BE FINE.
KREEK
GASP
GOOD EVENING.
RAAGH!

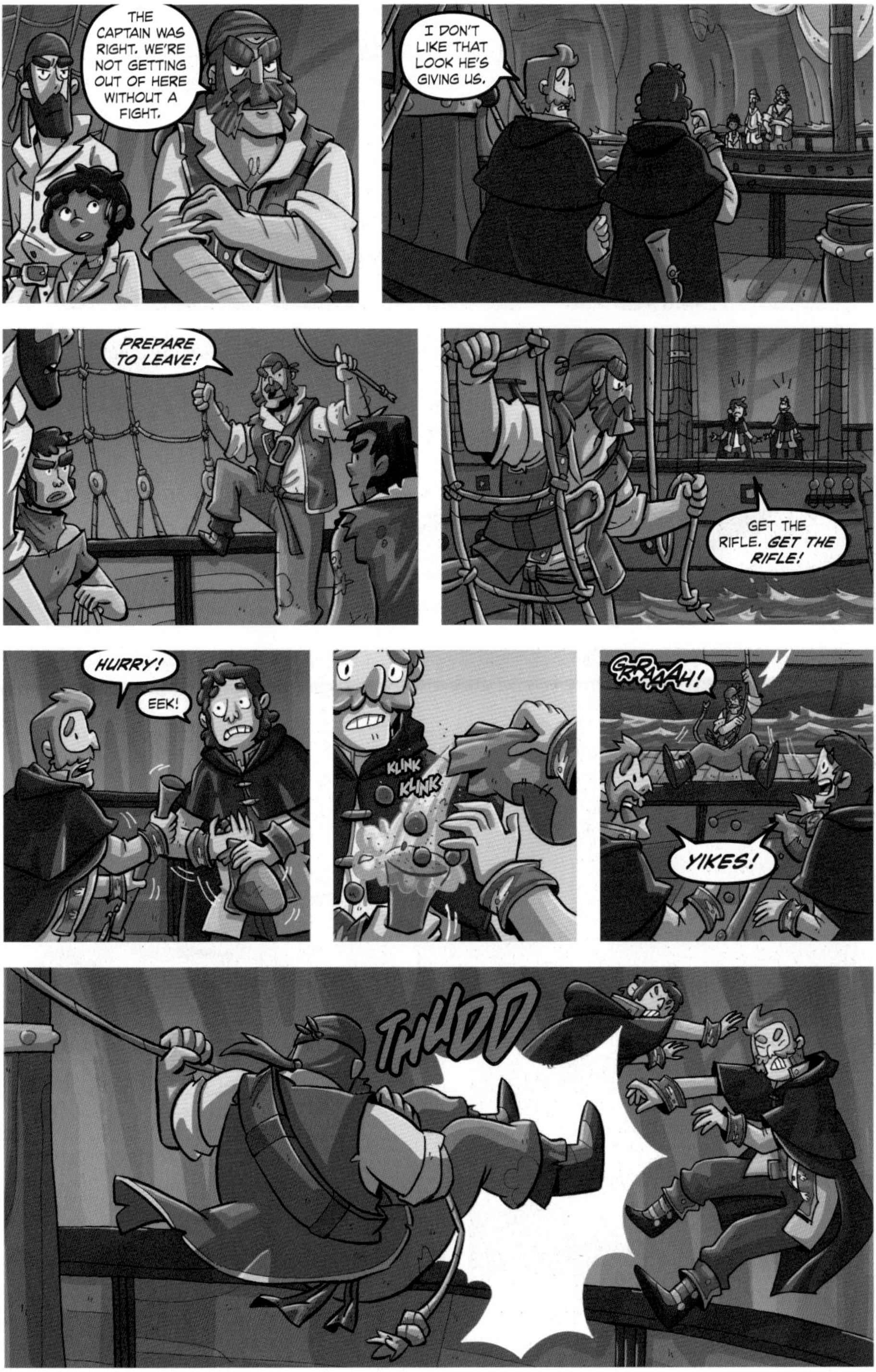
THE CAPTAIN WAS RIGHT. WE'RE NOT GETTING OUT OF HERE WITHOUT A FIGHT.
I DON'T LIKE THAT LOOK HE'S GIVING US.
PREPARE TO LEAVE!
GET THE RIFLE. GET THE RIFLE!
HURRY!
EEK!
KLINK
KLINK
GRRAAAH!
YIKES!
THUDD

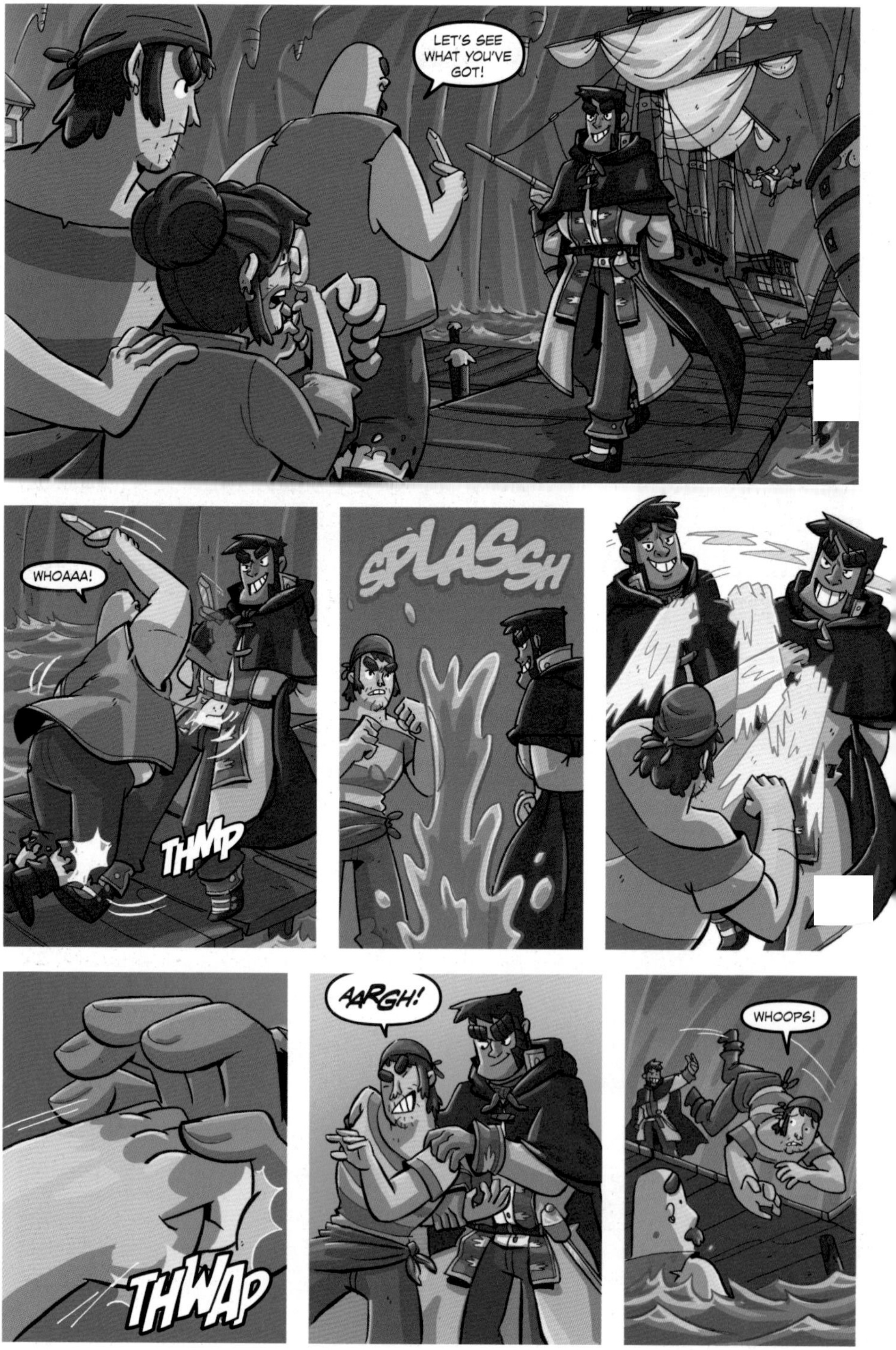
LET'S SEE WHAT YOU'VE GOT!
WHOAAA!
THMP
SPLASSH
THWAP
AARGH!
WHOOPS!

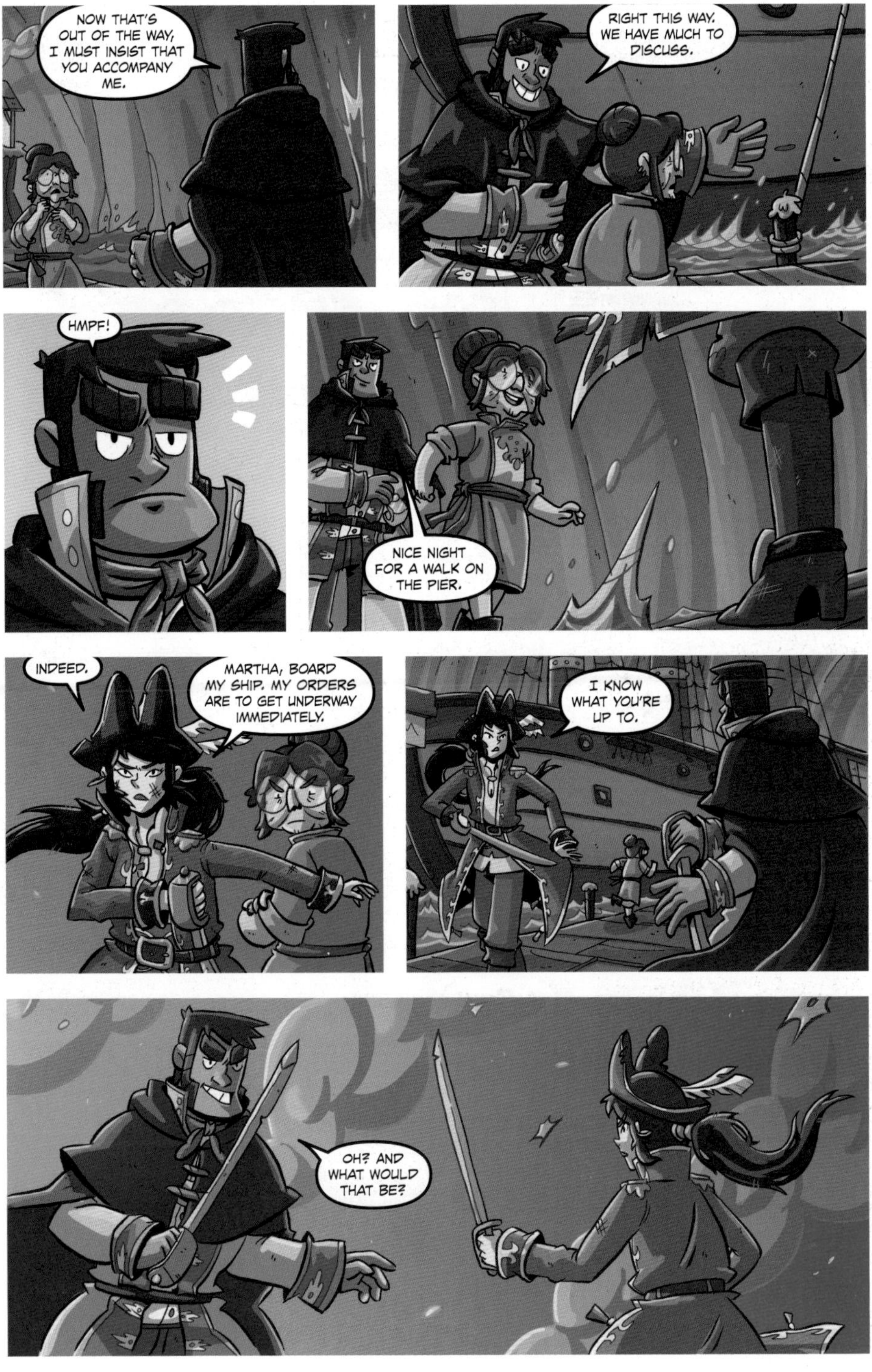
NOW THAT'S OUT OF THE WAY, I MUST INSIST THAT YOU ACCOMPANY ME.
RIGHT THIS WAY. WE HAVE MUCH TO DISCUSS.
HMPF!
NICE NIGHT FOR A WALK ON THE PIER.
INDEED.
MARTHA, BOARD MY SHIP. MY ORDERS ARE TO GET UNDERWAY IMMEDIATELY.
I KNOW WHAT YOU'RE UP TO.
OH? AND WHAT WOULD THAT BE?

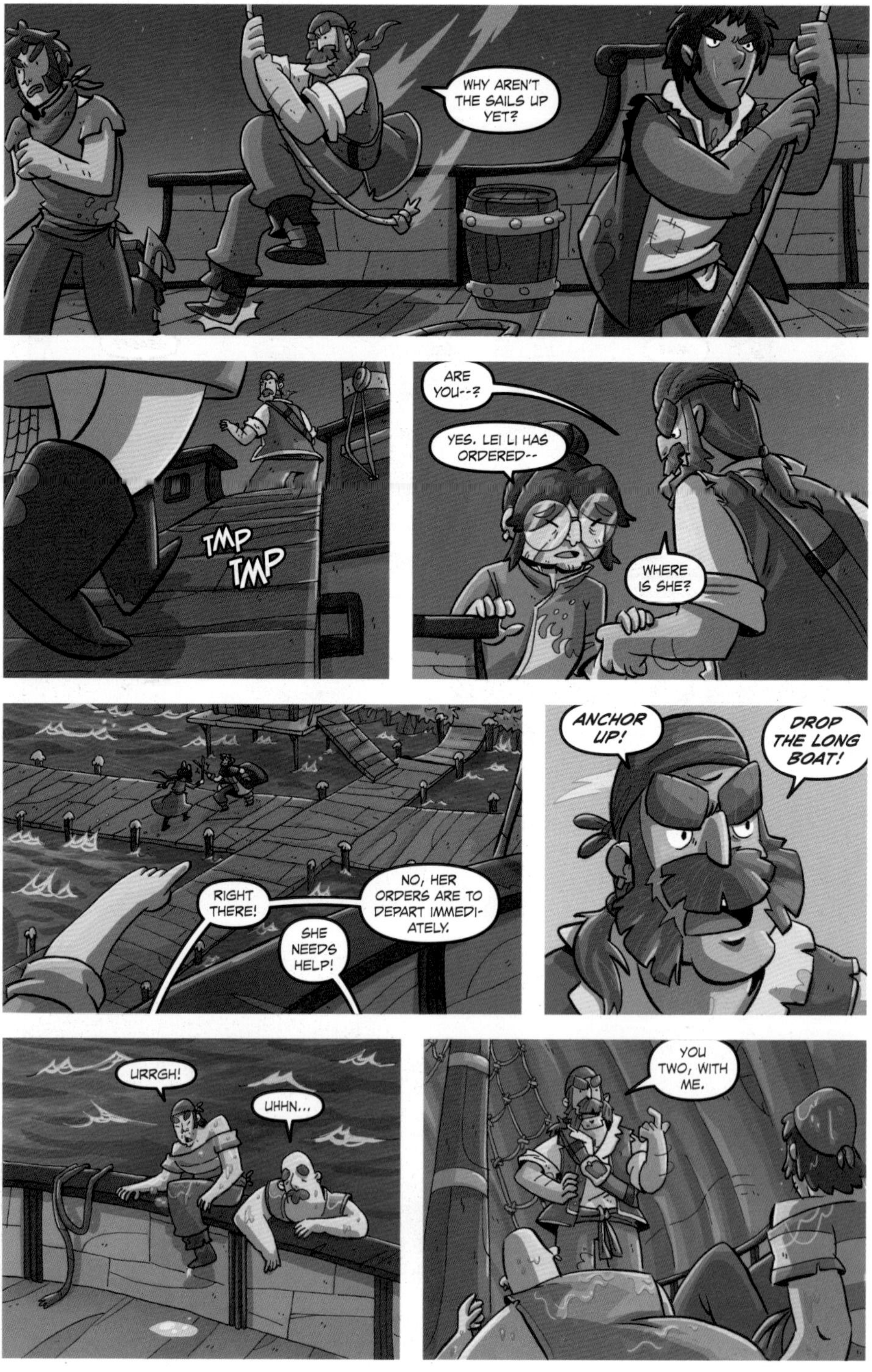
WHY AREN'T THE SAILS UP YET?
TMP TMP
ARE YOU--?
YES. LEI LI HAS ORDERED--
WHERE IS SHE?
RIGHT THERE!
NO, HER ORDERS ARE TO DEPART IMMEDIATELY.
SHE NEEDS HELP!
ANCHOR UP!
DROP THE LONG BOAT!
URRGH!
UHHN...
YOU TWO, WITH ME.

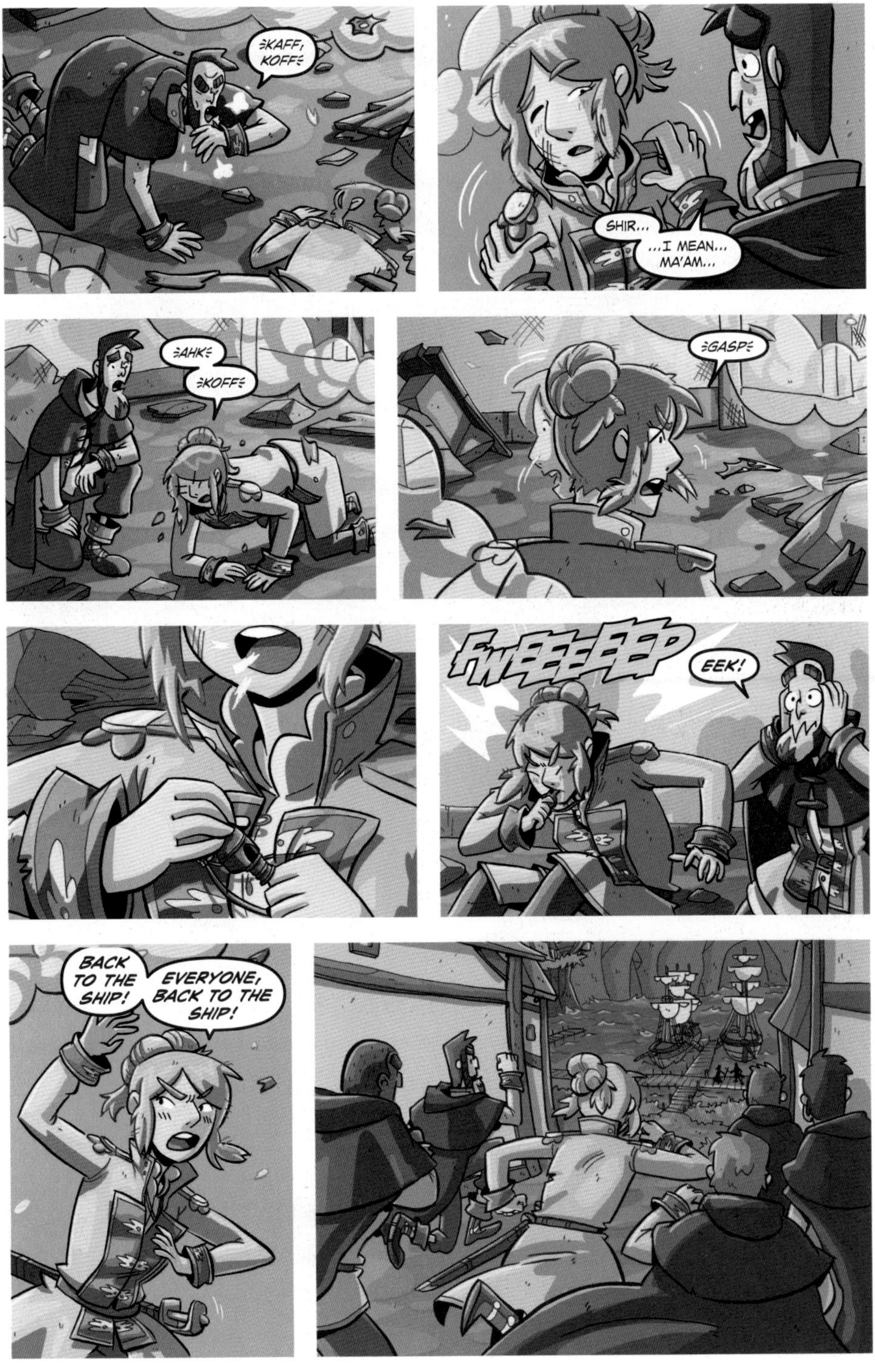
KAFF, KOFF
SHIR...
...I MEAN... MA'AM...
AHK
KOFF
GASP
FWEEEEEP
EEK!
BACK TO THE SHIP!
EVERYONE, BACK TO THE SHIP!

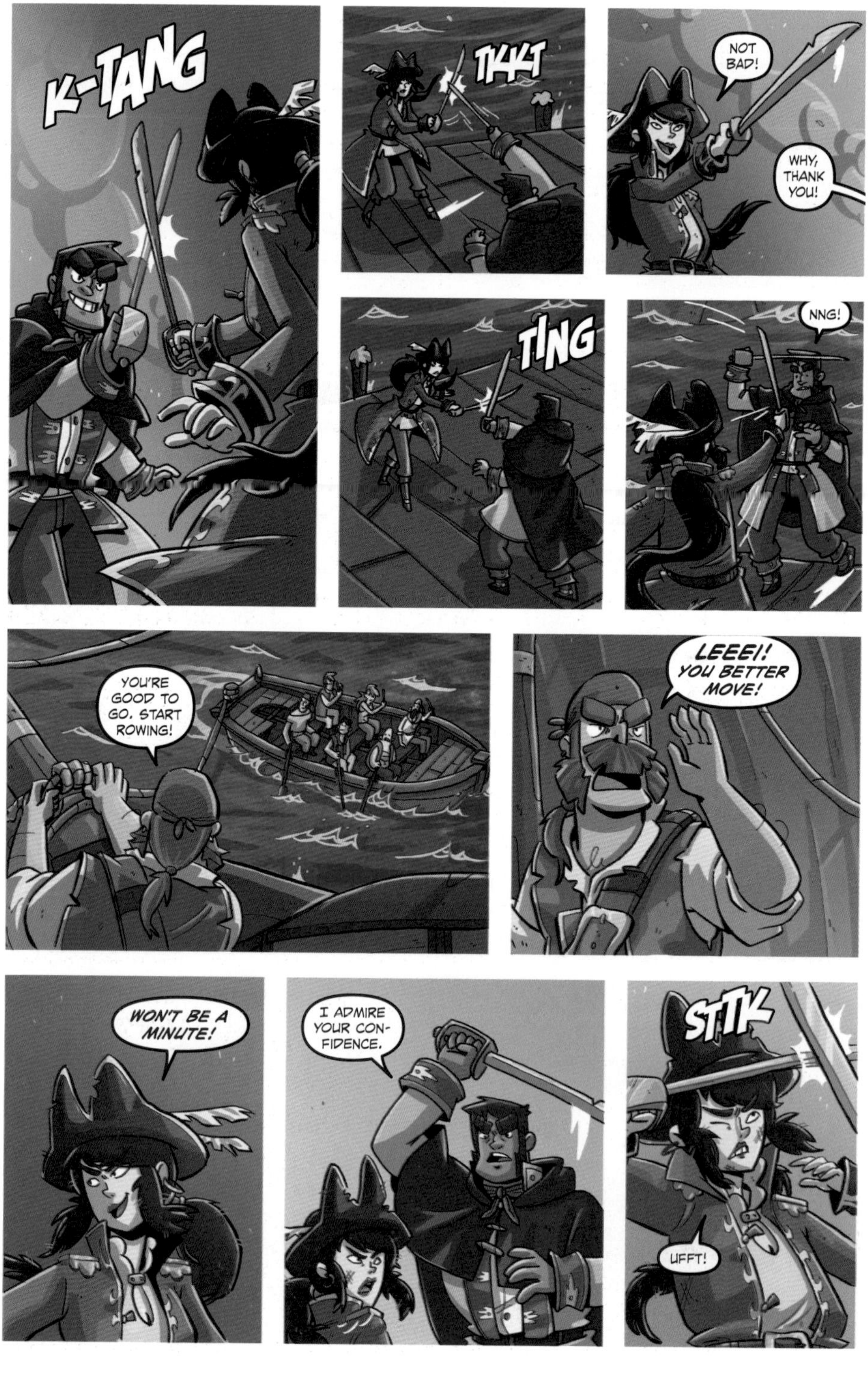
K-TANG
TKKT
NOT BAD!
WHY, THANK YOU!
TING
NNG!
YOU'RE GOOD TO GO. START ROWING!
LEEEI! YOU BETTER MOVE!
WON'T BE A MINUTE!
I ADMIRE YOUR CON-FIDENCE.
STTK
UFFT!

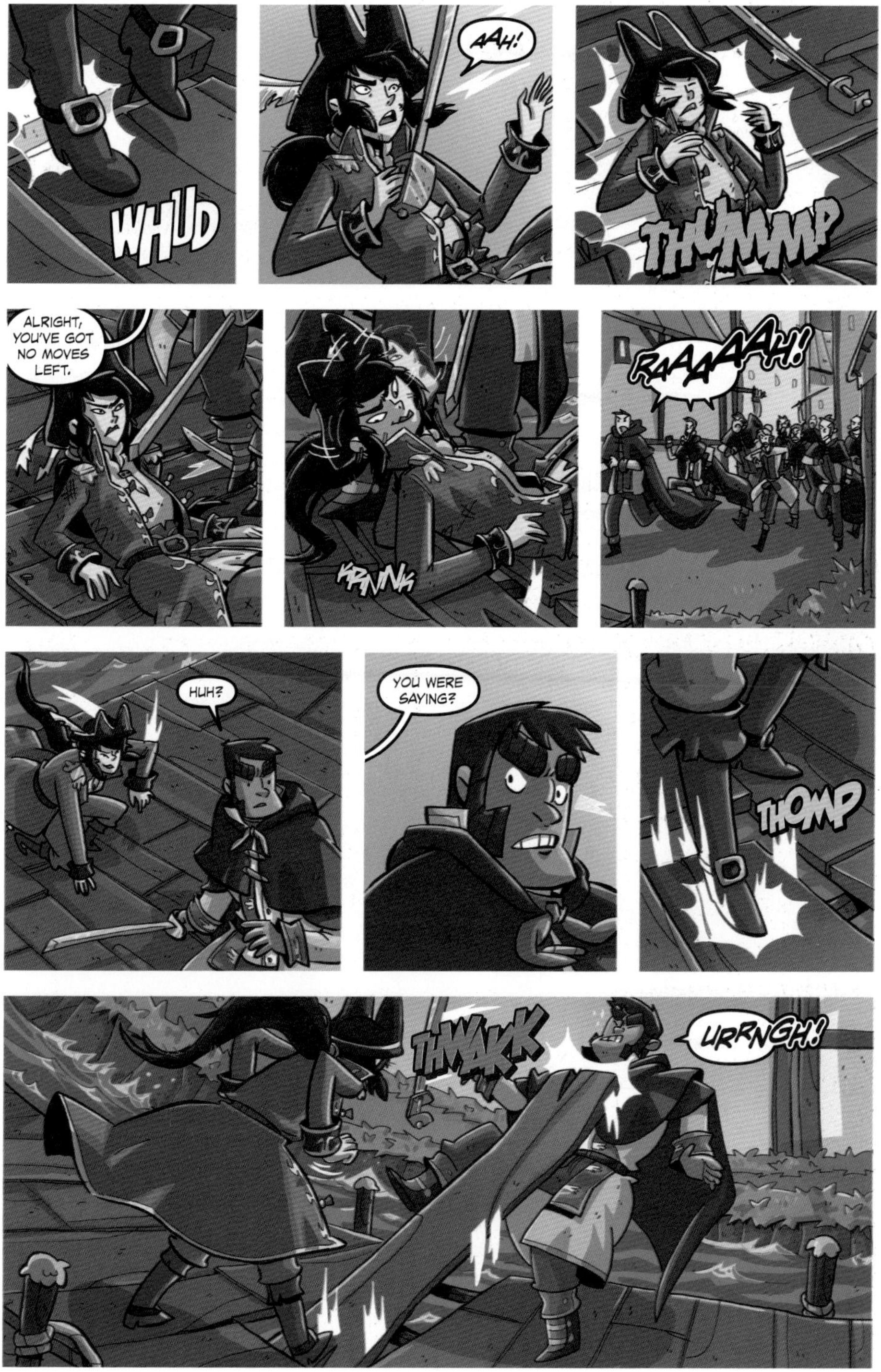
WHUD
AAH!
THUMMP
ALRIGHT, YOU'VE GOT NO MOVES LEFT.
KRNNK
RAAAAAH!
HUH?
YOU WERE SAYING?
THOMP
THWAKK
URRNGH!

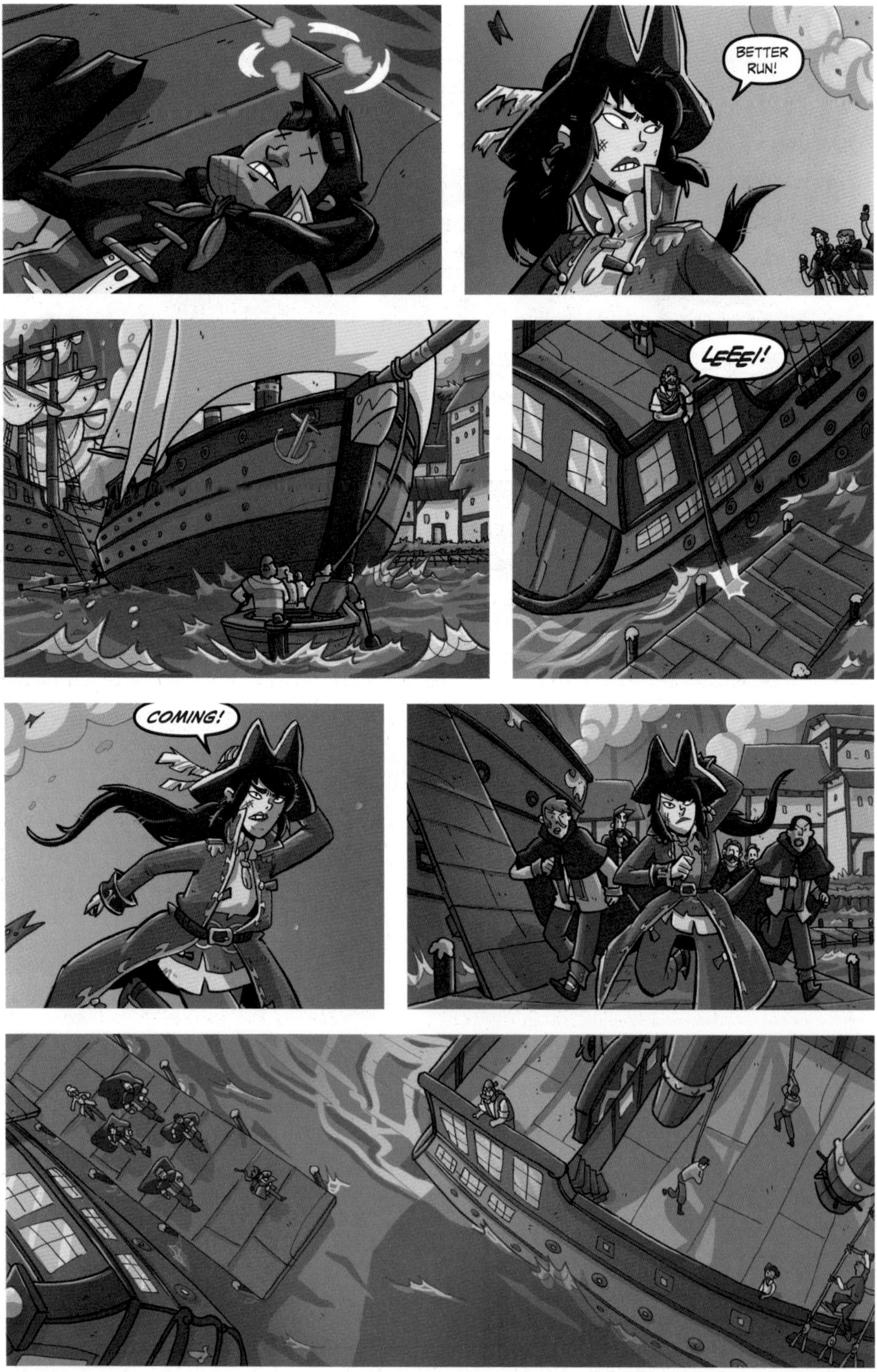
BETTER RUN!
LEEEE!!
COMING!

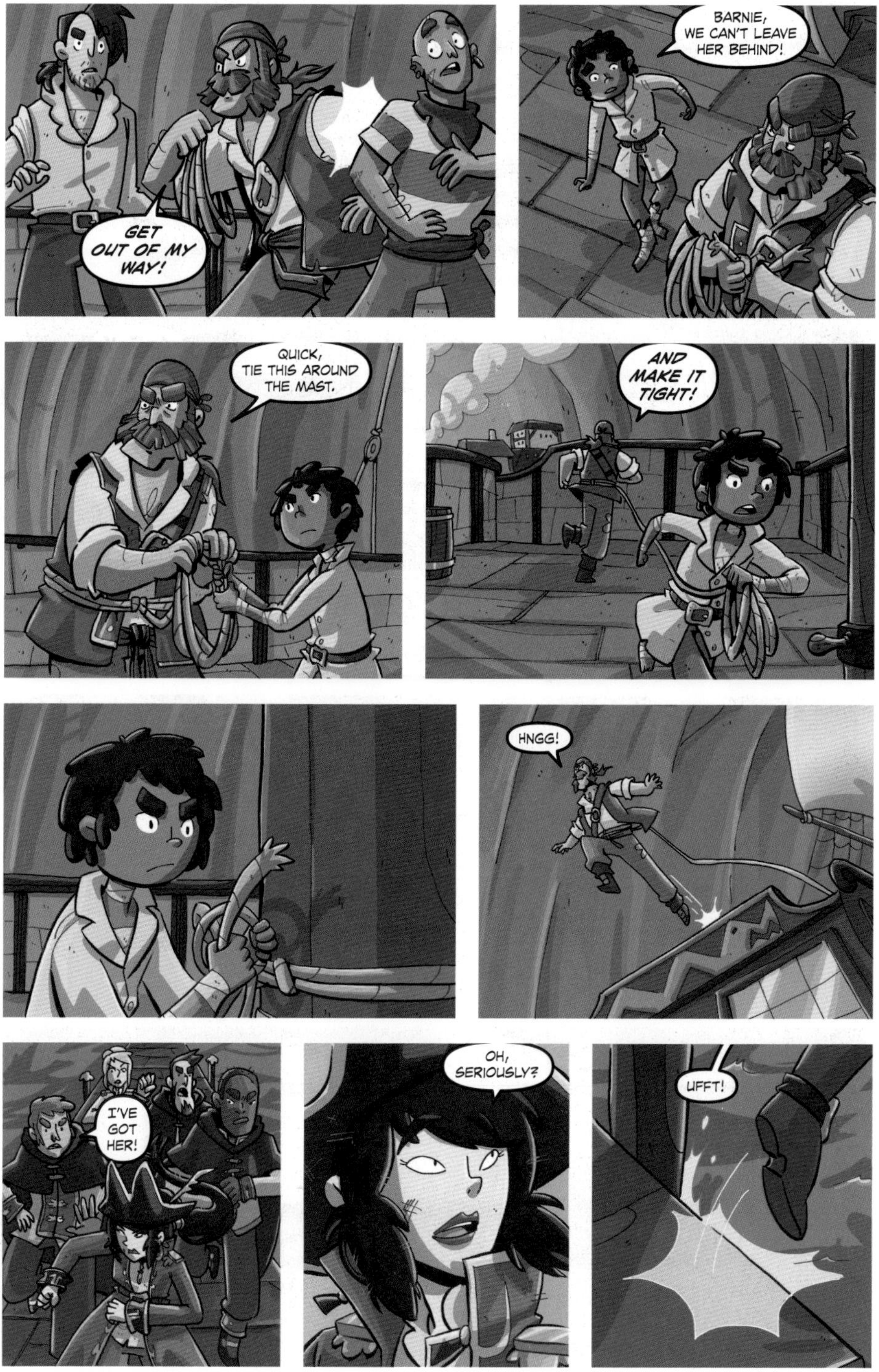
GET OUT OF MY WAY!
BARNIE, WE CAN'T LEAVE HER BEHIND!
QUICK, TIE THIS AROUND THE MAST.
AND MAKE IT TIGHT!
HNGG!
I'VE GOT HER!
OH, SERIOUSLY?
UFFT!

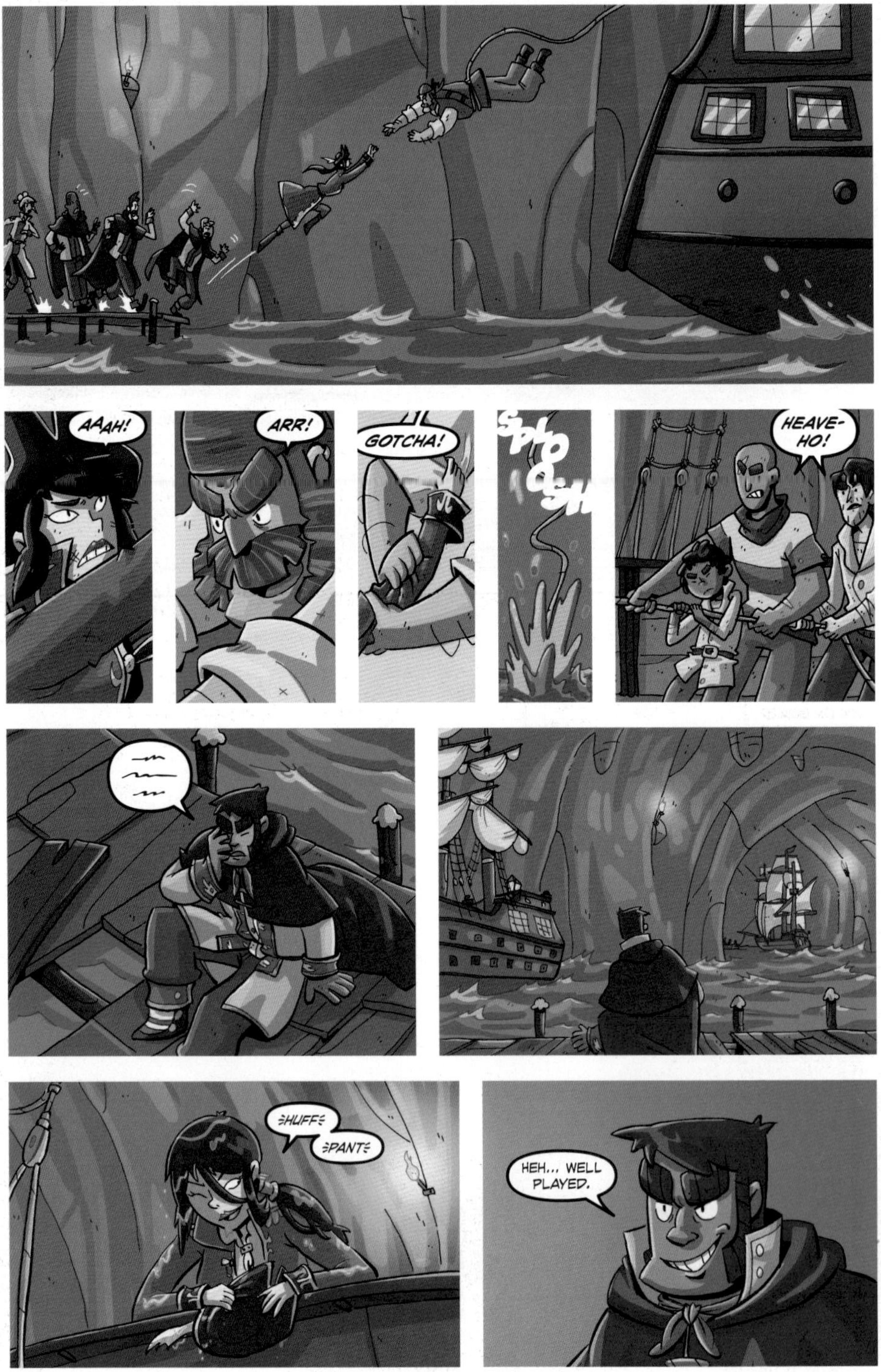
AAAH!
ARR!
GOTCHA!
SPLOOSH
HEAVE-HO!
HUFF
PANT
HEH... WELL PLAYED.

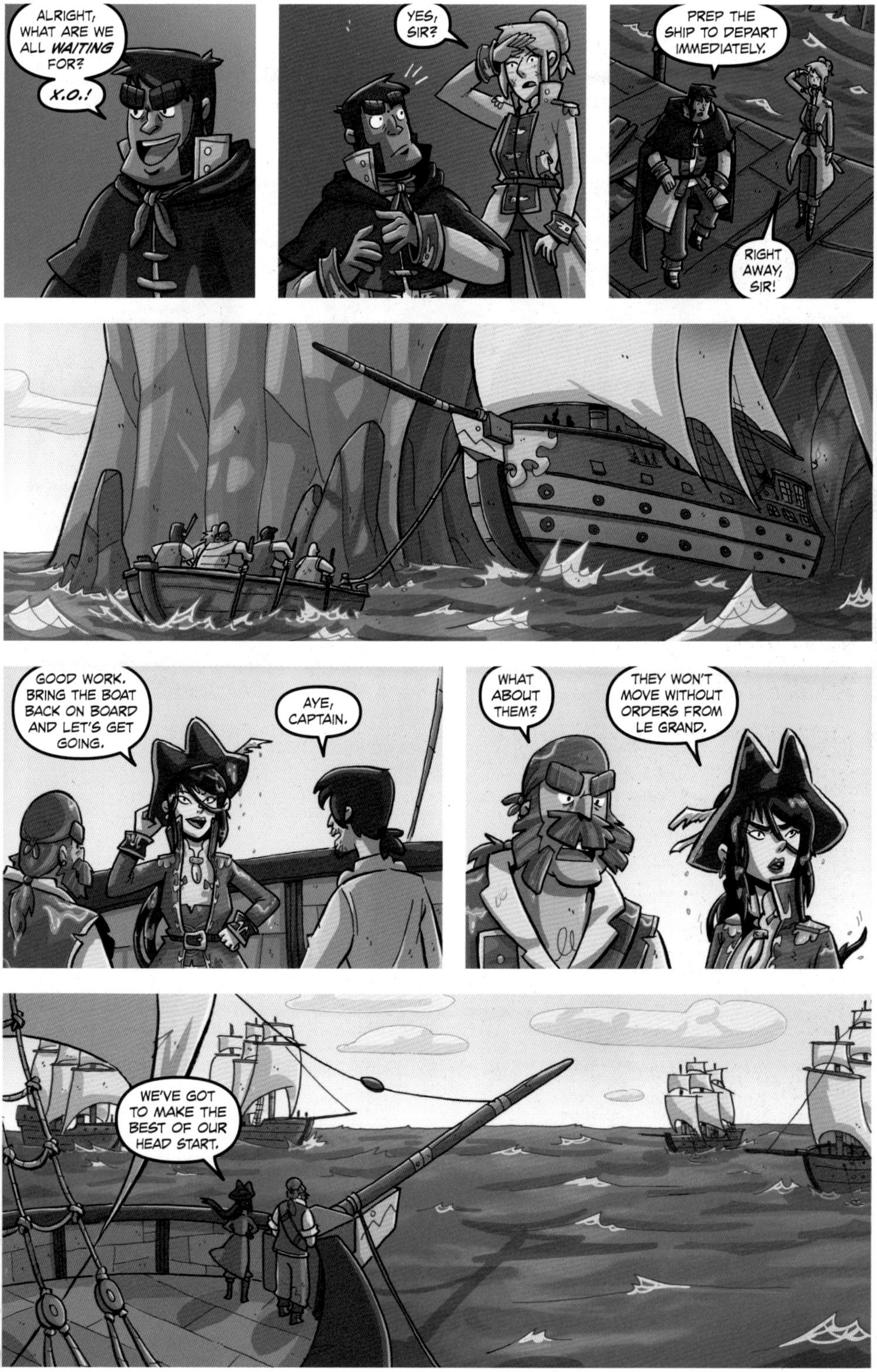
ALRIGHT, WHAT ARE WE ALL *WAITING* FOR?
X.O.!
YES, SIR?
PREP THE SHIP TO DEPART IMMEDIATELY.
RIGHT AWAY, SIR!
GOOD WORK. BRING THE BOAT BACK ON BOARD AND LET'S GET GOING.
AYE, CAPTAIN.
WHAT ABOUT THEM?
THEY WON'T MOVE WITHOUT ORDERS FROM LE GRAND.
WE'VE GOT TO MAKE THE BEST OF OUR HEAD START.

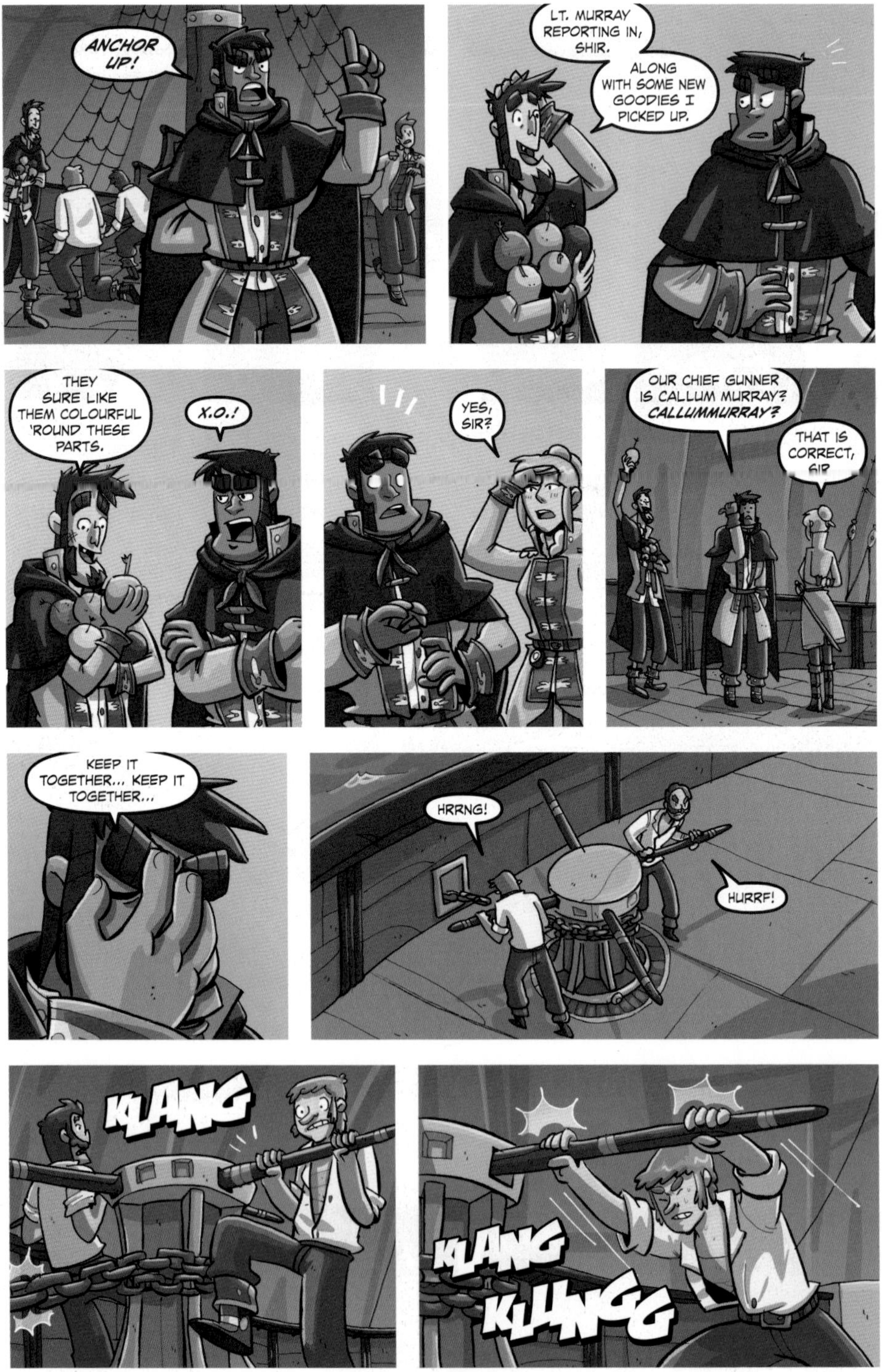
ANCHOR UP!
LT. MURRAY REPORTING IN, SHIR.
ALONG WITH SOME NEW GOODIES I PICKED UP.
THEY SURE LIKE THEM COLOURFUL 'ROUND THESE PARTS.
X.O.!
YES, SIR?
OUR CHIEF GUNNER IS CALLUM MURRAY? CALLUMMURRAY?
THAT IS CORRECT, SIR
KEEP IT TOGETHER... KEEP IT TOGETHER...
HRRNG!
HURRF!
KLANG
KLANG
KLLANGG

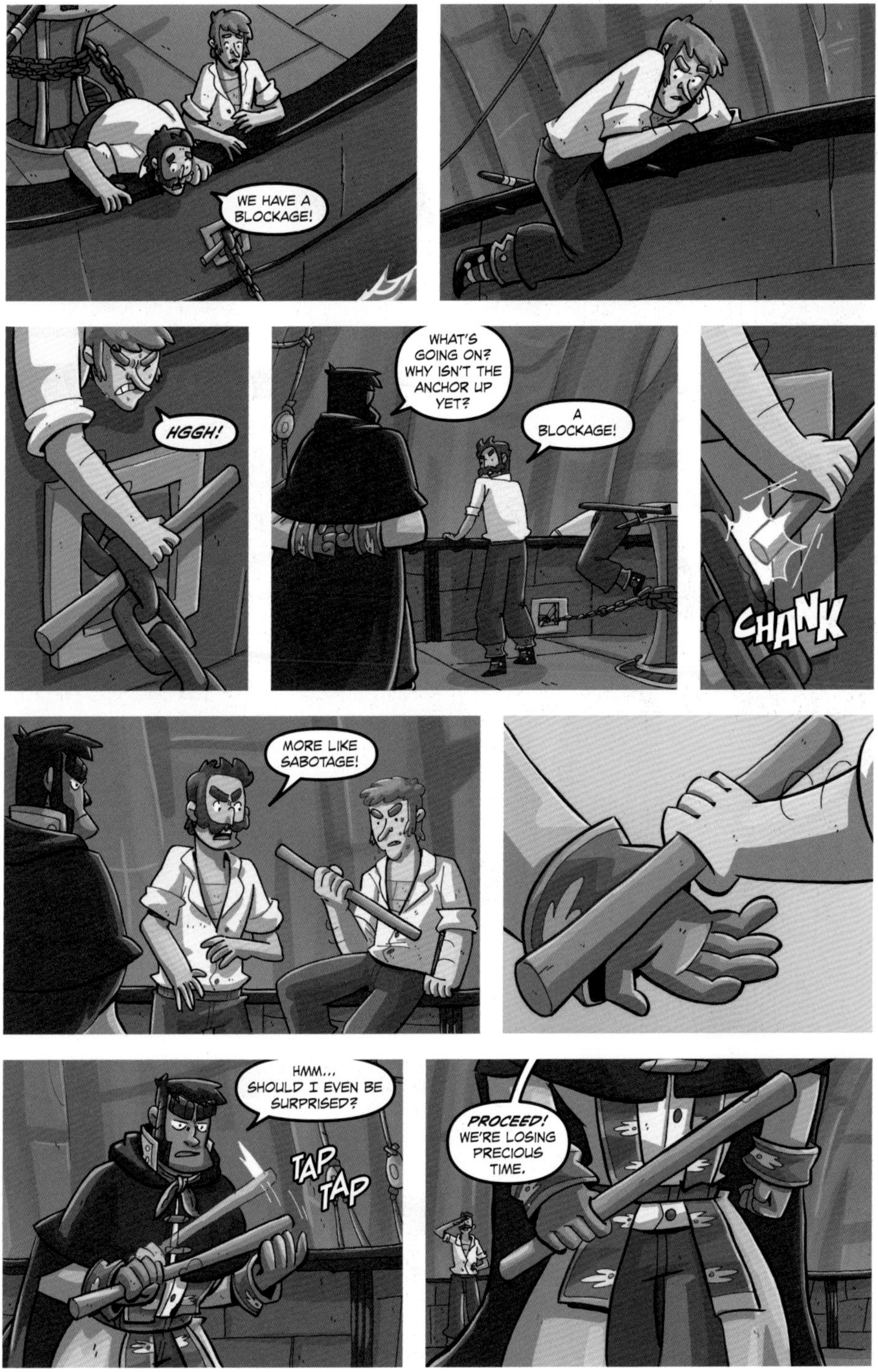
WE HAVE A BLOCKAGE!
HGGH!
WHAT'S GOING ON? WHY ISN'T THE ANCHOR UP YET?
A BLOCKAGE!
CHANK
MORE LIKE SABOTAGE!
HMM... SHOULD I EVEN BE SURPRISED?
TAP TAP
PROCEED! WE'RE LOSING PRECIOUS TIME.

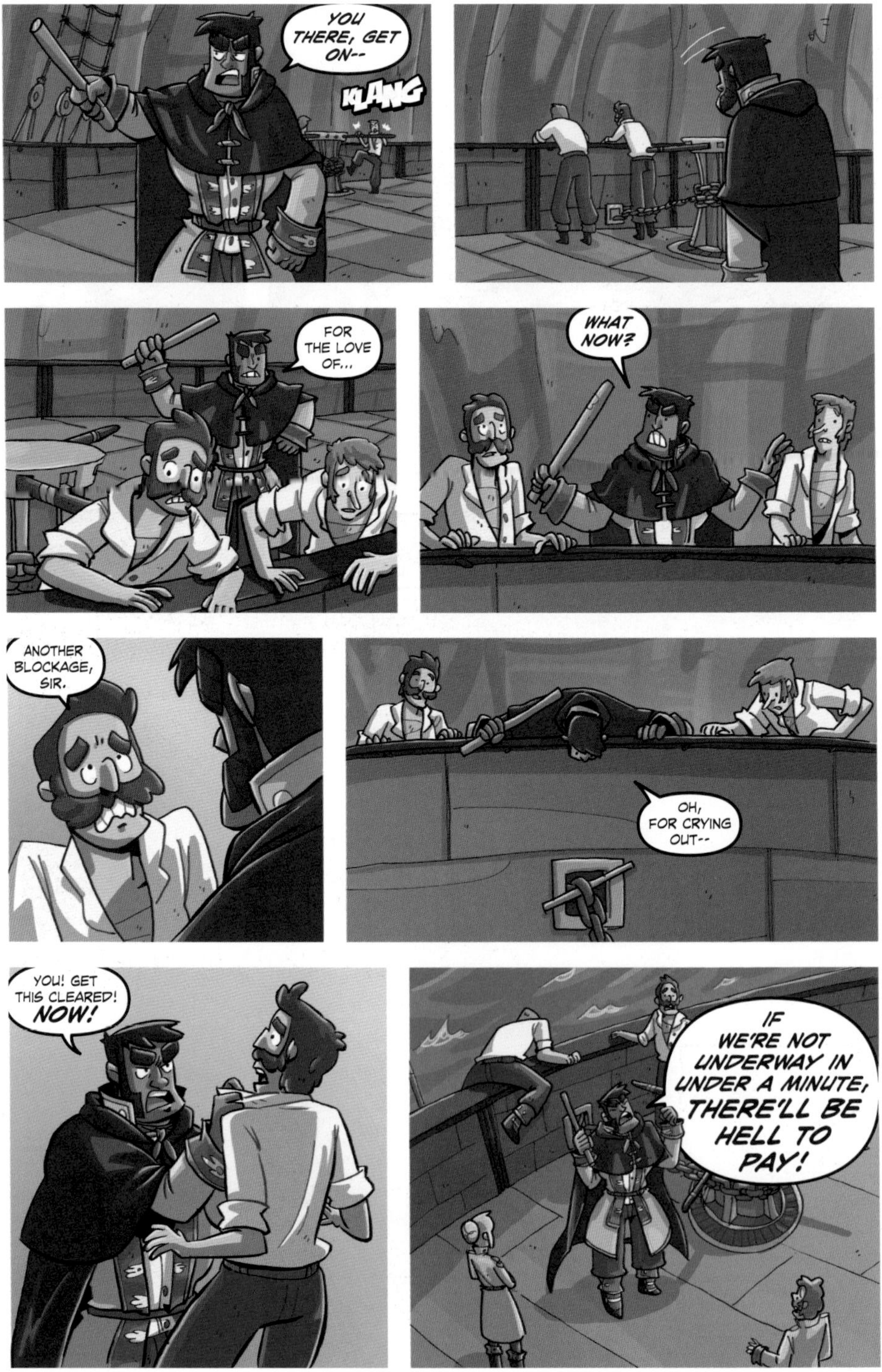

YOU THERE, GET ON--
KLANG
FOR THE LOVE OF...
WHAT NOW?
ANOTHER BLOCKAGE, SIR.
OH, FOR CRYING OUT--
YOU! GET THIS CLEARED! NOW!
IF WE'RE NOT UNDERWAY IN UNDER A MINUTE, THERE'LL BE HELL TO PAY!

JUST A MATTER OF TIME BEFORE THE CHASE BEGINS.

HANG ON, OLD FRIEND.

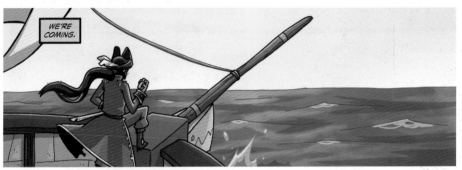

WE'RE COMING.

HURRY, LEI.

WE **CANNOT** LET THE KING GET HIS HANDS ON THE ORB.

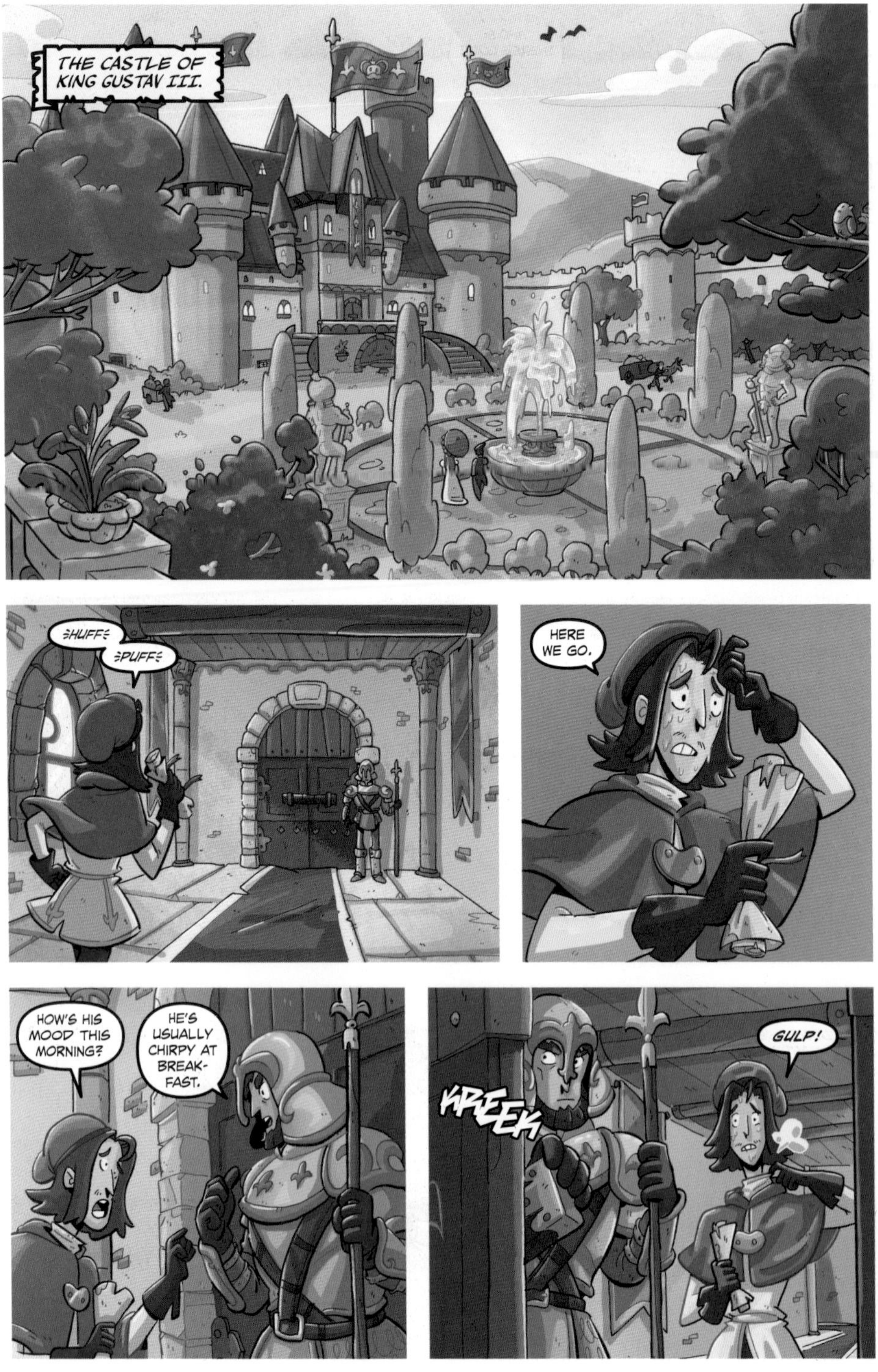

THE CASTLE OF KING GUSTAV III.
HUFF
PUFF
HERE WE GO.
HOW'S HIS MOOD THIS MORNING?
HE'S USUALLY CHIRPY AT BREAK-FAST.
KREEK
GULP!

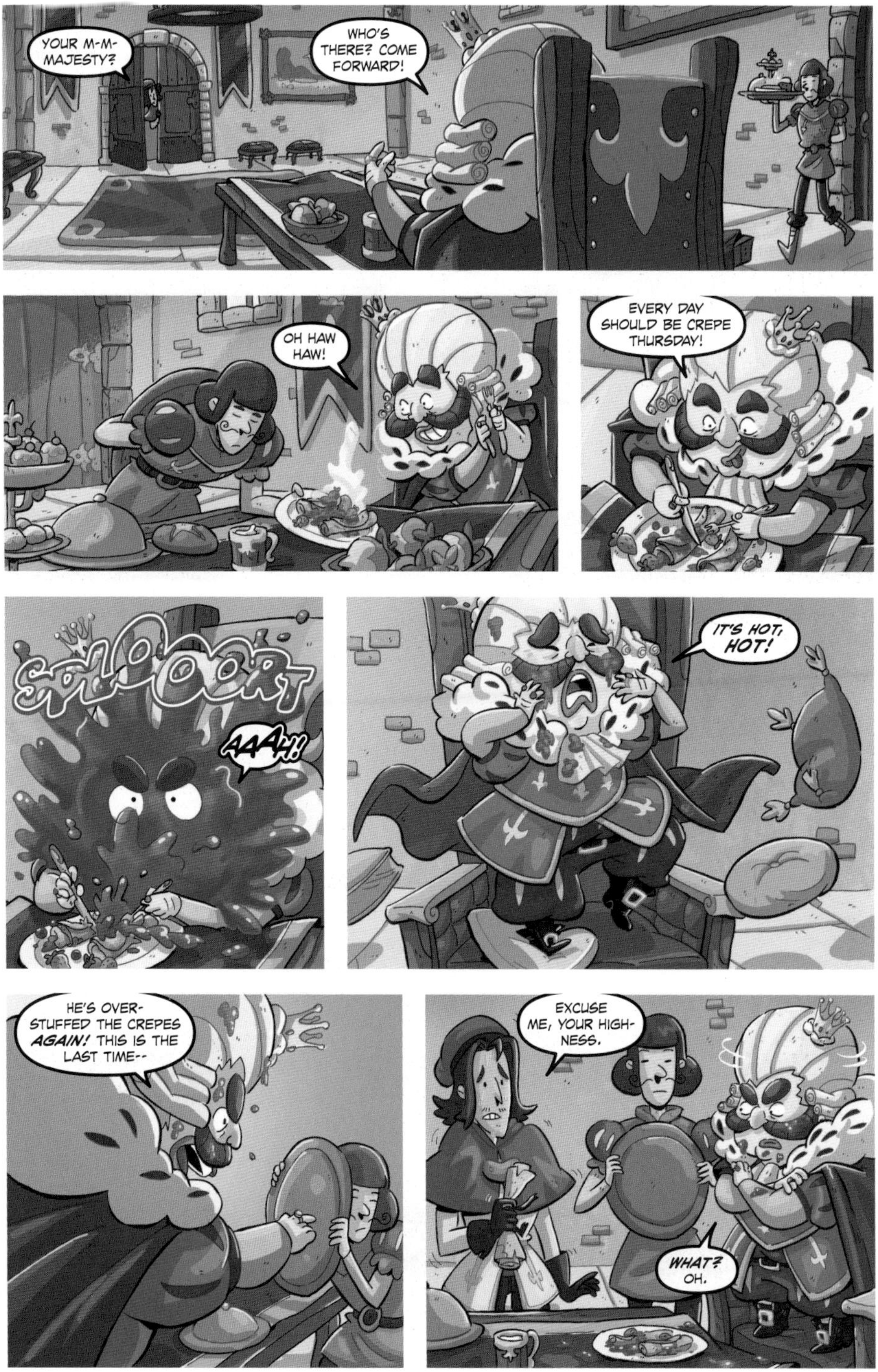
YOUR M-M-MAJESTY?
WHO'S THERE? COME FORWARD!
OH HAW HAW!
EVERY DAY SHOULD BE CREPE THURSDAY!
SPLOOORT
AAAH!
IT'S HOT, HOT!
HE'S OVER-STUFFED THE CREPES AGAIN! THIS IS THE LAST TIME--
EXCUSE ME, YOUR HIGH-NESS.
WHAT? OH.

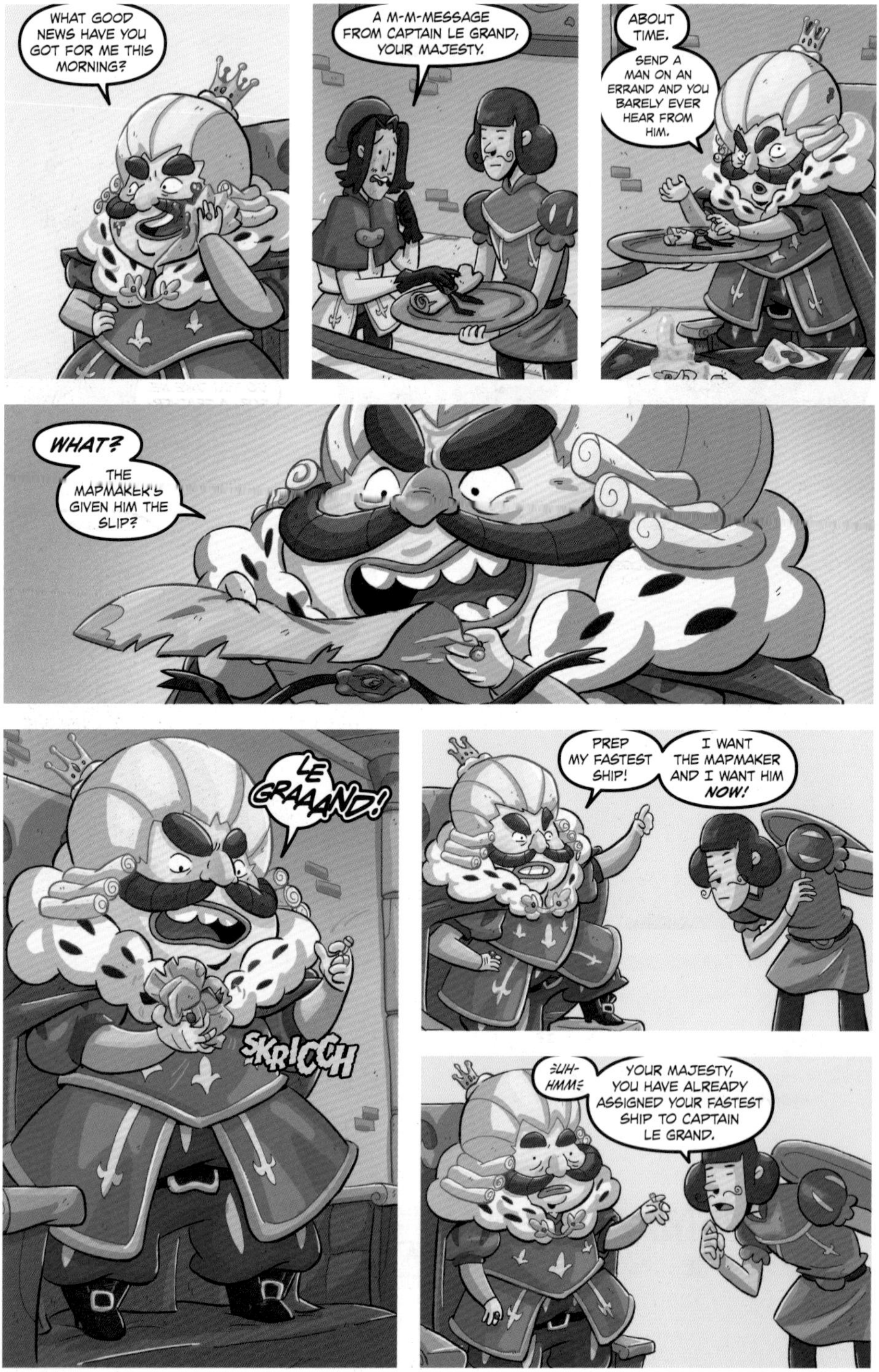
WHAT GOOD NEWS HAVE YOU GOT FOR ME THIS MORNING?
A M-M-MESSAGE FROM CAPTAIN LE GRAND, YOUR MAJESTY.
ABOUT TIME.
SEND A MAN ON AN ERRAND AND YOU BARELY EVER HEAR FROM HIM.
WHAT?
THE MAPMAKER'S GIVEN HIM THE SLIP?
LE GRAAAND!
SKRICCH
PREP MY FASTEST SHIP!
I WANT THE MAPMAKER AND I WANT HIM NOW!
-UH-HMM-
YOUR MAJESTY, YOU HAVE ALREADY ASSIGNED YOUR FASTEST SHIP TO CAPTAIN LE GRAND.

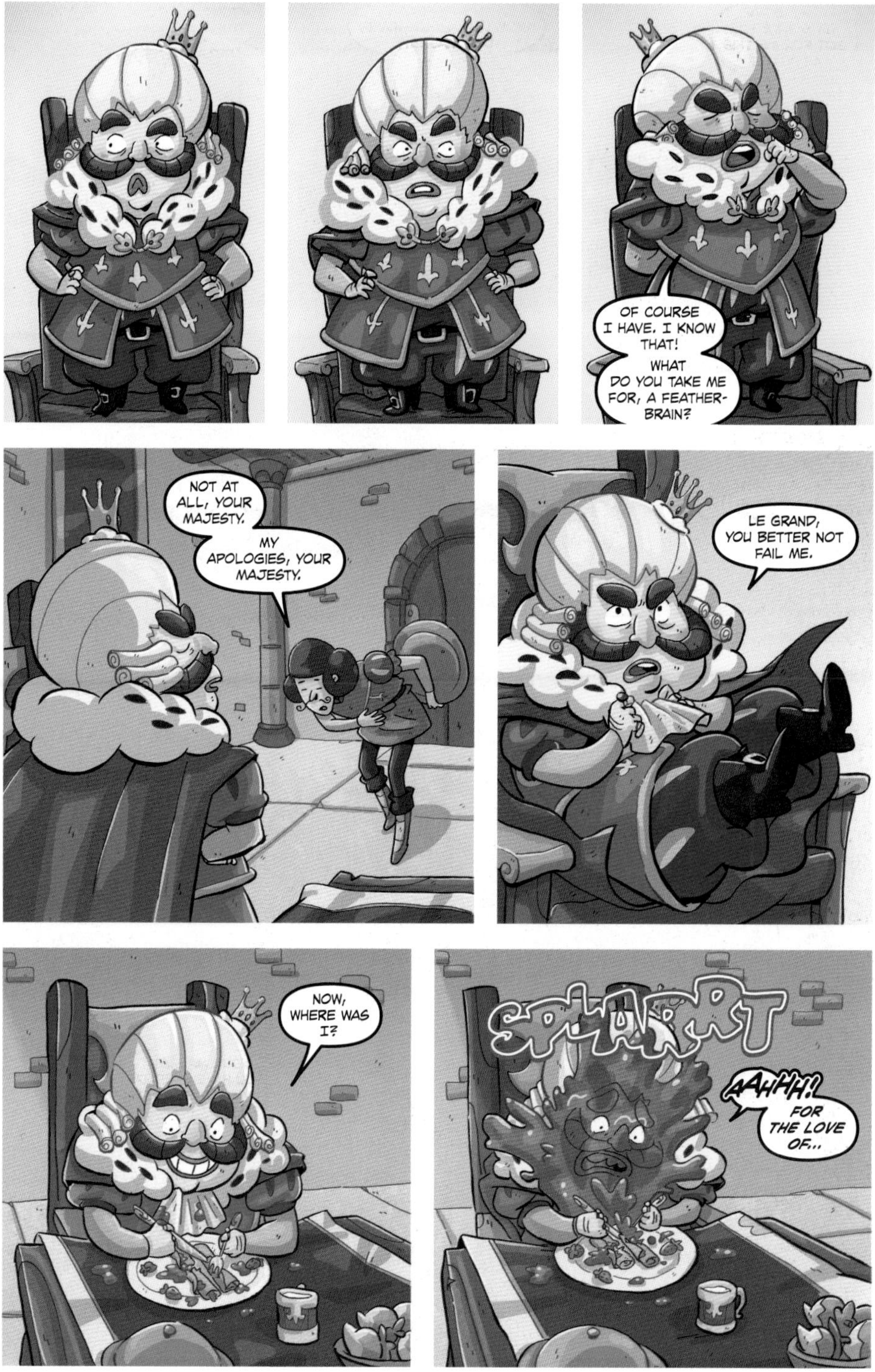
OF COURSE I HAVE. I KNOW THAT!
WHAT DO YOU TAKE ME FOR, A FEATHER-BRAIN?
NOT AT ALL, YOUR MAJESTY.
MY APOLOGIES, YOUR MAJESTY.
LE GRAND, YOU BETTER NOT FAIL ME.
NOW, WHERE WAS I?
SPLAPRT
AAHHH!
FOR THE LOVE OF...

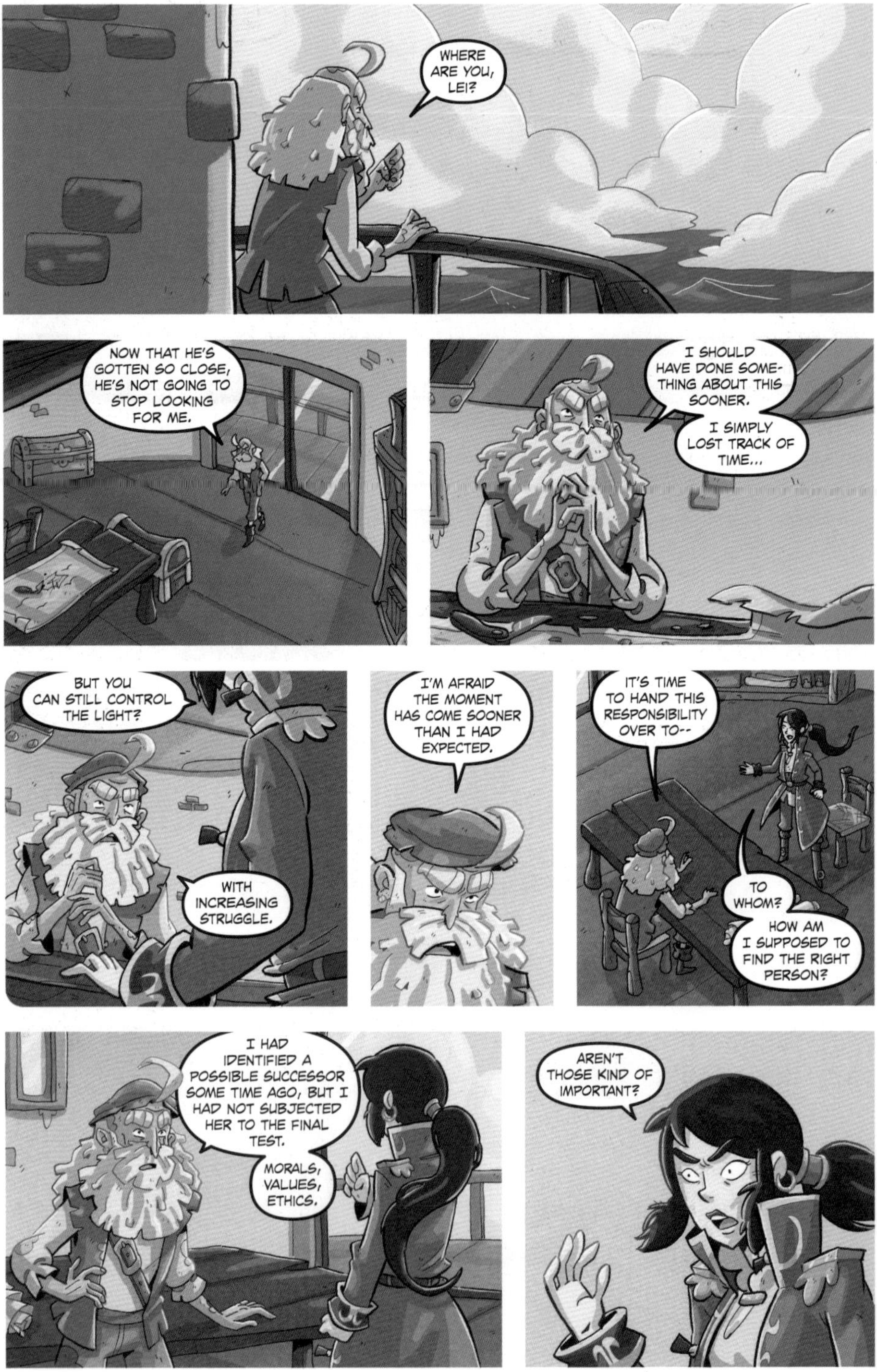

WHERE ARE YOU, LEI?
NOW THAT HE'S GOTTEN SO CLOSE, HE'S NOT GOING TO STOP LOOKING FOR ME.
I SHOULD HAVE DONE SOME-THING ABOUT THIS SOONER.
I SIMPLY LOST TRACK OF TIME...
BUT YOU CAN STILL CONTROL THE LIGHT?
WITH INCREASING STRUGGLE.
I'M AFRAID THE MOMENT HAS COME SOONER THAN I HAD EXPECTED.
IT'S TIME TO HAND THIS RESPONSIBILITY OVER TO--
TO WHOM?
HOW AM I SUPPOSED TO FIND THE RIGHT PERSON?
I HAD IDENTIFIED A POSSIBLE SUCCESSOR SOME TIME AGO, BUT I HAD NOT SUBJECTED HER TO THE FINAL TEST.
MORALS, VALUES, ETHICS.
AREN'T THOSE KIND OF IMPORTANT?

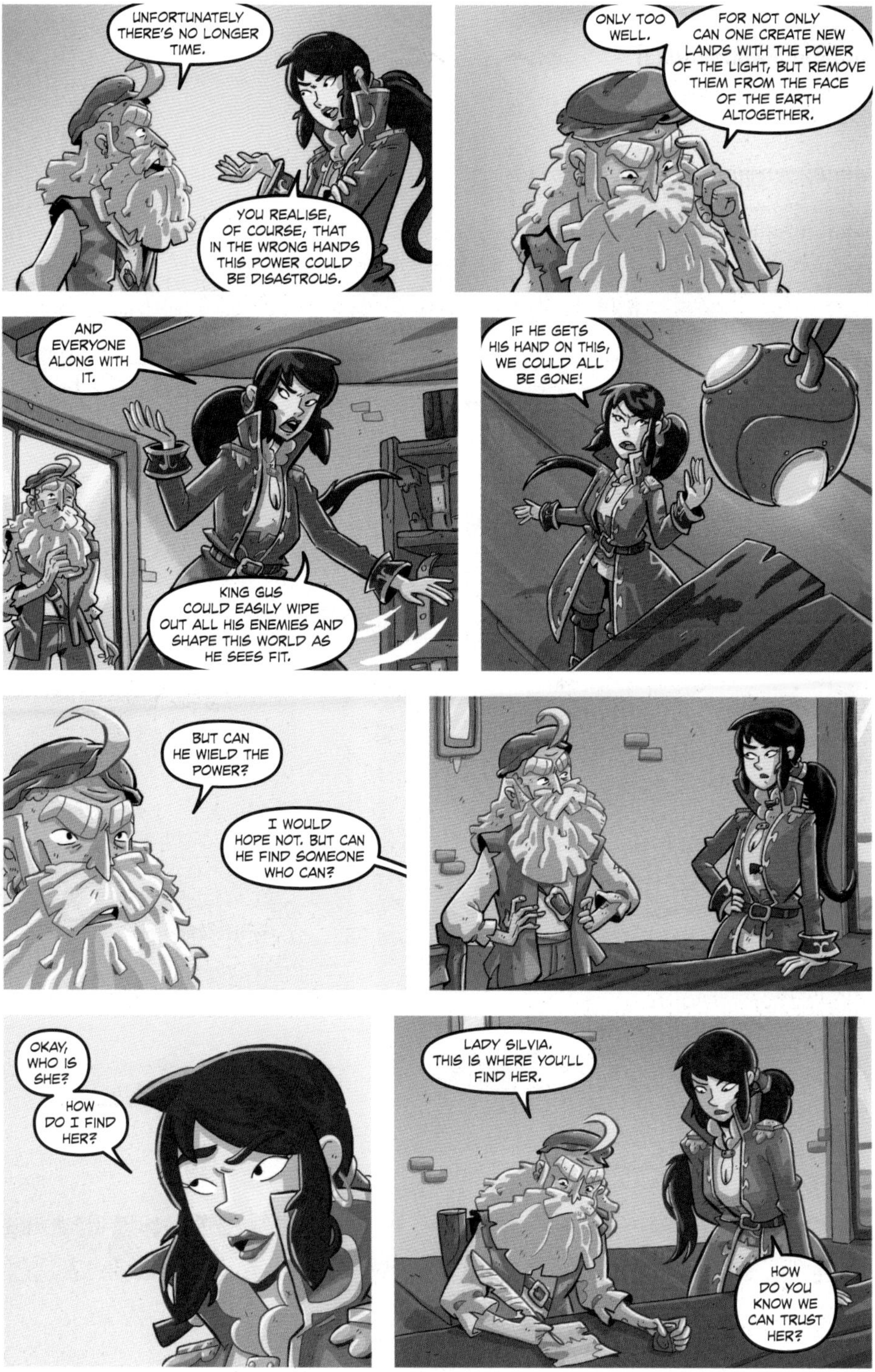
UNFORTUNATELY THERE'S NO LONGER TIME.
YOU REALISE, OF COURSE, THAT IN THE WRONG HANDS THIS POWER COULD BE DISASTROUS.
ONLY TOO WELL.
FOR NOT ONLY CAN ONE CREATE NEW LANDS WITH THE POWER OF THE LIGHT, BUT REMOVE THEM FROM THE FACE OF THE EARTH ALTOGETHER.
AND EVERYONE ALONG WITH IT.
KING GUS COULD EASILY WIPE OUT ALL HIS ENEMIES AND SHAPE THIS WORLD AS HE SEES FIT.
IF HE GETS HIS HAND ON THIS, WE COULD ALL BE GONE!
BUT CAN HE WIELD THE POWER?
I WOULD HOPE NOT. BUT CAN HE FIND SOMEONE WHO CAN?
OKAY, WHO IS SHE?
HOW DO I FIND HER?
LADY SILVIA. THIS IS WHERE YOU'LL FIND HER.
HOW DO YOU KNOW WE CAN TRUST HER?

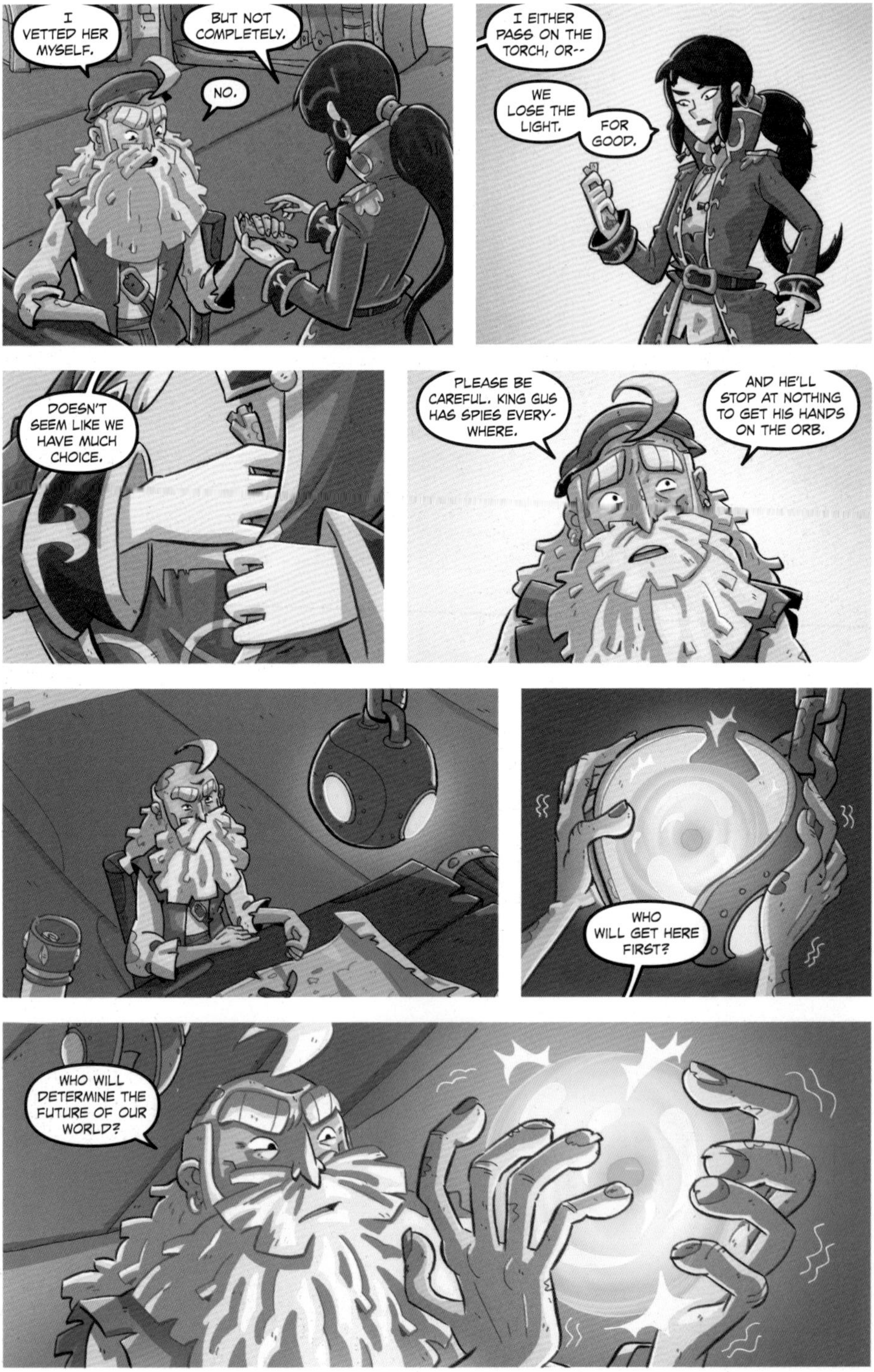
I VETTED HER MYSELF.
BUT NOT COMPLETELY.
NO.
I EITHER PASS ON THE TORCH, OR--
WE LOSE THE LIGHT.
FOR GOOD.
DOESN'T SEEM LIKE WE HAVE MUCH CHOICE.
PLEASE BE CAREFUL. KING GUS HAS SPIES EVERY-WHERE.
AND HE'LL STOP AT NOTHING TO GET HIS HANDS ON THE ORB.
WHO WILL GET HERE FIRST?
WHO WILL DETERMINE THE FUTURE OF OUR WORLD?

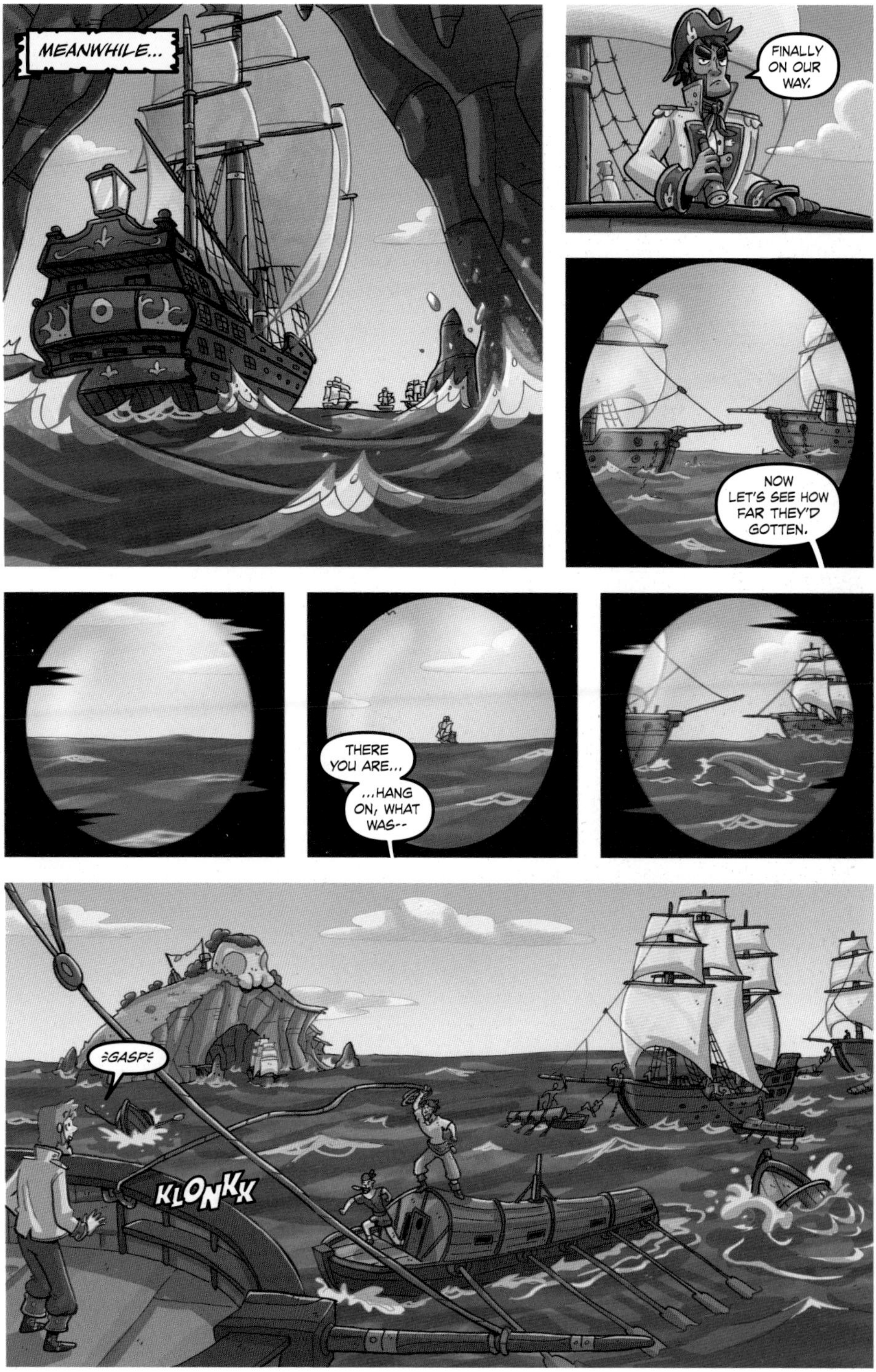
MEANWHILE...
FINALLY ON OUR WAY.
NOW LET'S SEE HOW FAR THEY'D GOTTEN.
THERE YOU ARE...
...HANG ON, WHAT WAS--
GASP
KLONKK

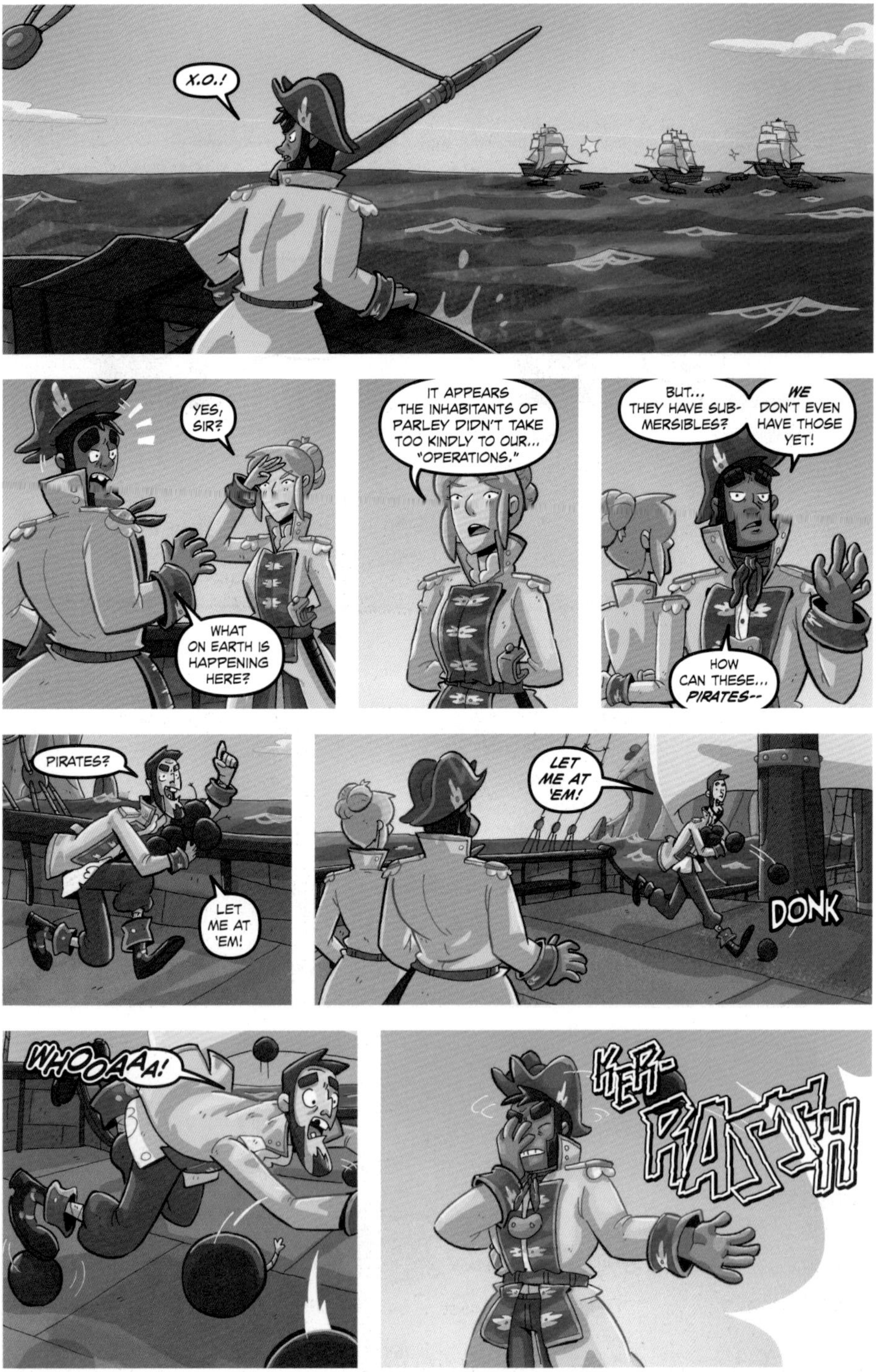
X.O.!
YES, SIR?
WHAT ON EARTH IS HAPPENING HERE?
IT APPEARS THE INHABITANTS OF PARLEY DIDN'T TAKE TOO KINDLY TO OUR... "OPERATIONS."
BUT... THEY HAVE SUB-MERSIBLES?
WE DON'T EVEN HAVE THOSE YET!
HOW CAN THESE... PIRATES--
PIRATES?
LET ME AT 'EM!
LET ME AT 'EM!
DONK
WHOOAAA!
KER-RASH

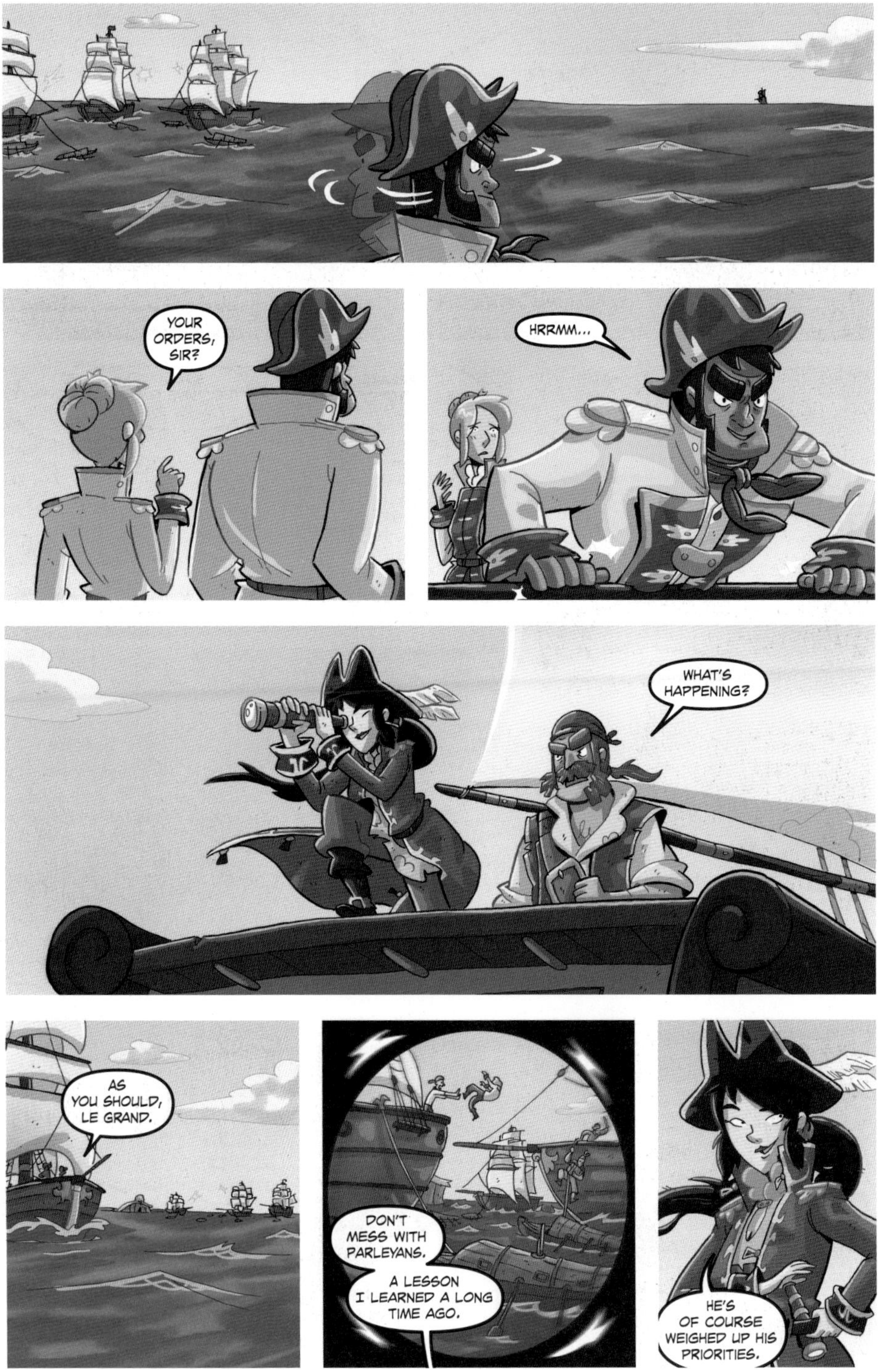
YOUR ORDERS, SIR?
HRRMM...
WHAT'S HAPPENING?
AS YOU SHOULD, LE GRAND.
DON'T MESS WITH PARLEYANS.
A LESSON I LEARNED A LONG TIME AGO.
HE'S OF COURSE WEIGHED UP HIS PRIORITIES.

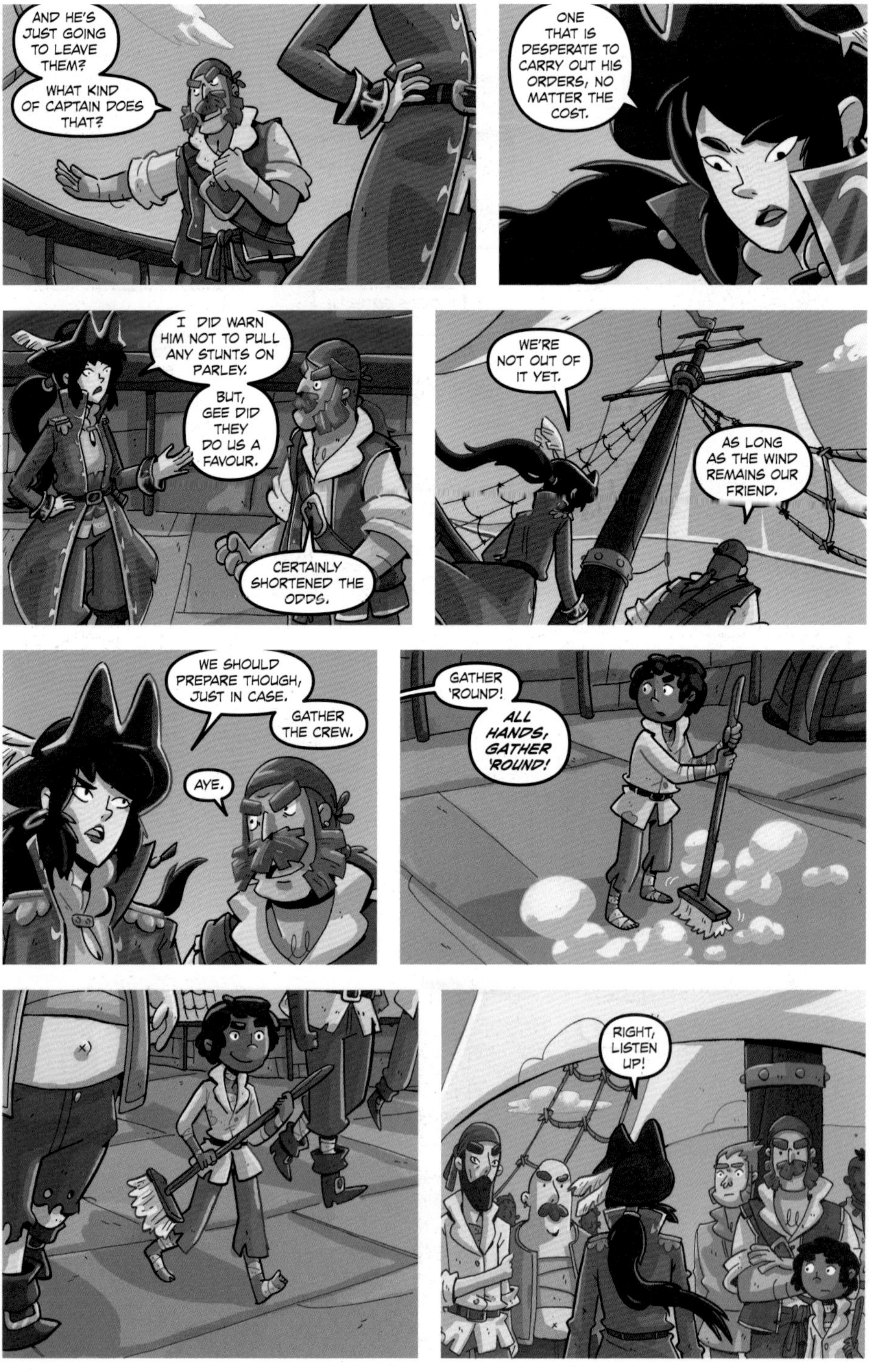
AND HE'S JUST GOING TO LEAVE THEM?
WHAT KIND OF CAPTAIN DOES THAT?
ONE THAT IS DESPERATE TO CARRY OUT HIS ORDERS, NO MATTER THE COST.
I DID WARN HIM NOT TO PULL ANY STUNTS ON PARLEY.
BUT, GEE DID THEY DO US A FAVOUR.
CERTAINLY SHORTENED THE ODDS.
WE'RE NOT OUT OF IT YET.
AS LONG AS THE WIND REMAINS OUR FRIEND.
WE SHOULD PREPARE THOUGH, JUST IN CASE.
GATHER THE CREW.
AYE.
GATHER 'ROUND!
ALL HANDS, GATHER 'ROUND!
RIGHT, LISTEN UP!

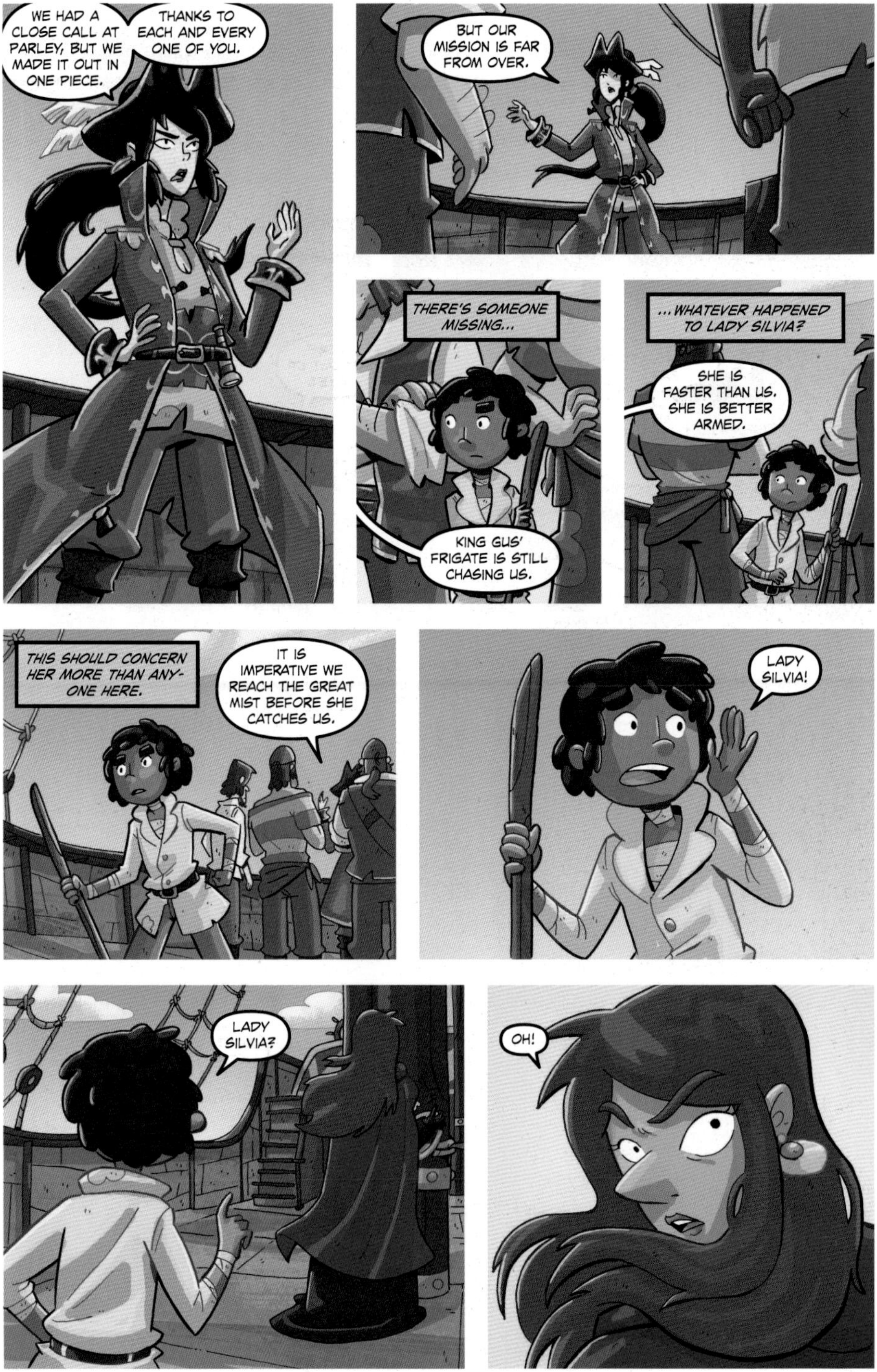
WE HAD A CLOSE CALL AT PARLEY, BUT WE MADE IT OUT IN ONE PIECE.
THANKS TO EACH AND EVERY ONE OF YOU.
BUT OUR MISSION IS FAR FROM OVER.
THERE'S SOMEONE MISSING...
KING GUS' FRIGATE IS STILL CHASING US.
...WHATEVER HAPPENED TO LADY SILVIA?
SHE IS FASTER THAN US. SHE IS BETTER ARMED.
THIS SHOULD CONCERN HER MORE THAN ANY-ONE HERE.
IT IS IMPERATIVE WE REACH THE GREAT MIST BEFORE SHE CATCHES US.
LADY SILVIA!
LADY SILVIA?
OH!

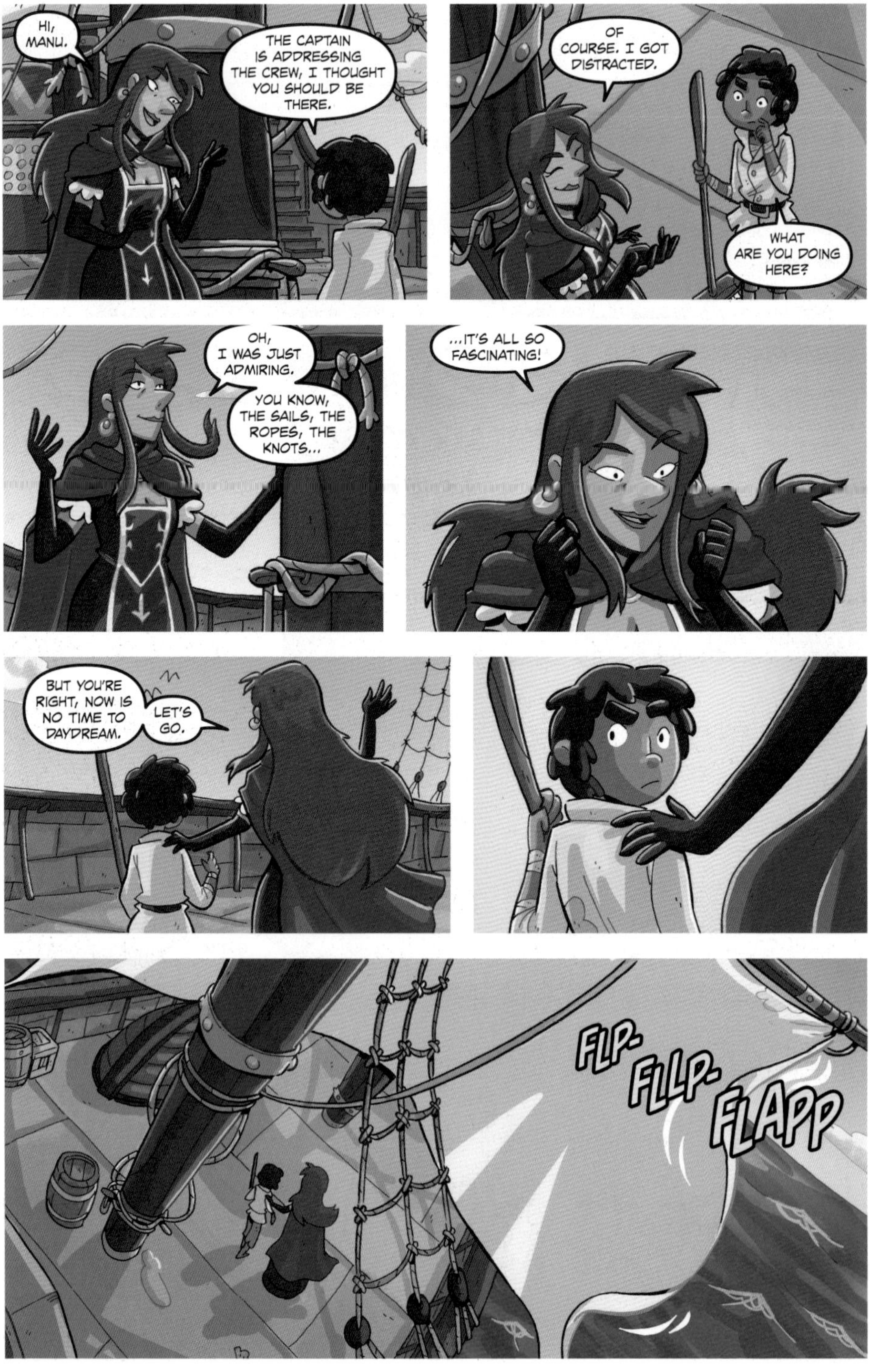
HI, MANU.
THE CAPTAIN IS ADDRESSING THE CREW; I THOUGHT YOU SHOULD BE THERE.
OF COURSE. I GOT DISTRACTED.
WHAT ARE YOU DOING HERE?
OH, I WAS JUST ADMIRING.
YOU KNOW, THE SAILS, THE ROPES, THE KNOTS...
...IT'S ALL SO FASCINATING!
BUT YOU'RE RIGHT, NOW IS NO TIME TO DAYDREAM.
LET'S GO.
FLP-
FLLP-
FLAPP

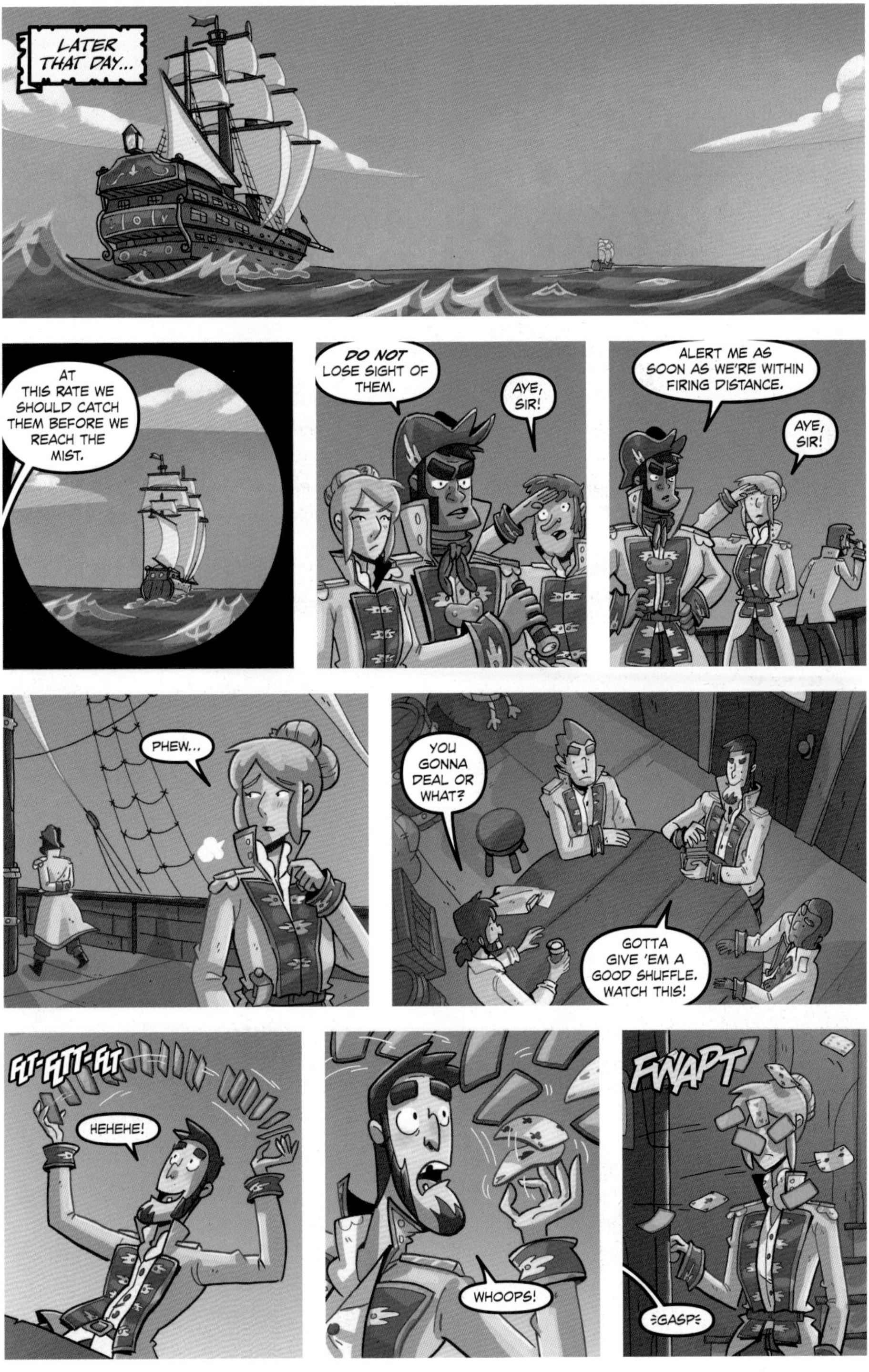
LATER THAT DAY...
AT THIS RATE WE SHOULD CATCH THEM BEFORE WE REACH THE MIST.
DO NOT LOSE SIGHT OF THEM.
AYE, SIR!
ALERT ME AS SOON AS WE'RE WITHIN FIRING DISTANCE.
AYE, SIR!
PHEW...
YOU GONNA DEAL OR WHAT?
GOTTA GIVE 'EM A GOOD SHUFFLE. WATCH THIS!
FLT-FLTT-FLT
HEHEHE!
WHOOPS!
FWAPT
GASP

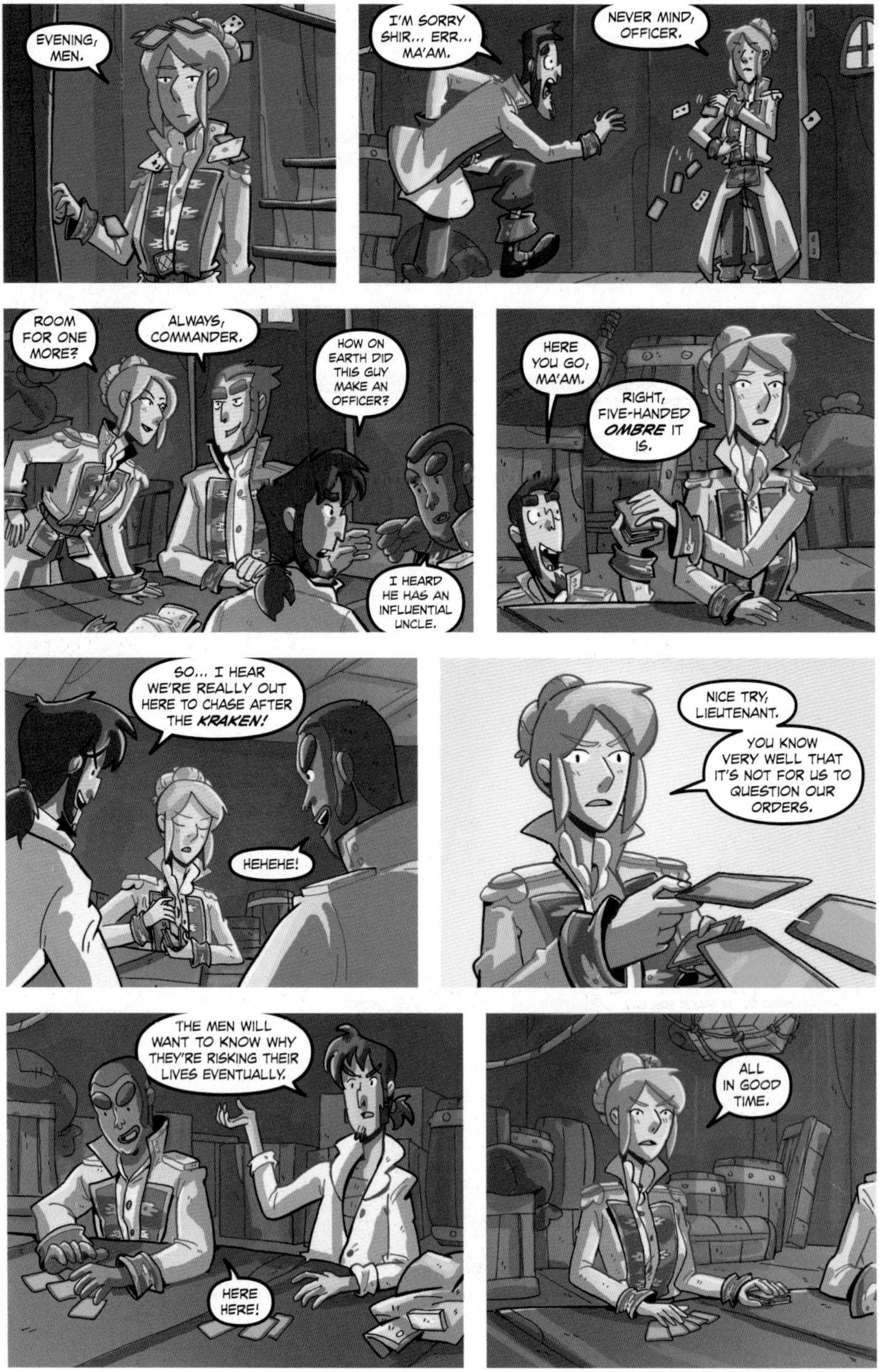

EVENING, MEN.
I'M SORRY SHIR... ERR... MA'AM.
NEVER MIND, OFFICER.
ROOM FOR ONE MORE?
ALWAYS, COMMANDER.
HOW ON EARTH DID THIS GUY MAKE AN OFFICER?
I HEARD HE HAS AN INFLUENTIAL UNCLE.
HERE YOU GO, MA'AM.
RIGHT, FIVE-HANDED *OMBRE* IT IS.
SO... I HEAR WE'RE REALLY OUT HERE TO CHASE AFTER THE *KRAKEN!*
HEHEHE!
NICE TRY, LIEUTENANT.
YOU KNOW VERY WELL THAT IT'S NOT FOR US TO QUESTION OUR ORDERS.
THE MEN WILL WANT TO KNOW WHY THEY'RE RISKING THEIR LIVES EVENTUALLY.
HERE HERE!
ALL IN GOOD TIME.

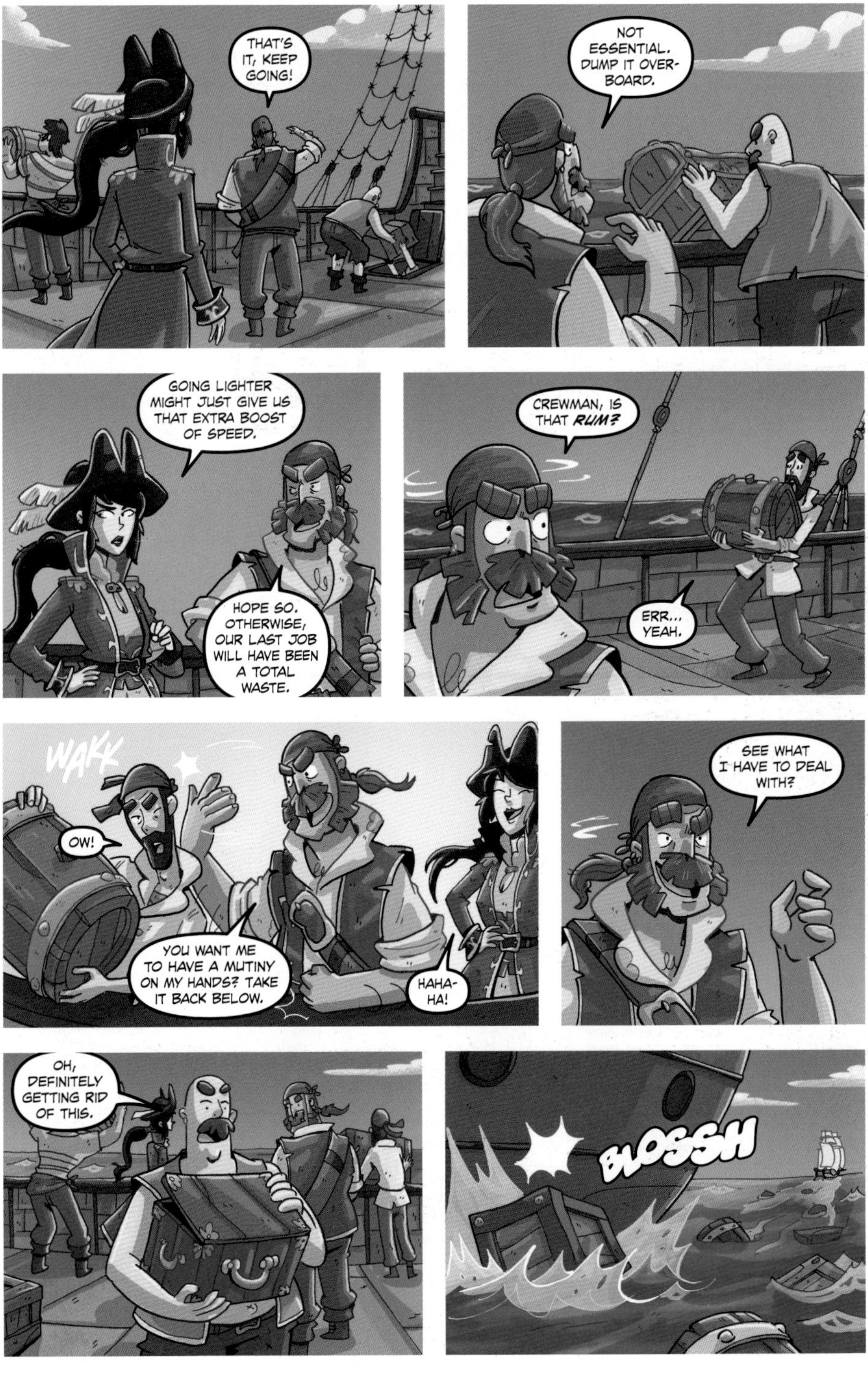
THAT'S IT, KEEP GOING!
NOT ESSENTIAL. DUMP IT OVER-BOARD.
GOING LIGHTER MIGHT JUST GIVE US THAT EXTRA BOOST OF SPEED.
HOPE SO. OTHERWISE, OUR LAST JOB WILL HAVE BEEN A TOTAL WASTE.
CREWMAN, IS THAT RUM?
ERR... YEAH.
WAKK
OW!
YOU WANT ME TO HAVE A MUTINY ON MY HANDS? TAKE IT BACK BELOW.
HAHA-HA!
SEE WHAT I HAVE TO DEAL WITH?
OH, DEFINITELY GETTING RID OF THIS.
BLOSSH

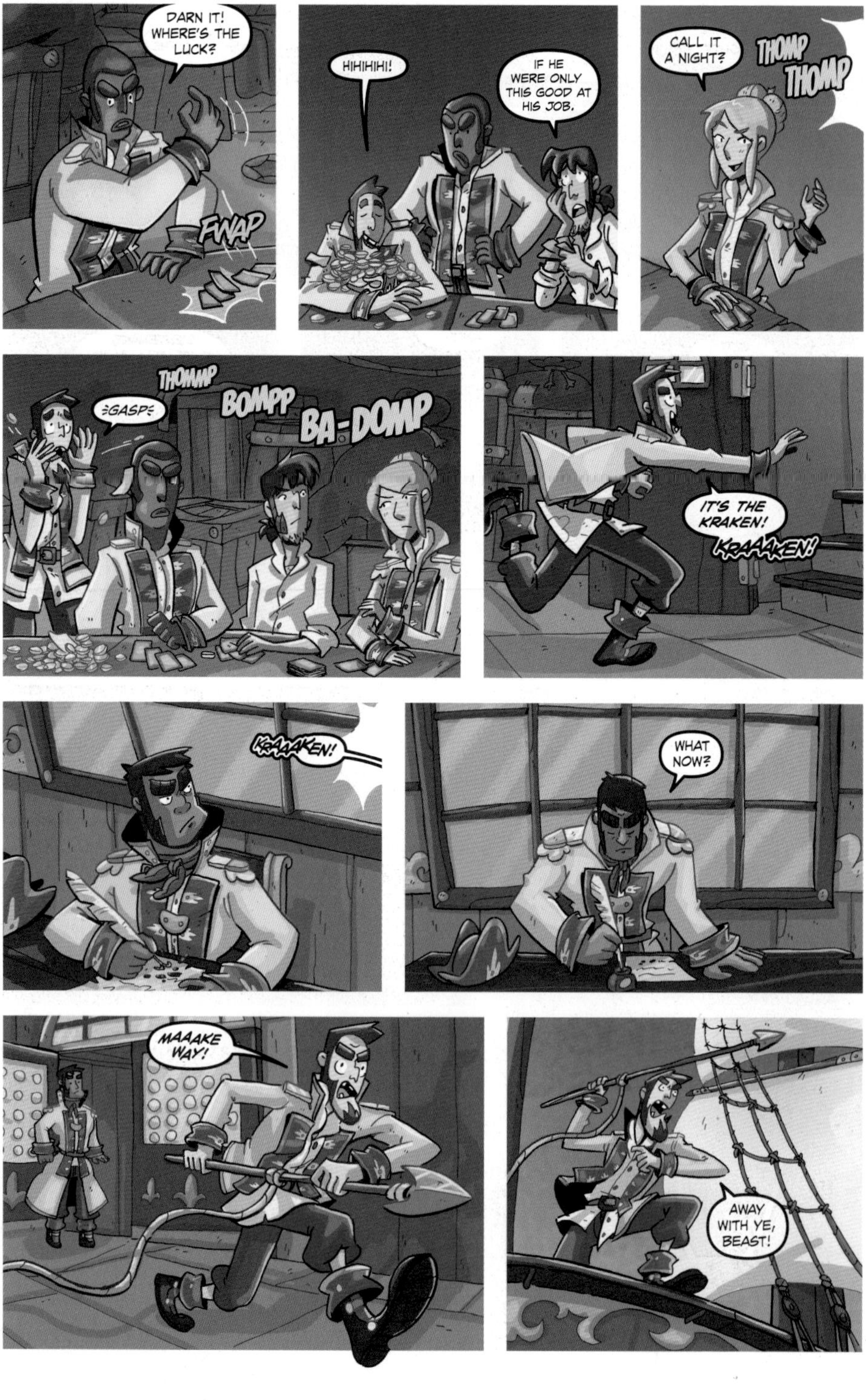

DARN IT! WHERE'S THE LUCK?
FWAP
HIHIHIHI!
IF HE WERE ONLY THIS GOOD AT HIS JOB.
CALL IT A NIGHT?
THOMP THOMP
GASP
THOMMP
BOMPP
BA-DOMP
IT'S THE KRAKEN!
KRAAAKEN!
KRAAAKEN!
WHAT NOW?
MAAAKE WAY!
AWAY WITH YE, BEAST!

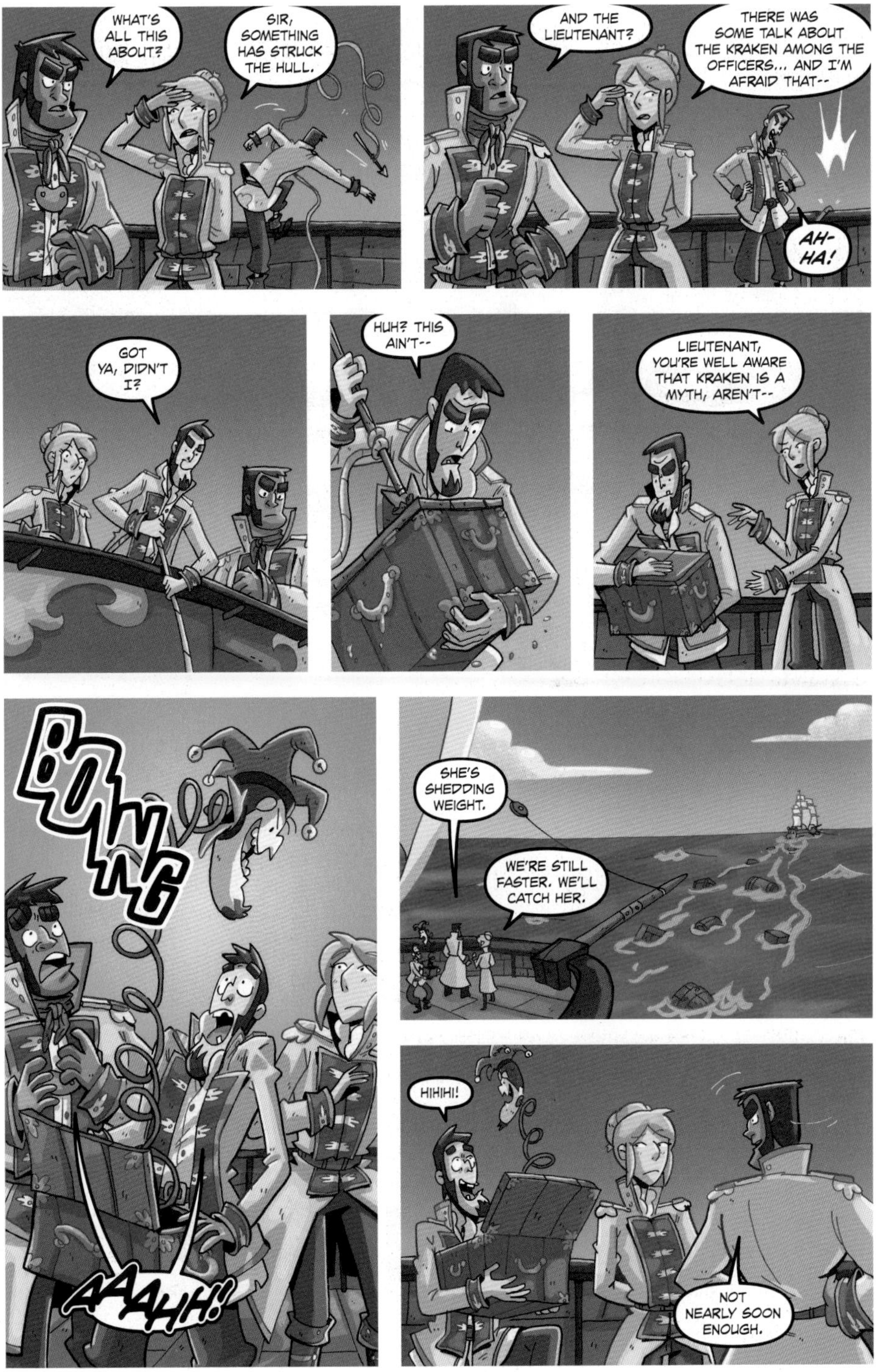

WHAT'S ALL THIS ABOUT?
SIR, SOMETHING HAS STRUCK THE HULL.
AND THE LIEUTENANT?
THERE WAS SOME TALK ABOUT THE KRAKEN AMONG THE OFFICERS... AND I'M AFRAID THAT--
AH-HA!
GOT YA, DIDN'T I?
HUH? THIS AIN'T--
LIEUTENANT, YOU'RE WELL AWARE THAT KRAKEN IS A MYTH, AREN'T--
BOING
AAAHH!
SHE'S SHEDDING WEIGHT.
WE'RE STILL FASTER. WE'LL CATCH HER.
HIHIHI!
NOT NEARLY SOON ENOUGH.

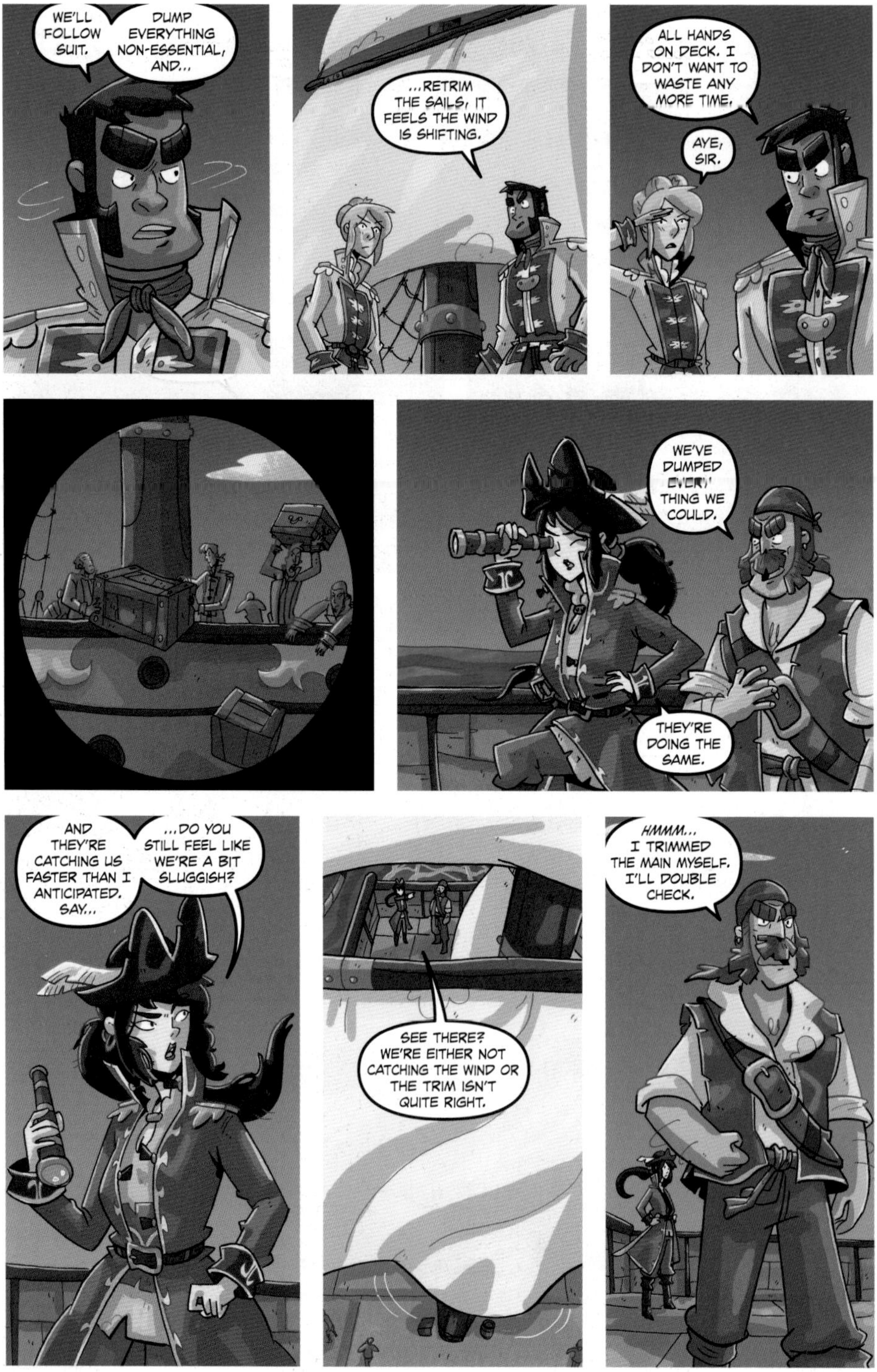
WE'LL FOLLOW SUIT.
DUMP EVERYTHING NON-ESSENTIAL, AND...
...RETRIM THE SAILS, IT FEELS THE WIND IS SHIFTING.
ALL HANDS ON DECK. I DON'T WANT TO WASTE ANY MORE TIME.
AYE, SIR.
WE'VE DUMPED EVERY THING WE COULD.
THEY'RE DOING THE SAME.
AND THEY'RE CATCHING US FASTER THAN I ANTICIPATED. SAY...
...DO YOU STILL FEEL LIKE WE'RE A BIT SLUGGISH?
SEE THERE? WE'RE EITHER NOT CATCHING THE WIND OR THE TRIM ISN'T QUITE RIGHT.
HMMM... I TRIMMED THE MAIN MYSELF. I'LL DOUBLE CHECK.

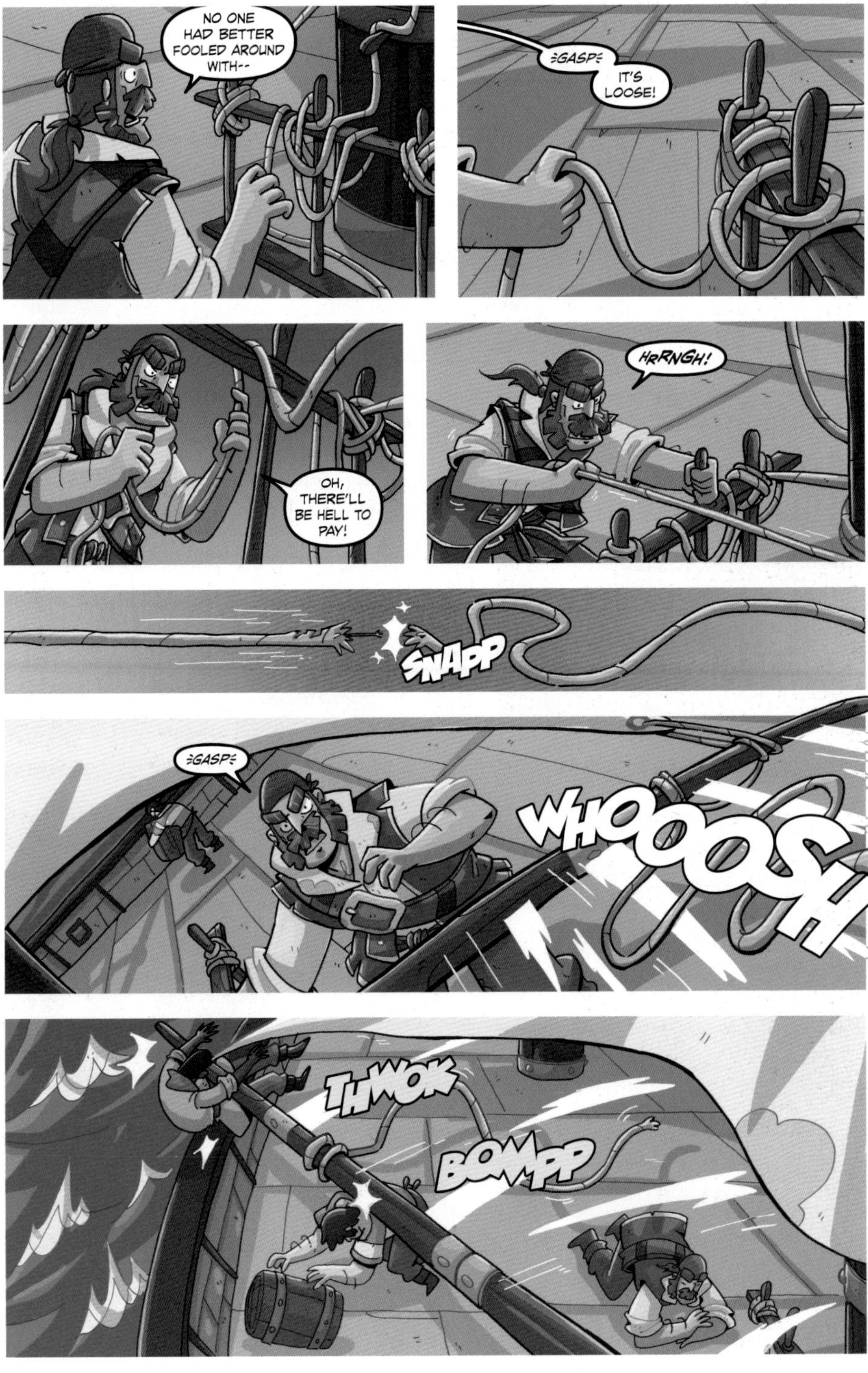
NO ONE HAD BETTER FOOLED AROUND WITH--
GASP
IT'S LOOSE!
OH, THERE'LL BE HELL TO PAY!
HRRNGH!
SNAPP
GASP
WHOOOOSH
THWOK
BOMPP

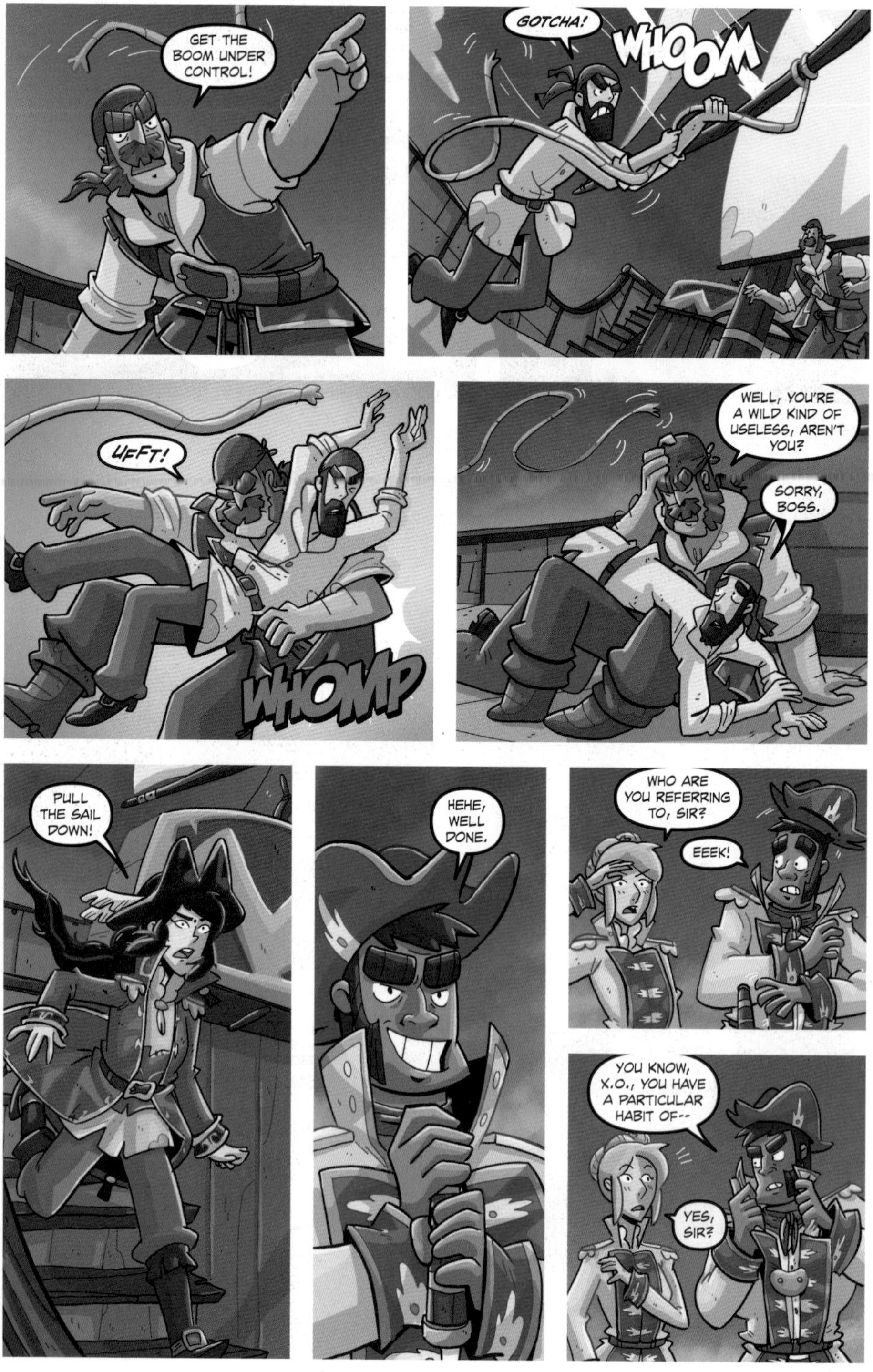
GET THE BOOM UNDER CONTROL!
GOTCHA!
WHOOM
UFFT!
WHOMP
WELL, YOU'RE A WILD KIND OF USELESS, AREN'T YOU?
SORRY, BOSS.
PULL THE SAIL DOWN!
HEHE, WELL DONE.
WHO ARE YOU REFERRING TO, SIR?
EEEK!
YOU KNOW, X.O., YOU HAVE A PARTICULAR HABIT OF--
YES, SIR?

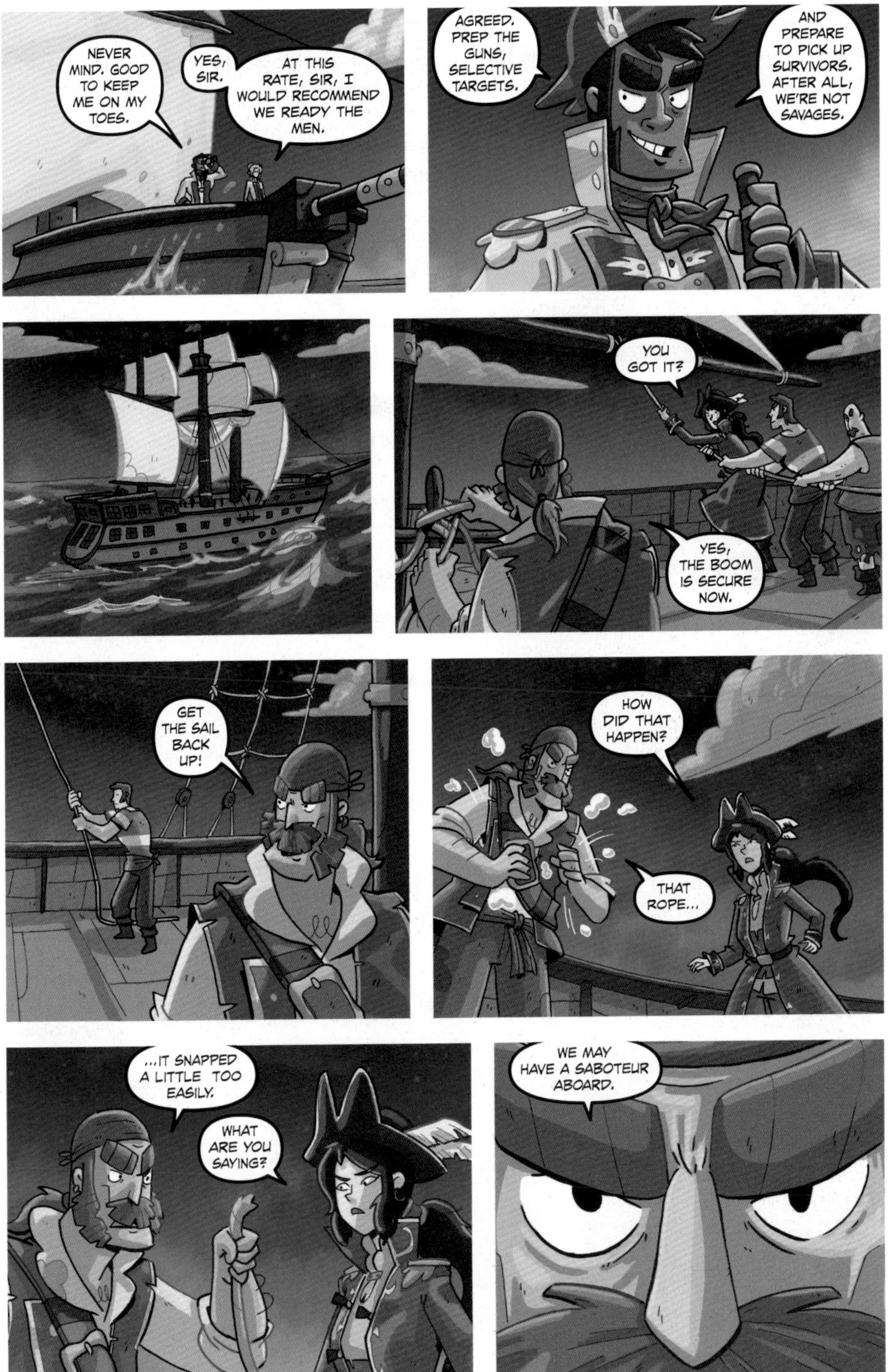
NEVER MIND. GOOD TO KEEP ME ON MY TOES.
YES, SIR.
AT THIS RATE, SIR, I WOULD RECOMMEND WE READY THE MEN.
AGREED. PREP THE GUNS, SELECTIVE TARGETS.
AND PREPARE TO PICK UP SURVIVORS. AFTER ALL, WE'RE NOT SAVAGES.
YOU GOT IT?
YES, THE BOOM IS SECURE NOW.
GET THE SAIL BACK UP!
HOW DID THAT HAPPEN?
THAT ROPE...
...IT SNAPPED A LITTLE TOO EASILY.
WHAT ARE YOU SAYING?
WE MAY HAVE A SABOTEUR ABOARD.

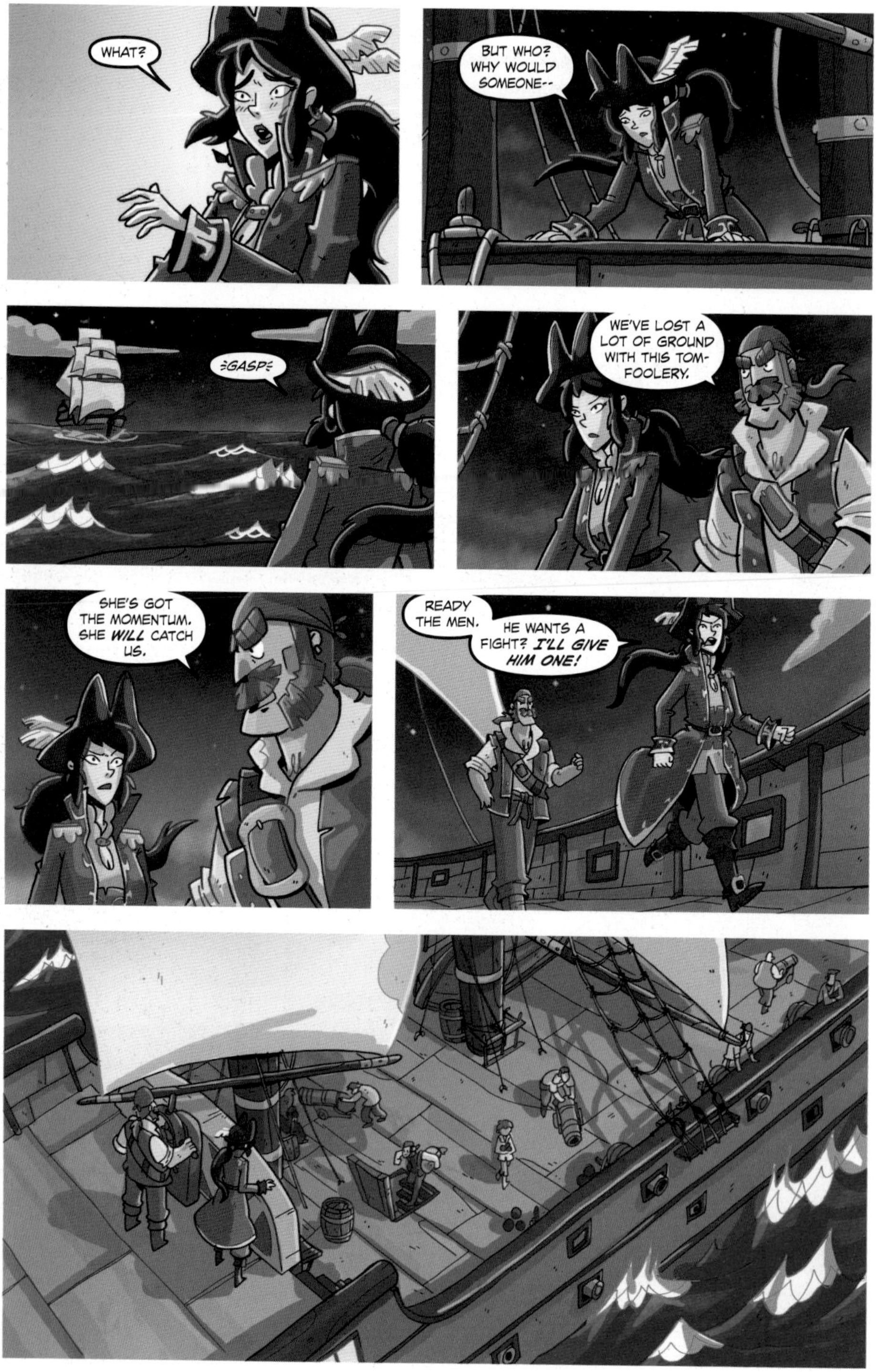
WHAT?
BUT WHO? WHY WOULD SOMEONE--
GASP
WE'VE LOST A LOT OF GROUND WITH THIS TOM-FOOLERY.
SHE'S GOT THE MOMENTUM. SHE *WILL* CATCH US.
READY THE MEN.
HE WANTS A FIGHT? ***I'LL GIVE HIM ONE!***

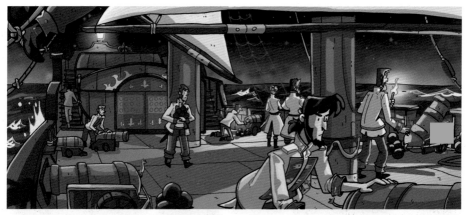

CAPTAIN, WE'RE IN FIRING RANGE.

GOOD, LET'S GIVE THEM A TASTE.

MASTER GUNNER, A WARNING SHOT OFF THE STERN!

AYE SHIR... I MEAN, MA'AM!

HEH HEH...

BOOM

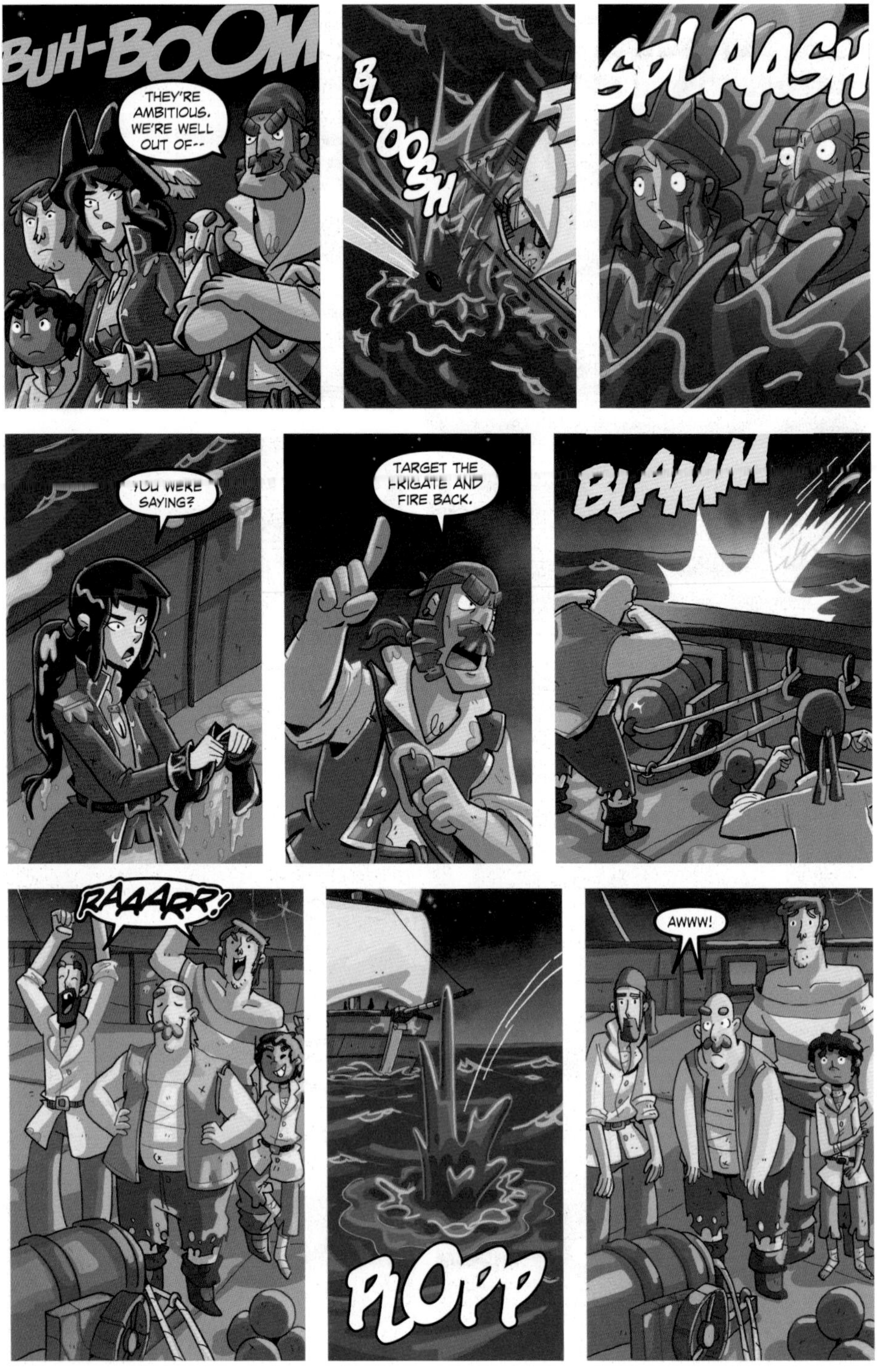
BUH-BOOM
THEY'RE AMBITIOUS. WE'RE WELL OUT OF--
BLOOOSH
SPLAASH
YOU WERE SAYING?
TARGET THE FRIGATE AND FIRE BACK.
BLAMM
RAAARR!
PLOPP
AWWW!

≥YAWN≥

THAT WAS RATHER LAME.

GIVE THE ORDER.

MASTER GUNNER, FIRE AT WILL.

≥MWA≥

I'VE BEEN LOOKING FORWARD TO SEEING THESE PARLEY BABIES IN ACTION.

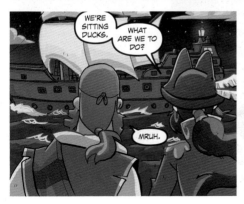

WE'RE SITTING DUCKS.

WHAT ARE WE TO DO?

MRUH.

I FEAR SHE MAY HAVE BESTED US ON THIS--

AHOY!

THE GREAT MIST DEAD AHEAD!

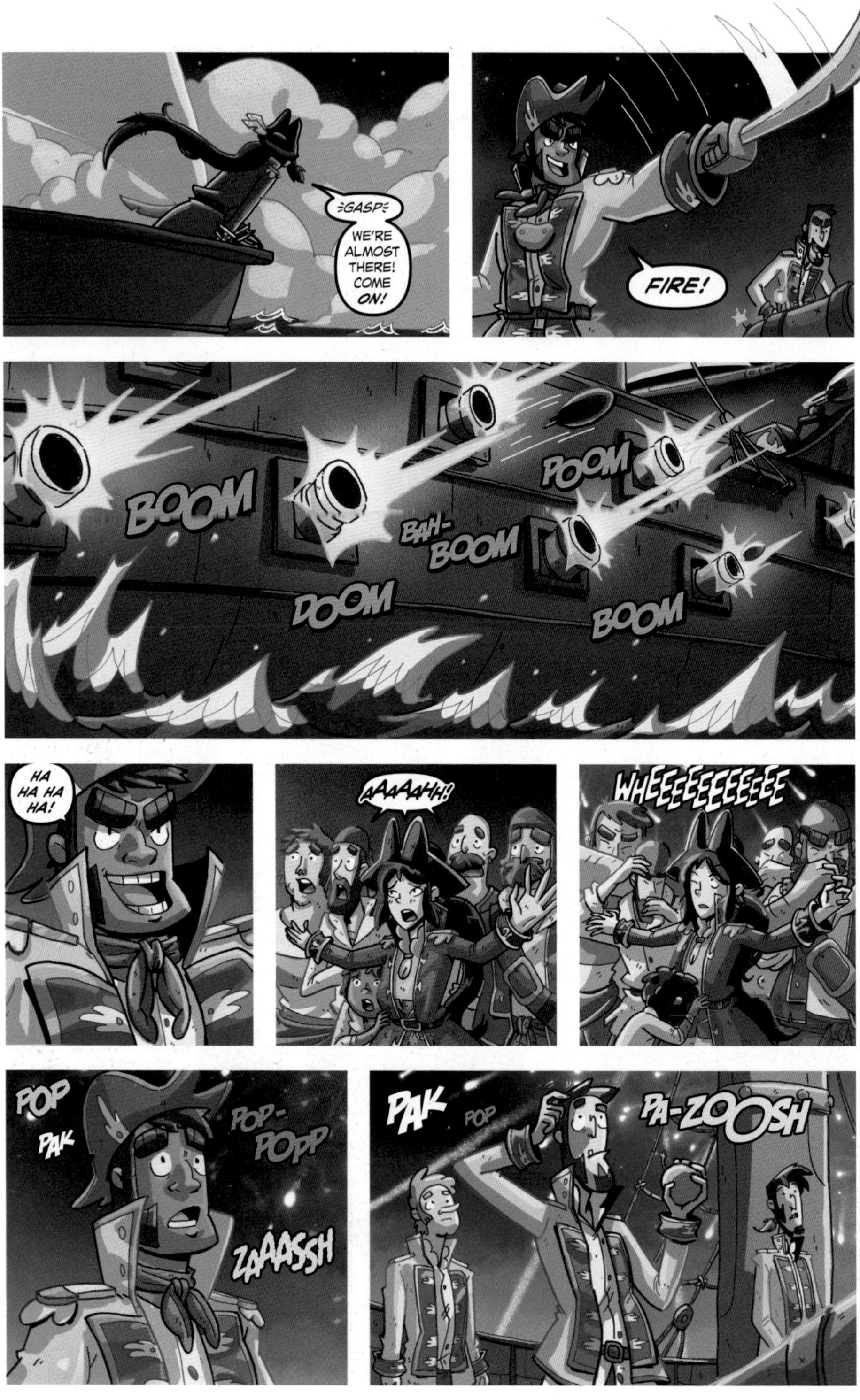

GASP
WE'RE ALMOST THERE! COME ON!
FIRE!
BOOM
POOM
BAH-BOOM
DOOM
BOOM
HA HA HA HA!
AAAAAHH!
WHEEEEEEEEEEE
POP
PAK
POP-POPP
ZAAASSH
PAK
POP
PA-ZOOSH

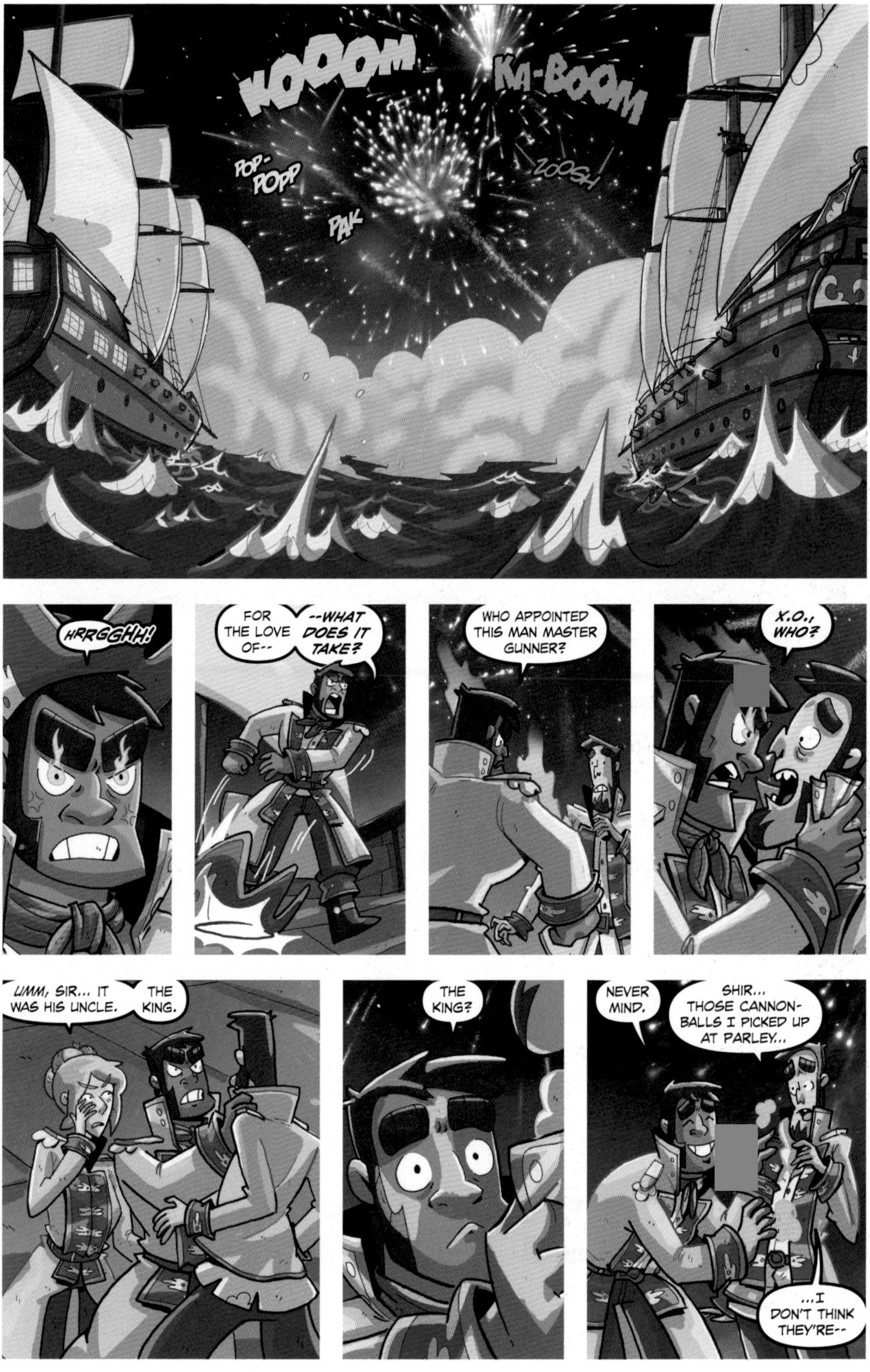
KOOOM
KA-BOOM
POP-POPP
ZOOSH
PAK
HRRGGHH!
FOR THE LOVE OF--
--WHAT DOES IT TAKE?
WHO APPOINTED THIS MAN MASTER GUNNER?
X.O., WHO?
UMM, SIR... IT WAS HIS UNCLE.
THE KING.
THE KING?
NEVER MIND.
SHIR... THOSE CANNON-BALLS I PICKED UP AT PARLEY...
...I DON'T THINK THEY'RE--

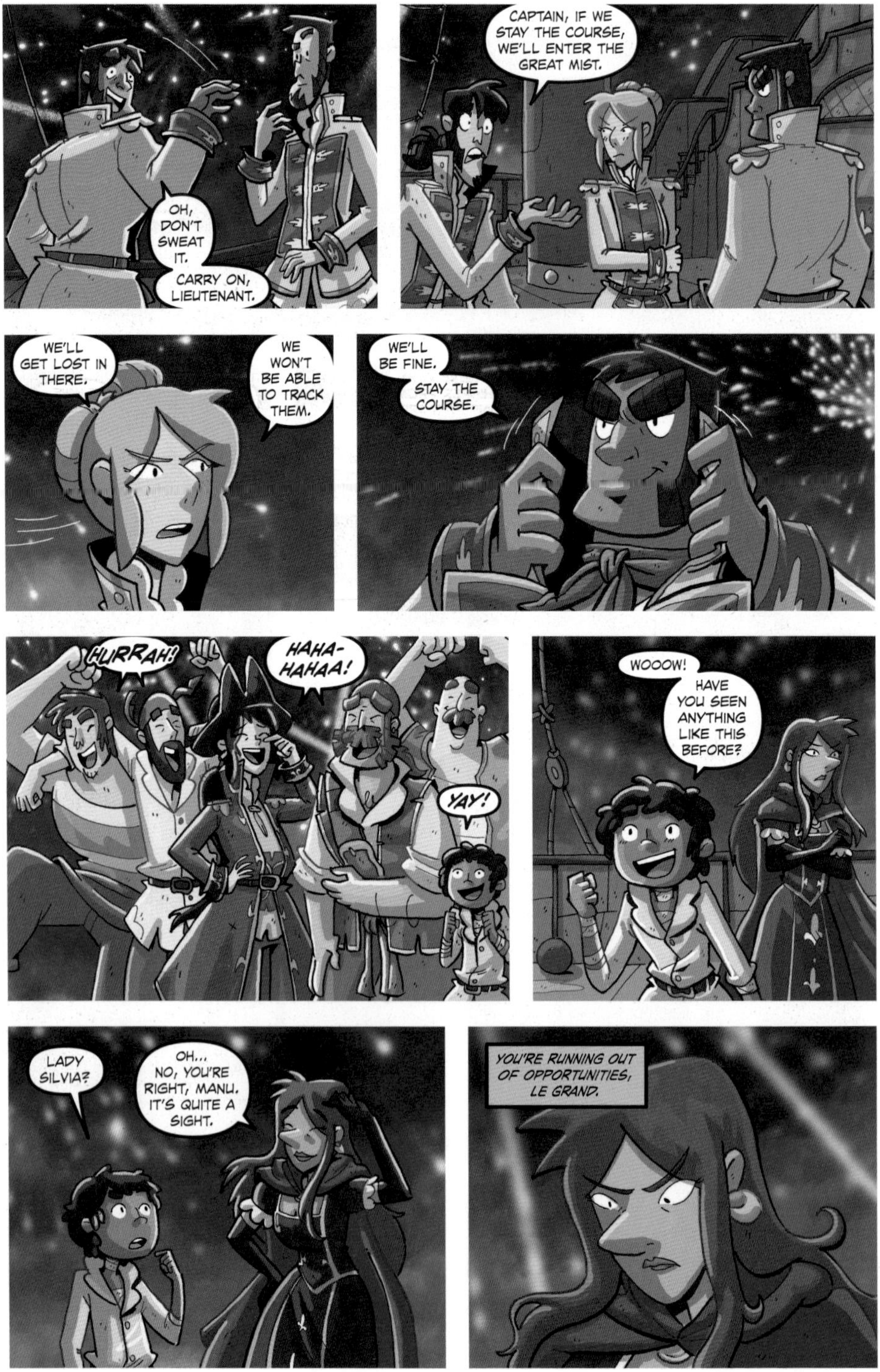

OH, DON'T SWEAT IT.
CARRY ON, LIEUTENANT.
CAPTAIN, IF WE STAY THE COURSE, WE'LL ENTER THE GREAT MIST.
WE'LL GET LOST IN THERE.
WE WON'T BE ABLE TO TRACK THEM.
WE'LL BE FINE.
STAY THE COURSE.
HURRAH!
HAHA-HAHAA!
YAY!
WOOOW!
HAVE YOU SEEN ANYTHING LIKE THIS BEFORE?
LADY SILVIA?
OH... NO, YOU'RE RIGHT, MANU. IT'S QUITE A SIGHT.
YOU'RE RUNNING OUT OF OPPORTUNITIES, LE GRAND.

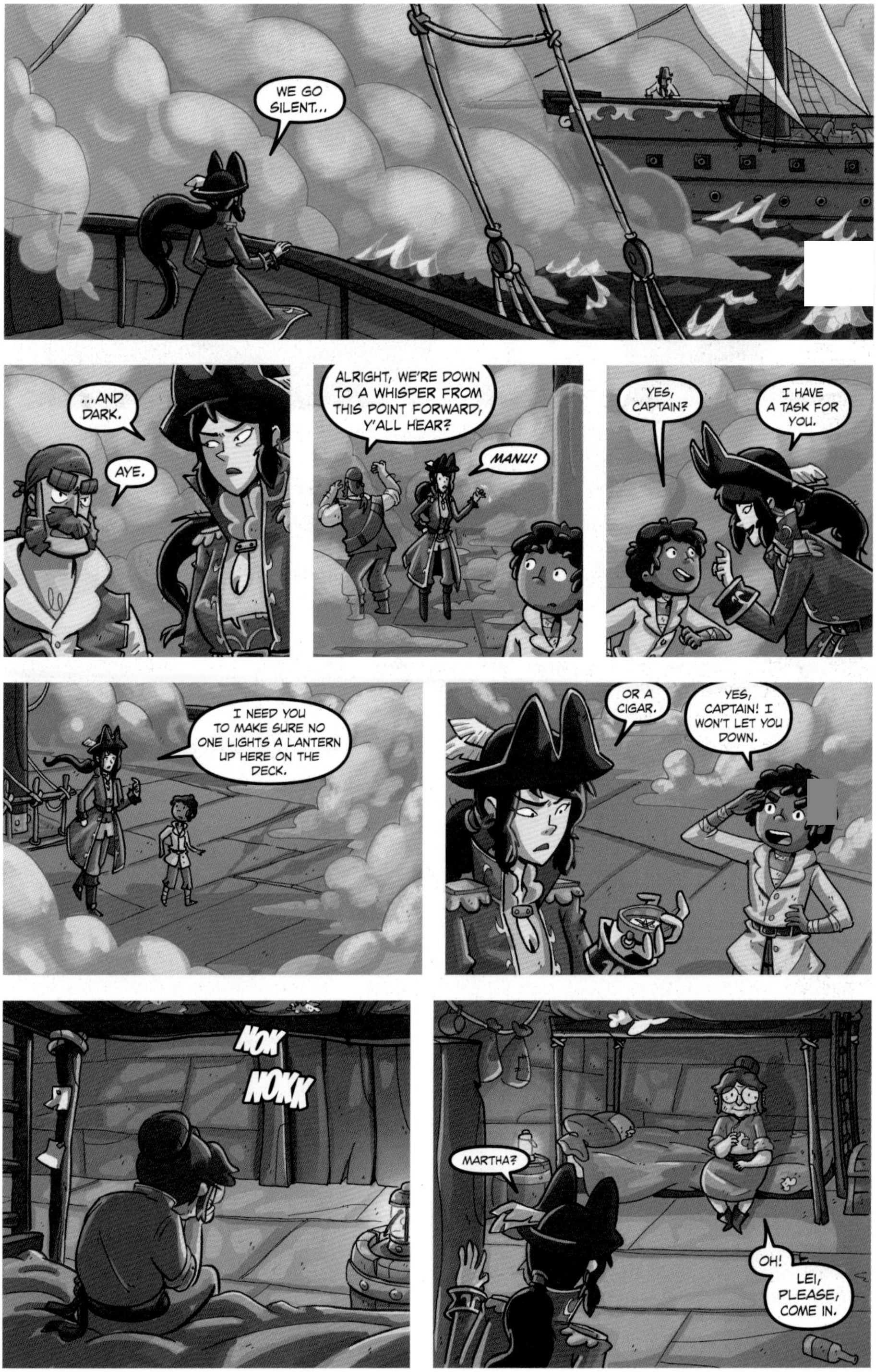
WE GO SILENT...
...AND DARK.
AYE.
ALRIGHT, WE'RE DOWN TO A WHISPER FROM THIS POINT FORWARD, Y'ALL HEAR?
MANU!
YES, CAPTAIN?
I HAVE A TASK FOR YOU.
I NEED YOU TO MAKE SURE NO ONE LIGHTS A LANTERN UP HERE ON THE DECK.
OR A CIGAR.
YES, CAPTAIN! I WON'T LET YOU DOWN.
NOK
NOKK
MARTHA?
OH!
LEI, PLEASE, COME IN.

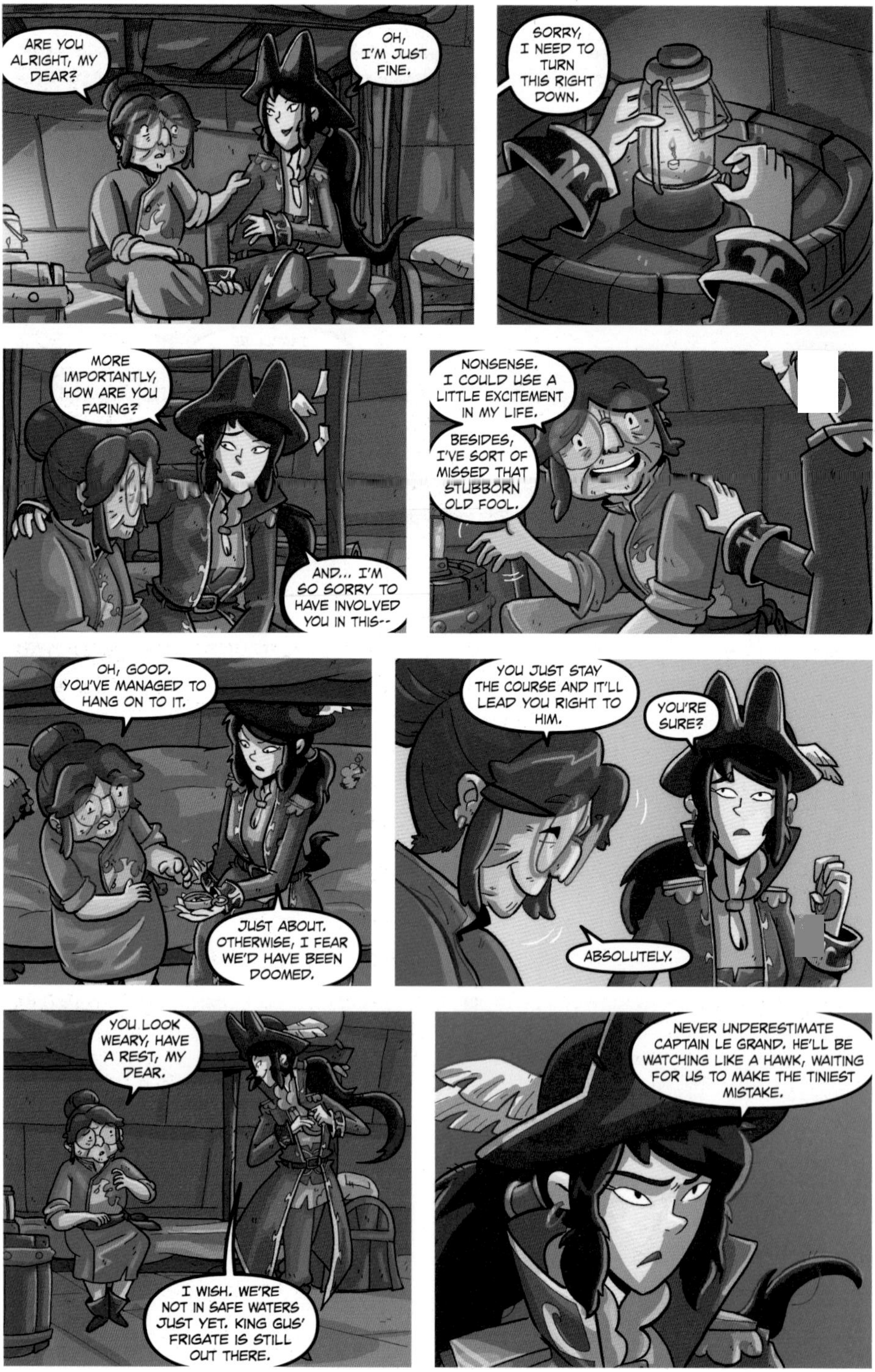

ARE YOU ALRIGHT, MY DEAR?
OH, I'M JUST FINE.
SORRY, I NEED TO TURN THIS RIGHT DOWN.
MORE IMPORTANTLY, HOW ARE YOU FARING?
AND... I'M SO SORRY TO HAVE INVOLVED YOU IN THIS--
NONSENSE. I COULD USE A LITTLE EXCITEMENT IN MY LIFE.
BESIDES, I'VE SORT OF MISSED THAT STUBBORN OLD FOOL.
OH, GOOD. YOU'VE MANAGED TO HANG ON TO IT.
JUST ABOUT. OTHERWISE, I FEAR WE'D HAVE BEEN DOOMED.
YOU JUST STAY THE COURSE AND IT'LL LEAD YOU RIGHT TO HIM.
YOU'RE SURE?
ABSOLUTELY.
YOU LOOK WEARY, HAVE A REST, MY DEAR.
I WISH. WE'RE NOT IN SAFE WATERS JUST YET. KING GUS' FRIGATE IS STILL OUT THERE.
NEVER UNDERESTIMATE CAPTAIN LE GRAND. HE'LL BE WATCHING LIKE A HAWK, WAITING FOR US TO MAKE THE TINIEST MISTAKE.

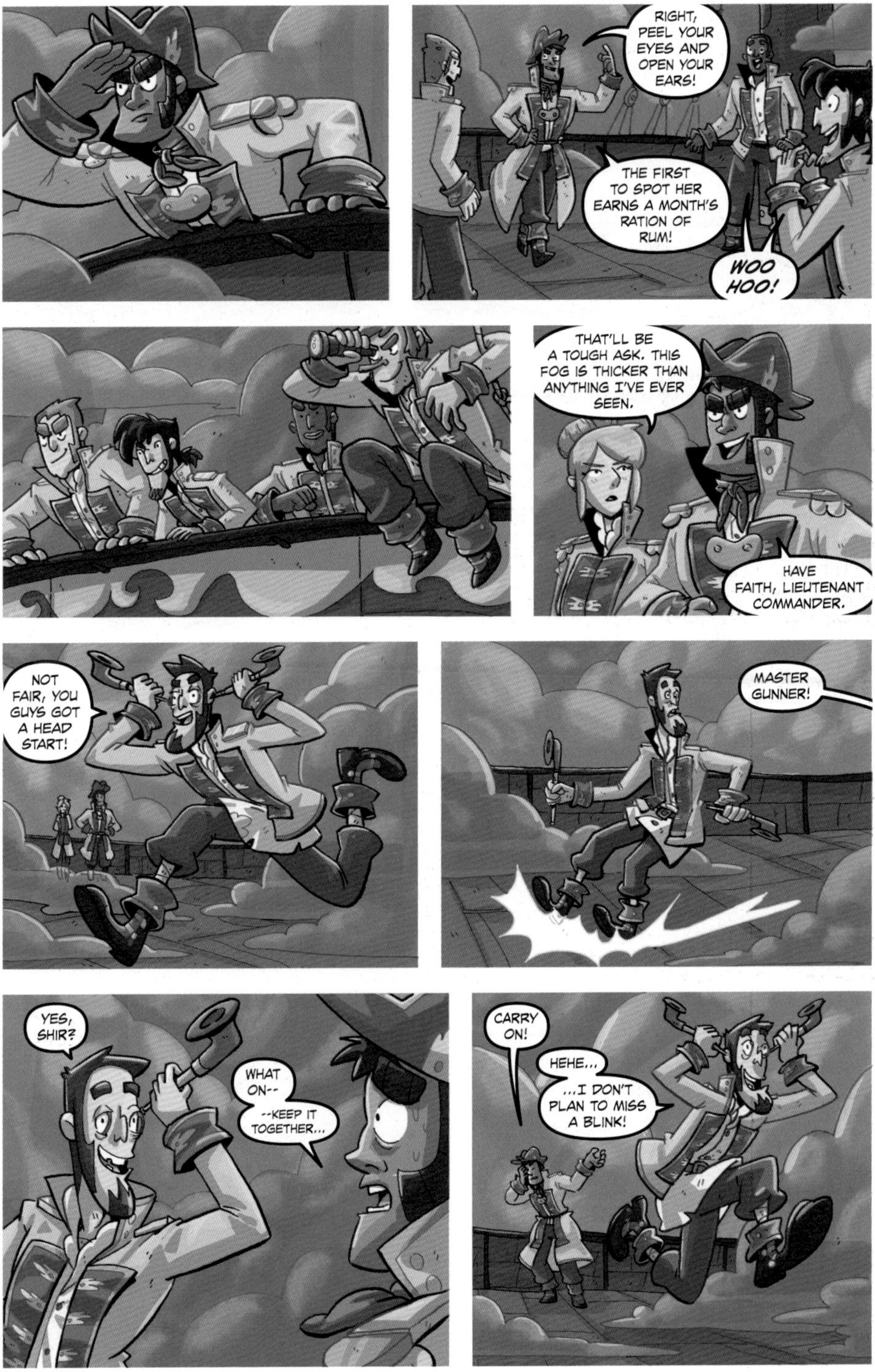
RIGHT, PEEL YOUR EYES AND OPEN YOUR EARS!
THE FIRST TO SPOT HER EARNS A MONTH'S RATION OF RUM!
WOO HOO!
THAT'LL BE A TOUGH ASK. THIS FOG IS THICKER THAN ANYTHING I'VE EVER SEEN.
HAVE FAITH, LIEUTENANT COMMANDER.
NOT FAIR, YOU GUYS GOT A HEAD START!
MASTER GUNNER!
YES, SHIR?
WHAT ON--
--KEEP IT TOGETHER...
CARRY ON!
HEHE...
...I DON'T PLAN TO MISS A BLINK!

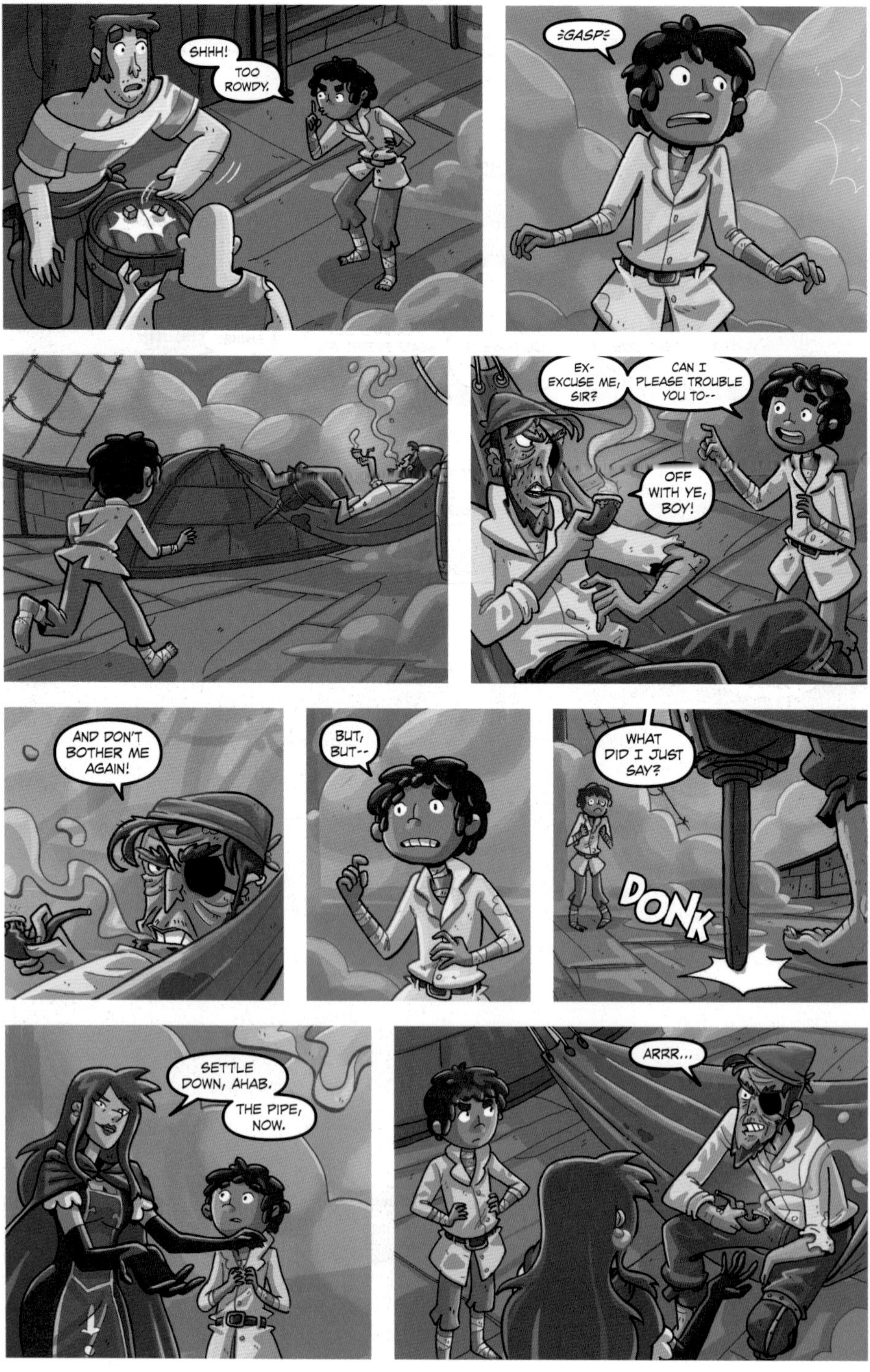
SHHH!
TOO ROWDY.
GASP
EX-EXCUSE ME, SIR?
CAN I PLEASE TROUBLE YOU TO--
OFF WITH YE, BOY!
AND DON'T BOTHER ME AGAIN!
BUT, BUT--
WHAT DID I JUST SAY?
DONK
SETTLE DOWN, AHAB.
THE PIPE, NOW.
ARRR...

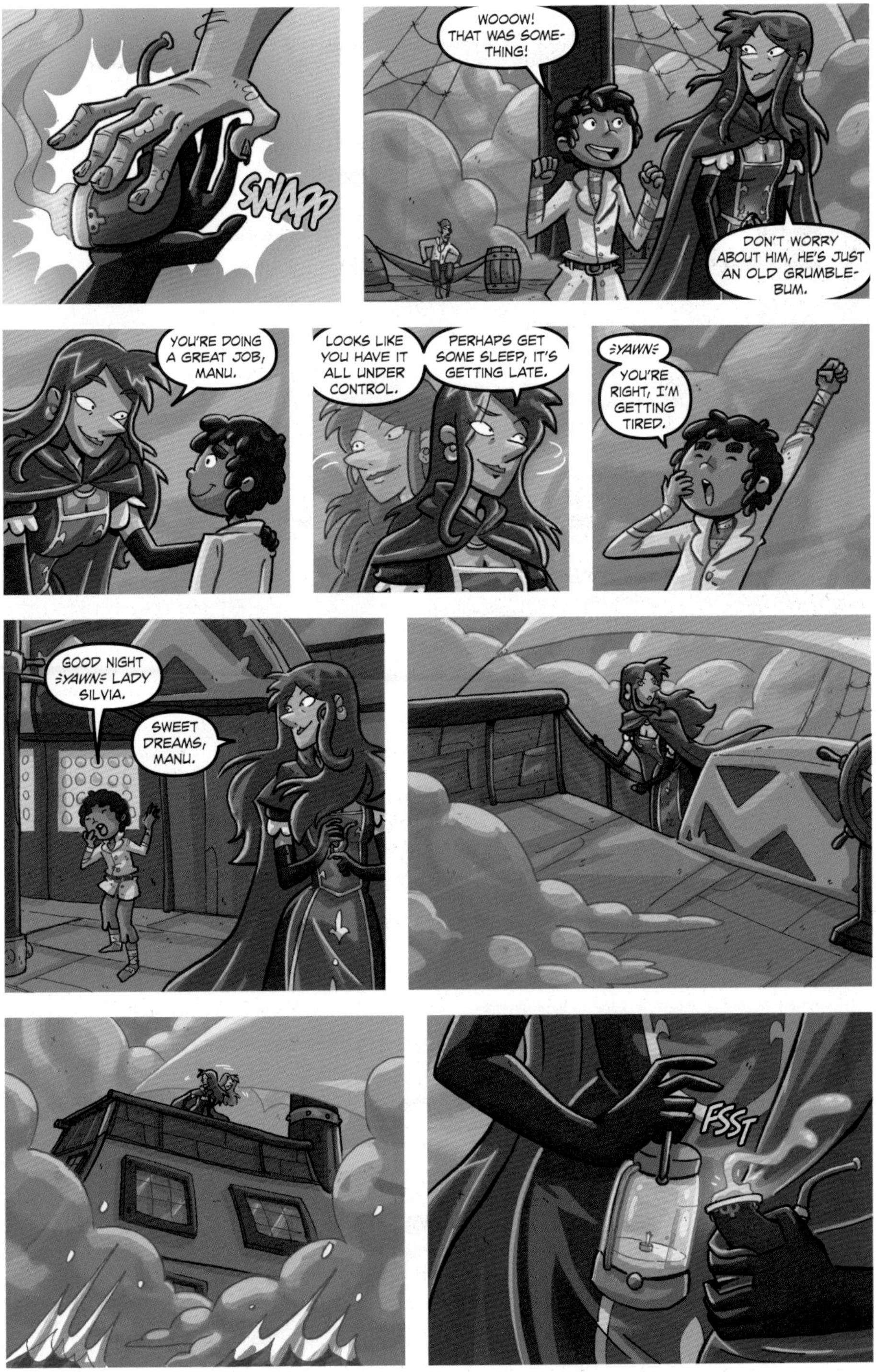

SWAPP
WOOOW! THAT WAS SOME-THING!
DON'T WORRY ABOUT HIM, HE'S JUST AN OLD GRUMBLE-BUM.
YOU'RE DOING A GREAT JOB, MANU.
LOOKS LIKE YOU HAVE IT ALL UNDER CONTROL.
PERHAPS GET SOME SLEEP, IT'S GETTING LATE.
YAWN
YOU'RE RIGHT, I'M GETTING TIRED.
GOOD NIGHT YAWN LADY SILVIA.
SWEET DREAMS, MANU.
FSST

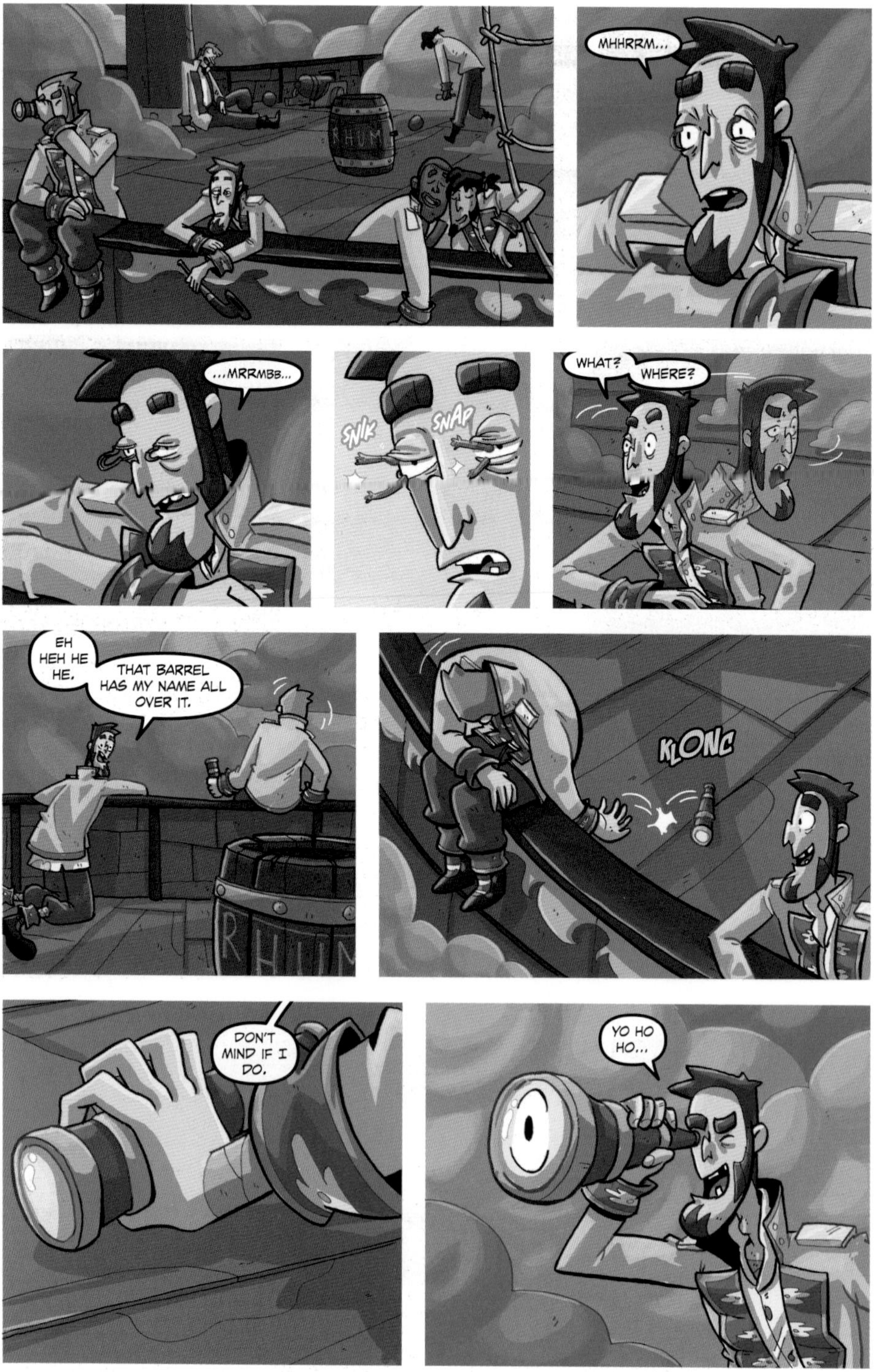
MHHRRM...
...MRRMBB...
SNIK
SNAP
WHAT?
WHERE?
EH HEH HE HE.
THAT BARREL HAS MY NAME ALL OVER IT.
RHUM
KLONC
DON'T MIND IF I DO.
YO HO HO...

...AND A BARREL OF RUM!

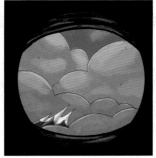

≥GASP≤

THERE SHE IS!

I'VE GOT 'EM!

HUH?

WHAT?

THIS BETTER BE IT.

TEN O'CLOCK, SHIR!

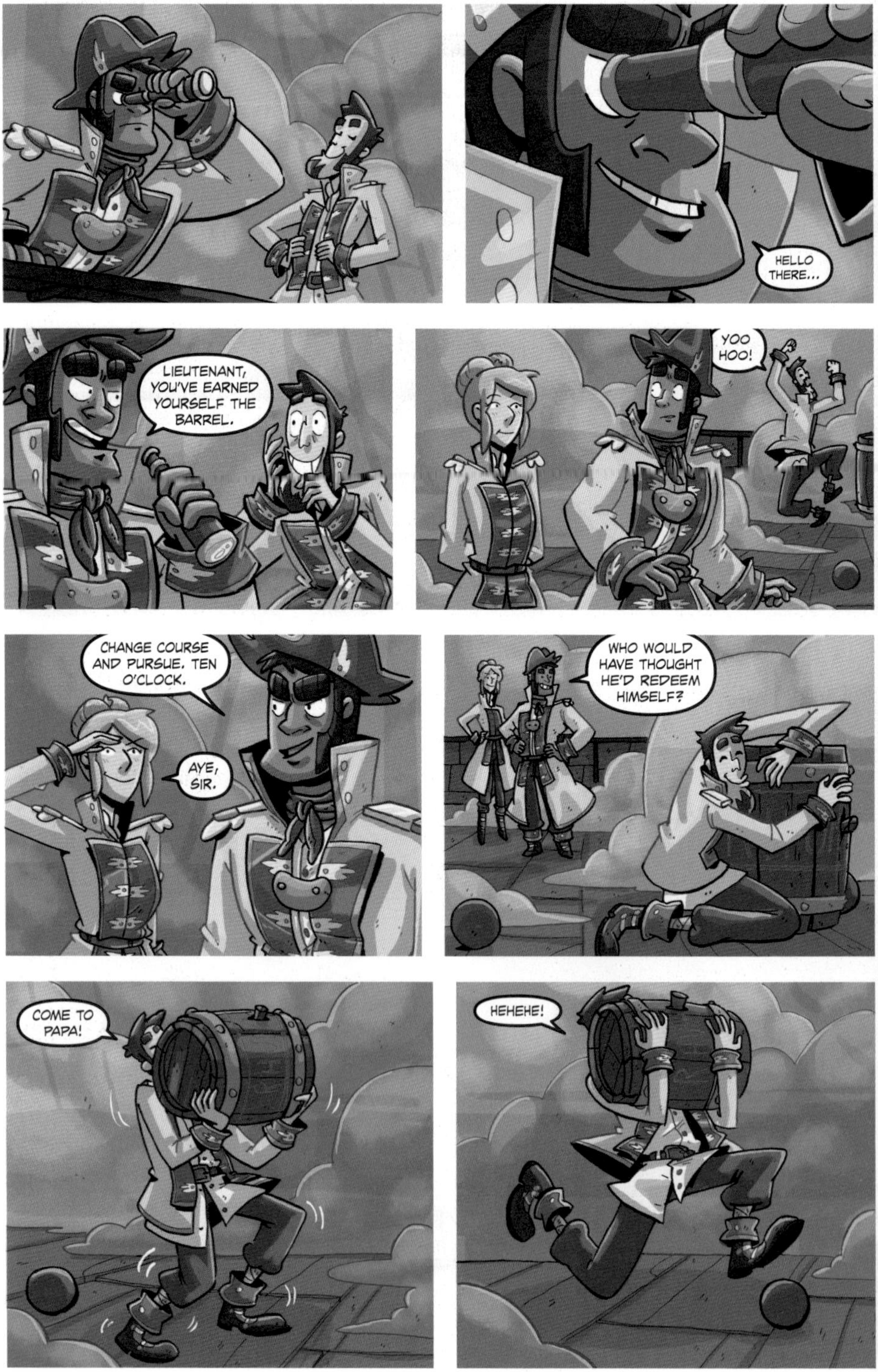
HELLO THERE...
LIEUTENANT, YOU'VE EARNED YOURSELF THE BARREL.
YOO HOO!
CHANGE COURSE AND PURSUE. TEN O'CLOCK.
AYE, SIR.
WHO WOULD HAVE THOUGHT HE'D REDEEM HIMSELF?
COME TO PAPA!
HEHEHE!

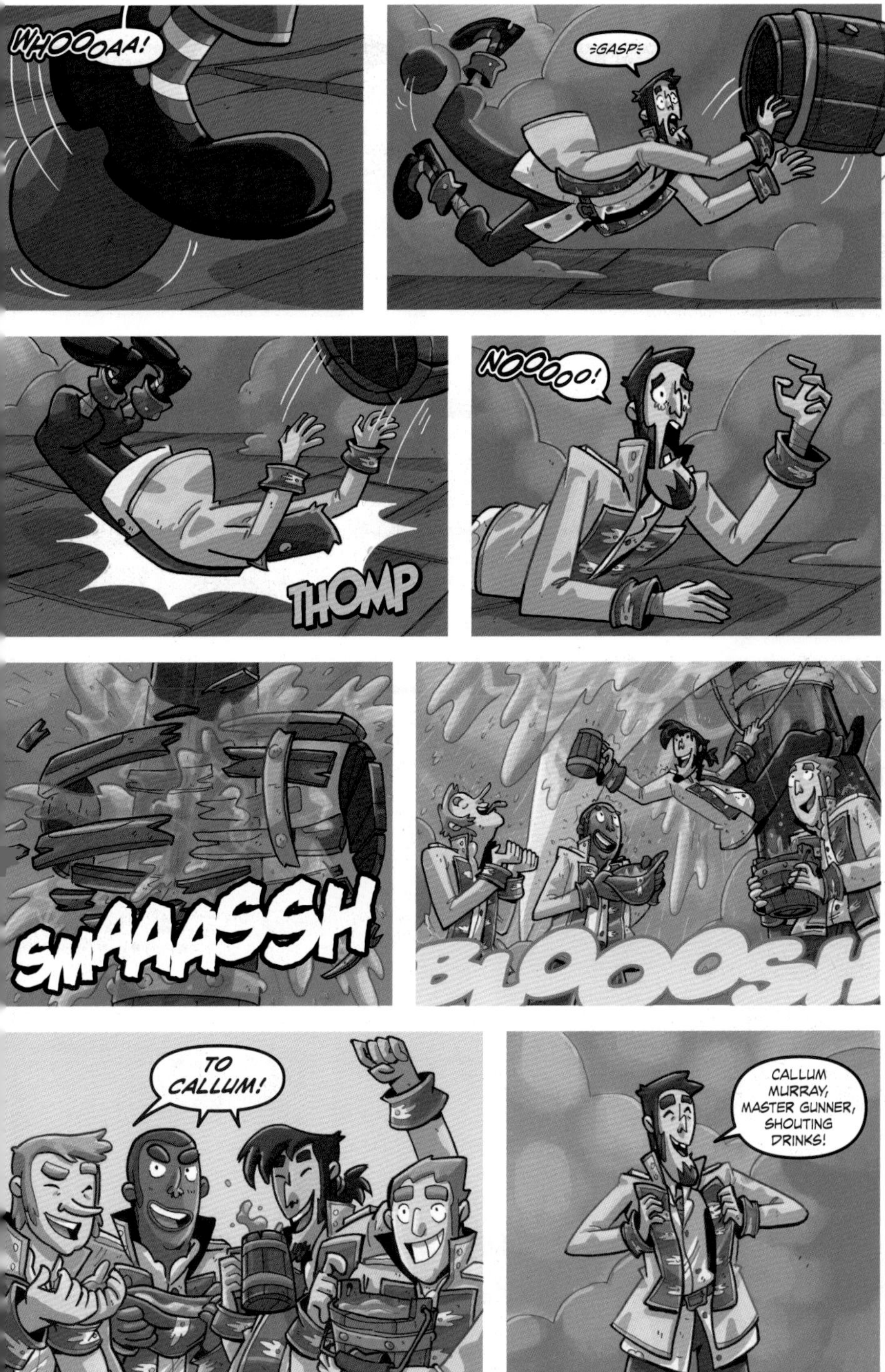
WHOOOOAA!
=GASP=
THOMP
NOOOOO!
SMAAASSH
BLOOOSH
TO CALLUM!
CALLUM MURRAY, MASTER GUNNER, SHOUTING DRINKS!

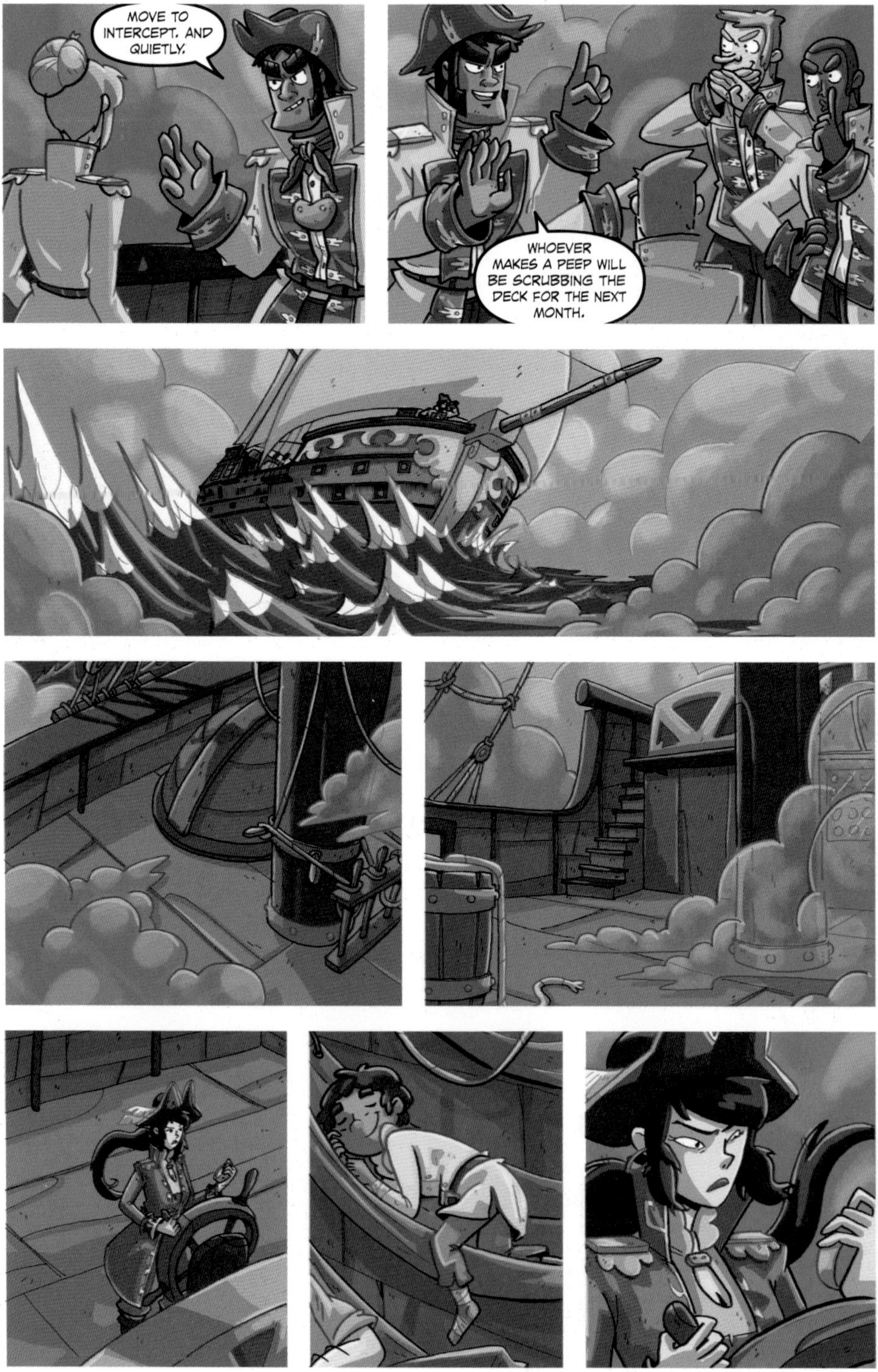
MOVE TO INTERCEPT. AND QUIETLY.
WHOEVER MAKES A PEEP WILL BE SCRUBBING THE DECK FOR THE NEXT MONTH.

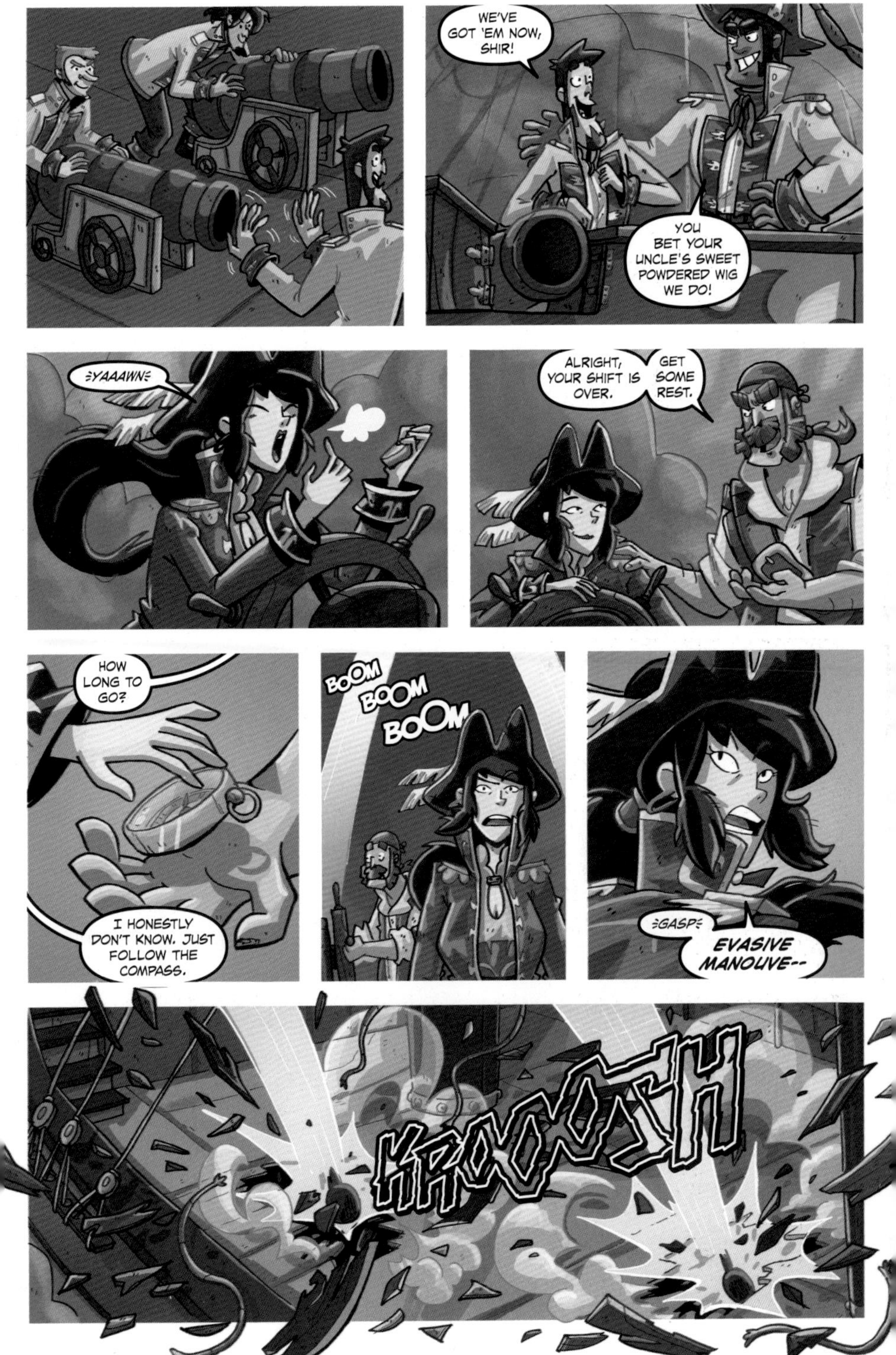
WE'VE GOT 'EM NOW, SHIR!
YOU BET YOUR UNCLE'S SWEET POWDERED WIG WE DO!
YAAAWN
ALRIGHT, YOUR SHIFT IS OVER.
GET SOME REST.
HOW LONG TO GO?
I HONESTLY DON'T KNOW. JUST FOLLOW THE COMPASS.
BOOM
BOOM
BOOM
GASP
EVASIVE MANOUVE--
KROOOSH

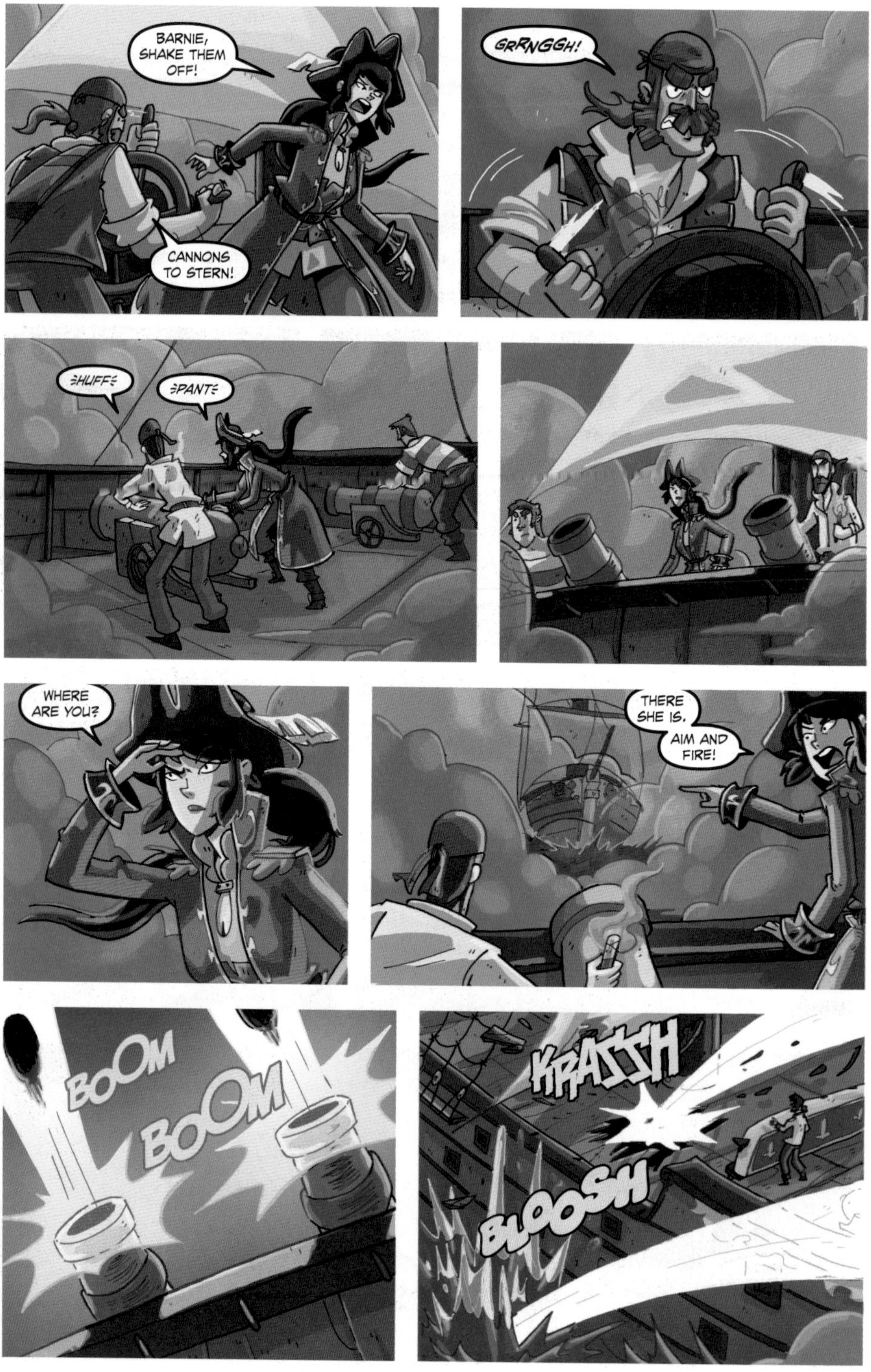
BARNIE, SHAKE THEM OFF!
CANNONS TO STERN!
GRRNGGH!
HUFF
PANT
WHERE ARE YOU?
THERE SHE IS.
AIM AND FIRE!
BOOM
BOOM
KRASSH
BLOOSH

BOOM
BOOM

HUH?
WHAT WAS
THAT?

THAT
SOUNDED
LIKE...

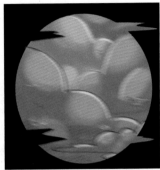

≥GASP≤
IT IS!

THEY'RE HERE,
AND THEY'RE BEING
PURSUED!

I MUST
HELP THEM,
SOMEHOW.

SKRIT
SKRIT

I KNOW
I'VE SQUEEZED
EVERY BIT OF
JUICE OUT OF
YOU...

...BUT THERE
MUST BE A TEENY
TINY BIT LEFT.

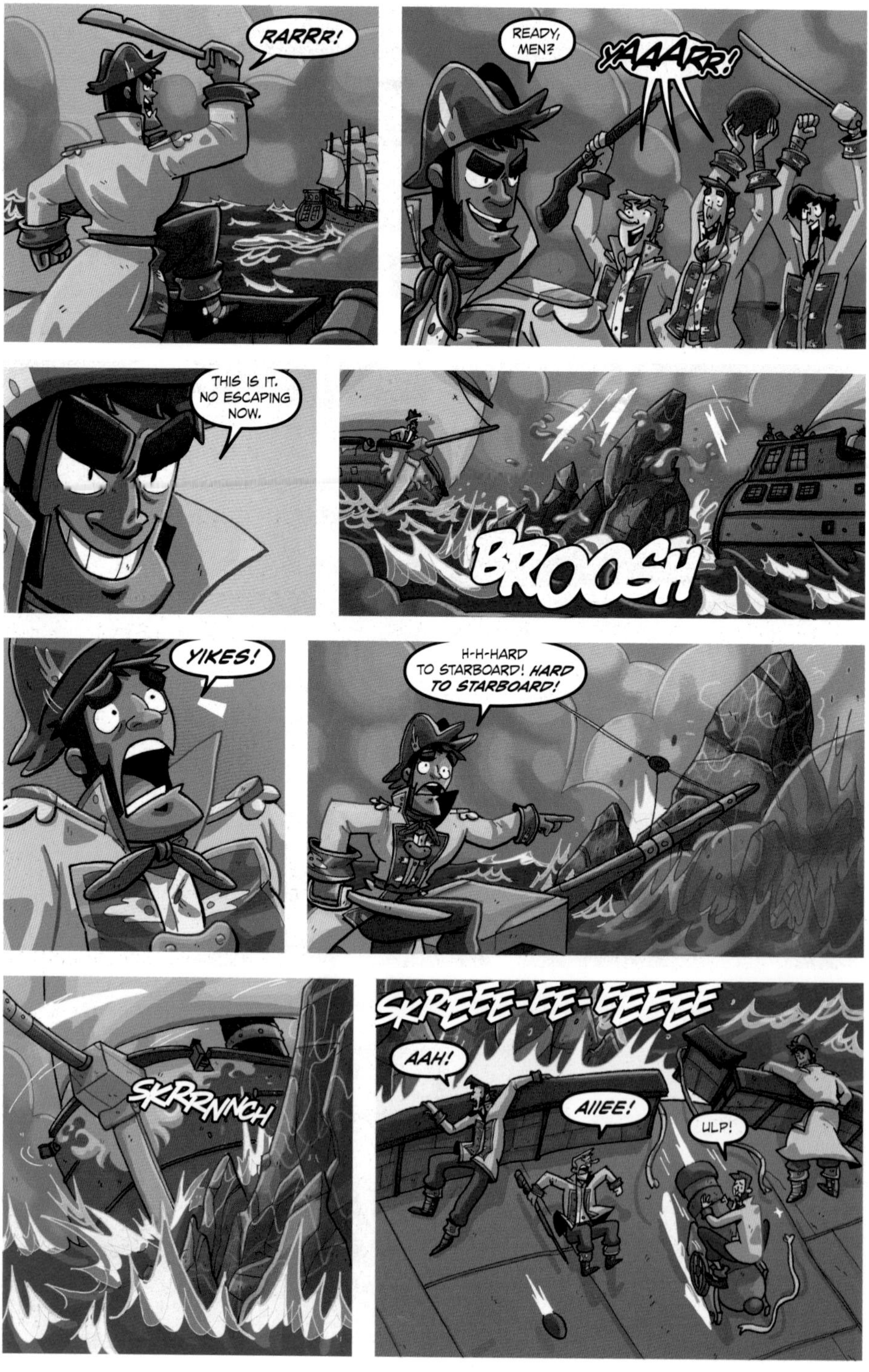
RARRR!
READY, MEN?
YAAARR!
THIS IS IT. NO ESCAPING NOW.
BROOSH
YIKES!
H-H-HARD TO STARBOARD! HARD TO STARBOARD!
SKRRNNCH
SKREEEE-EE-EEEEE
AAH!
AIIEE!
ULP!

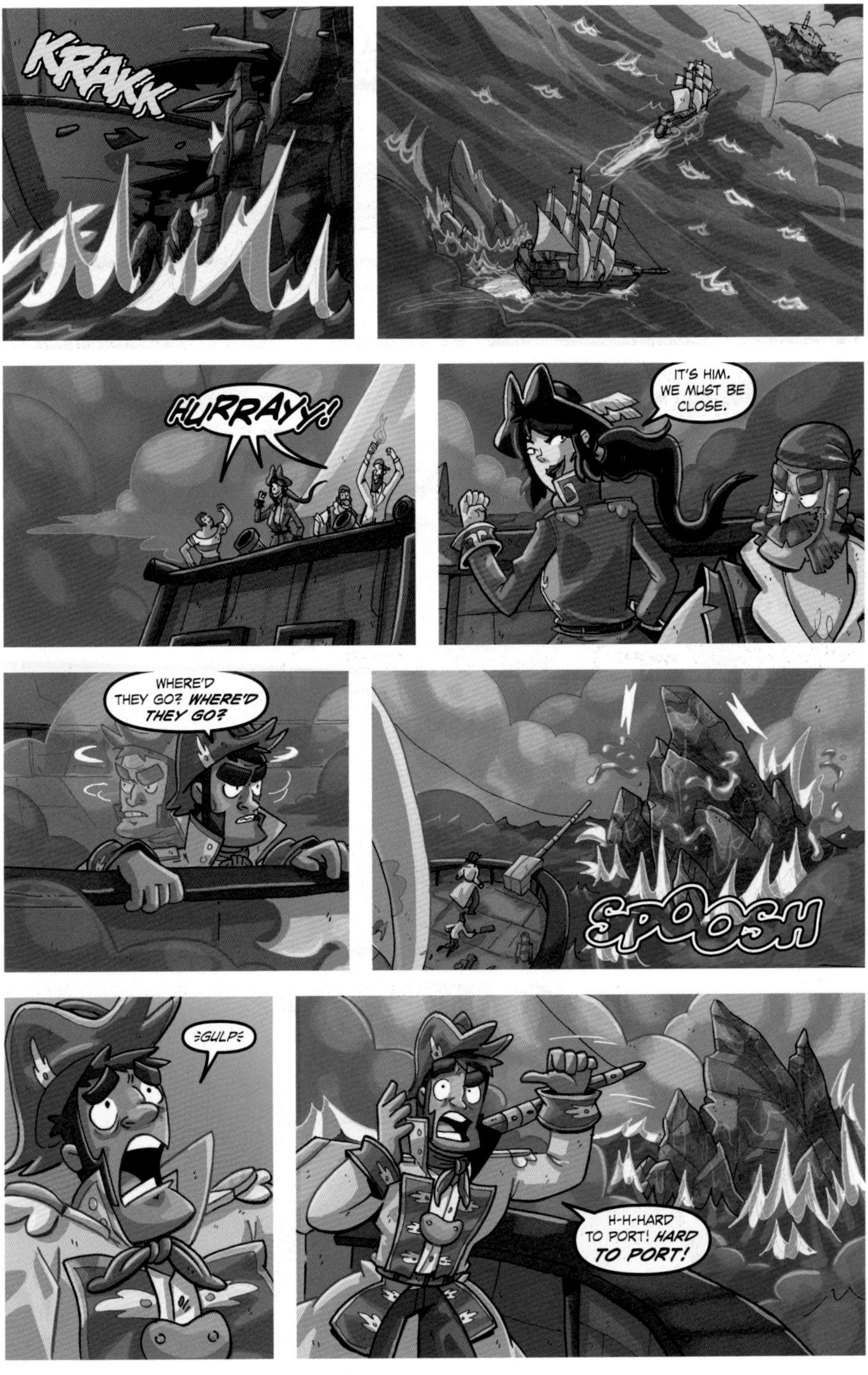
KRAKK
HURRAYY!
IT'S HIM. WE MUST BE CLOSE.
WHERE'D THEY GO? WHERE'D THEY GO?
SPOOSH
GULP
H-H-HARD TO PORT! HARD TO PORT!

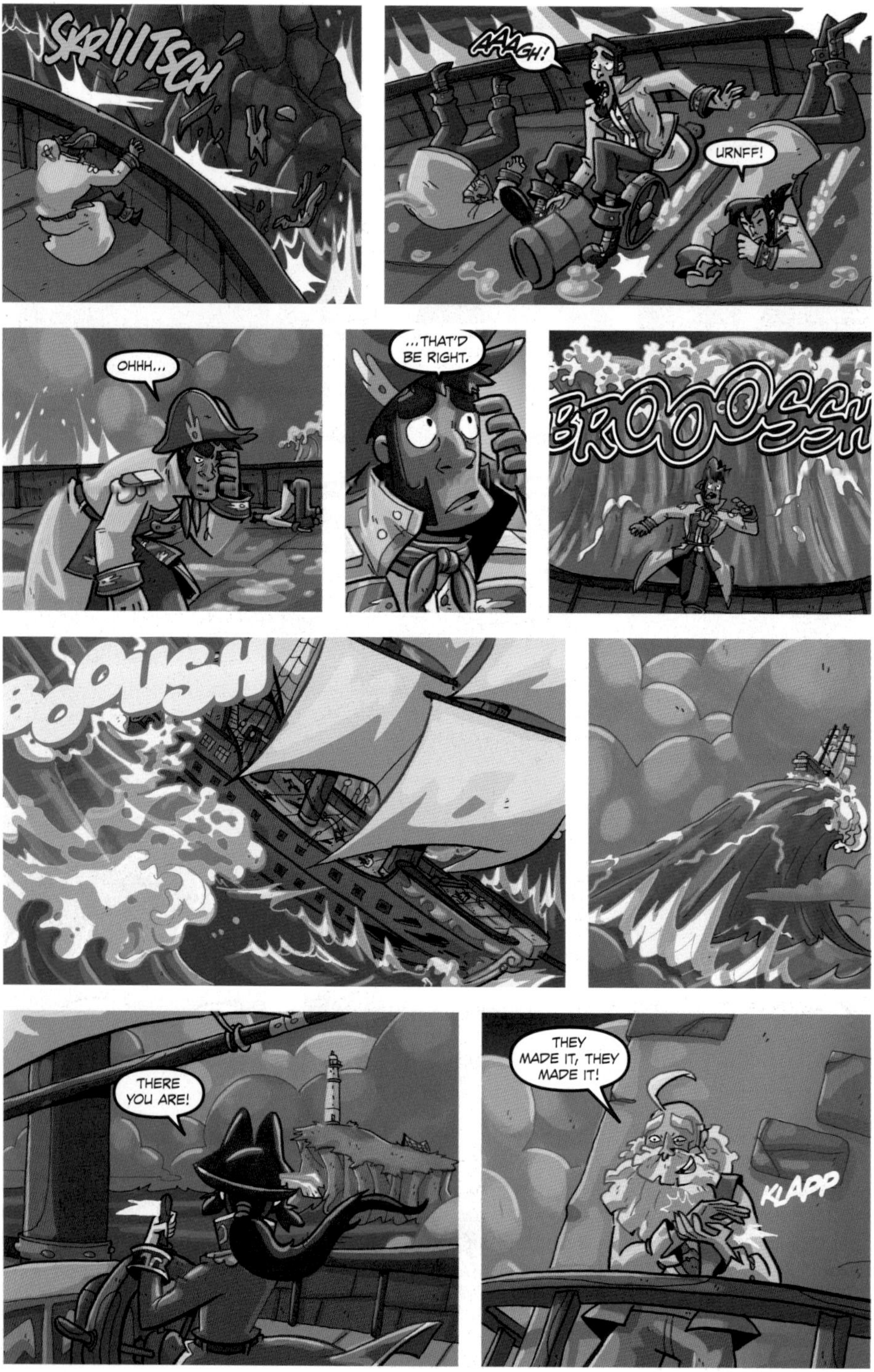
SKRIIITSCH
AAAGH!
URNFF!
OHHH...
...THAT'D BE RIGHT.
BROOOSCH
BOOUSH
THERE YOU ARE!
THEY MADE IT, THEY MADE IT!
KLAPP

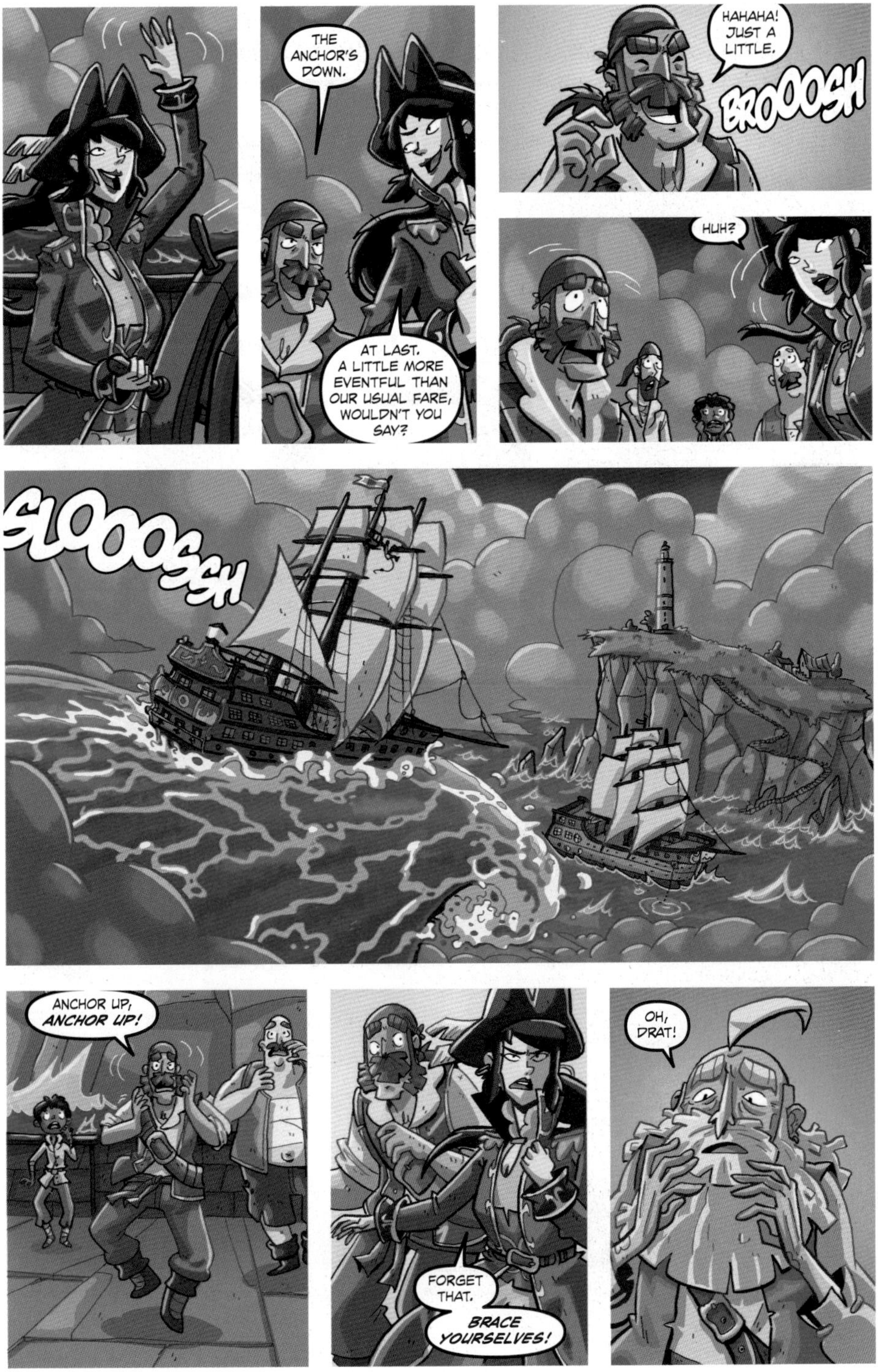
THE ANCHOR'S DOWN.
AT LAST. A LITTLE MORE EVENTFUL THAN OUR USUAL FARE, WOULDN'T YOU SAY?
HAHAHA! JUST A LITTLE.
BROOOSH
HUH?
SLOOOSSH
ANCHOR UP, *ANCHOR UP!*
FORGET THAT. ***BRACE YOURSELVES!***
OH, DRAT!

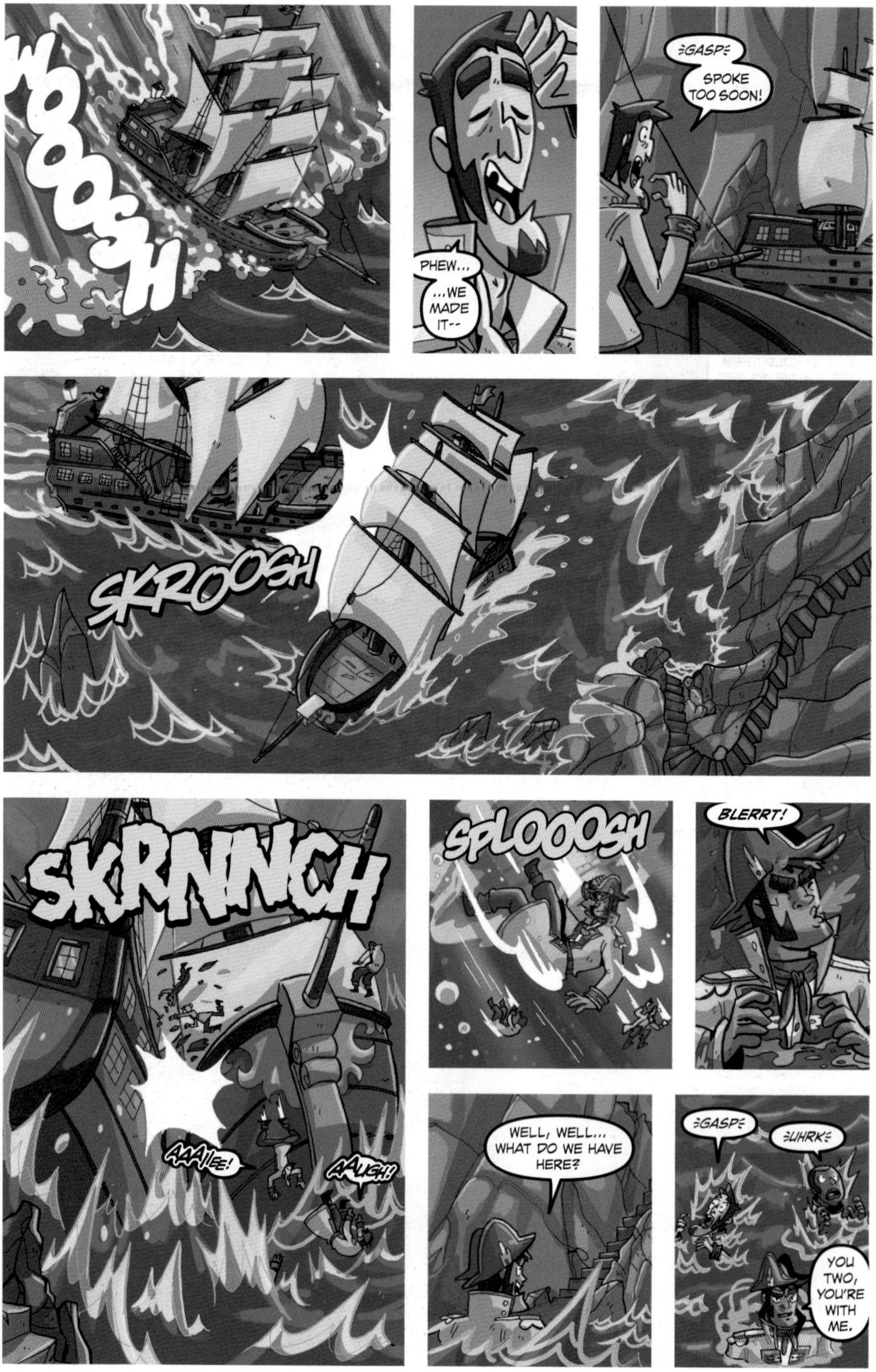
WOOOOSH
PHEW...
...WE MADE IT--
GASP
SPOKE TOO SOON!
SKROOSH
SKRNNCH
AAAIIEE!
AAUGH!
SPLOOOSH
BLERRT!
WELL, WELL... WHAT DO WE HAVE HERE?
GASP
UHRK
YOU TWO, YOU'RE WITH ME.

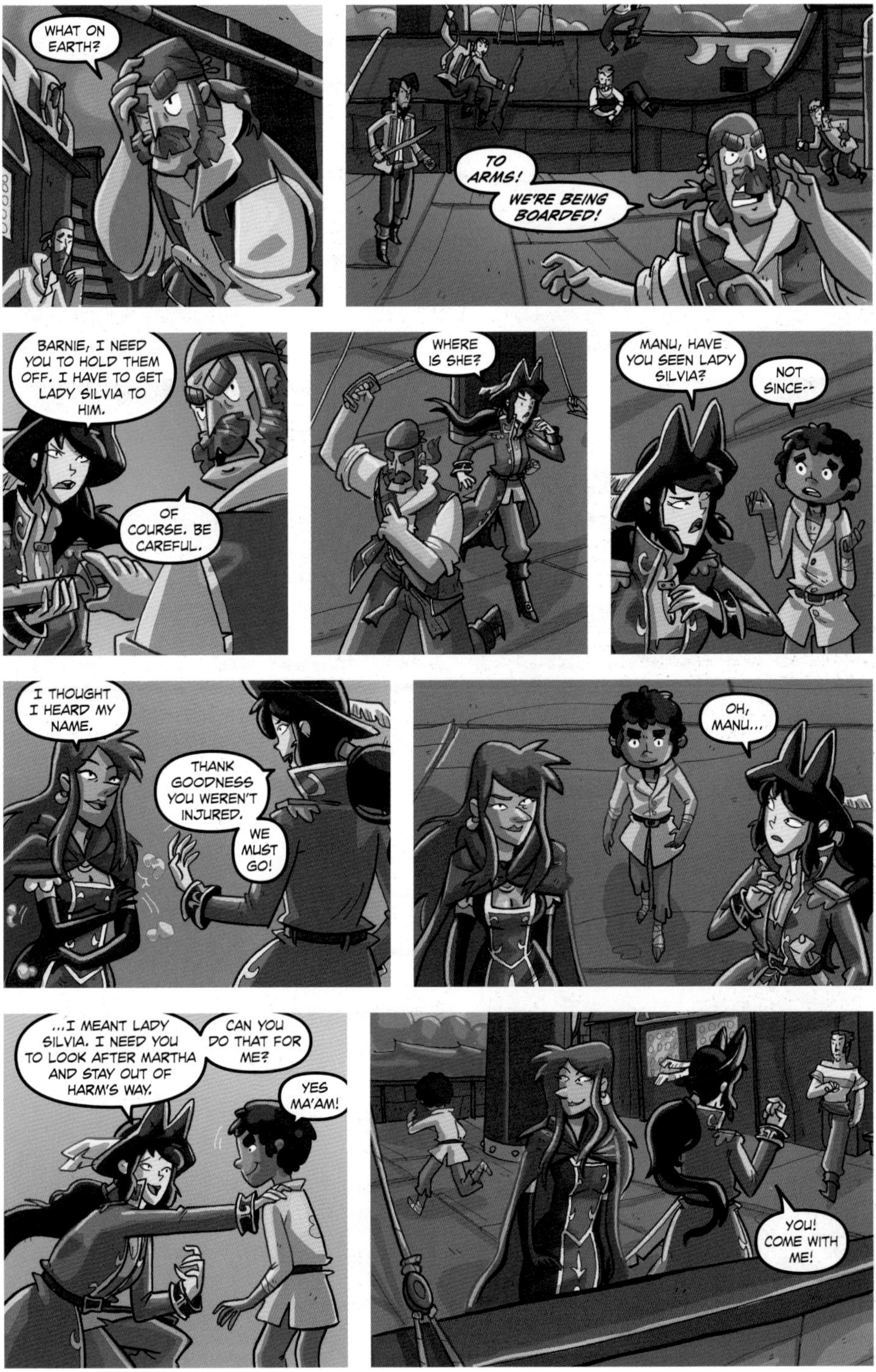
WHAT ON EARTH?
TO ARMS!
WE'RE BEING BOARDED!
BARNIE, I NEED YOU TO HOLD THEM OFF. I HAVE TO GET LADY SILVIA TO HIM.
OF COURSE. BE CAREFUL.
WHERE IS SHE?
MANU, HAVE YOU SEEN LADY SILVIA?
NOT SINCE--
I THOUGHT I HEARD MY NAME.
THANK GOODNESS YOU WEREN'T INJURED.
WE MUST GO!
OH, MANU...
...I MEANT LADY SILVIA. I NEED YOU TO LOOK AFTER MARTHA AND STAY OUT OF HARM'S WAY.
CAN YOU DO THAT FOR ME?
YES MA'AM!
YOU! COME WITH ME!

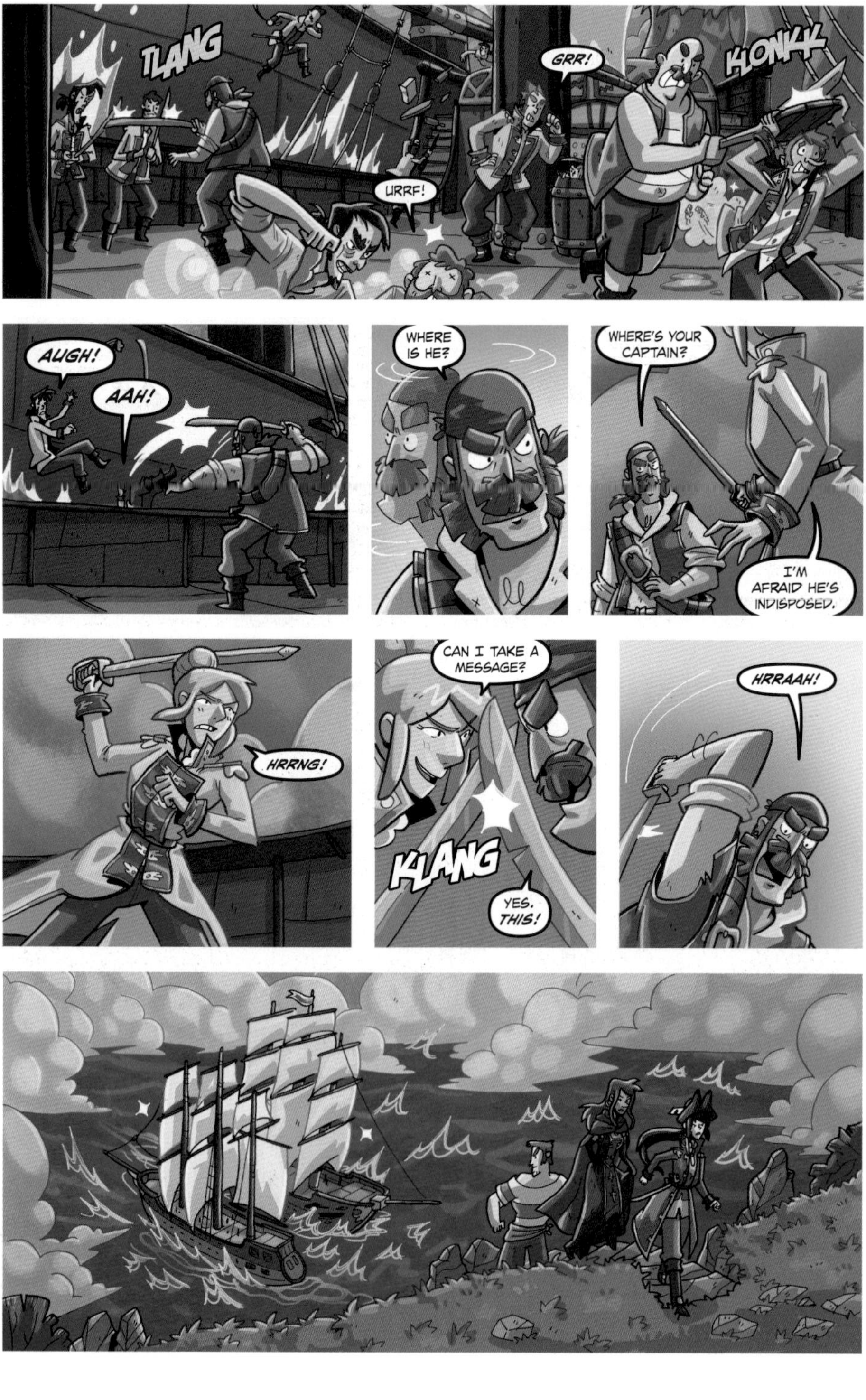
TLANG
GRR!
KLONKK
URRF!
AUGH!
AAH!
WHERE IS HE?
WHERE'S YOUR CAPTAIN?
I'M AFRAID HE'S INDISPOSED.
HRRNG!
CAN I TAKE A MESSAGE?
KLANG
YES. THIS!
HRRAAH!

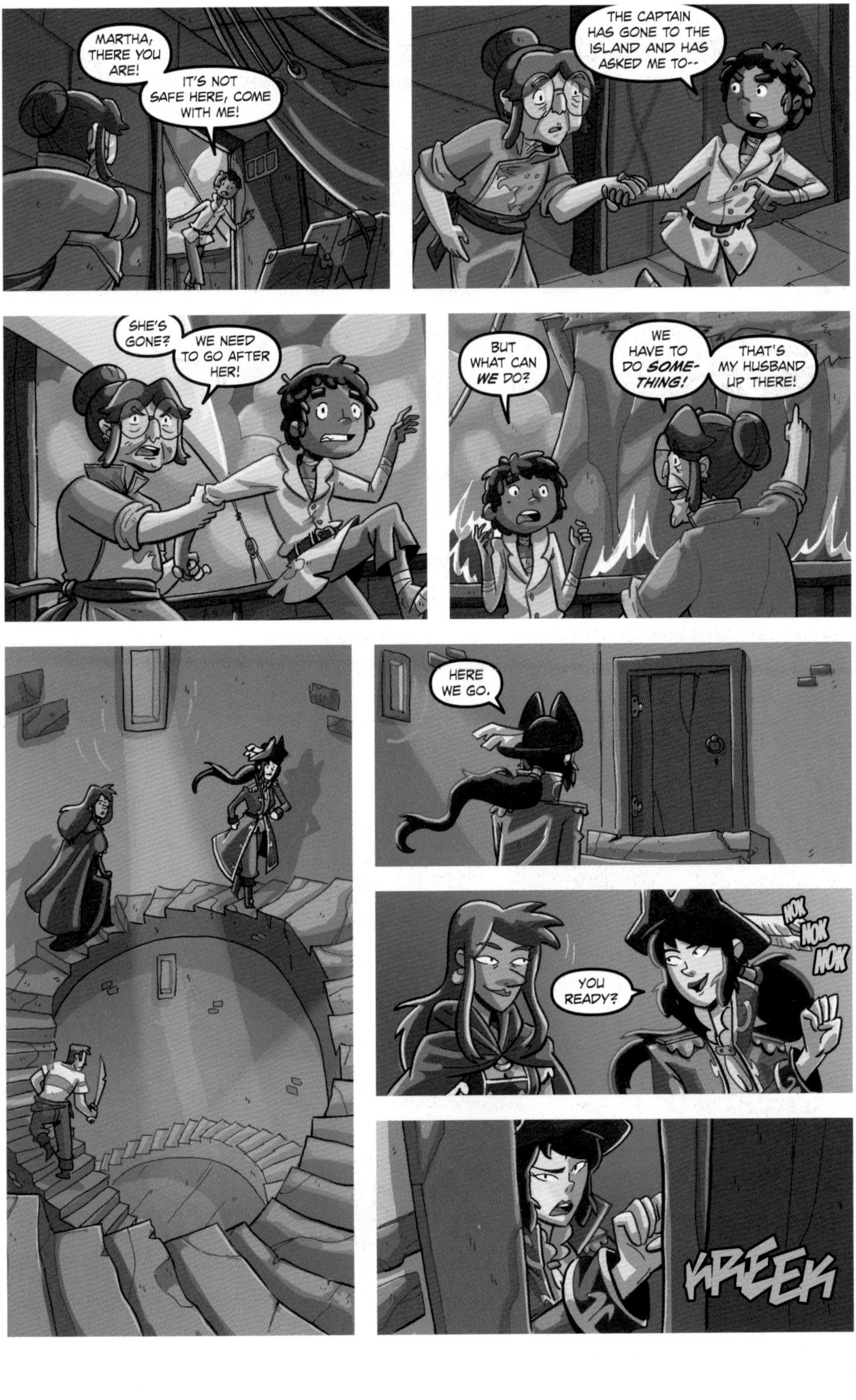
MARTHA, THERE YOU ARE!
IT'S NOT SAFE HERE, COME WITH ME!
THE CAPTAIN HAS GONE TO THE ISLAND AND HAS ASKED ME TO--
SHE'S GONE?
WE NEED TO GO AFTER HER!
BUT WHAT CAN WE DO?
WE HAVE TO DO SOME-THING!
THAT'S MY HUSBAND UP THERE!
HERE WE GO.
NOK
NOK
NOK
YOU READY?
KREEK

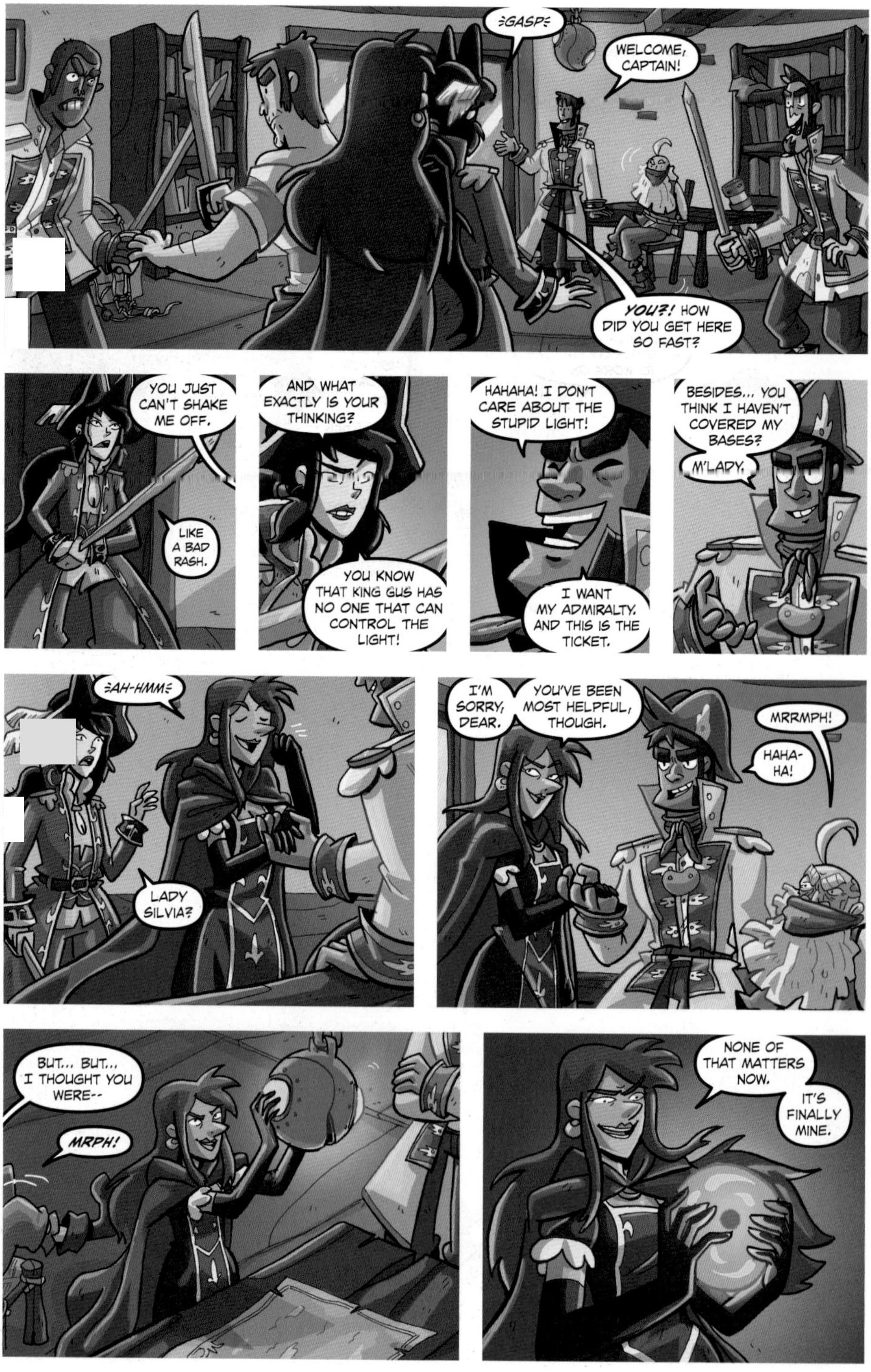

≥GASP≤
WELCOME, CAPTAIN!
YOU?! HOW DID YOU GET HERE SO FAST?
YOU JUST CAN'T SHAKE ME OFF.
LIKE A BAD RASH.
AND WHAT EXACTLY IS YOUR THINKING?
YOU KNOW THAT KING GUS HAS NO ONE THAT CAN CONTROL THE LIGHT!
HAHAHA! I DON'T CARE ABOUT THE STUPID LIGHT!
I WANT MY ADMIRALTY. AND THIS IS THE TICKET.
BESIDES... YOU THINK I HAVEN'T COVERED MY BASES?
M'LADY.
≥AH-HMM≤
LADY SILVIA?
I'M SORRY, DEAR.
YOU'VE BEEN MOST HELPFUL, THOUGH.
MRRMPH!
HAHA-HA!
BUT... BUT... I THOUGHT YOU WERE--
MRPH!
NONE OF THAT MATTERS NOW.
IT'S FINALLY MINE.

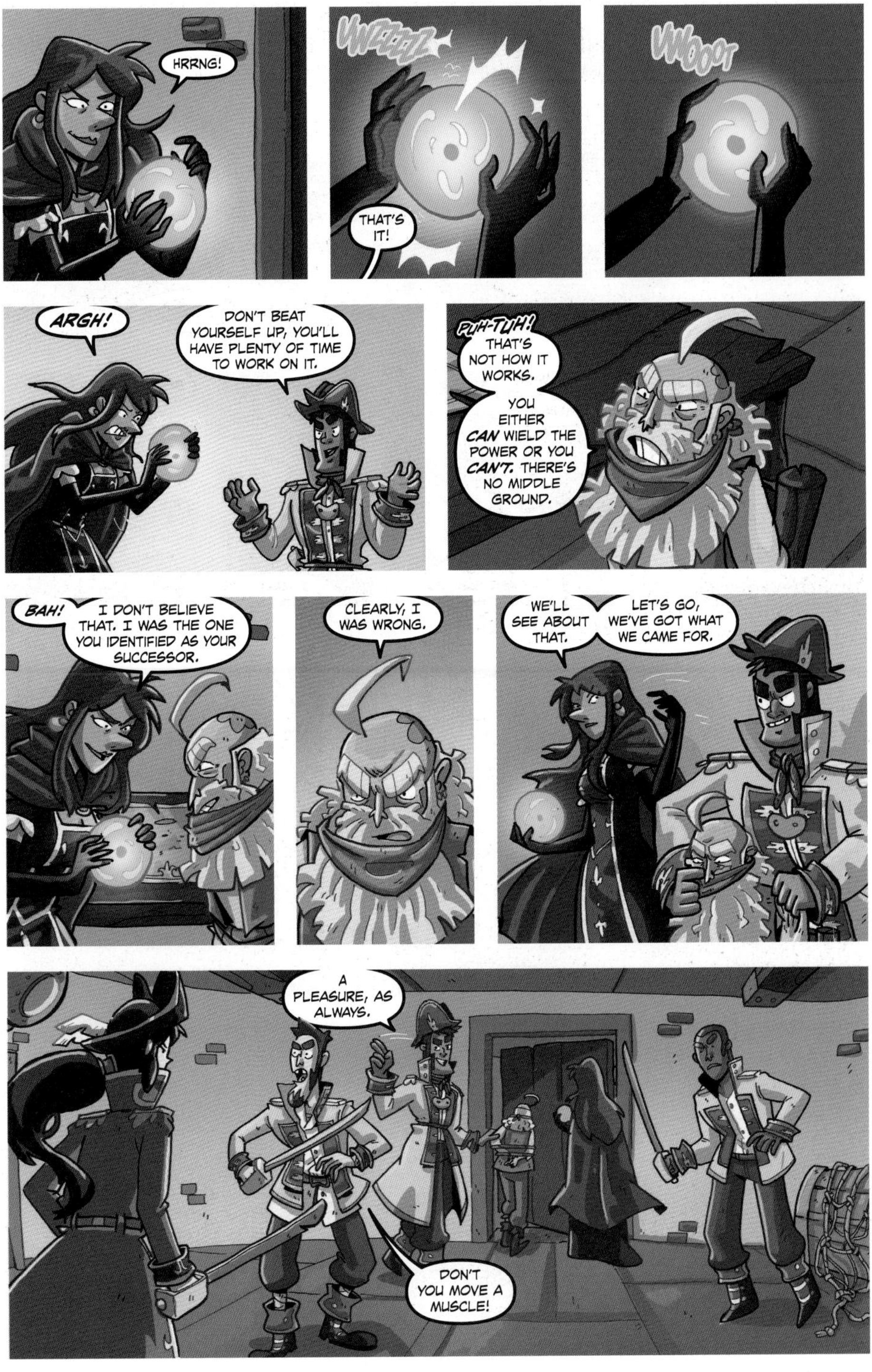
HRRNG!
VWZZZZZ
THAT'S IT!
VWOOOT
ARGH!
DON'T BEAT YOURSELF UP, YOU'LL HAVE PLENTY OF TIME TO WORK ON IT.
PUH-TUH! THAT'S NOT HOW IT WORKS.
YOU EITHER CAN WIELD THE POWER OR YOU CAN'T. THERE'S NO MIDDLE GROUND.
BAH!
I DON'T BELIEVE THAT. I WAS THE ONE YOU IDENTIFIED AS YOUR SUCCESSOR.
CLEARLY, I WAS WRONG.
WE'LL SEE ABOUT THAT.
LET'S GO, WE'VE GOT WHAT WE CAME FOR.
A PLEASURE, AS ALWAYS.
DON'T YOU MOVE A MUSCLE!

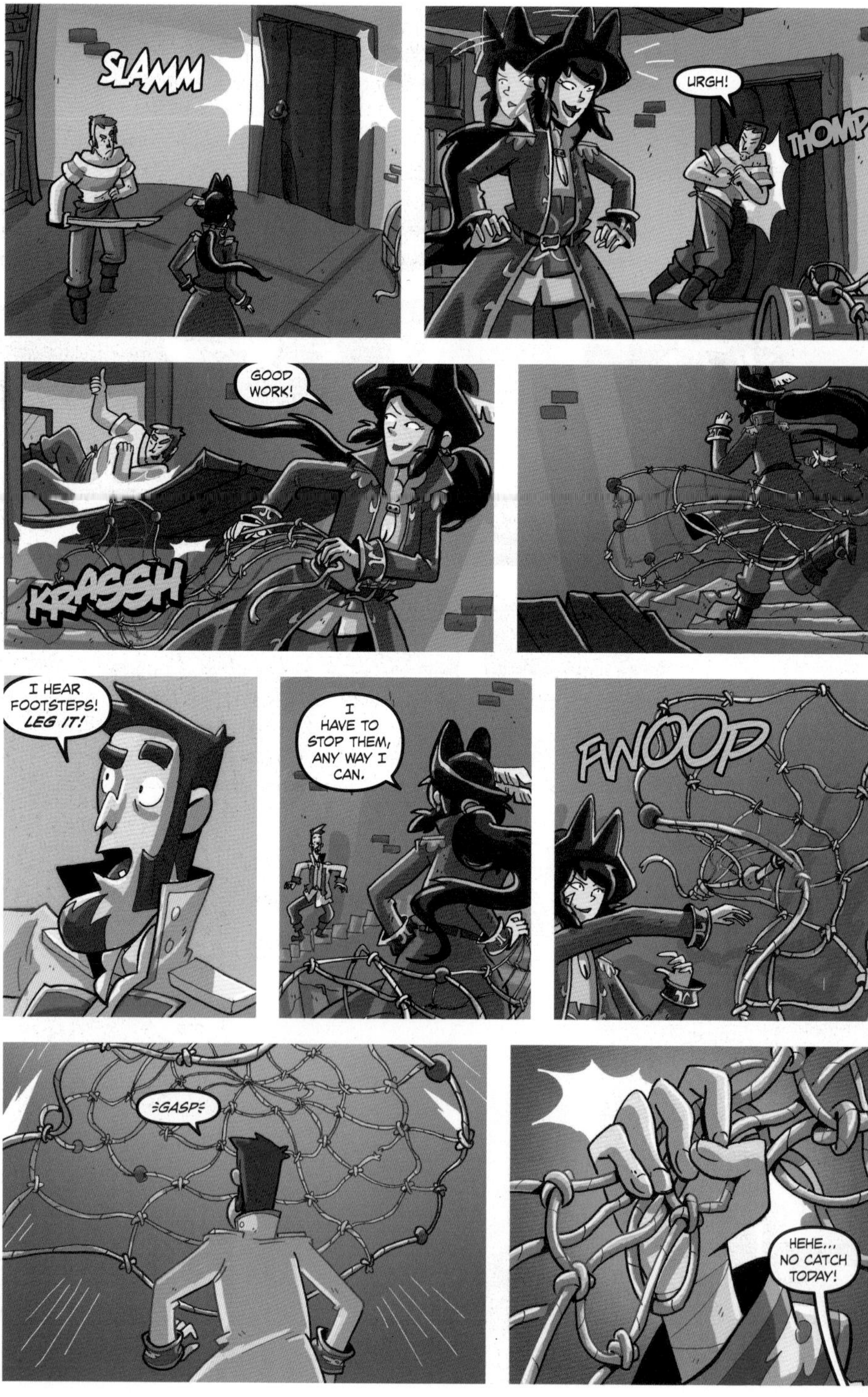
SLAMM
URGH!
THOMP
GOOD WORK!
KRASSH
I HEAR FOOTSTEPS! LEG IT!
I HAVE TO STOP THEM, ANY WAY I CAN.
FWOOP
GASP
HEHE... NO CATCH TODAY!

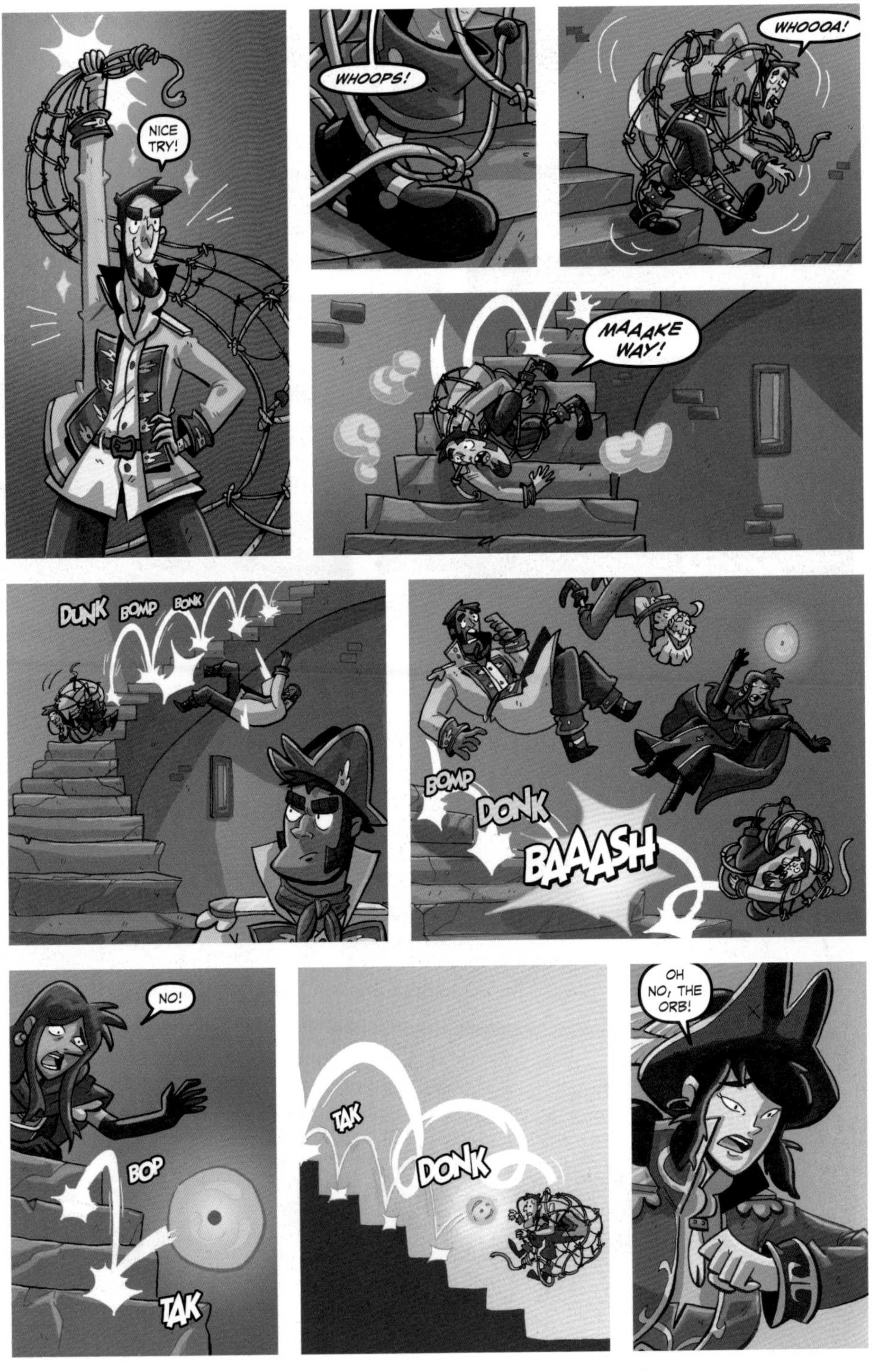
NICE TRY!
WHOOPS!
WHOOOA!
MAAAKE WAY!
DUNK
BOMP
BONK
BOMP
DONK
BAAASH
NO!
BOP
TAK
TAK
DONK
OH NO, THE ORB!

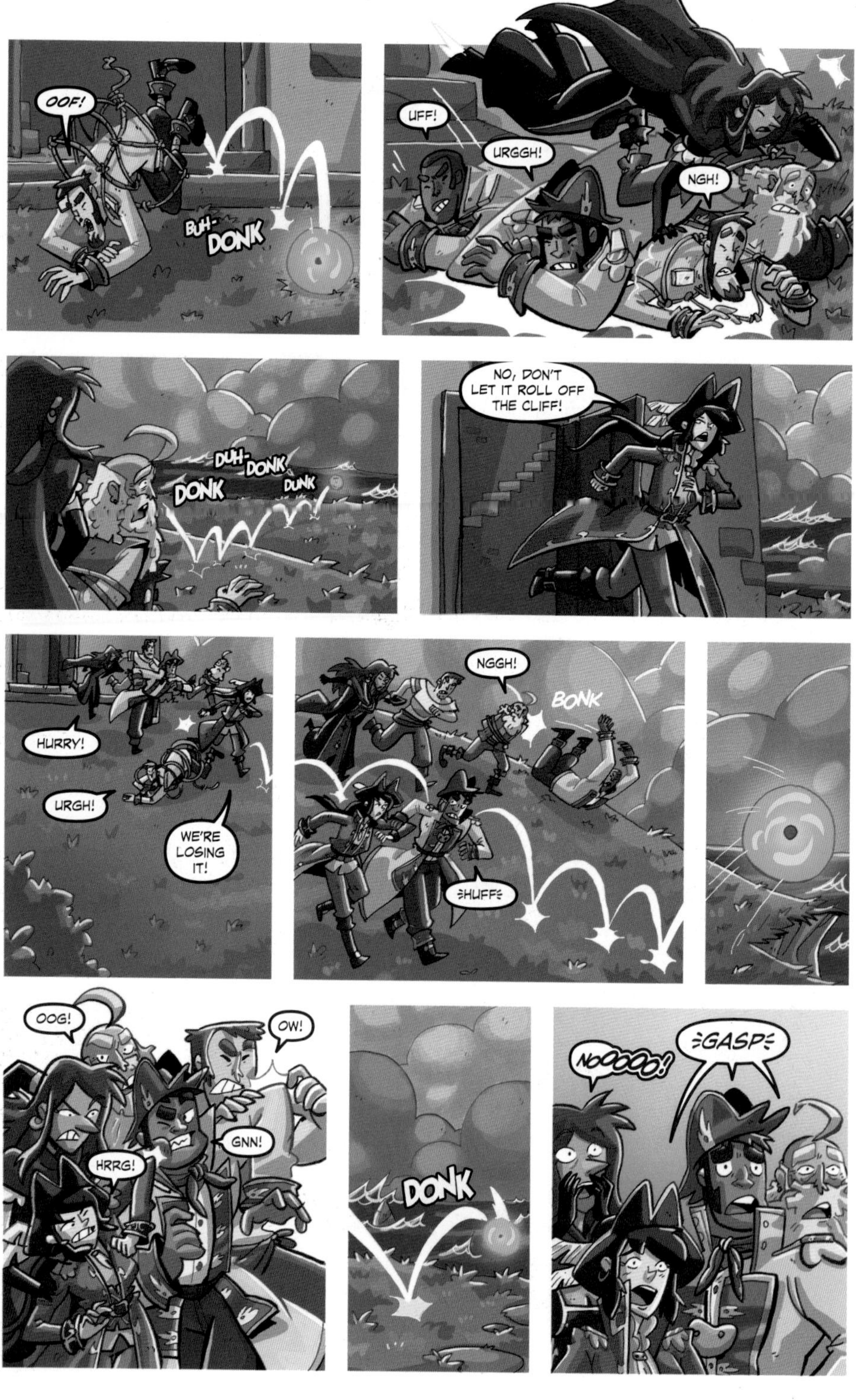
OOF!
BUH-DONK
UFF!
URGGH!
NGH!
DUH-DONK
DONK
DUNK
NO, DON'T LET IT ROLL OFF THE CLIFF!
HURRY!
URGH!
WE'RE LOSING IT!
NGGH!
BONK
HUFF
OOG!
OW!
GNN!
HRRG!
DONK
NOOOOO!
GASP

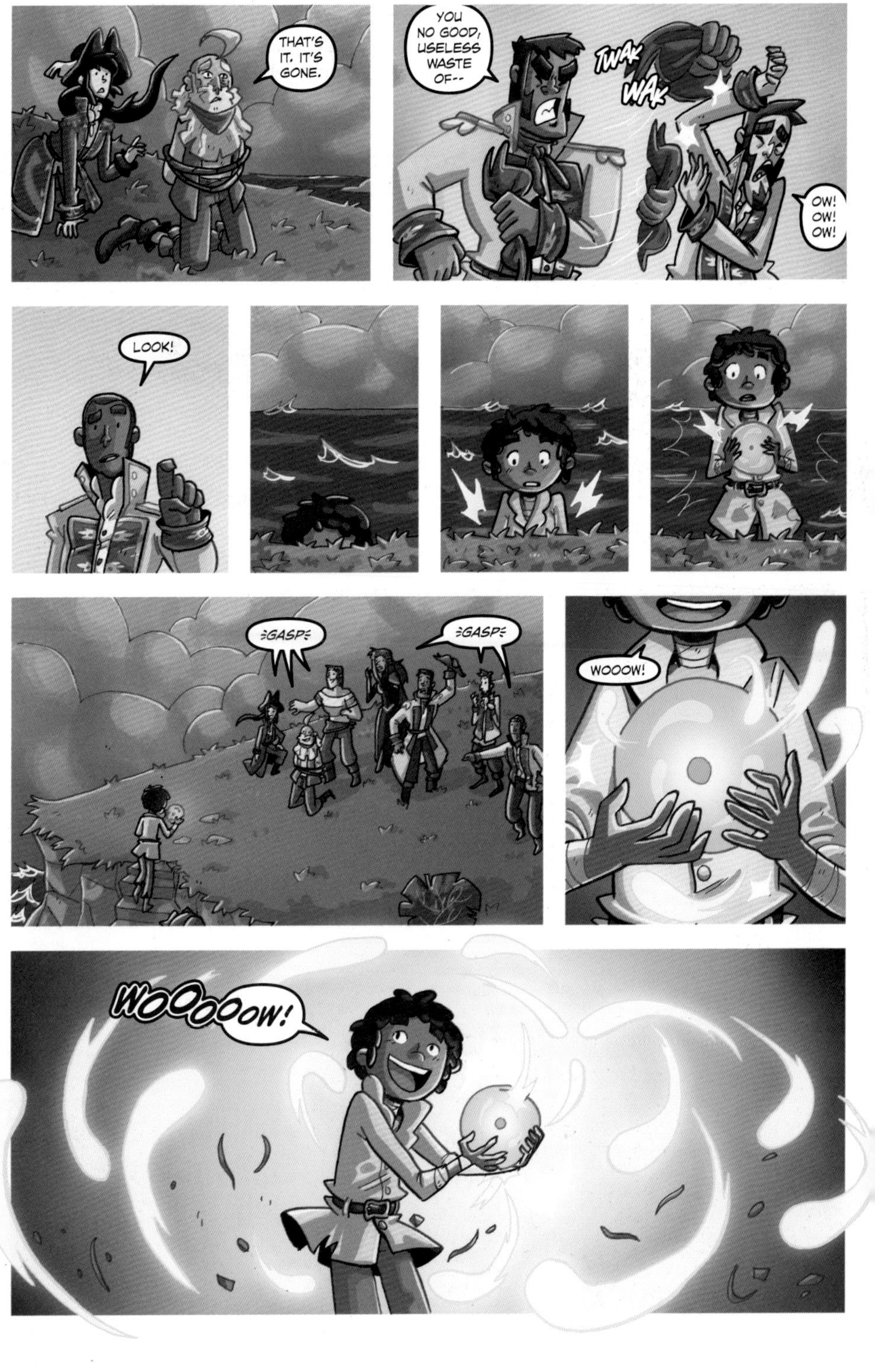
THAT'S IT. IT'S GONE.
YOU NO GOOD, USELESS WASTE OF--
TWAK
WAK
OW! OW! OW!
LOOK!
GASP
GASP
WOOOW!
WOOOOOW!

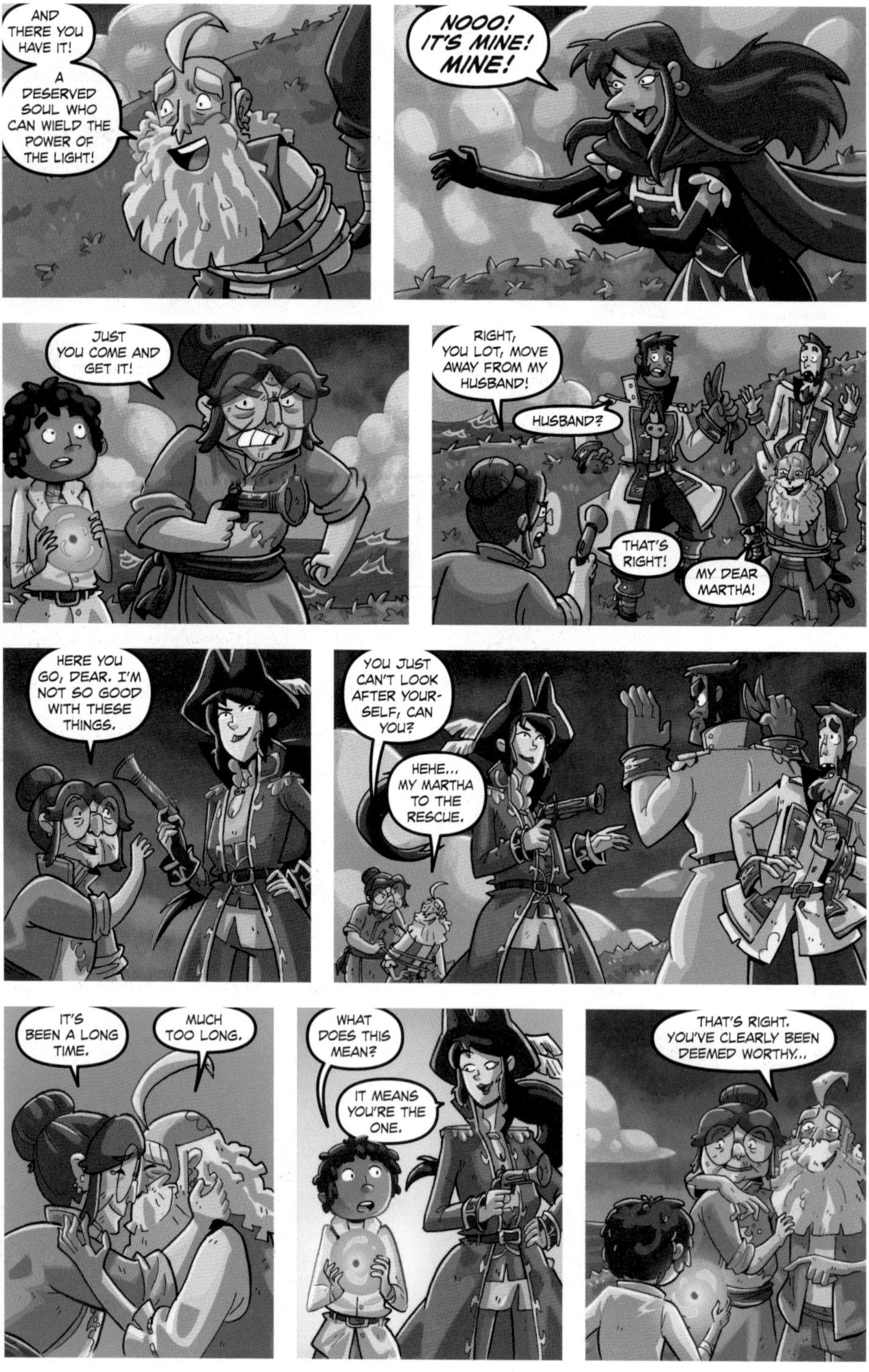
AND THERE YOU HAVE IT!
A DESERVED SOUL WHO CAN WIELD THE POWER OF THE LIGHT!
NOOO! IT'S MINE! MINE!
JUST YOU COME AND GET IT!
RIGHT, YOU LOT, MOVE AWAY FROM MY HUSBAND!
HUSBAND?
THAT'S RIGHT!
MY DEAR MARTHA!
HERE YOU GO, DEAR. I'M NOT SO GOOD WITH THESE THINGS.
YOU JUST CAN'T LOOK AFTER YOUR-SELF, CAN YOU?
HEHE... MY MARTHA TO THE RESCUE.
IT'S BEEN A LONG TIME.
MUCH TOO LONG.
WHAT DOES THIS MEAN?
IT MEANS YOU'RE THE ONE.
THAT'S RIGHT. YOU'VE CLEARLY BEEN DEEMED WORTHY...

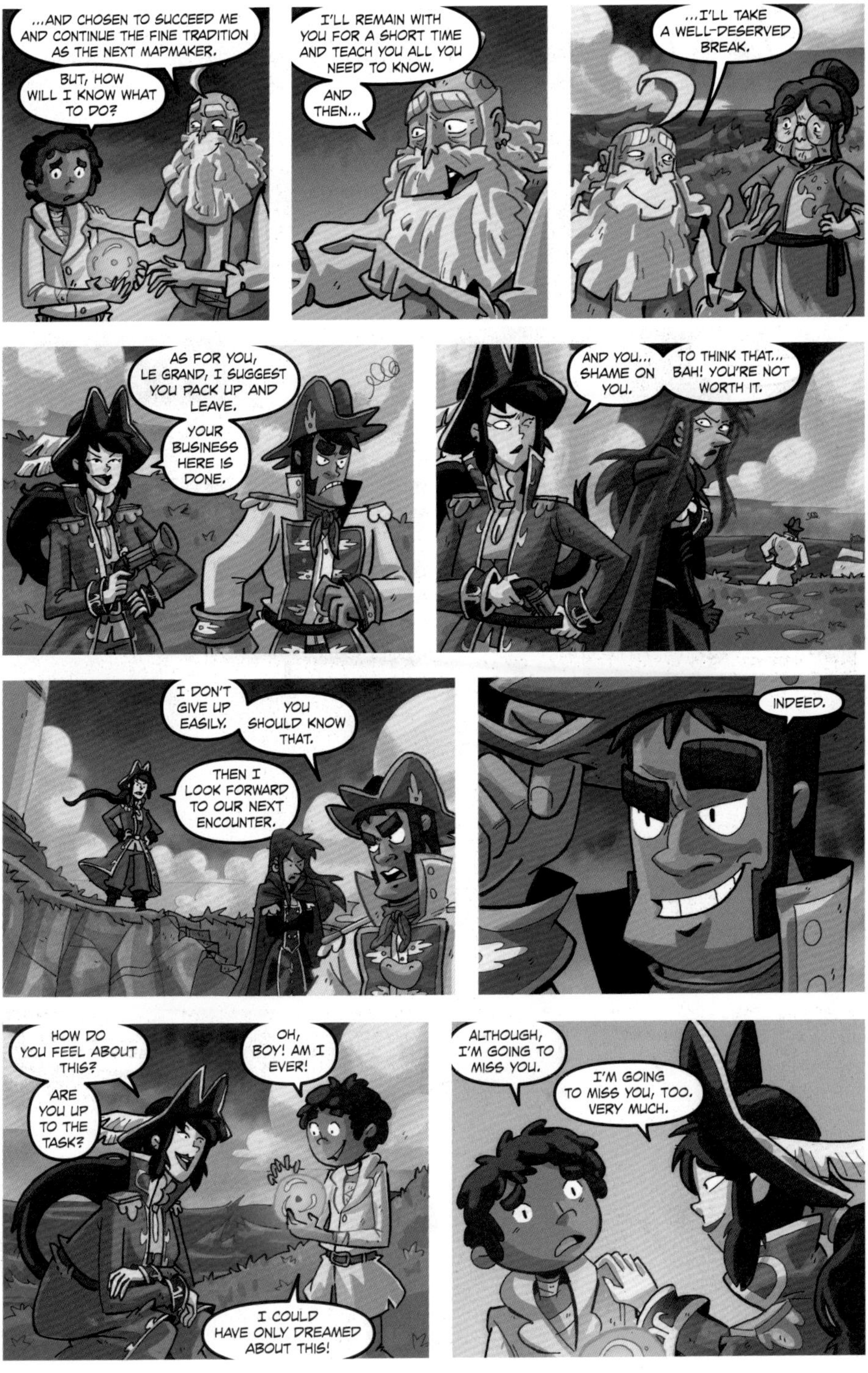
...AND CHOSEN TO SUCCEED ME AND CONTINUE THE FINE TRADITION AS THE NEXT MAPMAKER.
BUT, HOW WILL I KNOW WHAT TO DO?
I'LL REMAIN WITH YOU FOR A SHORT TIME AND TEACH YOU ALL YOU NEED TO KNOW.
AND THEN...
...I'LL TAKE A WELL-DESERVED BREAK.
AS FOR YOU, LE GRAND, I SUGGEST YOU PACK UP AND LEAVE.
YOUR BUSINESS HERE IS DONE.
AND YOU... SHAME ON YOU.
TO THINK THAT... BAH! YOU'RE NOT WORTH IT.
I DON'T GIVE UP EASILY.
YOU SHOULD KNOW THAT.
THEN I LOOK FORWARD TO OUR NEXT ENCOUNTER.
INDEED.
HOW DO YOU FEEL ABOUT THIS?
ARE YOU UP TO THE TASK?
OH, BOY! AM I EVER!
I COULD HAVE ONLY DREAMED ABOUT THIS!
ALTHOUGH, I'M GOING TO MISS YOU.
I'M GOING TO MISS YOU, TOO. VERY MUCH.

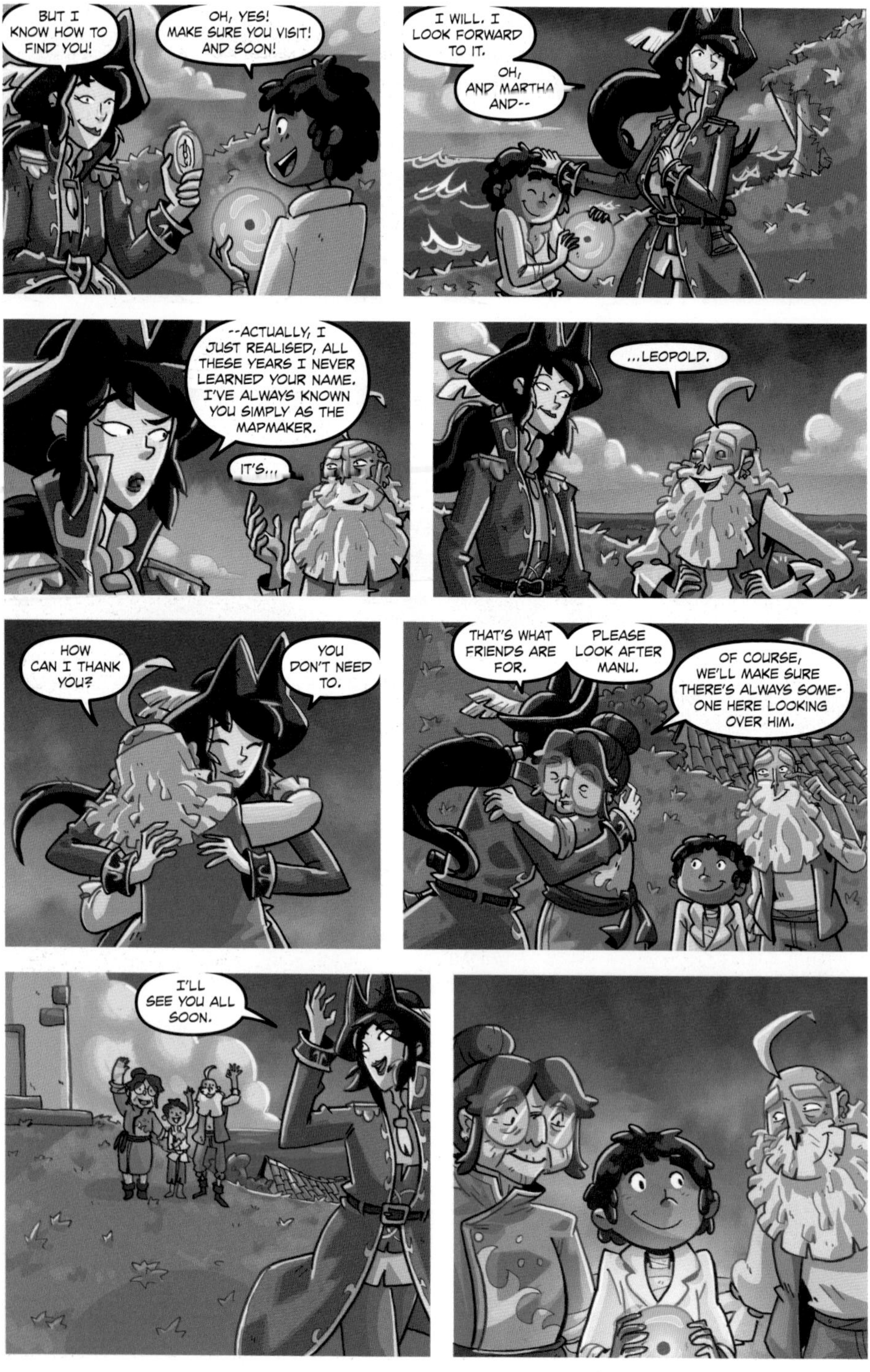
BUT I KNOW HOW TO FIND YOU!
OH, YES! MAKE SURE YOU VISIT! AND SOON!
I WILL. I LOOK FORWARD TO IT.
OH, AND MARTHA AND--
--ACTUALLY, I JUST REALISED, ALL THESE YEARS I NEVER LEARNED YOUR NAME. I'VE ALWAYS KNOWN YOU SIMPLY AS THE MAPMAKER.
IT'S...
...LEOPOLD.
HOW CAN I THANK YOU?
YOU DON'T NEED TO.
THAT'S WHAT FRIENDS ARE FOR.
PLEASE LOOK AFTER MANU.
OF COURSE, WE'LL MAKE SURE THERE'S ALWAYS SOME-ONE HERE LOOKING OVER HIM.
I'LL SEE YOU ALL SOON.

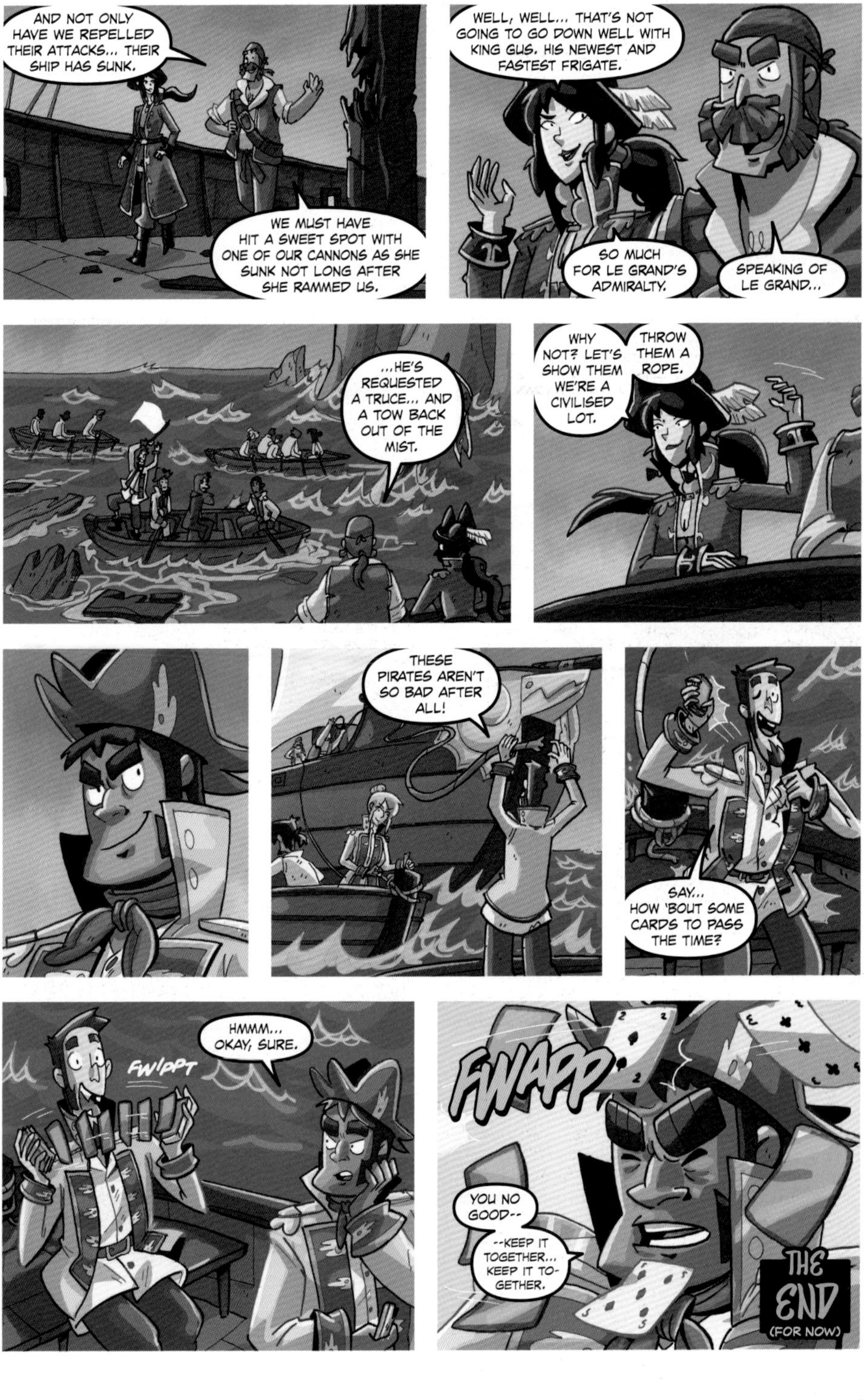
AND NOT ONLY HAVE WE REPELLED THEIR ATTACKS... THEIR SHIP HAS SUNK.
WE MUST HAVE HIT A SWEET SPOT WITH ONE OF OUR CANNONS AS SHE SUNK NOT LONG AFTER SHE RAMMED US.
WELL, WELL... THAT'S NOT GOING TO GO DOWN WELL WITH KING GUS. HIS NEWEST AND FASTEST FRIGATE.
SO MUCH FOR LE GRAND'S ADMIRALTY.
SPEAKING OF LE GRAND...
...HE'S REQUESTED A TRUCE... AND A TOW BACK OUT OF THE MIST.
WHY NOT? LET'S SHOW THEM WE'RE A CIVILISED LOT.
THROW THEM A ROPE.
THESE PIRATES AREN'T SO BAD AFTER ALL!
SAY... HOW 'BOUT SOME CARDS TO PASS THE TIME?
FWIPPT
HMMM... OKAY, SURE.
FWAPP
YOU NO GOOD--
--KEEP IT TOGETHER... KEEP IT TO-GETHER.
THE END (FOR NOW)

A word from the author

'*I wisely started with a map and made the story fit*,' J.R.R. Tolkien once wrote. He was, of course, referring to the now-iconic map of Middle Earth that is the setting of one of the most well known and most beloved works of fiction (and one of my personal favourites), the three-volume fantasy novel *The Lord of the Rings*.

Maps often feature in literary works, and they do not necessarily have to show real places. They help with the world-building by laying out the geography of locations that the various characters inhabit, and allow the readers to immerse themselves in these new worlds.

I have been drawn to maps, particularly to those from the bygone era, and have been captivated by them ever since I was a little kid. They continue, to this day, to bring a sense of wonder about new and faraway places. This goes perfectly in hand with my passion for history. Many of my stories, such as the *Trail* and *Trail: New World* series, as well as the upcoming graphic novels *1566 A.D.* and *Ahmose*, are inspired by real-life historical figures and events. When it came to *The Mapmaker*, however, I took a different approach.

For some years, I had been toying with the idea where one could, with the aid of special power or energy that only that individual can command, create new lands simply through drawing maps. An ability that would naturally be highly desirable and sought after. This premise laid the early foundation of the story of *The Mapmaker*.

A concept sketch of the Mapmaker doing what he does best - create maps!

I chose to set the story in a middle-ages type era on a fictional Earth during the age of discovery of new worlds by daring seafarers. At this point, the central character, the Mapmaker, had been losing the ability to control the extraordinary power that allows him to create new lands, known as 'The Light'. While awaiting a successor he nominated, the Mapmaker is startled by the sight of a fleet of ships at his doorstep. Sent by the power-hungry King Gustav, the advancing fleet leaves the Mapmaker with little choice. He summons what little control he has of 'The Light' and shifts himself and his entire island to an uncharted part of the Earth that is covered by a

thick fog dubbed, aptly enough, 'The Great Mist'. What follows is a tale of fun, action, and adventure, which I hope you enjoyed. I have had a lot of fun writing it and collaborating with the very talented Francesca Carità, who illustrated and coloured the book.

I grew up reading predominantly Italian and Franco-Belgian comics and graphic novels. The style of *The Mapmaker*, featuring some slapstick humour, is very much inspired by the likes of *Asterix*, *Tintin*, and *Lucky Luke*. I am hoping that the fans of these iconic works, in particular, will enjoy *The Mapmaker*.

Even though the story is finished, this does not mean it's the end. There will be more stories from the world of *The Mapmaker* in the future, and I myself am looking forward to them.

The Mapmaker uses 'The Light' to shift his island into 'The Great Mist' and escape capture

I originally launched the first issue of *The Mapmaker* at my favourite comic con event of the year - the great New York Comic Con back in 2018. It sold out at the event, striking a chord with readers of all ages, and that's what I aimed to achieve when I set out to produce *The Mapmaker*.

The Mapmaker was subsequently signed by the US-based publisher Scout Comics, specifically their all-ages imprint, Scoot, who have made this collected edition possible. I couldn't be more thrilled to be working with such a great publisher in bringing *The Mapmaker* to a wider, international audience.

If you are interested in following any of my other work, you can keep up with the latest on Facebook, Twitter, and Instagram, where you can find me under 'BenSlabak', as well as on my website site at BenSlabak.com.

Until next time, happy reading!

- Ben Slabak, May 2021, Sydney, Australia

Page #17 step-by-step process

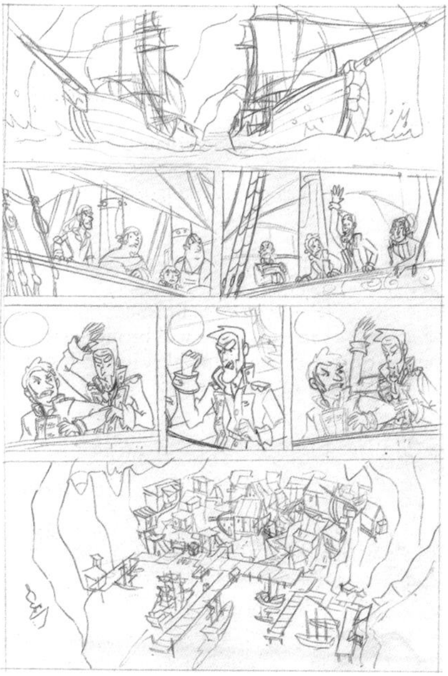

Step 1: Rough layout is sketched out

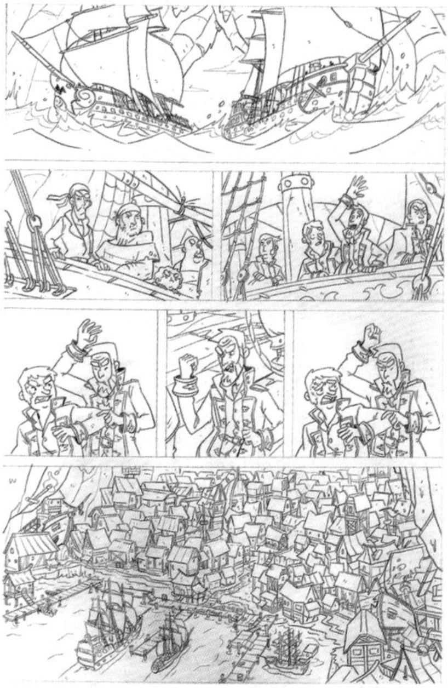

Step 2: More detailed, pencilled artwork

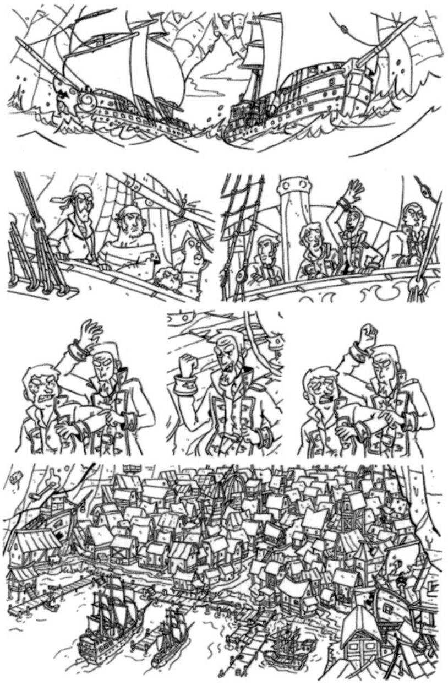

Step 3: Inks

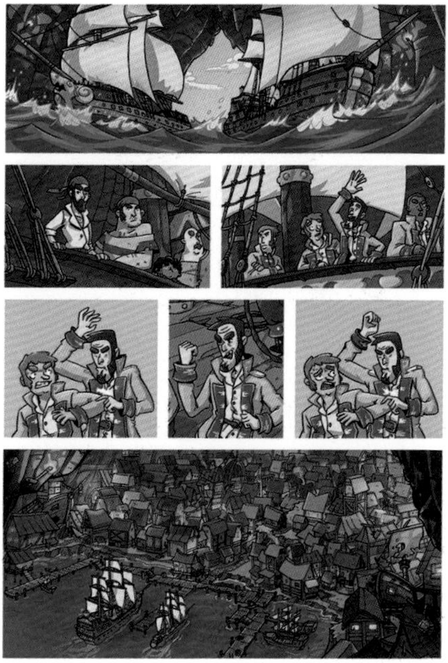

Step 4: Colours

Character Studies

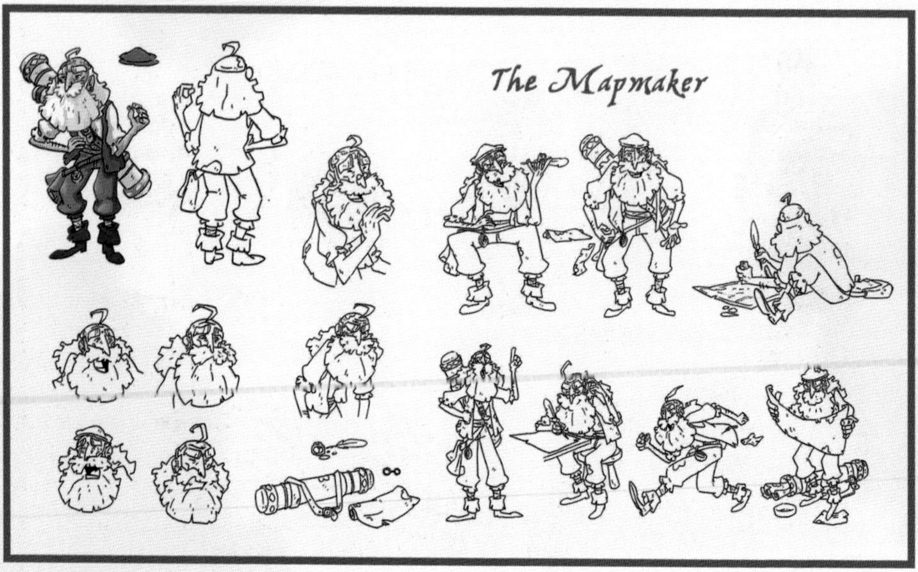
The Mapmaker

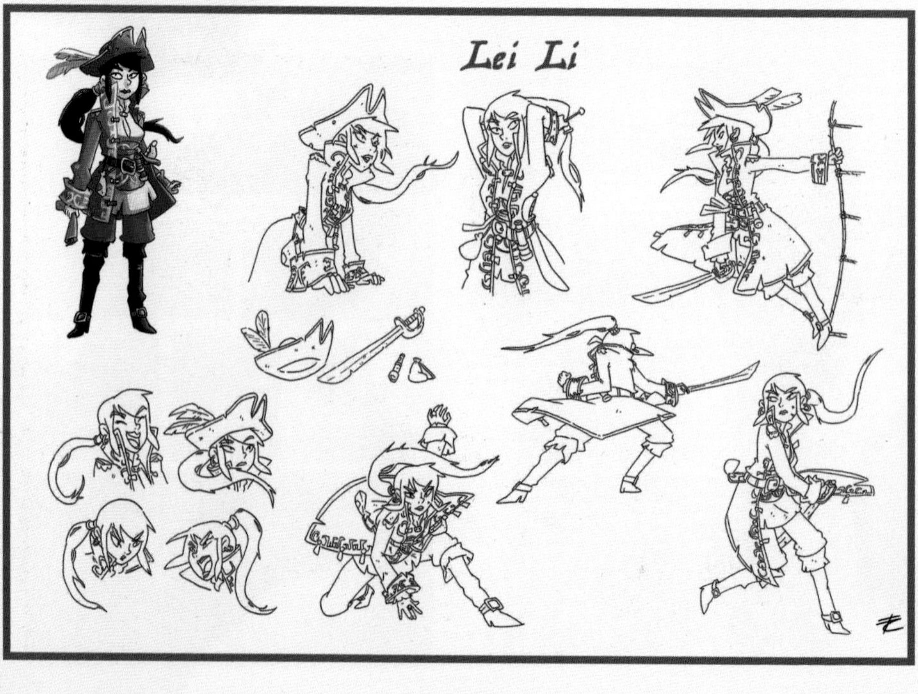
Lei Li

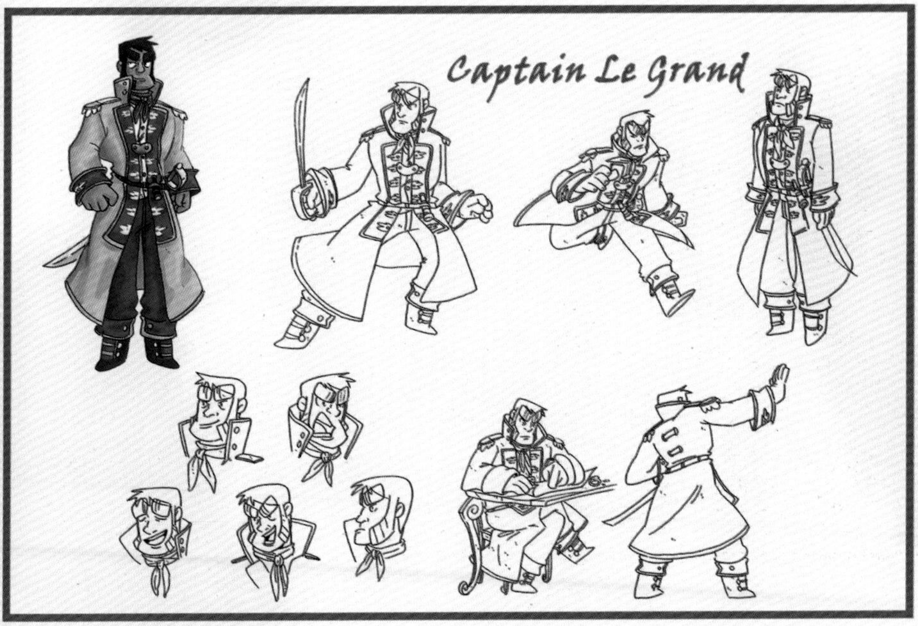
Captain Le Grand

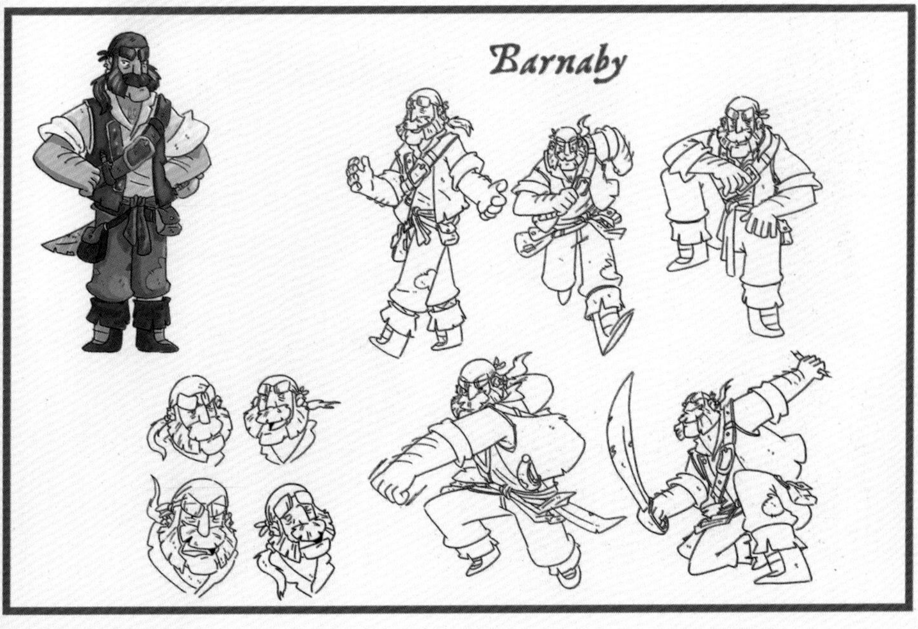
Barnaby

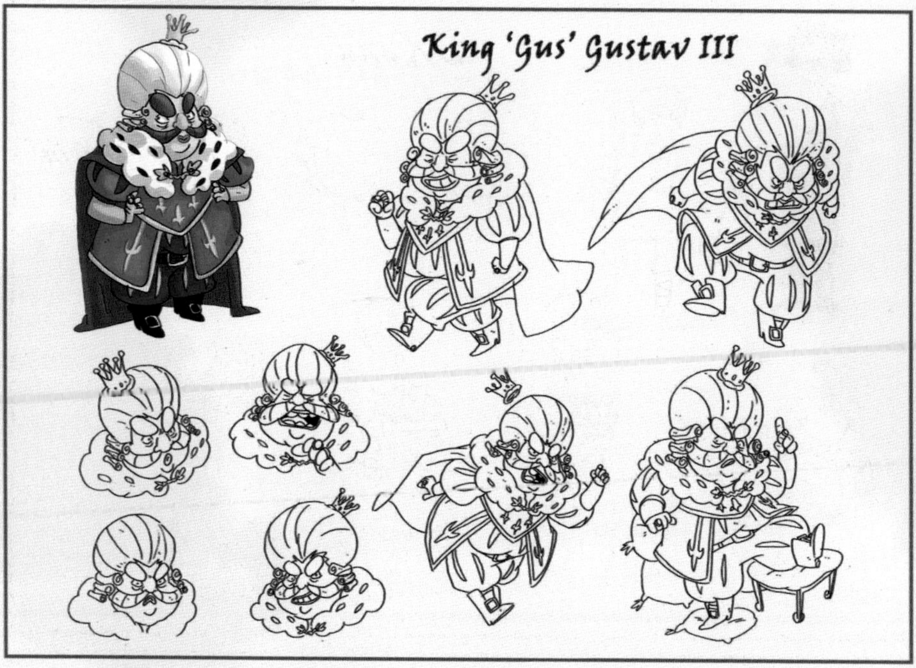
King 'Gus' Gustav III

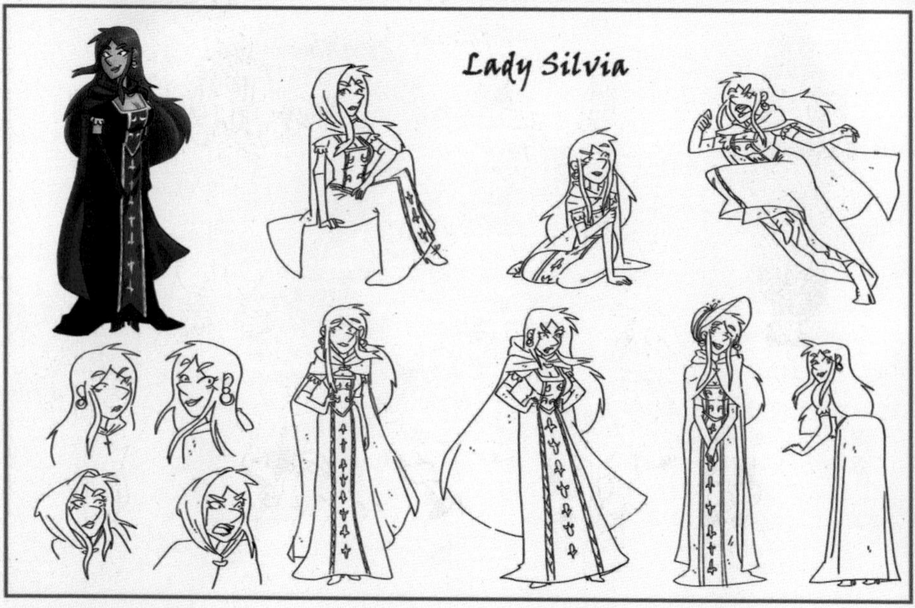
Lady Silvia

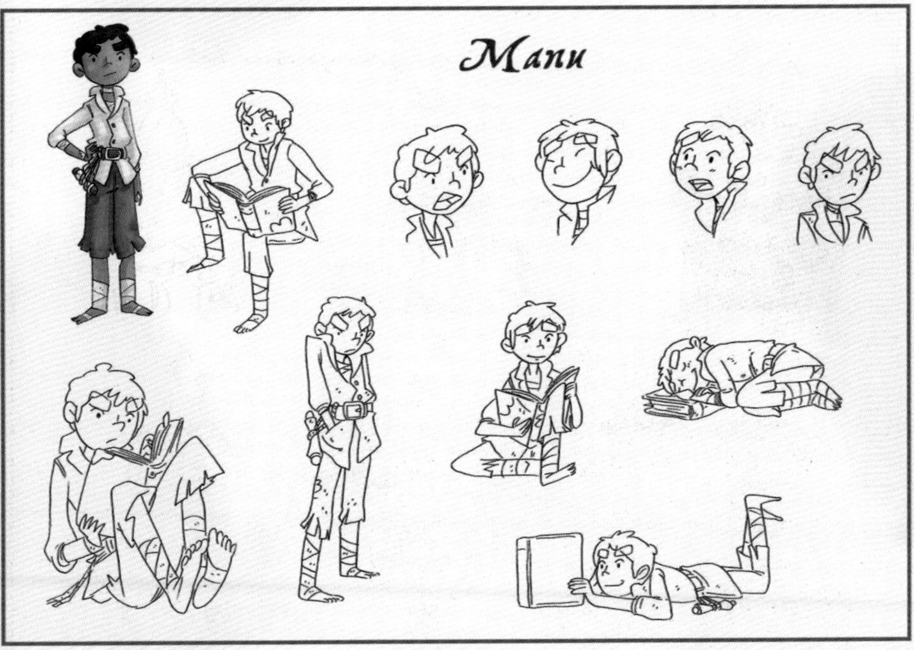
Manu

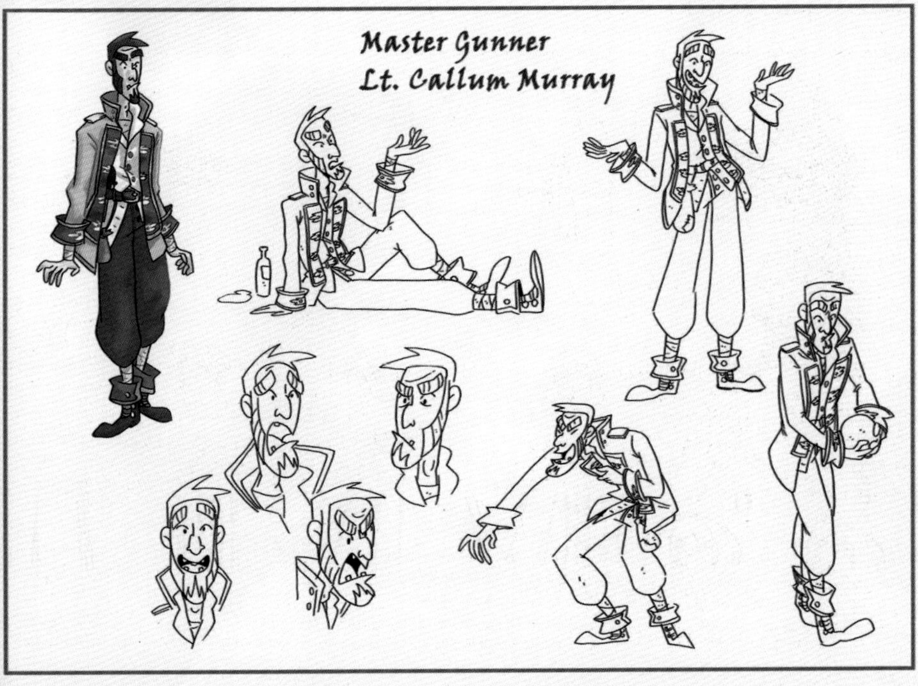
Master Gunner
Lt. Callum Murray

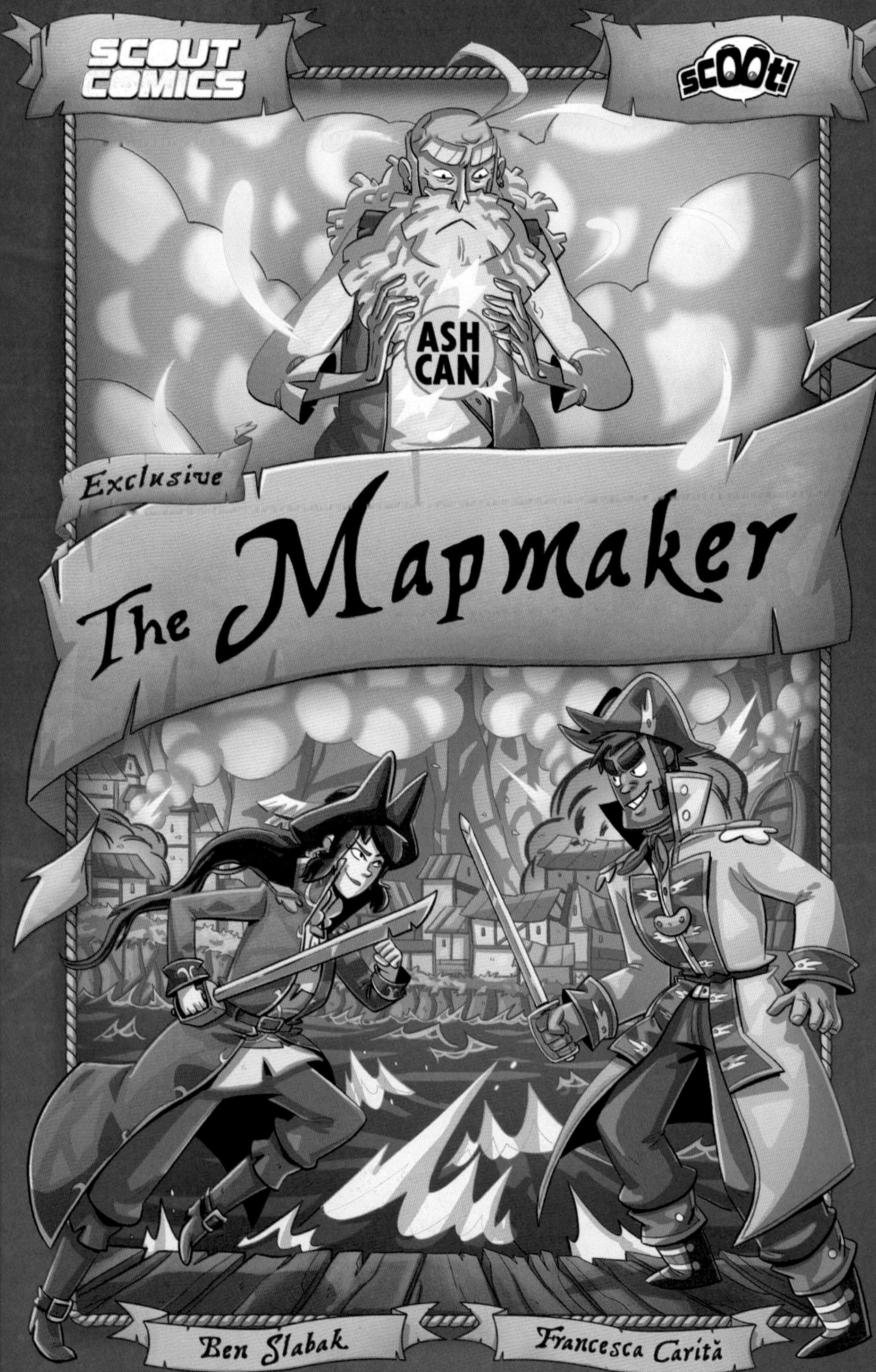
SCOUT COMICS
scOOt!
ASH CAN
Exclusive
The Mapmaker
Ben Slabak
Francesca Carità

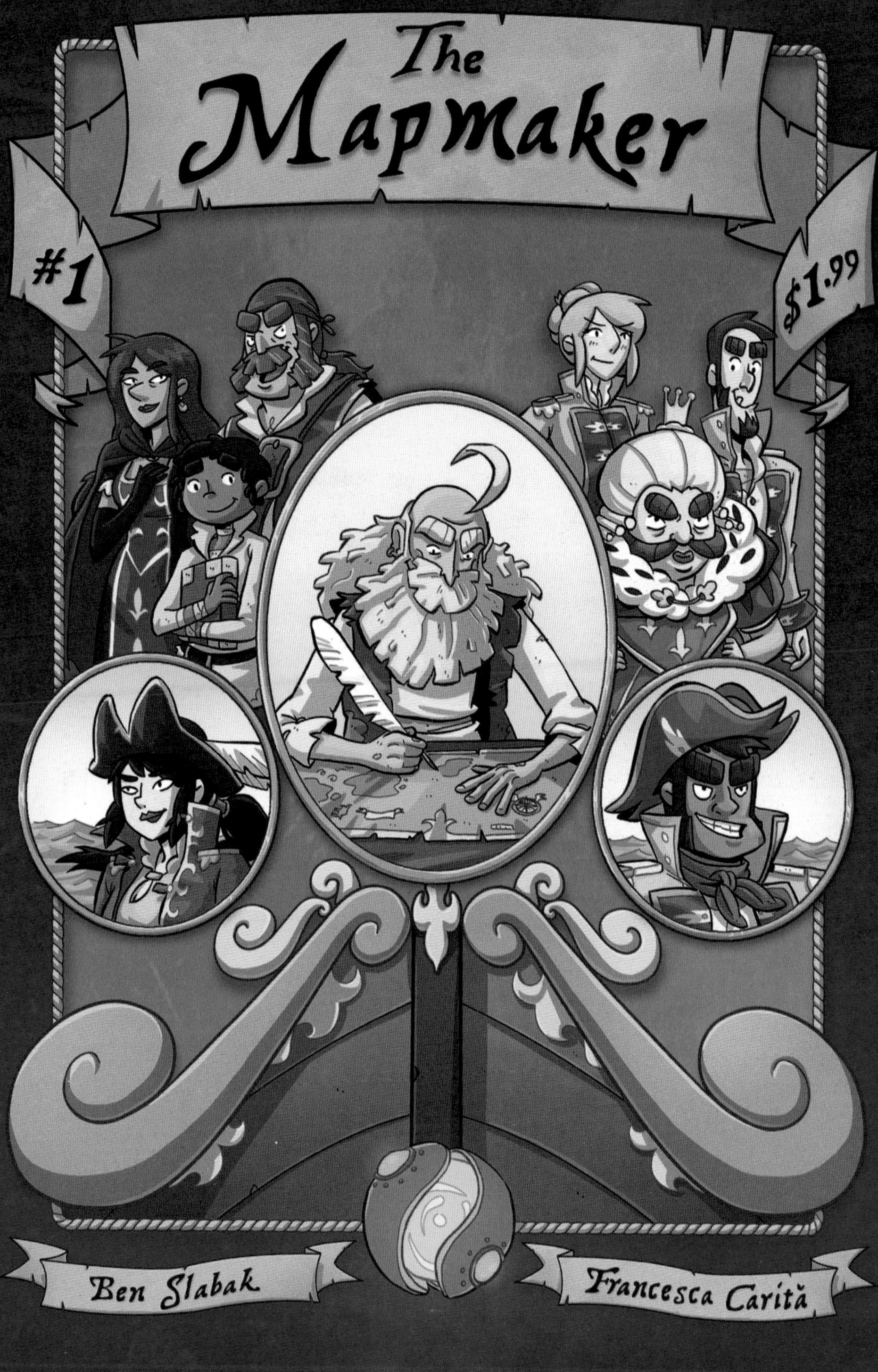

The Mapmaker
#1
$1.99
Ben Slabak
Francesca Carită

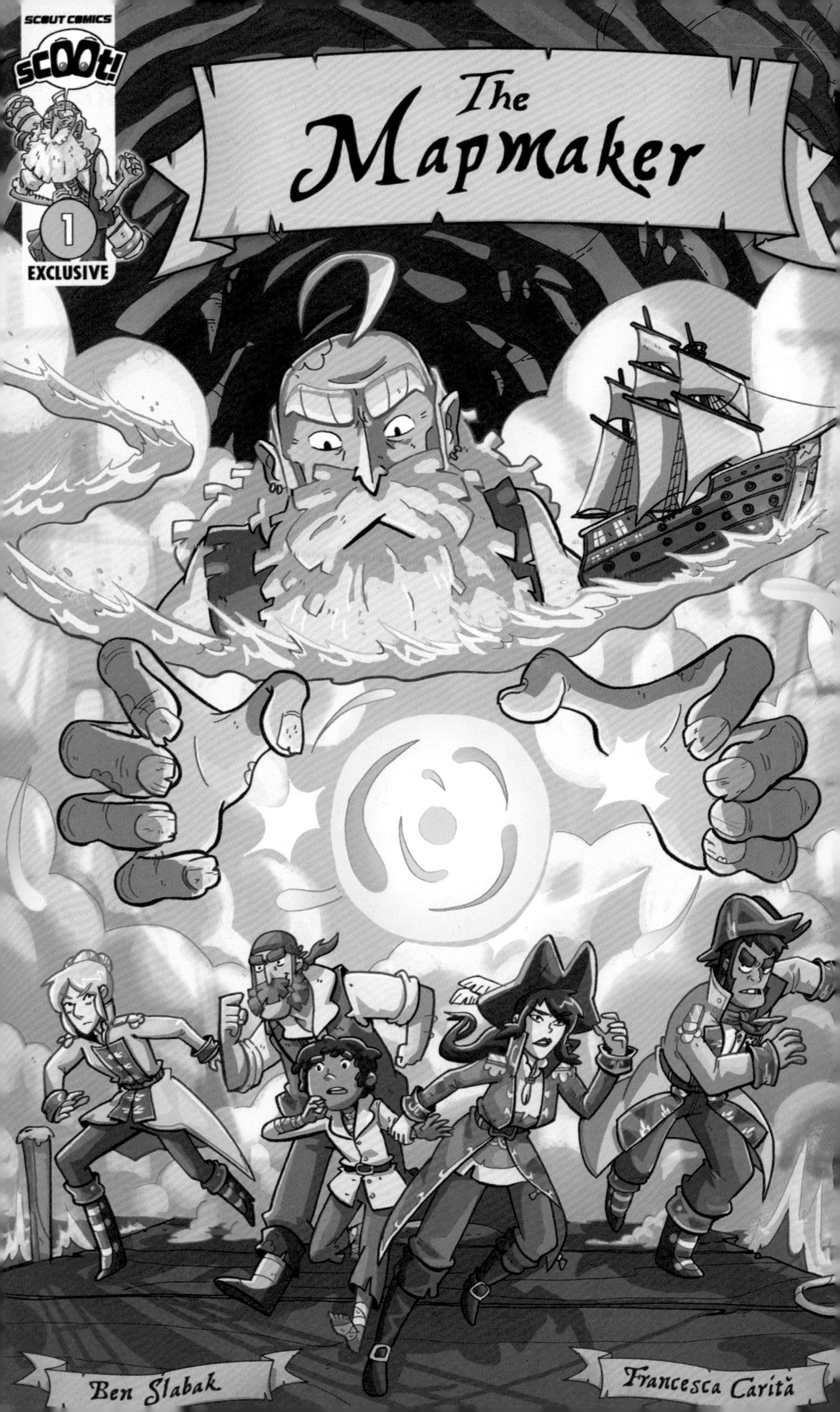
SCOUT COMICS
SCOOT!
The Mapmaker
1
EXCLUSIVE
Ben Slabak
Francesca Carità

Variant cover design process - homage to Marvel's Fantastic Four #49

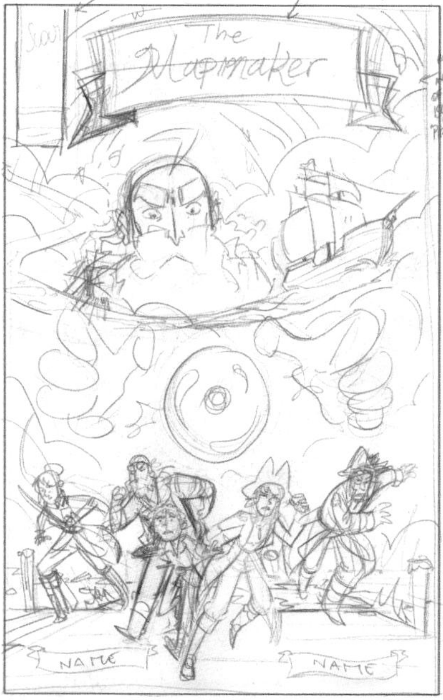
The
Mapmaker
NAME
NAME

Step 1: Sketch of a rough layout

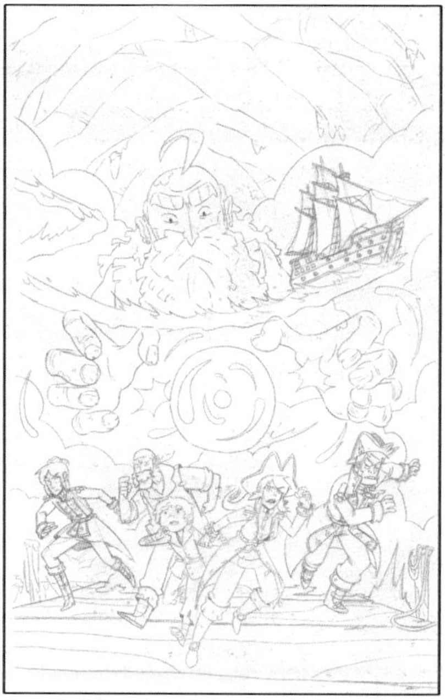

Step 2: More detailed, pencilled artwork

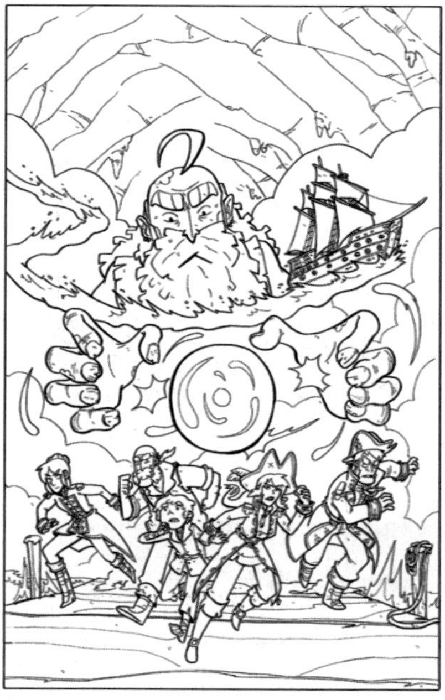

Step 3: Inks

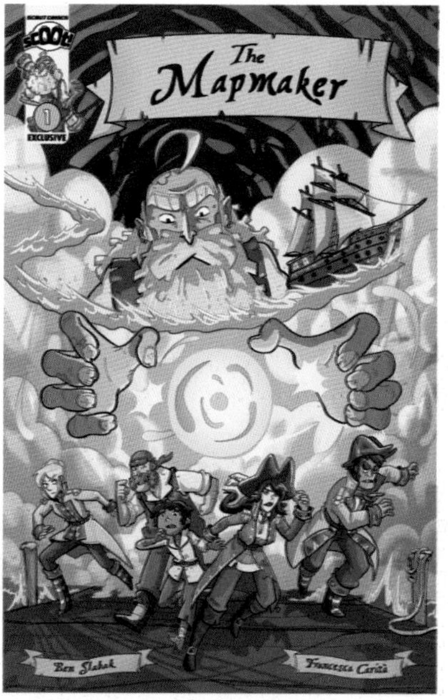
scOOt!
1
EXCLUSIVE
The Mapmaker
Ben Slabak
Francesca Carità

Step 4: Colours and dressing

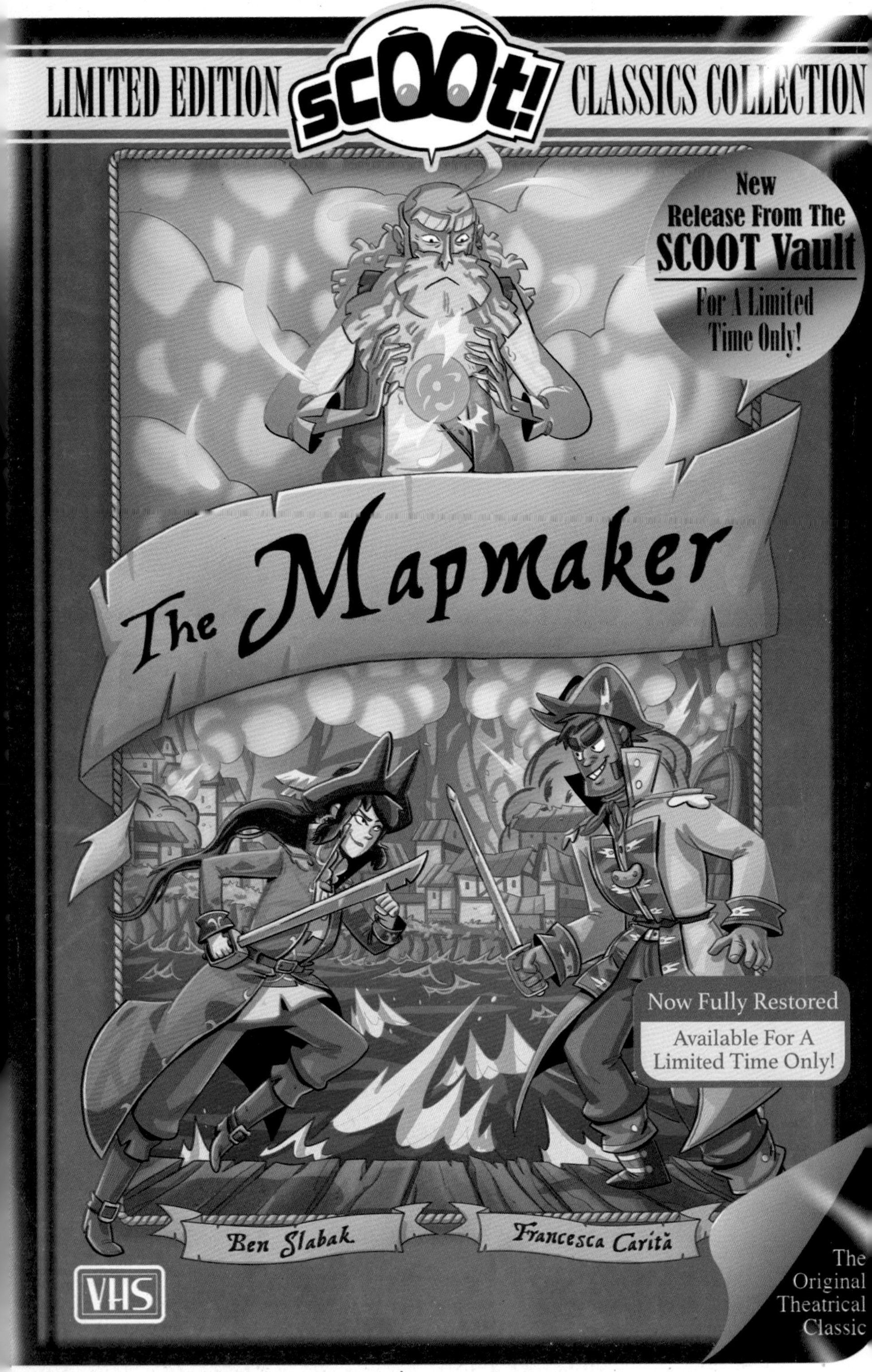
LIMITED EDITION
scOOt!
CLASSICS COLLECTION
New
Release From The
SCOOT Vault
For A Limited
Time Only!
The Mapmaker
Now Fully Restored
Available For A
Limited Time Only!
Ben Slabak
Francesca Carità
VHS
The
Original
Theatrical
Classic